CLOCKWORK SHERLOCK

IAN W. SAINSBURY

CHAPTER ONE

This nightmare starts *with the boy's face.*
Hard to say which of us is more terrified.
Our makeshift prison is a drug lab in a bombed-out school. Goalposts have been painted on one of the outside walls and when I creep around the corner, the boy comes flying out of the darkness, unleashing a kick that sends the ball smacking against the brickwork.
I put his age at nine or ten. I can't understand how a child can be here, in this place of torture and death. It's not until later that I realise he must have been the child of an ope producer, or one of the warlords who control them. To us they are dangerous criminals: ruthless and unfeeling. Barely human. Even if a soldier isn't explicitly encouraged to dehumanise the enemy, we do it anyway. How else could we bring ourselves to kill them?
The boy doesn't see me immediately. There are no lights, and the moon gives him barely enough illumination to make out the football. He performs a small victory dance, encouraging the invisible crowd to acknowledge his goal. He holds his arms aloft, appealing to the home supporters behind the goalmouth. Then he turns to do the same to those in the east stand and comes face to face with me.

When he sees my face – bloody, filthy and shit-stained, but still recognisably that of a foreigner – he thinks he's going to die.

I hold up my hands to show him I won't hurt him. He looks at the dirty, makeshift splints on my left hand in confusion. It might have been his father who had snapped the bones, his uncle who made the splints, his mother who was ready to break them again before they could heal.

They started on my fingers four days ago, one guard holding my hand on the table, the other wielding the hammer. They left me till last. I listened to the screams of the others for ten days before they came to me.

The boy's eyes dart to my right hand. I'm still holding the knife. I think he's about to scream, so I throw it into the bushes, shaking my head, a mute appeal in my eyes.

The boy edges backwards as I continue towards the road, my hands still in front of me. He doesn't cry out, just retreats slowly, never taking his eyes off me, fear distorting his face.

A door opens inside the building. The sudden light makes me freeze. That's when I see Hughes – just for a second – before the door swings closed and the light disappears. But it's long enough. Not that anyone believes me later. But I know what I saw. Chatting with one of the guards, laughing, unhurt, unbound. Hughes. I don't want to believe it, but I have no choice. He's with them.

I look for the boy, but he's melted into the shadows.

As soon as I reach the road I start to run, ready to dive into the trees on either side when the alarm is raised. It doesn't happen for another ten minutes, by which time I've heard the rush of the Kokcha River and veered away from the road.

I follow the river north to the border, crying with the pain of running on feet bruised from beatings.

It isn't hope that keeps me running. It isn't love. I don't think of my father. I think of my dead squad, their bodies dragged past my cell so that I could see them. After I saw the first body – Boone, his eyes open, his expression puzzled – I was glad to hear the screams of the others, because it meant they were still alive. After Boone, I knew they were going to kill us all.

I kept count as each scream was cut short by a bullet. I kept count until there were two of us left alive. Me and my betrayer.

The dream ends there, as I run alongside the river, my body delaying its inevitable collapse until I reach the border. As I run, it's Hughes I'm thinking of.

It's hate that keeps me running. Hate, and the promise of revenge.

I woke up shaking, slick with sweat, phantom pain lancing through long-healed fingers.

There were no alerts on my smotch, but I unfolded my noter and thumbed through the emails anyway. Nothing new. I flicked over to the news, giving the nightmare time to fade. The counsellor assigned by the army before I quit told me talking about what had happened would, over time, mean the nightmares would stop. She was wrong. Talking about it doesn't help at all. And I don't want to stop the nightmares, not yet. It keeps the hate fresh.

I put the empty bottles in the bin in the leaden grey light of another London dawn. Grunt-level nanomeds won't stop a hangover, but they reduce it to a dull ache that accompanies my first waking hour.

The wind changed direction and rain speckled the window. The skyline was washed out, incoherent, all colours leeched away by the low, heavy clouds.

I drank the first coffee of many and stared out into the morning.

I was no closer to finding Hughes than I had been the day I handed in my stripes and became a civilian again.

The day stretched before me. I needed a job, if only to

service the debt I'd amassed. Maybe call in on some private security firms run by ex-soldiers.

My reflection stared back at me, as dark as the shadows in the corners of my apartment. I turned away.

As far as I was concerned, it was a day like any other.

I was wrong.

CHAPTER TWO

'Him? He doesn't exist.'

'I assure you he does, Miss Barnes.'

'*Captain* Barnes. So, tell me who he is then. I can't work for someone who hides their identity.'

'I'm afraid that's not possible, Ms Barnes. Nobody can know who he, she, or it is.'

I yawned.

'Then I'm not interested. I'm sorry, but you're wasting your . . . your . . .'

'My . . . ?'

'Weird. Can't think of the right worm. What's happening to my. . . you know. . . my. . .'

'Just relax, Ms Barnes.'

'Mait a wicket. Have you drudged me, you muggle fudger?'

I woke up in the wrong century. There was a newspaper in front of my face. I had seen newspapers as a child but I couldn't remember ever holding one. The last physical novel had been printed when I was still in infant school. And this newspaper was huge, impractically so. For a start, it was almost impossible to hold. To see the contents of both pages, my arms had to be held out at full stretch. Even then, the print was so small, I could only comfortably read the story closest to my face.

Reluctant Conscript Joins Consulting Detective To Fight The Rising Tide Of Crime In London And Abroad

A man coughed in a nearby room. I froze. A few seconds later, someone began playing the violin.

Three questions. Where was I? How had I got there? And why the hell were the backs of my hands hairy?

The next few breaths I took were through my nose, exhaling through my mouth. The counsellor swore by this simple technique. Apparently, it allowed me to calm myself whenever I felt overwhelmed. In practice, it might give whoever was pissing me off an extra three seconds to run before I beat the crap out of them.

I looked down at my legs. Tweed trousers. FFS, as my father still said.

When I lowered the newspaper, my mind refused to cooperate with the evidence of my senses. The disconnect made me nauseous. I brought a hand to my mouth, where it encountered a moustache.

There are two paths you can follow in situations when you have limited information. You can panic, or you can go along with the ride until you work out what's going on. I was considering a third option: find who's responsible for giving tweed trousers and a moustache to a female ex-army captain with a penchant for violence, and repeatedly smash their face into a wall until they're sorry.

First thing to do would be to find out where the hell I was. I screwed up the newspaper and tossed it across the room, where it landed in the fire, producing a brief but impressive lick of flame.

The violin stopped. 'Oh, I say, good shot. Bravo! Be with you in a moment.' The music continued.

Right. I stood up.

Well, I tried to.

It didn't work.

My brain sent the correct signals, but my tweed-clad, moustached body refused to obey them.

The slow breathing, if it had ever contributed to keeping me calm, wasn't doing so now.

At least my head could move, so I scanned my surroundings. To my right was a table covered in a heavy ivory-coloured cloth, behind which was a wall with a bookcase containing large, leather-bound volumes. To my left, two vast bay windows. In front of the left window was a high-backed armchair, similar to the one in which I was trapped. A brass and wood telescope on a tripod stood in front of the other window. The view was unremarkable: many London streets featured similar terraces, although these were particularly dirty and soot-blackened. The fireplace was directly ahead of me. A poker lay in front of it, too bent to fit in the stand with the other fire irons. The mantelpiece above held a dark wooden box, a pile of envelopes and – oddly – some kind of shoe or slipper. And, over that, a large mirror with a gilt frame. My tweedy body wouldn't let me look over my shoulder, but the mirror showed a partially open door leading to the violinist's room behind me.

The heavy wallpaper where the bookcase stood had been ruined by bullet holes, but these shots weren't the result of a firefight. They were placed precisely, spelling out the letters VR. I half smiled at that, despite my predicament. VR indeed.

Apparently, I was on the upper floor of a residential building in London, kitted out like a museum of Victoriana, even down to the open fire; an inefficient means of keeping warm, banned in the city well before I was born.

This was no dream. But Virtual Reality tech – as far as I knew – was not advanced enough to make a scene this convincing. Not yet, anyway.

'It's not what you think,' came the voice from the other room. The violin notes ceased a few seconds afterwards and I turned my head in time to see the voice's owner appear in the doorway.

He was tall – a hair above six foot two would be my guess. Wiry, thin almost to the point of gauntness. His black hair was slicked back in a style I hadn't seen outside a movie. His skin was pale, his nostrils were flared and there was a smile playing at his thin lips. Most striking of all were his eyes. They were dark and gunmetal grey, the grey of an approaching storm. He was wearing a black suit, a white shirt and a red cravat around his throat. With his violin bow, which he clutched in the long fingers of his right hand, he indicated the letters on the wall.

I had seen enough.

'Look, I don't know who you are, or what game you're playing, but you made a mistake bringing me here, you piece of –'

I didn't stop talking but the sound vanished as if muted by an unseen finger on a button. My rant continued for a few sentences before I gave up. After that, I attempted to communicate the depth of my ill-feeling through the stare with which I fixed the violinist. He didn't so much as glance in my direction.

'I imagine you think this stands for Virtual Reality,' said my captor, strolling over and indicating the bullet holes. He was wrong. The room, the bent poker and the tobacco-stuffed slipper on the mantelpiece had chimed somewhere deep in my memory. I knew what the letters stood for, and where I was supposed to be.

'Victoria Regina,' I said, although still on mute. The violinist placed his bow on the mantelpiece, propped the instrument on a chair and, folding his arms, regarded me with a broad smile.

'Correct,' he said. 'I *knew* you were the right choice, Captain Barnes.'

I tried, and failed, to speak again. Apparently he could understand what I was saying, despite the lack of sound. My facial expression deepened in intensity from glower to glare, but it had no effect on the man in front of me. He waved an elegant hand to indicate our surroundings.

'You were quite the reader once, were you not?' It would appear he was the sort of man who asked questions without necessarily expecting answers. 'Quite right; Victoria Regina. And yes, you have deduced the modern implication. You are indeed currently in virtual reality.'

He drew himself up to his full height then, eyes gleaming, and struck a dramatic pose. It was the sort of thing you practise in front of a mirror as an adolescent, until you either decide on a career in the theatre or grow up. Somehow, he pulled it off without looking like a complete wanker.

'I've been awfully rude,' he said, with what was either a wink or a facial tic. 'It's a pleasure to meet you, Captain Barnes. My name is, well . . . it's unimportant. But you can call me Sherlock Holmes.'

CHAPTER THREE

I LAUGHED IN HIS FACE. The man standing in front of me in the upper rooms of 221b Baker Street was an urban myth, a simulacrum based on Conan Doyle's fictional detective. No one thought he actually existed. The Met used to have a crime database nicknamed Holmes, so most people thought the rumours referred to version 2.0. The most outlandish theory I'd heard so far was that a prototype of an advanced Artificial Intelligence was being let loose on cold cases in preparation for being given the real thing. But, like I said, no one thought we were talking about a real person.

'You're actually *real?*' I said, my voice now audible again, and the question of where, how, why and who I needed to punch for this temporarily forgotten. 'You're the cold-case guy.'

I tried to stand up, but my lower body was still refusing to play along. 'You're Clockwork Sherlock.'

The simulated detective winced. 'A puerile nickname and one that hardly does my abilities justice.'

He walked over to the bookshelves to my right and pulled down a thick, leather-bound volume. 'Not that it matters,

Watson, but you would do well to remember that the application of a nickname often reduces one's ability to see beyond the restrictions suggested by it.'

I wanted to say, 'I'm not Watson, you deranged lunatic,' but what came out was, 'Eh?'

'Take Knives McKeller,' said Holmes, flicking through the pages. 'What do you know about him?'

I knew nothing about Knives McKeller. Or Forks Flintlock and Spoons von Smiffy, for that matter. The initial shock of finding out Clockwork Sherlock was real had diminished and I was back to feeling angry and pissed off. Hungry and hungover from the sedative too. Not a good combination. I took a deep breath, then let loose a stream of invective. I pointed out that not only was it illegal to kidnap someone and hold them prisoner, but it was particularly unwise when your prisoner had been trained in a multitude of ways to cause pain, physical damage and death. Although I conceded that none of the above options might be available to me in a virtual environment, I expressed the certainty that I would shortly demonstrate my prowess in *real reality* to the fool hiding behind the persona of the famous detective. The actual words I used were mainly short and derived from the Anglo-Saxon side of Britain's etymological heritage.

Holmes ignored me, still scanning the book. His finger jabbed forward. 'Aha!' He shot me a look and shook his head. 'I'm sorry, Watson,' he said. 'I tuned you out I'm afraid. Literally. I have the option to mute you. It's one of the useful aspects of a virtual construct.'

He walked over to the fireside and leaned against the mantelpiece, holding the book in front of him.

'I'm not Watson,' I said with a sigh.

He shut the book and smiled. I wished I could mute him, the cocky twat. 'In the nineteen-thirties, Knives McKeller was feared across the East End because of his skill with a blade. It was said of Knives that he was so fast and so precise that if he killed you, you didn't know about it until you got home, removed your hat and your head fell off.'

I intensified my glare. It had been developed over fifteen years in the army and had ended careers. It didn't even seem to register on Holmes.

'When a rival criminal organisation decided to take down Knives McKeller, the assassins waited for him in an open place. They planned to use handguns before Knives got anywhere near them with his blades.' Holmes shut the book. 'Knives had a machine gun under his coat. It was a massacre.'

He arched an eyebrow at me. Since my glare wasn't working and creatively aggressive swearing had no effect, I opted for disdain.

'Are you going to get to the point?' I said. 'Or was I kidnapped so you could bore me to death?'

'Ah. Good. Your school, university and military records, as well as my investigations, suggested a keen intelligence. I was beginning to wonder if we'd picked up the wrong Captain Jo Barnes. Bravo, Watson.'

'I'm not Watson! You know my real name. What the hell's wrong with you? And I'm not a captain anymore.'

'True. Shame you're not a doctor, either, but one can't have verisimilitude in every aspect of a simulation. The point, Watson, is that my nickname –'

'Clockwork Sherlock,' I repeated, childishly enjoying the look of irritation it provoked.

'Quite.' He took a moment to resume his calm demeanour, looking up at the ceiling as he spoke. 'My nickname carries certain assumptions with it. The main one being that I am mechanical, a computer program, an algorithm. An AI. You yourself said so a few moments ago. A cerebral, logical, *detached* quality is attributed to my methods by those who know of my existence. This rather plays into my hands. The criminal underworld has recently become concerned about my presence. They have noted my success in solving the cold cases put my way by Scotland Yard, and they have fired a few warning shots across my bow.'

'If they think you're an algorithm, how do they fire warning shots? A sternly worded email? Did they block you on social media?'

He ignored that. I had read about terrorist cyber-attacks on the Yard's system. Maybe they'd been aimed at the ponce in the cravat.

'As I am confined to VR, my reach is limited, Watson. Hence, my enemies don't take me too seriously. However, they are making the same mistake as did the would-be assassins of Knives McKeller.'

'You have a sub-machine gun?'

'Very droll. Guess again.'

'Fine. You're not an algorithm. What are you, then?'

The hooded eyes flicked away from their examination of the ceiling and homed in on me. The look he gave me was intense and almost physically intimidating. It would give my glare a run for its money.

'I'm a consulting detective, Watson. That's all that need concern you. My nickname gives criminals the impression that my work is all done outside of Real Reality. They don't believe I can examine a crime scene, pursue a lead on foot, or turn up on their doorstep.'

He waited. I badly needed a drink, so I played along in the hope we might wrap this up. 'Are you telling me you can do all those things?' I said.

'No.' The intense gaze was joined by an incongruous smile, his thin lips twitching upwards. 'But you can. You're physically fit, an excellent shot, quick-witted, a good student, and capable of taking orders. One of the best hand-to-hand fighters in the army. All of this is useful to me, but two qualities in particular make you stand out.'

I smirked. 'My private life is none of your business.'

'Amusing. No, Watson, I'm referring to the intelligence that you hide behind those smart remarks. Your IQ test results put you in the top five percentile, but it's the way you apply that intelligence that interests me.'

If Clockwork Sherlock had been a character in a VR game, monologuing would have been listed as one of his strengths.

'You make decisions quickly. You are prepared to act on incomplete information in situations where inaction is dangerous. And when you do act, you do so without hesitation.'

I hadn't hesitated when I'd led the mission that ended with my comrades tortured and killed. I wasn't sure that was a personal quality I'd be bragging about any time soon.

'The other is your ability to survive. Physically and mentally. You ran eight miles barefoot through hostile territory at night, with a fractured skull, four broken fingers and bruising all over your body. You walked out of counselling after three sessions, then you walked out of the army. I've seen the report. After what you went through, the fact that you're still functioning at all shows a rare toughness of character.'

Even If I'd wanted to respond, I couldn't. I was thinking of the boy's face again.

'Your superiors believed you'd go far. There was talk of rapid career advancement. I require assistance, Captain Barnes, and you, despite your temporary psychological issues, are an excellent candidate.'

Temporary psychological issues. I'd punched a colonel. He'd needed punching. And, right now, it was taking every bit of my training not to throw myself across the room and batter the detective to death with his own violin, simulation or not. Of course, I still couldn't move, which didn't help improve my mood.

'I know what you're thinking,' he said. He sat down in the chair by the window and tilted his head back, placing his forefinger on his chin. His eyes were closed while he spoke. 'None of this is real, of course, which means the observational methods of deduction associated with the original Sherlock Holmes are not available to me. That's not strictly true. I can review documents, photographs and videos. Anywhere with a security camera can give me multiple points of view. And the way people behave in VR can often be as revealing as, say, spotting a series of scratches on the inside of a pocket watch.'

I remembered that story. I had been a big Sherlock Holmes fan in my teens. Not that I was going to give this charlatan the satisfaction of knowing that. In the story, Holmes had pegged Watson's brother as a drunk owing to the amount of scratches around the keyhole of his pocket watch where an unsteady hand had wound it every night.

One eye half opened and managed to express amusement before closing again.

'You recognise the reference. Of course, you don't have a brother, Captain Barnes. And if anyone in your family can be said to have a problem with alcohol, it's you.'

About ten seconds into my next tirade of abuse, the eyes opened, and Holmes fluttered his fingers in my direction. 'Get it out of your system, old man. I've muted you again, I'm afraid.'

I stopped. To be fair, he had a point about my relationship with alcohol. Not that he had any right to comment – if he knew about my past then he knew why I drank.

'Library and online shopping records are easily hacked.

Your military records weren't much harder, according to Miss Poplar.'

Who? It had been a man who drugged me, using the insultingly simple method of buying me a coffee and dropping something in my cup while leaning across for the sugar. When I started slurring my words, he helped me outside and bundled me into the back of an Egg as the world went dark around me. Huge bloke, mid-forties, possibly early fifties. Shaved head. Ex-military would be my guess. That made at least three of them, including Clockwork Pillock.

'I apologise for bringing you here like this, but I need help now, and your name is at the top of a very short list. I tried various methods to contact you. I imagine you thought my emails were a hoax.'

Apart from the occasional note from Dad, my inbox was full of reminders for unpaid bills. Everything went straight in the trash, unread. I wondered how Holmes's colossal ego would like that?

I forced myself to focus on what was important. I wanted to know who had the wherewithal to drug and kidnap me so efficiently.

I tried standing up again, my legs obeying me this time. I wasn't moving realistically. My real body was upright, but it felt unnatural. For the first time, the simulation lost some of its power. It might be more sophisticated than any VR I'd ever heard of, but even this environment had its limits. It wasn't real.

The room flickered and my head throbbed.

There was a mirror on the far side of the hatstand. I walked over, ignoring Holmes.

I looked at what they'd turned me into: the wrong gender *and* the wrong colour.

A fit, middle-aged white man stared back at me, eyebrows raised. His hair was sandy and thick, flecked with grey, as was his moustache. His eyes were clear and intelligent – a cornflower blue, rather than my own brown. I put him in his mid-forties. Over a decade older than me. He had the kind of face people warm to easily: open, trustworthy, loyal. Or was I superimposing what I knew of the fictional John Watson? Stolid, reliable, an everyman who marvelled at his companion's remarkable intellect.

I flexed my left leg. The stiffness wasn't due to any real-world injury. It was another gift from the virtual environment, like mutton-chop sideburns and bad teeth. I ignored a momentary urge to rummage around in the front of my trousers. Always wondered what owning one of those must be like.

Another strange flicker, this time in the mirror. Not a digital glitch, but something unexpected and disconcerting. The room behind Watson's reflected face lost its sharpness at the same time as my hearing dulled, the space around me suddenly claustrophobic. I stumbled across the room and sat down.

'What's happening?'

Before the detective could answer, everything went crazy.

3

'Stay calm, Watson. Placing a subject in VR while sedated makes it far more likely that the brain – particularly one as keen as yours – will reject the environment as the sedative wears off.'

'Brain? The sedative?' I don't usually repeat questions like a trained bird, but it had been an unusually trying day.

Holmes was looking at his watch. 'Vital signs?' he said to nobody. A slip of paper materialised in his hand.

'Thank you, Miss Poplar.' Holmes scanned the paper and shook his head. 'I'd hoped for longer. You're bumping yourself out of VR. Damnation. We'll speak again soon. I need an answer, and you really would make a first-rate –'

I wasn't listening anymore. I was fighting a sudden bout of nausea as two realities competed for dominance. My brain was telling me I was in a different room to the one I could see, that the chair underneath my thighs was nothing like the upholstered furniture I'd been sitting on. I could sense movement around me – not in Baker Street, but in the real world.

My vision blurred for a moment, then I started seeing double.

'Miss Poplar?' There was a note of urgency in Holmes's voice. 'Quickly, now.'

I could still see the detective, pipe in hand, his brow furrowed as he looked at me. But simultaneously, I was aware of a young woman, one side of her scalp shaved close, the other a curtain of blue hair, bending over me with a syringe.

I tried to bat her hand away. In Baker Street, my tweedy forearm waved in the air, but in the other reality, Bluehair got closer still. This was definitely Real Reality, my brain finally informed me, and my wrists were secured to the arms of a chair. I blinked and Holmes faded, although his voice was as clear as ever.

'Captain Barnes, please don't struggle. It's really for the best if you let Miss Poplar do her job.'

Miss Poplar – she of the blue hair and the syringe – was trying to do just that. The chair I was in was designed for comfort, not restraint, which meant there was padding along the arms and legs. While Holmes was talking and my new surroundings were coming into focus, I struggled, jerking my arms against their restraints.

Presented with a wildly thrashing angry woman had made Miss Poplar hesitate. No military training there. I noted the information for future reference. She paused, before leaning forward again, aiming the syringe at my neck. By then, I was pushing down on the spongy upholstery under my right arm with all my strength and, with one last effort, pulled my arm free.

Bluehair realised what I'd done, but her reactions were hopeless. She should have got in close and sedated me. I only had one arm free – the advantage was still hers. Instead, she tried to get out of range, leaning back.

I grabbed her wrist, twisting it down. She screamed and dropped the syringe. My head was free to move, so I pulled her close enough to see the fear in her eyes, then headbutted her. She dropped onto my chest, then slid to the floor. Something fell off my face and the last trace of Baker Street vanished.

I was in a small room. Clean. Clinical, even. My restraints were just Velcro snaps around my ankles and wrists, and I made short work of releasing them.

'Owwwww . . .' Bluehair was touching her nose. 'What did you do that for? I was trying to *help*.'

I ignored her. Next to her was the piece of equipment that had dropped off my face. It looked like an oversized pair of swimming goggles, although from the soft, slow blink of a blue light on the side, they were wirelessly connected to a computer powerful enough to run the Baker Street simulation. I stood on them, twisting my foot until they cracked and shattered.

'Really, Watson, that's quite unnecessary.' The voice came from the wall.

I took a step away from the chair. The broken high-tech goggles stuck to the sole of my foot.

The room was windowless with one door. It wasn't a big space. The chair dominated half of it. I had time to take in a few details – the chair was sophisticated tech, an array of multi-hinged rods that looked as if they could move independently, rising like branches from a solid stand. I had been sitting down, but the device could manipulate the occupant into almost any position.

There were cameras mounted in all four corners of the ceiling, and the other half of the room featured the biggest computer monitor I'd ever seen. Seventy or eighty inches, curved, swivelled on the desk at right angles so that I could see a pin-sharp rendition of the Baker Street apartment I had just occupied. Clockwork Sherlock's voice came from flat speakers on the walls, any of which would have cost more than my monthly pay in the army.

'Captain Barnes, please try to remain calm. You are in no danger, no one is trying to hurt you. It isn't unusual for a subject to revert to a fight-or-flight mentality under these circumstances. On reflection, it might have been wiser to approach you more circumspectly, but you refused to engage with any of . . . Miss Poplar, are you injured?'

Bluehair had shuffled herself into a corner and was touching her cheekbone. She would have a black eye to show off later.

'She attacked me.'

'I'm leaving now,' I said to the detective on the screen, who was staring out at me from his position by the mantlepiece. It really seemed as if he could see me. Ah. That was what the cameras were for.

He pointed the stem of his pipe at me. 'You haven't heard my offer yet.'

'Not interested.'

I started checking the room for weapons, or something I could use as one. I didn't know what was on the other side of that door and I didn't want to find out without a blunt instrument in my hands. Behind me, Bluehair – Miss Poplar –was moving.

As I turned, she spotted the syringe a few feet away. I got there first, knelt on her arm and pushed it against her neck.

No needle, it was a hyjector, one of those fancy air-pressure jobs, a single button at the end. I held it to her neck and pressed the button. The hiss sounded familiar; it had been the last sound I heard before I passed out in the back of the Egg and woke up in a Conan Doyle story.

'No. Don't do th—' she managed, then slumped and started snoring.

'Captain Barnes.' The detective's voice carried a strong natural authority and I almost came to attention. 'Please try to remain calm. Nobody who doesn't already work here knows our location, so I *cannot* let you leave until you have been sedated.'

'Yeah? And how exactly do you plan on doing that?'

On cue, the door opened. No light from outside spilled into the room because the entire doorframe was filled by my shaven-headed ex-military doping friend.

'Captain Barnes, this is Toby. Please allow him to sedate you without any further unpleasantness.'

I'm a good fighter. Better than good. Up close, I'm one of the best. I'm also a pragmatist, which means I avoid fights I can't win. We were in a confined space and my opponent, although at least a decade and a half my senior, was close to twice my weight. Besides, he'd already drugged me once today, spiking my coffee to get me here. I wasn't dealing with a slab of trained muscle.

'Is that how you hope to get a girlfriend one day?' I said. 'Drop a little something in their drink when they're not looking?'

He had the good grace to look ashamed.

'I'm sorry about that. But Mr Holmes is insistent that you are the ideal candidate.' His voice didn't fit his body, or his face. With his weightlifter's physique – his neck was like a tree stump – his physical presence was intimidating, but there was also a quiet intelligence at work that made him dangerous. And attractive, of course. No point in denying it. I'd let him buy me a coffee, after all, and let my guard slip enough that he could spike it without me catching him. I blushed at the memory.

'Mr Holmes is seldom mistaken,' he said.

'Seldom?' The voice from the speakers was outraged. Toby smiled.

I stepped towards him. This was a fight I was going to avoid. For now.

'Do as your master says, Toby, there's a good boy.'

He nodded, bringing up his right hand, the syringe looking tiny in his huge fingers. I tilted my head like a virgin offering her neck to a vampire. There was a hiss, a pinprick of pressure on my skin, then I dropped.

CHAPTER FOUR

WHATEVER THEY GAVE me to knock me out didn't last long. Long enough to get me out of the building and into an Egg. When I opened my eyes, the vehicle was in dark mode, all muted pastels and ambient music. I knew we were still in central London from the stop-start nature of its movements as it negotiated the traffic.

'Light mode, show view,' I said. The Egg stayed dark. 'Stop. Let me out.' No response.

I raised my voice. 'Emergency stop.'

I was only half surprised when the electric vehicle continued without pause. The emergency stop protocol was supposed to be impossible to override, but Clockwork Sherlock's virtual reality demonstration proved he had access to technology I'd thought was still years away. If anyone could hack TFL, it was him – or whoever he was working with.

There was a small cloth bag on the seat beside me. I tipped the contents onto my palm. It was my smotch – powered down, of course, to make it untrackable. I slipped it on to my wrist and looked at the face. The welcome message flashed up. There were no missed calls or messages. Had anyone even noticed I was missing?

As if hearing my thoughts, the screen in the Egg brightened. There was a call coming in, but I didn't recognise the ident.

'Reject call.'

The screen went blank for less than a second, then another call came in. Same ident.

'Reject call,' I said again. This time the screen brightened, showing the Baker Street apartment where I'd spent the morning. Holmes was sitting in the high-backed armchair by the window, smoking a pipe.

'Captain Barnes, I want to apologise for my handling of our meeting. I thought it best to approach you directly. I'm convinced that, with you by my side as Watson, we could –'

'Apology not accepted. End call.'

The line stayed open, Holmes drawing deep on his pipe, his dark, piercing eyes looking straight out into mine.

I tried again. 'End call!' Nothing. I folded my arms. 'You're not helping yourself. You've seen my service files, you knew where to find me. You even know I read the Sherlock Holmes books because you hacked the library system. Your violation of my privacy should have given you at least a tiny insight into how I might react to being drugged, kidnapped and held against my will.'

A thin smile from the detective. 'A fair point, Ms Barnes. I also know you have a logical, tenacious mind, and a keen sense of justice. If you could learn to rein in your –'

I kicked the screen in. I was hoping for a satisfying explosion of glass and complast, but it buckled, the screen splintering. The image of Holmes remained, his face folded in on itself like bad origami.

'– temper, Watson,' he said, one eyebrow raised. I kicked

it a second time. The screen went dark at the same instant as the privacy glass cleared and the Egg rolled to a stop. My efforts prevented the screen from showing the bill, but the Egg's voice functions were unimpaired.

'Journey time ninety-seven minutes.' Which meant either that Holmes was holed up beyond Greater London, or the Egg had been asked to drive in circles until I woke up. 'This journey, and the cost of the screen, will be billed to the account used to book it. All criminal damage is reported to the Metropoli—'

I'd never heard an Egg's programmed voice hesitate before. It was only for a fraction of a second, but it was there.

'The account has been settled. Goodbye.'

The shell rotated and the sliding door opened, the sill flush with the kerb. A blast of cold air hit me, accompanied by the kind of rain that contrives to fall diagonally, finding its way through collars and cuffs, and insinuating itself inside all forms of footwear. I climbed out and checked the doorway of my building. No one hanging around. I turned in a circle, cursing the Egg for dropping me directly in front of the door.

My economic circumstances usually precluded travelling in single seaters. I got around in Cartons, like ninety per cent of Londoners, making sure I got off a few streets from home so I could recce the neighbourhood before approaching my flat. I owed money, and some of my creditors were impatient.

As the Egg's door hummed back into place, I checked all the obvious places someone might use to watch my door. All clear.

The Egg accelerated back into the passing traffic at a speed no human driver would have risked, slotting into a space made available for it between a Carton and a cement truck. London had been driverless for twenty-three years, the rest of the country for fifteen, but I was old enough to remember sitting behind Dad and Mum on a rare car journey to the coast, watching him make occasional adjustments to the on-screen route plan. Once we were out of the city and off the motorway network, he had to take full control of the vehicle. It seems incredible now that we trusted ourselves to drive without help, that we accepted the loss of life that came with it, never mind the colossal inefficiency. Dad still moaned about the nanny state, even when I reminded him it once took us eight hours to get from Brick Lane to Margate.

I pulled the hood over my head and adopted the universal gait of the disaffected teenager, somewhere between a lope and a shuffle. I'm at least a decade too old to move or dress this way, but I'm small enough to get away with it, and it's cheap camouflage. I passed my door without slowing, shooting a look into the communal hallway. Also clear. Good.

The neighbouring building had been visited by the New Ludds' poster crew. The walls had been treated with anti-graffiti surfaces, but paper sheets and paste did the job nicely. I hadn't seen this one before. A salt-of-the-earth, honest male face, weathered and lined, stared out at me. Behind him, driverless diggers, earth-movers, rollers and cranes prepared the land for housing or industry. The caption was typically unsubtle.

SEVEN GENERATIONS OF MY FAMILY FARMED THIS LAND. OUR WAY OF LIFE IS BEING STOLEN. FIGHT THE MACHINES!

Their slogan may not have been catchy, but everyone recognised the New Luddite logo, with a pair of high-tech handcuffs representing the two 'D's in their name.

Personally, I was grateful for whatever tech I could access, and this moment was a good example. At the rear of the building, I checked my smotch, flicking past the missed calls to the heat sensor app linked to my flat. It showed someone had entered at 14:52. And they were still there.

The fence at the rear was easy to vault from the saddle of a wheel-less bicycle rusting in the long weeds. I ducked behind the sagging potting shed, looked up at the house, then jogged through the waist-high grass to the back door. When I'd moved in six months earlier, it had creaked like a horror film prop, so I'd smothered its hinges in oil. Hope for the best, prepare for the worst. I'd read that somewhere. Made sense to me.

The stairs were hardwood and as noisy as the door. Unless, as I did now, you took them at a run, four at a time. When I reached the third floor, I was light-headed. I'd missed lunch and had been drugged twice. Monochrome fireworks crowded my vision. I squatted, let my head hang between my knees.

'One elephant, two elephant, three elephant.'

Clockwork Shithead.

I swiped the smotch face, scrolling through the camera feeds inside the flat. All of them were still operational, which meant that my unwanted guest was either supremely confident, or an idiot. The final camera shot gave me my answer: he was both.

I walked into the tiny hall and hung up my hoodie, slipping off my boots. The kitchen was twice the size of the hall, meaning I couldn't quite touch both walls with arms outstretched. The living-room door was ajar, just as I'd left it.

I looked at my smotch again. The intruder was standing with his back to the door in front of the bookcase, holding a book.

I entered the living room silently, waiting until I was close enough for his astringent aftershave to dry my throat out.

'Mehmet,' I said, 'you're trespassing.'

He had probably imagined a different opening to our conversation while he'd been waiting. The only chair in the living room boasted a dent in the upholstery the same size as his sizeable behind. No doubt he had prepared a witty greeting for when I showed up, hoping to deliver it like a movie villain, seated in the shadows. At some point, he'd got bored, half opened the curtains and looked through my bookshelf.

The book he dropped when I spoke to him was a hardback copy of Mervyn Peake's *Gormenghast* trilogy. It wasn't just heavy in a literary sense, and Mehmet howled when the corner landed squarely on his slippered toes.

'Aaaagh!' He hopped comically around the room, massaging his injured foot.

'You remember I was a soldier, don't you, Mehmet?' I said, picking up the book. Fortunately, my intruder's toes had prevented any damage to the spine. I replaced it on the shelf. 'Trained to kill.'

He sat heavily, gingerly removing his slipper to check the damage.

'Is it broken?' he moaned. 'I think it's broken.'

'Can you wiggle your toes?'

He tried. He could, but the movement was accompanied by another shriek.

'Yeah, probably broken,' I said.

'I need a doctor. You have assaulted me.'

'For a broken toe? No. You don't need a doctor. They'll make you wait all day then tell you there's nothing they can do. I've broken all my toes, some more than once. Your nanites will help it heal. You'll be fine in a week. And you're lucky it's only your toe. You broke into my flat. After which you assaulted yourself with my book.'

He gave me a hurt look. It looked much more natural on his jowly features than the angry look he'd been practising for my return.

'*My* flat,' he said. 'And I used a key to enter the premises.

You are three months behind with the rent. I am taking it back. I cannot trespass on my own property.'

He had a point.

'Tea?' I suggested. 'Or would you prefer a beer?'

'I am serious, Joanna.'

'So am I. And sort those toenails out, Mehmet. Seriously. They're disgusting.'

He put his slipper back on while I filled up the kettle and got myself a beer from the fridge. It was after lunch, I told myself, even if I hadn't eaten any lunch.

'You have to pay, Joanna. I am not running a charity.'

'It's Jo.'

'And you should call me The Turk.'

I laughed and took a swig from the beer.

'No one calls you The Turk, Mehmet. You need to stop watching all those police procedurals. You own a couple of buildings and three kebab shops. You're not Tony Soprano.'

'Who?'

I rolled my eyes. No one watches the classics anymore.

Halfway down that first bottle, I knew it would take another couple to feel human again. Mehmet stood in the doorway as I made his tea, wrinkling his nose as he saw the teabag. 'How can you drink that? It's not really tea. No, no, don't put milk in it, what are you doing? Do you have any honey, at least? No? Sugar?'

I opened a drawer and handed him a packet of sweetener. He handed it straight back.

'A glass of water will be fine, thank you. I worry about you, Joanna. You do not pay your rent. You disappear for days at a time.'

The rent money and the missing days were both spent looking for Hughes. Chasing leads, bribing officials in a dozen countries. I'd been in Benidorm at the weekend, after an email tip-off, only to find a sixty-year-old ex-pat running a hydroponic marijuana farm. I was no closer to finding the traitor than I'd been when he disappeared in Afghanistan nearly two years earlier. And now my money had run out. Clockwork Git had done his homework. He knew I needed cash. Didn't mean I was going to help him.

'Are you eating properly?'

Mehmet was standing in front of the fridge. His bulk hid the contents, but I knew what was in there. Two dozen eggs, a bag of spinach, milk, peanut butter, beer, lemons and tonic water. The freezer was just big enough to hold two bottles of vodka.

'What are you, my mother?'

Mehmet shut the door. 'No. But you have been here a year now. I think you are a good person – you help my wife carry her shopping, you play with the children – but you are not looking after yourself. You look tired. And you've stopped paying your rent.'

'I'm fine. And you'll get your rent. By the end of the week. I promise.' It was a promise I'd struggle to keep. The only well-paid work I'd been offered was as muscle for local characters on the wrong side of the law. There weren't many legit opportunities for employment for ex-military types with a black mark on their record, and the few gigs I picked up here and there barely kept me in vodka.

'Nicky Gambon's men were here. Asking for you.'

Shit. Nicky didn't need a nickname like The Turk to convince anyone to take him seriously. Everyone knew who Nicky was, and everyone hoped Nicky would never want to know who they were. Extortion, prostitution, drugs, money laundering, Nicky Gambon had a hand in all of it. He'd served sometime early on, but he was too smart to go back to prison. He'd built an organisation. When he'd deposed the previous gang boss who ran things in Whitechapel, he'd done it in a typically brutal fashion, littering the streets with corpses. The boss himself was found hanged from a hotel window opposite the police station. Nicky Gambon was smart, careful, and probably the most dangerous man in East London. If you wanted a long life, you avoided him. So what the hell did he want with me?

'He says you owe him money, Joanna.'

Shit, shit, shit. I'd deliberately crossed the city when I needed a loan. The banks wouldn't touch me, not with my credit record, so it was either take a job protecting the local dealers, or get cash from a shark. I'd been careful. There was no connection with Nicky. None.

Mehmet drained his water and went to the front door.

'You cannot stay here, Joanna. It's not safe. Do you understand?'

I nodded.

'I don't know what you were thinking, going to him.'

I protested, but he waved away my excuses. 'I know you won't pay me the rent you owe.'

'I will, Mehmet, I just need a couple of days to –'

'But this is different. Joanna, a man like Nicky Gambon doesn't accept late payments.'

'Mehmet, I didn't go to him for money.'

Mehmet nodded. 'So you say. But he knows who you are. You took a loan from someone, yes?'

'Yes, south of the river. *Well* south. I'm not stupid.'

'Then Mr Gambon must have known about your financial situation and bought your debt. For whatever reason, this means he has taken an interest in you. He wants to see you, Joanna.'

Mehmet looked around the tiny kitchen, shaking his head. Great. I owed Nicky Gambon twenty grand, and he wanted to talk to me.

I needed another drink.

'Tomorrow,' I said. 'I'll move out tomorrow. If I box up my books, is there any chance you could . . .?'

'I will store them in the office for you. Only for a week. Then I will sell them.'

No, he wouldn't.

'You're a good man, Mehmet.'

He limped to the door. 'No, Joanna, only Allah is good. I am a careful man. Please return your key in the morning.'

CHAPTER FIVE

When I ran out of patience and threw my first punch, it wasn't aimed at the giant, bearded halitosis champion who'd put his meaty hand on my thigh. He was slow and would be easy to disable. Unless he was planning on poisoning me with his breath, which was so bad even the flies were rerouting.

No, of the three charmers who had been watching me drink, it was the small man with the widow's peak who would need taking down first. He was the quietest, the most watchful, the slowest drinker. He sat very still, a lizard on a rock, unblinking. I'd clocked the three of them in the reflection provided by the dirty glass of a faded Picasso print on the wall.

The small man spoke less than the other two, but when he did comment, they paid attention. Ten minutes ago, he had steered his cronies to a nearby booth at the back of the pub and I had caught a nod between him and the landlord.

If I was going to leave, that would have been the moment to do it. I assumed they were cheap thugs sent by Seamus, who was probably the cheapest of the loan sharks I owed money to. The last time Seamus had tried to collect, I'd been stoned. He'd tried to pin me against a wall. I should've let him. There were witnesses, and status means everything to bottom-feeding loan sharks. I'd left him with a dislocated shoulder for his trouble.

Looked like he'd sent others to do his dirty work for him.

I stayed put. I was pretty drunk. Right at the stage where I get mean.

It was late. The last paying customer had been shaken awake and directed to the street two minutes earlier, the landlord locking the door behind him. Two bolts and a deadlock. It wasn't the only exit. A breeze blew through the bar when the front door was open. There must be an open door at the back of the building.

Fistfuls of rain rattled the window. I looked at the three of them. Cheap muscle. They were at the budget end of the thug market. Part-time, probably.

I was smaller than them and look misleadingly young. This, combined with being born female, means I'm fair game to certain men. If you think I'm exaggerating, you must drink in far nicer places than I do.

They sat down in my booth without invitation, boxing me in. Nobody spoke for a while. When I finished my beer, I kept the bottle in my hand.

The lizard sneered. 'You're coming with us, sweetheart.'

It was clear he made up for his reptilian looks with a line in witty repartee.

I changed my mind about who to hit first when Beardy's hand squeezed my thigh. I snapped his middle finger. Whether it was a by-product of alcohol, or that his sluggishness of mind was mirrored by his nervous system, the interval between his sharp intake of breath and the scream was 5.6 seconds. Which gave me plenty of time to act.

The table went over first, sending drinks sliding towards the small man, who leapt to his feet to avoid being drenched.

His eyes flicked down to the tide of alcohol and glass crashing at his feet, then back up to me. Bad idea. The bottle I'd thrown connected squarely with the bridge of his nose, flattening it. Cartilage cracked and blood spurted.

Beardy was sobbing. He was out of the equation for now. The third man was on my left. His unsightly habit of sitting with legs spread as if to advertise his wares or, possibly to allow airflow around a fusty, unused area, presented too easy a target. I dropped, one arm braced across my chest. My elbow neatly pinned his genitals to the hard, wooden bench. He toppled onto his side, emitted a series of short stuttering gasps and curled up like a fortune-telling fish on a sweaty palm.

I vaulted the table, my senses singing. All the fuzziness was gone and I was smiling. I *needed* this.

The lizard scuttled backwards as I moved, his hand going to the small of his back. My intuition was bang on the money. He was more capable than his cronies. He had reassessed the situation fast. He'd been sloppy and he knew it.

His reflexes suggested time spent in the military, and the way he handled the blade, which he pulled from behind his back, suggested he had seen combat. I was weaponless, and glad of it. I'd seen enough death in the army.

The small man was all business now. Unfortunately, adrenaline turned him into a talker.

'A bit of a live one, eh? I don't mind that. I don't mind that at all. Just ask Big Bob.'

Did real people actually talk this way? Really? I wondered if all of them had alliterative nicknames. Lizardy Lenny? Halitosis Harry?

He tilted his head towards the bar, upon which the landlord's impressive man boobs rested while he leaned forward with interest. I wasn't going to be distracted. My eyes stayed locked on the lizard and I advanced, never taking my eyes off his face.

He hawked and spat a red wad of liquid onto the planks between us. He wasn't showy with his blade. His stance was comfortable, assured. He was confident he had regained the upper hand. As he edged to one side, I mirrored his movements. We prescribed a cautious arc around each other.

I let him manoeuvre into the open, away from the booth. He thought he could take me down more easily in a less confined space, away from the pool of beer and glass. Fine with me. I was as happy to beat him up in the middle of the pub as in the corner. I nudged one of the broken glasses, hooking it with the toe of my shoe. It rolled towards me. The small man froze, guessing my intention. We were eight feet apart and both of us knew I'd have time to scoop up the glass and throw it before he reached me.

'You *really* don't want to mess with me,' he said as a smile twitched at the corner of his mouth.

He was too confident. What had I missed?

The answer came immediately, and I cursed my complacency a split second before falling, sudden pain lancing through my side.

The landlord. Shit. I had dismissed him as a threat because of his distance from me. I failed to anticipate the taser he kept behind the bar.

I twitched like a landed fish, muscles clenching, spasming, and cramping, my cheek bleeding where I'd bitten it. I watched the beer-soaked trainers of the small man approach, tiny shards of glass crunching with each step.

A taser strike is a very effective, non-lethal way of immobilising an opponent. No one gets up for minutes after being tasered.

Almost no one, that is.

Much of the efficiency of the taser is down to the physical

shock suffered by the victim. Fifty-thousand volts of electricity leave the weapon, but considerably less than that actually passes into the target. Even so, the voltage is enough to drop the victim and send their muscles into spasm. Most people who've been tasered are keen to avoid a second helping.

I'm not most people.

The first time I was tasered was part of an initiation ceremony favoured by my old army unit. The loss of control had been so humiliating, I'd vowed to train myself to endure it. For weeks, I spent my free time with a commandeered taser, inflicting its coiled pulsed shocks to my body over and over, building my resistance. The advantage the small man and Big Bob thought they had gained was more precarious than they knew.

I let my eyelids flutter and twitch, keeping an eye on the enemy as he squatted in front of me. The third man was still curled up on the bench. He was no threat. Beardy was crying like a child while examining his finger. The danger from that quarter might not be eliminated, but he was preoccupied. Behind me, I heard the heavier tread of the landlord as he approached, no doubt to extract the prongs from my side, or – if necessary – give me a second blast.

'Not quite as clever as you thought, eh, babe?' my attacker said, prodding me with his shoe.

Lizard man had a point. The sober, match-fit Jo would have noted Big Bob as a potential threat and kept him in her field of vision. Sober Jo would not have underestimated her assailants. Then again, Sober Jo would be at home working out, staring blankly at the TV screen, or lying awake in her flat, rather than kicking the crap out of lowlife shitbags in the darkest, dodgiest corners of Whitechapel.

The small man held his knife in front of my face. I would have to make my next move count. Once they saw how quickly I could recover from being tasered, they would probably hit me with something heavy to make sure I stayed down. The lizard angled the knife, then placed it on my cheek. Putting his thumb on the flat blade to give him finer control, he pushed hard enough to hurt, not hard enough to cut.

'Nicky wants a word.'

Nicky. Oh. Oh, *shit*.

The small man's fingers danced across the face of his smotch. He took a photo of me, then held his wrist close to his mouth to dictate a message.

It had to be now.

I rolled on to my side and pedalled my legs, pivoting on my pelvis. My shin caught the barman first, sweeping his legs from under him. His smaller colleague reacted, but not fast enough. As soon as I had swept his feet out from under him, I rolled back to face Big Bob, just in time to see the back of his stubbled head smack the floor. With an explosion of breath, his limbs relaxed and his eyes rolled up. Lucky.

I spun back to face the other threat. Not so lucky. He was facing me. He punched me in the stomach. I raised a fist to retaliate and gasped at the pain that followed.

'Oh.'

The small man hadn't punched me; he had stabbed me. I put my hand to my stomach.

The small man got up. 'Let's go.'

I twisted my head too late to prevent Halitoisis Harry, still snivelling, plunging a needle into my neck. The room started to dance, but I couldn't join in as my limbs had been dipped in concrete.

Drugged for the third time in a day. Surely a record.

CHAPTER SIX

'You'd better go.'

I nudge Hughes and he grunts, turns on to his side. I nudge him again, harder. 'Yeah, yeah. I'm going.' His voice thick with sleep.

Sexual relationships aren't officially allowed between serving officers in a war zone, but the brass turns a blind eye. When there's a possibility of imminent death, humans like to remind themselves that they're still alive.

Hughes rolls out of bed and stretches, a bone clicking in his long, lean legs. 'You know I always obey orders, Captain.'

That last statement is technically true. He does obey orders, but if he doesn't like them, he lets everyone know about it.

Hughes is a strange candidate for the army. Intelligent, questioning, cynical, apparently devoid of any ambition to rise above lance corporal. He jokes about it, even refers to sex with me as the only time he wants to climb the ranks.

He fumbles for his clothes in the half-light. I prop myself up on one elbow. 'We leave in an hour. You OK?'

This is as close as I come to admitting to harbouring any feelings for Hughes more significant than mild pleasure at his availability when I'm horny. It's better to keep some distance between us. I'm his *commanding officer and we're about to cross the border into Afghanistan on a mission that – should it go pear-shaped – the British army will deny ever happened.*

As I watch him find his underpants and pull them on, I wonder how well I'm doing at maintaining that professional distance. I still call him Hughes. Surely that counts.

Something drops onto the hard floor. Hughes scoops it up, flashing a look in my direction. Too late.

I turn on a light. 'Is that a smotch?'

He carries on dressing. The moment of panic is gone. He's as laid-back and cool as always.

'Hughes. I asked you a question.'

He pulls a T-shirt over his head, then smooths his hair down. 'I heard you, Captain.'

My own smotch, like every other in the camp, was powered down and locked inside the quartermaster's safe the day I arrived. Military communication in danger zones is old-school, shortwave, coded. Even the best smotch tech might be vulnerable to hackers.

Hughes handed his in along with everyone else. So what had I just seen?

He puts his jacket on and squats next to the low camp bed. He takes the smotch out of his pocket. The wrist strap has been removed. It's an old model, chunkier than mine. He touches the screen. It's off.

'It doesn't work. Hasn't done for years. It's personal, Jo.'

He's never used my first name before. My skin prickles.

He looks away from me, down at the floor. Waits a few seconds before speaking again.

'It belonged to my sister. She was three years older than me. Died when I was seventeen.'

Hughes rolls the smotch between his fingers. 'Stupid, I know. Sentimental. But I think it brings me luck. I always have it on me.'

He looks into my eyes. I could insist he hands it over. I could press and hold the power button; check he's telling the truth. Or I could trust him. I choose the latter.

Bad choice.

'Wake her up, will you?'

It was a male voice, East-London accent. I was already awake. I'd heard a key turn in a padlock, then a chain being pulled through metal. Next, a squeak of hinges as a door swung open. Footsteps echoing. Hard to tell how many there were. The air that followed them in was warm and fetid.

My head was hanging on my chest. My eyes were half open. From that angle I could see a concrete floor and little else. There was one natural light source, but either it was miserable outside, or the only window was small and dirty.

My hands and legs were attached to the wooden chair with cable ties, pulled tight.

Someone turned on a tap. The sound of running water was an uncomfortable reminder that I badly needed to pee. One more piece of information about my cell: it had plumbing.

The bucketful of cold water drenched my head and upper body and I snapped upright, gasping.

'Rise and shine, Captain, rise and shine.'

I blinked water out of my eyes. A muscled goon, buzz-cut red hair, with skin so white he was almost translucent, stood on my right. He was wearing a brown shirt. After treating me to a cold, unfriendly glance, he put the empty bucket in the corner by a sink. The room was about the size of what an estate agent would call a third bedroom and I'd call a cupboard. Four walls, a sink, the chair I was sitting on and nothing else. I didn't much like the look of the stains on the floor, and there was a spatter of dark paint up one wall. At least, I hoped it was paint.

We were in a basement. The single window was about

twelve feet above me and the size of a shoebox lid. I wouldn't be getting out that way.

Another goon stood in the doorway. Black, broad, tall, and dressed in brown like his partner. They both looked as if they could handle themselves. Professionals, with bodies built by free weights and punch bags, not protein shakes and cross-trainers.

'I think brown shirts have already been done,' I said. 'You might want to try something new. I hear pink is in.'

No answer. I've never been very good at the smart-arse chat, despite reading boxfuls of American hard-boiled detective stories in the back of Dad's shop when I was ten or eleven.

'What do I call you?' No response to that, either. 'Fine. I'm going to go with Adolf and Benito.'

Nothing. I hadn't expected to get a rise out of them. Only the lowest thugs in the food chain can be wound up that easily.

The guy at the door – Benito – stepped outside. He was back almost immediately, holding a paper bag in one hand and a gun in the other. He dropped the bag next to the sink.

'Lunch,' said Adolf, crouching next to me. Cold metal pressed against my wrist and I tensed. There was a *snick* and the pressure released as he cut through the cable tie. He repeated the procedure while Benito watched, the gun pointing at the floor. He and I both knew he could shoot me before I took a single step.

Adolf fetched a pile of clothes from outside, dropped them next to the sink and placed my smotch on top.

After they'd left, I rubbed some life back into my hands and feet, then hobbled to the sink, sloshing water on my face, and drinking out of my cupped hands.

I pulled up my shirt and checked the mesh of the stab

vest beneath. It had done its job, but my stomach already boasted a blue-black bruise.

The clothes were my size and clean. Jeans and a maroon sweatshirt. I kicked off last night's clothes and got changed. I kept the stab vest on, of course. It was the most expensive fashion item I owned.

The smotch buzzed into life as it made contact with my skin and powered on fully when I looked into the camera. Battery at 0.5 per cent, flashing red. No net. Not even the hint of a signal, even when I stood on the chair under the tiny window and held my hand towards the muddy light. Seconds later, what was left of the battery died and the screen went blank.

I was off the grid then, stuck here at Nicky Gambon's pleasure. Not a good feeling at all.

I checked the room thoroughly. Twelve seconds well spent. The only unusual feature was the door, which had a sliding metal grille at eye level, like a prison. I wondered where rich criminals picked up this kind of specialist furniture. The Dark Web? Car boot sales?

The paper bag contained a peanut butter sandwich and a banana. Protein. Carbs. Good. I ate them, then wasted ten minutes trying to conceive an escape plan utilising a paper bag and a banana skin.

I used the bucket, and wondered whether chucking its contents at the goons might buy me the time to escape, or make them more likely to shoot me.

I was tired. I'd been drugged, spent a couple of hours in virtual reality with a lunatic who thought he was Sherlock Holmes, been drugged a second time for the trip home, got myself evicted, had a fight in a pub where I was tasered, stabbed, and – for good measure – drugged again, then spent the night tied to a chair at the behest of the most notorious gangster in London. And I'd just taken a shit in a bucket.

A habit developed during years of military service kicked in. Get your rest while you can. I curled up on the concrete floor and shut my eyes.

I enjoyed what I estimated to be nine minutes of deep sleep before snapping awake at the sound of breaking glass.

CHAPTER SEVEN

I REACHED for a gun that wasn't there.

Broken glass glinted in the corner of the room. The window above was missing a disc of about six centimetres in diameter. It was a perfect circle. I thought of spy films where assassins cut holes in glass through which they poked the barrel of a gun. There was no gun now, and surely the idea was to pull the circle of glass back out silently, not drop it twelve feet onto a concrete floor. I flattened myself against the wall so that I couldn't be seen.

A whisper from above. 'Sorry!'

Probably not here to assassinate me then. Something was pushed through the hole and lowered towards the floor on the end of a piece of string. I shuffled closer.

It was a box the size of a pencil case. Complast, the kind that biodegrades in days. I undid the string looped around it and an unseen hand pulled it up.

'Hey,' I hissed as the end of the string disappeared through the hole in the window. No reply.

Inside the case was a small thin pen, two flesh-coloured

buttons marked L and R, a contact lens case, a single-use antiseptic wipe and a lump of something wrapped in paper.

When I unwrapped the lump, I had an urge to squat on the bucket again. Plastic explosive. It was blue-grey, soft, heavy. When I held it up to my nose, it smelled like a newly tarred road on a hot summer day. PE-4x. The strong stuff. This lump was the size of my thumb. The detonator was underneath – a metallic rod with a button at one end.

Interesting. Not only did someone know I was here, they had access to devices only the military or police were legally allowed to use. And the military or police were unlikely to be sneaking around outside one of Nicky Gambon's houses helping me out. I unfolded the paper wrapped around the explosive. It was a note.

1. Put the monitors into your ears using the soft end of the pen to push them inside. The opposite end is a magnet to help you extract them later.

I rested the tip of the pen against one of the fleshy buttons. It stuck to it.

2. Use the contact lenses.

Holmes

Binary choices are easy. People sometimes think it's difficult to make decisions in a firefight, but it's not. You don't have time to think. If you're caught in the open when the shots start, you don't analyse the pros and cons of alternate escape routes. You shout an order, you run, and your team follows. Left or right. Find cover or make a break for it. Hold your fire or shoot to kill. Binary decisions.

Trust Clockwork Sherlock or don't trust him. Put the monitors in my ears or leave them in the box.

Binary.

I put the monitors in my ears. It was a strange, invasive sensation. I expected them to act like earplugs and block all sound, but they didn't. I could still hear as normal. Some sort of porous material.

I heard nothing other than clunks from the sink's pipes and the murmur of distant traffic, London's background hum of a million electric motors.

I'd never tried contact lenses before. They were fashion accessories, used to change eye colour and shape. Corrective laser surgery was cheap, so no one popped contacts in unless they were attending a fancy dress party dressed as a cat.

I didn't much like the look of these. Each lens shimmered like a pond on a windy day, ripples skipping across their surface. I cleaned my right index finger and thumb with the wipe, then lifted the first lens out of the liquid in which it rested. The ripples were still moving as I held it up to my eye.

It was either this or take my chances with Nicky.

Holding my eyelids open with my left hand, I moved my finger closer. The ripples looked like worms now. I tried not to think about it. The lens made contact with my eyeball and I blinked. My vision was unaffected, and the worms were gone. I repeated the procedure with my right eye.

Within a few seconds it was as if the lenses weren't there. I couldn't really feel the buttons in my ears, either. They were as snug as if they'd been specifically designed for me. I frowned at that thought. I'd been unconscious before waking up in the Baker Street VR. Plenty of time to take moulds of my inner ear. I was going to have something to say to Clockwork Sherlock if I ever saw him again.

There was a tiny click and a whine as the in-ear monitors turned on. At the same moment my vision blurred, then cleared.

I looked up at the broken window, taking a pace backwards and tilting my head to see if I could make anything out through the hole. To my surprise, I could. There was a small tripod outside. On top of it was what looked like a microphone – one of the long, thin, cigar-shaped ones I'd seen on twentieth-century TV shows.

'It's a camera, a microphone and a net booster, Watson.'

I swung around in shock. Sitting in the only chair, legs crossed, a cherrywood pipe in one hand, which he was filling with tobacco from a leather pouch, was Clockwork Sherlock.

'Wha—?'

Before lighting the pipe, he pointed its stem at the explosive in my hands. 'Might be best if you put that down, Watson. We wouldn't want an accident. It's rather powerful stuff.'

I did as he asked, then sat on the floor. I needed to be next to something solid.

'The booster we're using is only effective at short range, I'm afraid, so I've adapted the plan accordingly.'

He leaned forward and fixed me with a penetrating glare. 'Look, old man, the technology 221b uses is rather more advanced than you, or anyone else, is used to.'

I found my voice. 'AR.' Augmented Reality had fallen out of fashion along with glasses and smartphones a generation ago, only recently making a comeback as part of every smotch OS. Any noter linked to a smotch could now act as a virtual window, with information about the real world superimposed onto the images. It was heralded as a game changer, but people mostly used it to compare restaurant ratings.

Holmes fractionally dipped his head. It took only two strides of those long legs to reach the door, and he went straight through it like a ghost on a children's television programme.

'I could have just used the in-ear monitors to give you instructions, but AR gives us the option of non-verbal communication without anyone being aware of it.'

The voice came from my right. I swivelled round, but there was no one there.

'Only you can see me, Watson. It would be as well to remember that when you're in AR. You'll be supplied with additional wearable technology when we work together, but for now, we shall keep things simple. I'll explain more later. Let's effect your escape first.'

He was back in the chair, clouds of smoke coming from the pipe as he puffed at it. 'Are you with me?'

Unlike my father, I was a fan of technology. Under other circumstances, I would be deriving a geeky thrill from having access to devices such as the ones in my ears and perched on my eyeballs.

'Yes. Yes, I'm bloody with you. Stop calling me Watson.'

He did that dismissive hand wave again. I experienced a useless urge to break his fingers. 'I can see you're talking, Watson, but even this level of equipment has limitations. I know what way you're facing, and I can speak to you. However, due to the lack of signal down here, the only way I can hear you is via the mic attached to the signal booster above you. I'm not getting much, I'm afraid. Too much ambient noise. I will do the talking, and you will follow my instructions. Understood?'

A few choice responses came to mind, but I wasn't given the opportunity to use them. A green tick appeared in the top left corner of the room, a red cross opposite on the right. When I moved my head and looked at the tick, I heard a soft chime and it vanished. It was like playing a retro video game.

'Good,' said Holmes. 'Now listen carefully. As long as you obey my directions, I am confident we can extract you from the clutches of this ne'er-do-well.'

If he was going to talk like this all the time, we were going to have a problem. Fortunately, I was saved by the sound of a distant door being unbolted.

'Ah,' said Holmes, 'your host approaches. Good.'

'Good? Easy for you to say. You're not even here.'

The detective either couldn't hear, or chose to ignore me. 'We may learn something from Mr Gambon.'

Footsteps echoed outside. Holmes put his pipe between his teeth, then – as the padlock was unlocked – withdrew it again. 'Don't look at me anymore, old man,' he said. 'Don't want to give away our advantage, do we?'

'Will you stop calling me old –'

A heavy fist banged on the door and the metal grill slid open.

'Stop talking to yourself and stand against the far wall or I'll shoot you in the knee.'

I did as I was asked, moving the bucket to cover the broken glass. The window was high enough that they likely wouldn't notice the fact that it had been broken. I hoped.

The chain was pulled away and my two favourite henchmen entered. As before, Adolf – the pasty redhead – came in while his taciturn colleague stayed at the door. He drew his gun, thumbed off the safety and held it ready.

Adolf was carrying an item I struggled to identify. It was a black box about the same size as an old phone. It wasn't a phone, though. It was a bit chunkier, and there was no screen I could see.

Nicky Gambon stepped into the room.

CHAPTER EIGHT

'Sit down, Captain Barnes. We need to have a little chat.'

Nicky Gambon was physically unremarkable. Average height, brogues, chinos, an untucked white shirt. His white hair was shaved close and his goatee was neat. It was a bland face, but there was no mistaking those infamous doe-like brown eyes.

I said nothing. No point threatening him or demanding to be released. If I lost my temper, it would either make him angry or feed his sense of superiority – neither of which were attractive options when I was unarmed and held captive by two gorillas and the most famous psychopath in London.

Staying quiet, I looked at the gun Benito was pointing at me, and walked to the chair, wondering if I was going to have to sit on the virtual detective's lap. I supposed the fact that Holmes wasn't actually there meant I could ignore his presence, but it would still be weird.

Fortunately, he had anticipated Gambon's request and was now standing by the wall.

I sat down and winced as the bruise from the knife wound caught. Gambon noticed.

'Sorry about the trouble last night.' He sounded like he was discussing a party that had got too rowdy. 'The boys got a bit carried away. Still, you did give them more than they bargained for, didn't ya?'

Again, I chose not to respond. Nicky nodded. I couldn't tell if he was impressed, annoyed or bored.

Adolf put the phone-shaped object on the sink and pulled new cable ties out of his pocket. I let him tie me to the chair, then both he and his fellow brownshirt left the room, closing the metal door behind them.

Gambon walked over to the sink and the phone-shaped object Adolf had left.

I glanced at Holmes, but he was puffing happily on his pipe, paying no attention. I remembered he couldn't see what was going on.

I watched as the detective blew a cloud of smoke above his head and that was when it happened.

There was a click behind me and the smoke vanished. So did Holmes.

'Wouldn't want anyone listening in, would we?' said Nicky.

I have a pretty good poker face. I needed it as I stretched my neck, eyes half closed, scanning the room. No Holmes. No voice in my ear.

Shit. A blocker. I hadn't seen one outside the army. They were illegal in most countries, the UK included. Did Nicky suspect I might have help, or was he just being thorough? It didn't really matter either way as the result was the same. Any piece of tech nearby was now unable to connect with anything else.

I was on my own.

Nicky smiled. It was a perfectly ordinary, unreadable smile. That was the secret of Nicky's rapid rise to the top. He was rumoured to be one of the best card players in the country because his decisions were never emotional. If he got angry, disappointed, stressed or excited, it didn't show. There were plenty of stories about him, but the one that stuck in my mind was the time he took a meat cleaver to a rival at the same time as discussing dinner plans with a girlfriend on speaker phone. 'The lads are watching a horror film, darling,' he'd said as he hacked off his victim's hands and feet. 'Turn it down, lads, will ya?' Then he'd taken off the head with one swing, while suggesting his mistress book a table for nine o'clock.

His hands hung loosely at his sides. Big hands. I tried not to imagine them holding a meat cleaver.

'You don't expect me to show no interest in who lives in my neighbourhood, do ya, Jo?'

Hard to tell if he was being rhetorical. I cleared my throat, but he carried on talking. Right. Rhetorical, then.

'Military background, couple of medals, deployed to another one of our little wars with the Afghans, then all of a sudden, you're back home. Still, you might have led a quiet life, kept yourself to yourself. But you attracted my attention. Want to know why?'

Nicky evidently went in for rhetorical questions in a big way. I waited.

'Well?' he said. 'Do ya want to know, or are ya not bothered?'

Oh. Not rhetorical this time.

'Yes,' I said, my mouth as dry as sun-bleached paper. 'I want to know.' I coughed, careful not to wince again at the pain in my stomach.

'You asked questions, the sort of questions that get reported back to me. You're looking for someone, *someone* you thought might have gone to ground in London, right?'

Rhetorical or not? I nodded, hoping it would cover either eventuality.

'This bloke you're looking for. He was in your unit. You're

the only two left from your squad. The rest are dead. You left the army. He disappeared.

'You lost your whole squad. That can't look good on your record. Sold ya out, did he?'

He was fishing. The investigation had been held *in camera*. The army liked to clean up its own messes. My pulse climbed all the same.

'I can find him, Jo. Not only that, I can arrange for you to have a nice chat with him in a room like this one.'

I didn't say anything. Although I imagined it. Oh boy, did I imagine it.

'Have a think about that. There's a little job you can do for me. Do it right and I'll forget all about the thirty grand you owe me, plus I'll give you your old army pal. It's a hell of a deal, Jo.'

'*Thirty* grand?'

He fixed me with a steady look. 'Interest.'

I stared back at him. He was trying to intimidate me, and he was succeeding. There was no way I was going to let him see that, though.

Nicky called his goons back in, then returned his attention to me.

'I'll give you some time to think it over. I'll be back the same time tomorrow morning and we'll have a chat about what you can do for me. I'm not going to hurt you. It's a business proposition, that's all.'

He looked at Adolf. 'Cut her out of those ties, will ya? And leave the bucket in case she needs another shit.' He winked.

Two seconds after he'd left, his face reappeared in the doorway. 'You do know who I am, don't you, Jo?'

I thought about the meat cleaver and nodded.

'Good. See ya tomorrow.'

After he'd left, the ginger heavy stepped up, taking a knife from his boot. I tensed again as he prepared to cut the first cable tie, but when I glanced at the doorway, his partner waved the heavy pistol at me.

I'd have to think of something else.

CHAPTER NINE

THREE MINUTES after Gambon and his boys had left, taking the blocker with them, Holmes reappeared. He was standing where Nicky had stood in front of the sink, his intense stare levelled at me.

'Blocker?' he said.

I nodded and his face briefly twisted into a frown before returning to a passive, still state – like a computer character on pause. No tension in the muscles of the face, no twitches, no glances around him. He was utterly still.

'Nicky Gambon is an exceptionally dangerous man,' he said eventually. 'He knows how to distance himself from the activities of his criminal organisation. It's been years since he did his own dirty work. What is his interest in you, Captain Barnes?'

He turned those piercing eyes on me, and I experienced a momentary urge to tell him everything.

'I don't know.' It was the truth. I decided to omit the mysterious job offer and his promise of delivering Hughes. 'He's coming back tomorrow.'

'Really? It might be wise to wait until after then to break you out. If we learn what he wants, we can work to –'

I looked up at the net booster behind the hole in the window. He'd said it was a camera too. I made sure my expression was easy to interpret, accompanying it with a well-known hand gesture to make sure.

'Ah. You'd rather get out now. Perfectly understandable. My apologies. Let me explain what you need to do.'

I listened while he outlined his plan. Yesterday, Holmes had claimed to have researched my suitability for the role of Watson. I remembered from the books that the good doctor had always gone along with the instructions of his more famous friend, even if he didn't understand them. I wouldn't be such a walkover. However, I couldn't think of a better course of action than the one he was suggesting, so grudgingly agreed. It was lacking in finesse, but so was I.

After the briefing, I placed the plastic explosive on the door lock and pushed the detonator into the soft material. Then I lay back down on the floor, tensing and relaxing each muscle group individually, keeping my attention on what I was doing and trying not to think ahead. Overthinking would hinder rather than help. I'd seen the same in combat. When you've absorbed the information, far better to turn off and do something else. If you can.

My internal clock is better than the ridiculous antique timepieces Dad insists on wearing. It was just before 1 p.m. when I heard a door open and close, followed by footsteps. I stood up. The room was empty.

'Holmes?'

Nothing happened. No detective appeared. The footsteps came closer.

'Holmes.' I hissed the word through my teeth, then jumped as he appeared at my shoulder. 'Shit!'

'Ready, old man? Excellent.'

Holmes moved in front of me.

'Once we're through, we'll lose signal. I'll be gone until you get outside and pick up the net again. Take your position.'

I put my thumb on the detonator button. Seconds passed. Time took on the unreliable quality common to highly charged, adrenaline-rich moments.

'Now!' His voice was an urgent whisper.

The explosion blew the heavy door into the corridor, taking the red-haired Adolf with it. I followed, rolling into the cloud of brick dust and flakes of old paint. The skin on my stomach flexed, sending a sharp reminder of the knife wound. I ignored it.

The corridor was clear. Tomato soup dripped down the wall opposite and a smashed bowl lay next to the body. I checked his pulse. It was steady. His shoulder was dislocated, and he'd have a hell of a headache, but he'd live to explain to Nicky Gambon how an unarmed prisoner had somehow got her hands on plastic explosives.

As the dust cleared, I looked back into my cell. Holmes was watching me, his body flickering and glitching. 'This is where we part company.' His voice stuttered and faded in and out. 'There's a locked door at the top of the stairs. Check him for keys.'

He disappeared. I checked the redhead's pockets, muttering to myself. 'Wasn't born yesterday. I knew he'd have keys. Patronising arsehole.'

Big heavy doors with big heavy keys were an ancient, low-tech solution to security, but were remarkably effective against hackers. I found the keys and sprinted for the stone stairs, taking them two at a time. As I ran, I looked ahead at the keyhole on the metal door at the top. It was big and old-fashioned. Good. Only one key on the bunch I'd taken would fit it. I gripped it between thumb and finger.

The keyhole rattled when I was two steps from the top. There was nowhere to hide, so I crouched behind the opening door. Twin shotgun barrels appeared, advancing inch by inch.

Benito's voice echoed down the stairs.

'Talk to me. Is she out?'

No names. Smarter than they looked.

He was in no hurry to come down and check. Smart again. There was no answer from Adolf, so he'd assume he was unconscious, dead or a hostage. A cloud of dust in the corridor after the sound of an explosion. Only one exit, which was under his control. Benito was about to realise his best move was to retreat, lock the door and cover it until reinforcements arrived.

The shotgun moved backwards. I reacted.

Bracing one leg against the wall I pushed the door shut on the gun. I got lucky. He screamed as his fingers broke. Before he had time to swap the weapon to his good hand, I opened the door again and stepped into view. His right hand was useless, so he punched with his left. It was a good attempt under the circumstances – a straight jab at where he expected my face to be. But by that time the door was between us as I'd slammed it again.

The howl of pain from this second injury rose in pitch and intensity when, crouching, I opened the door again and punched him in the gut. He folded over and I grabbed his collar, using his momentum to pull him hard towards me, then twisting aside as he fell.

He was quicker than I expected, trying to regain control as he hit the stairs at speed. He managed to get a hand on my shirt, tearing it at the shoulder as he passed. His right foot slapped down on a step and he broke into a stumbling run, in an attempt to get his balance, but he was travelling too fast.

I didn't wait to see the result. He still had the shotgun,

after all. I stepped through the door, locked it after me and ran. No shots or shouts followed.

The room outside the stairs was nothing more than a four-sided box with a bare lightbulb. An open door took me into a kitchen, half a bowl of tomato soup still steaming. Before trying the only other door, I scanned the room for weapons, settling on a kitchen knife with a five-inch blade.

Holmes had told me where I was and that my best course of action was to brazen it out. I didn't know who was on the other side of the door, or how many of them there were; what I did know, however, was that — directly or indirectly — they were in the pay of Nicky Gambon. They might not be trained fighters like the goons in the basement, but they weren't on my side.

I took a breath, held it, and walked out.

The room I stepped into was another kitchen, but this one was four times the size and smelled of basil and garlic. The double door at the far end was still swinging and I caught a glimpse of the restaurant beyond. It was busy. I knew it well, had eaten here myself when I could still afford it.

There were two people to get past in the kitchen. To my left, on the other side of a rack full of hanging pans, was a large woman, her dark hair tucked into a net, loading a dishwasher. She had her back to me and was wearing headphones. Five feet in front of me was a tall, thin guy in his twenties. He was wearing striped trousers, a white jacket and an apron. Both his hands were wrapped around the handle of a flat shovel as he took a pizza out of the oven. He stared at me, then at the knife.

My shirt was ripped, my jeans were dirty, and my face and hair were full of dust from the explosion.

I shook my head at him and raised a finger to my lips. He nodded his understanding.

My stomach rumbled. I couldn't remember the last time

I'd eaten anything. Spinach, capers and a baked egg topped the steaming pizza. I pointed the knife at the stacked takeaway boxes on a shelf.

'To go,' I said, before adding, 'please.' I wasn't brought up in a barn.

A striped apron hung on a hook. I borrowed it, dropped the knife into the pocket, and nudged one side of the double doors open with my hip, holding the pizza box at shoulder height to conceal my face. The only customer who noticed me was a toddler, dark ringlets framing a face smothered in tomato sauce. I winked at her as I left.

The pizza place was half a mile from my flat, but I couldn't risk going back there. I turned right instead, heading towards Limehouse.

Before I reached the end of the street, Holmes appeared beside me, a dark green overcoat buttoned over his black suit.

'What's that, old man?' He indicated the cardboard box on my shoulder.

'Lunch. And quit calling me that.' Something occurred to me. 'How can you see me?'

In answer, the detective pointed first at the top of a lamppost, then above a shop doorway. Cameras.

'You're hacking the CCTV network?'

'Hacking is an ugly word, Watson. My consulting work has not gone unrewarded. Access to our glorious nation's surveillance network has been granted at the highest level, partly in thanks for services rendered and partly in anticipation of my help in future cases.'

He gave me a hurry up signal. 'The chef will have called his boss by now and Gambon has eyes everywhere in this borough. This way.'

I followed him into an alleyway. It was a dead end. Not a smart choice. I stopped and Holmes looked back over his shoulder.

'I know what I'm doing. Come on.'

Behind a skip was a nondescript door with a more common keypad entry. Holmes stopped in front of it and waited. When I didn't move, he pushed his virtual fingers through the keypad.

'If I could do it myself, why would I need you?'

'Tetchy.' I stepped forward.

'Eight seven six nine four.' I pressed the keys and, when the door clicked, went inside. Lights flickered into life overhead, revealing a large warehouse.

'Don't tell me,' I said. 'You own the building.'

'Wrong,' he said, filling his pipe. 'But the woman who does had infra-red cameras installed for extra security. Ironically, this enabled me to discover her door code by taking a still photograph of the keypad immediately after she'd used it.'

I shrugged, but was impressed. Especially as the building was only a few hundred yards away from where I'd been held.

'How many of these –' I began.

'Enough for my purposes. London is full of empty or under-used buildings. I have amassed quite a portfolio.'

Holmes indicated a staircase behind a row of clothes rails along the wall. 'At the far end of the upper floor is a fire escape down to another alley. At the end of that alley is a Carton rank. Let me take you back to 221b. You'll be safe from Nicky Gambon there. I understand you have a cashflow issue and have fallen somewhat behind with your rent. Board and lodging can be made available when you join us, Watson.'

It was time to stop this. 'There is no *us*. You had me drugged and kidnapped. I don't know what you think I can do for you.'

He sat down on thin air, leaned back and crossed his long legs. 'Please forgive the blunt nature of my approach. I felt it necessary. After all, you ignored my emails, and when I sent a colleague to speak to you on my behalf, you threw him in a canal.'

I thought back. Actually, that did sound familiar. A few weeks ago, a lead on Hughes that turned out to be nothing, then a lost weekend of vodka, cocaine and revenge fantasies. Going home after an all-nighter. Ah.

'He was stalking me.'

'He was looking for you.'

'He sneaked up on me.'

'He crossed the street towards you, saying your name.'

'He threatened me.'

'He said, *Excuse me, Captain Barnes, may I speak with you for a moment?*'

I reviewed my memory of the incident and conceded that Holmes's version might be accurate. Not that I would admit it.

'It was dark and he looked dangerous.'

'It was eleven fifteen on a Sunday morning. Jonathan is a retired police officer who runs the odd errand for me. He's seventy-four and walks with a stick.'

I winced. 'Is he . . .?'

'Yes. He is. Tougher than he looks, fortunately. He actually praised you. Called you feisty, said you reminded him of his daughter.'

That was when what had been nagging at me finally made itself clear. I remembered how thorough Nicky Gambon was reputed to be. How many times he had slaughtered a whole family to avenge a betrayal.

Dad.

'Shit.'

. . .

I dropped the pizza, took the box from my pocket and used the magnetic end of the pen to extract the first earpiece, placing it on the crate alongside the virtual Holmes.

'Please, Captain Barnes. Hear me out. I didn't pick your name out of a hat. I didn't come to you because I want the same Doctor Watson Conan Doyle gave us. It's not just your physical abilities, although they are considerable, it's your intelligence. Your skill set and moral code make you –'

The second earpiece joined the first and Holmes fell silent. I squeezed at the first contact lens and it sprang from my eyeball, landing somewhere on the dusty floor. I shrugged a half apology at Holmes, who stood, gave me a stern look that I refused to meet, then turned his back and walked away. The moment I had the second lens between thumb and finger, he vanished. I placed it beside the earpieces and ran for the staircase.

CHAPTER TEN

From where I was in Whitechapel to Dad's bookshop was a ten-minute walk, but I knew I could run it in six. I'd normally be quicker, but the bruising on my stomach made it harder to settle into my usual pattern of breathing.

When I rounded the corner of Princelet Street onto Brick Lane, I slowed to a walk, then stopped. The junction ahead was completely blocked with people. Scarves obscured the lower halves of hundreds of faces, goggles, sunglasses and hats preventing the CCTV cameras from capturing images clear enough to help facial recognition software.

I got close enough to see that all the scarves were black, and that each protestor had linked arms with their neighbour. Then I remembered the date.

'Shit.'

It was two days after the Iver Heath anniversary. The New Ludds went further than the rest of the country, not just marking the day, but planning traffic disruption during the week leading up to and following the 27th of January. They would be blocking carefully selected junctions around the city, coordinating their protests to cause maximum chaos. If the junction I had arrived at was the first to be blocked, the Fairfield algorithm that ran the driverless transport network would reroute traffic to avoid it. But the New Ludds, anticipating this, would block five or six junctions elsewhere, temporarily gridlocking the capital; Eggs and Cartons crawling, even bikes unable to penetrate the crowd-blocked streets.

Iver Heath was my generation's defining tragedy. Thirteen years ago, the unthinkable happened. At 6 p.m., Saturday evening, on a dark, wind- and rain-swept stretch of the motorway between Heathrow and the M40 exit, a mechanical failure in an Egg had caused the worst accident since human drivers were banned from the nation's motorways. The vehicle in question had joined the M25 normally, accelerating to its top speed of ninety miles an hour. A Feeder in the middle lane slowed and they were about to dock when it happened. The weather conditions disrupted the data connection, the Egg mistimed its approach and missed the Feeder. In itself, this should have caused no safety concerns, but as the Egg fell behind, it drifted across into the middle lane, crossing the white line – something we had all been assured could never happen. The protocol designed to protect passengers failed catastrophically.

Eggs are not designed to remain at high speed for long, so when it failed to dock, the smaller vehicle automatically reduced speed to a more stable fifty miles an hour. This would have been fine in the slow lane, but it was in the wrong lane. A second Feeder, which was increasing its speed to join a Roadtrain in the fast lane, struck the malfunctioning Egg at over two hundred miles an hour. The Egg, all but destroyed by the impact despite its tough construction, ricocheted away, breaking into pieces as it did so. Every single vehicle along the five-mile stretch behind automatically slowed to a crawl. If all the debris had spread across the middle and inside lanes, the disaster would have been averted. But the biggest piece, containing the body of Melissa Capstan, killed instantly by the impact, careered into the fast lane and struck the Roadtrain at its weakest point – the slip-streaming gap between carriages. Physics can't be denied; the Roadtrain was slowing, but it takes time to decelerate from three hundred miles an hour without injuring passengers. The carriage struck by the Egg was nudged out of the slipstream.

The footage of what happened next had been shown endlessly for months, an overhead traffic-drone shot showing the rear of the carriage twitching like the tail of a fish before tilting as it struck the central reservation, bounced onto its side, and was struck by the carriage behind, which was hit by the carriage behind that, and so on. Seventy-three people died that evening.

Sales of bicycles had tripled in the year that followed. Passenger numbers using the driverless network dipped briefly, but were back to normal within a month. There were documentaries, news stories, debates in Parliament. Software engineers, robotics experts and AI designers spoke about a billion-to-one chance, an unforeseeable tragedy. Changes were made, and they promised it could never happen again, but their explanations were impossible to follow.

The truth was, the kinds of decisions necessary to keep our transport network flowing had to be made in microseconds, and no human could do that. The network was run by artificial intelligence. And that was what the New Ludds found objectionable.

I'd observed the minute's silence with my fellow Londoners on Thursday evening. Like most of my fellow city dwellers, I respected anyone's right to peaceful protest, as long as it didn't inconvenience me too much. Right now, though, they were preventing me from reaching Dad. I unfolded my noter and smotched a map onto it, but the live feed showed that the market, and his shop, were completely boxed in by the protestors. I'd have to think of something else.

Shopkeepers and cafe owners stood in their doorways, watching the show. The air hummed with drones, both press and police. The Met would send squads of officers to the pinch points, but it was a game they couldn't win, and they knew it. As soon as one blockage was broken, accompanied by live footage and complaints of police brutality, the Ludds would block another junction elsewhere in the city. The New Ludds' leadership were careful to distance themselves from the protests, but they didn't condemn them. Londoners had come to accept the annual disruption, knowing it would last no longer than a week. The New Ludds didn't want to lose the political ground they had gained since Iver Heath by upsetting the grass roots.

It was an eerie sight, a crossroads filled nose to tail with Eggs and Cartons, silent and still, their occupants waiting for the disruption to cease.

All but the extreme New Ludds travelled in Eggs, Cartons, Feeders or Roadtrains, of course, since there was no alternative other than bikes, or walking. But their annual protests served to highlight their demand that humans take back control of their own transport. Iver Heath had played into their hands, despite traffic accidents since then dropping to 0.27 per cent of the annual average before the UK went driverless. Still, it made for good slogans: *Steering Our Own Future, Driving Humanity Forward* and so on. Many New Ludds kept a pair of fake handcuffs in their pockets so they could attach them to a seatbelt or hanging strap as a visible protest. Seemed daft to me. They could always just stay at home.

As I turned away from the protestors and into a side street, a cheer went up behind me. A police drone had come too close and a weighted net, thrown from an upper window, had snared it. I turned in time to see it spin and bob crazily, dipping in the air, before engaging emergency mode and sinking to the ground. The nearest protestors cleared a space for it to land, then relinked arms. Complast splintered and shattered, a wisp of black smoke threaded through the crowd and a ragged cheer went up.

I was sixteen on the first anniversary of Iver Heath. On that occasion, a national day of mourning was held. For twenty-four hours, no vehicles operated, not even private cars. A strange silence settled over the capital on that January day, lines of Eggs charging silently in depots and on side streets. I remembered walking through a familiar landscape that had suddenly become alien, everyone hushed, cold rain spattering the empty streets.

But Iver Heath had one unexpected consequence. The New Ludds, previously considered a borderline-laughable fringe pressure group, suddenly found themselves thrust into the limelight. They had been warning about the dangers of AI and the disastrous effects advanced technology would have on human progress for years. Greta Blackstone, the New Ludds' leader, had been the media's go-to anti-AI talking head for as long as I could remember. After Iver Heath, she went from being the butt of many stand-up routines to the focus of those who now saw her unease with technology as prescient. She articulated the unconscious fears of many, and she subtly fanned the flames of resistance until the New Ludds – who had embraced the mocking name given them by the press – were the fastest-growing movement in Europe.

Greta Blackstone had proved to be a cannier operator than most commentators had predicted, using the next decade to build support and distance herself from some of the extremists in the movement who advocated the use of violence. She used the media intelligently to spread a message of hope for the future based on human rejection of any technology that might supersede us as a species. No one had been surprised when, last year, the New Ludds had registered as a political party. Few doubted that Greta Blackstone would contest the next general election, and no pundit was prepared to bet against her picking up a handful of seats.

In the narrow street I had ducked into, I found what I was looking for. A young man in a hurry, late to the party, his black scarf hanging out of his jacket pocket, wearing an antique flying helmet and goggles. I stepped in front of him.

'Do me a favour?'

He didn't answer, but changed direction to avoid colliding with me. I moved too, side-stepping, grabbing the arm of his jacket. 'Asked you a question, Luddy.'

They don't like being called Luddies. Ludds, yes, New Ludds or Luddites, but not Luddies. He bristled.

'Let go. What do you want?'

'I'd like to borrow your scarf and your headgear, please.' Dad had brought me up to use my *please* and *thank yous*.

The Luddy gave me a quick up and down. He was a foot taller than me, maybe ten years younger. He looked fit and strong. The corner of his mouth twitched in a disbelieving smile. He dismissed me. His mistake.

He jerked his jacket to break my grip. When that failed, his temper flared and he gave me a good, hard push. Or he tried to. I pivoted on one heel and his hand missed me by three inches. He hadn't expected that, so he was off-balance. I used his momentum and weight to bring him down, sweeping a straight leg under his to help him on his way. He landed heavily, with no idea how to break his fall. His relative youth, and some seriously hurt pride, meant he ignored the pain of the fall, rolled, and tried to kick me. I'd moved, of course. His eyes filled with tears behind the ridiculous goggles when I punched him in the gut. I pulled it a little – didn't want to do any real damage.

'You're winded, that's all. Stay on your side. Bring your knees up to your chest. That's it. It'll pass soon, don't panic. Next time, don't get so rough.'

I peeled the helmet off his head and put it on my own, wrapping his scarf around my mouth and over my nose. Then I ran back the way I came.

'Let me through. My sister's at the front, there's an emergency!' It wasn't a brilliant ploy and some of the Ludds looked at me with suspicion, but I was a lone female, no threat. The line, six deep, parted to let me through, reforming behind me.

At the front, I didn't hesitate, using the sloping front of the nearest Egg to run onto its roof. Just like their namesakes, the Eggs are curved, offering no sure footing, so once I was up there, the best course of action was to keep moving.

As I leaped from Egg to Egg, weaving left or right to avoid the taller Cartons, the crowd responded, some cheering, others telling me to get down, berating what they saw as an individual act of criminal damage that could tarnish their protest. I ignored it all. As I approached the front line of the crowd on the other side of the street, I saw anger and confusion on the faces of some of the nearest Ludds. They were obviously considering tackling me, but since doing so would mean unlinking with their neighbours and breaking the line, they stayed put.

There were a few gasps of annoyance and shock when I didn't slow down. I jumped from the roof of the final Egg, landing squarely on the right shoulder of the biggest Ludd I could find. If he had intended to react, he was far too slow, as I continued on my way, picking my route across the protestors' shoulders. I hit the ground four feet behind the back line, barely slowing as I rolled, regained my feet and ran on.

I diverted into the covered market long enough to peel off my costume away from the cameras, then exited through a side door, within sight of Dad's shop.

Almost immediately, I smelled burning.

CHAPTER ELEVEN

DESPITE BEING, theoretically, part of the ever-trendy Brick Lane Market, Dad's shop – Ioawnat Booksellers – had managed to remain relatively obscure. It was greatly loved by the small number of loyal regulars who kept it solvent – just.

Part of its lack of success, despite appearing in at least three *London's hidden secrets*-type pieces on the big sites every year, was its forbidding exterior. There were no actual books in the window, just a huge poster. Large black letters set against a background of manuscript yellow, it read like a quote, but Dad insisted it wasn't.

YOU ENTER A BOOKSHOP. YOUR JOURNEY MAY BE BEGINNING, OR ENDING, OR BOTH.

People asked about the poster, just as they asked about the name *Ioawnat*. They received a different answer every time. I had heard dozens, and suspected the truth might be buried among them. I never asked Dad on my own account, choosing instead my favourite answer, which I'd overheard him outlining to a young literature student.

'Well, I'll tell you, but it must go no further. It's an anagram of a chapter title in one of Borges' hidden books –

novels he wrote in English under a pseudonym he never revealed.' He winked. 'I have a copy of it on the shelves, if you only knew where to look.'

That student, and many of his friends, were often to be found exploring the more obscure corners of Ioawnat after that conversation. My father could have run a successful, expanding business, but he chose not to. His needs were few. Enough money for business rates, food and two walking holidays a year. The only other necessity was a constant supply of reading material and, as the proprietor of a second-hand bookshop, that was taken care of.

He lived above the shop in a spartan bedsit full of books. No television, no computer, no smotch. He wasn't a zealot like the New Ludds, but he had no interest in technology. 'I have ten thousand universes on my shelves, Jo. When I am tired of exploring them, I'll look for new horizons.' Funny guy.

I hadn't associated the smell of burning with the bookshop until I saw the front door was held open by a hardback copy of *The Return of the Native*.

The front door of Ioawnat was *never* left open, not even in the dog days when it became unbearably stifling. While the shop boasted two enormous cast-steel radiators so ancient they might have warmed Charles Dickens' buttocks in his later years, the heat they gave out dissipated after four feet. At the end of January, Dad would be wearing a coat and fingerless gloves as he served the customers. He wouldn't leave the door open.

When I caught sight of the distinctive heavy, grey, ashy flakes produced by burning paper, I broke into a run.

Inside, Dad was surveying the damage, arms folded, frowning. He turned as I came in and lifted his arm, hugging me to his side. His beard tickled my forehead when he kissed me.

'It's not as bad as it looks, Jo.'

It looked bad. An angry black streak marked the spot where a set of shelves had been pulled away. The shelves themselves were ruined. The books that had survived were coated in the white residue left by the fire extinguisher standing nearby.

Dad smiled. 'Lucky, really. Probably lost fewer than thirty books, and the damage is only cosmetic.'

'How did it start?'

'No idea. The first I knew about it was the sound of the fire extinguisher.'

'The alarm didn't go off?' I looked at the sensors I had insisted he install. The lights weren't blinking. 'You get these checked, right?'

'Yes, Jo, I get them checked. Twice a year. As instructed. Last time was December – a month ago.' He shrugged. 'Technology failure. What happened to you?'

I was confused for a moment until I remembered my ripped shirt. I was about to explain when I looked down and saw I was still wearing the pizza restaurant apron. I took it off.

'I was baking.'

'You? Baking?' Dad eyed me quizzically. I smoothed down my clothes and smeared dust and dirt from the explosion onto my fingers.

'Yeah. I know. I'll stick to takeaways.'

I was about to check the alarm system myself when movement at the back of the shop in the sacrosanct space behind the counter caught my eye. I tensed, my hand automatically dropping to my side for a weapon that wasn't there. 'Hey, stand down, soldier.' My Dad laughed. 'It's okay. It's just Mark.'

I didn't move. 'Who?'

'My guardian angel. If he hadn't acted as quickly as he did, the whole shop might have gone up. I was lost in *Siddhartha*. You know how I get.'

I knew. At five years old, I had walled him in at his desk while he read, using sets of Observer's books as bricks. He hadn't noticed until a customer had rung the bell on the desk, only to shriek when Dad's face materialised between *Manned Spaceflight* and *Freshwater Fishes of the British Isles*.

The shop might have burned around him before he noticed. That was why I had insisted on the modern alarm system. Fat lot of good it had done.

Dad's saviour walked out of the shadows.

Mark was small, wiry. Even without his distinctive widow's peak and the bandage across his nose where the bottle had broken it, I would have recognised him. I don't forget people who've stabbed me.

He winked, then sniffed his suit jacket. 'Blimey, I smell like a barbecue. I'd best be off, Mr Barnes.' He feigned surprise at my presence. He wasn't much of an actor. I moved into a fighting stance and his smile widened. He was Nicky Gambon's man and he knew I understood what that meant.

I was dismayed at how fast Nicky had acted. He must have had his henchman primed and ready to act immediately in the event I refused to play ball.

Dad walked past me and clapped 'Mark' on the shoulder. Mark took an involuntary step forward. Dad is six foot three and broad as a bouncer. He tells me my mother always called him Heffalump.

'I'll pay for the dry cleaning, Mark. Send me a bill. I insist.'

'No, no, Mr Barnes, I couldn't. I just did what anyone would have done. I couldn't bear the thought of losing these wonderful books.'

I scowled at him, guessing the only books he'd ever read, if any, prioritised illustrations over text.

'Mark, this is Jo, my daughter.'

The little creep held out his hand. 'A pleasure, Jo.' I ignored him, so he turned his outstretched hand into a clumsy wave towards the ruined shelves. 'Can't believe I've never been here before, what with how much I love reading and everything, but good job I chose today to take a look-see. I reckon it was faulty wiring. I spotted the fire extinguisher and that was that. You might want to get those smoke detectors checked, though. It could easily happen again. Would be awful if you were asleep upstairs. Really awful. Right, Jo? It was Jo, wasn't it?'

Being punched in the nose when it was already freshly broken would, I guessed, be extraordinarily painful. I clenched my fist.

The antiquated phone rang in the back. 'Ah,' said Dad, 'probably the insurance company. Please excuse me.'

The small man looked in my eyes, saw what was coming and backed away. I followed. 'Don't even think about it,' he hissed. 'Nicky's on his way to have a little chat with you. Just you bloody behave.'

He hadn't gone for his knife. He had his orders and they didn't involve hurting me. I couldn't decide if that was good news or not. When he backed into a shelf of French philosophy, I squared up to him, my face two inches from his.

A shout in a bookshop or library sounds twice as loud as anywhere else.

'Boo!'

He jumped. A leather-bound Rousseau fell from the top shelf and caught him squarely on the skull. 'Ow. You bloody . . .'

I grabbed his nose and squeezed. His eyes watered and he brought up both hands to my arm. I squeezed harder and shook my head. When he dropped them, I eased off a little.

'Just so you know,' I said, keeping my tone calm and even.

'If you even *think* about laying a finger on my father, or hurting him in any way, I will find you, kidnap you and dismember you while you're still conscious.'

He paled, tried to speak. I squeezed harder and he shut up.

'Now I know you're one of Nicky's boys, so you think you're protected, but I promise you you're not. Think about this. I escaped from two of Nicky's goons earlier, probably put them both in hospital.'

No response. I smiled. Not a nice smile.

'I broke your nose and beat up your buddies too. I did that when I was drunk. I'm not drunk now, and won't be when I come for you. Think on that.'

Through the open door, I saw a black car pull up.

CHAPTER TWELVE

THE CAR DOOR swung open as I approached. Most people who could afford to pay the insane level of tax required to own a private vehicle were keen to advertise the fact. The fastest-growing branch of the arts was among those who offered custom paint jobs. Because Eggs, Cartons and Road-trains sold advertising on their carbon-fibre hulls, the private market had gone the other way. If you owned your own vehicle, you made sure it was a work of art.

Not Nicky Gambon. His car was plain black. No art. No mods. No decals. One big, luxurious, hideously expensive understatement.

'Get in.'

I bent down. The back seat was empty. So was the front. The interior was leather. Deep red. I thought of blood.

'I haven't got all bloody day. Get in before the sodding Ludds march back this way.'

Mark waved from the shop doorway. He was smiling.

I sighed, getting into the car. The moment I was inside, the door hissed shut, the windows blacked out and we accelerated with a lick of speed that pushed me firmly back against the soft upholstery.

The lighting inside the darkened car was like a chill-out zone in a night club, all subdued blues and turquoises. If it was intended to have a calming effect, it wasn't working. Nicky Gambon had ordered people dismembered for disrespecting his cat. I wondered what he would do to me.

'You're not stupid, Jo. You know if I'd wanted you dead, we wouldn't be having this conversation.'

The voice came from a panel on the seat in front of me. A screen flickered into life and Nicky Gambon's face appeared, those soft, brown eyes staring unblinkingly into mine.

'Carl has a dislocated shoulder and a headache. Raul wasn't so lucky.'

I said nothing. He was trying to scare me, or make me uncomfortable. He was succeeding on both counts, but I wasn't going to let him see that.

'You broke three of his fingers and every rib on his right side. His pelvis shattered when he bounced down those stairs. Modern medicine being what it is, he'll walk again, but not for a while, and when he does, he'll limp for a few weeks. I imagine he'll be thinking of you throughout his recovery.'

I shrugged and yawned to cover the hasty swallowing I was suddenly compelled to do.

'Every act has consequences, Jo. You could have stayed in that room, waited for me to come and see you again.'

And take another shit in a bucket, I didn't add.

'Yeah. I have a reputation,' said Nicky. 'I know. You probably didn't take me at my word when I said you were safe. No one could blame you for that. To be honest, I wanted you to try to escape. I didn't expect you to succeed, though.'

A rueful smile from Nicky. Was he trying to flatter me?

'I'll come back to that. First of all, my business proposition. I'm not going to piss about. I'll show you what I'm offering. Then we'll talk about what I want from you.'

My smotch vibrated. It was at full power again. One thing you can say about living in the city – the wireless charging is everywhere. Everywhere there's a signal, at least. The less generous might say it's in the government's interest to keep their citizens' smotches charged, since it gives them a means of tracking us, but I just like knowing I can search for the nearest source of Stoli vodka twenty-four seven.

It was an image file. I cupped my hand to view it and stopped breathing. I'd know that face anywhere. I had so many reminders. The scars on my back, the itch in the soles of my feet before a thunderstorm, an after-effect of the electrodes they'd attached there; the nights I woke up after I'd thrown myself out of bed because I thought they were coming back to torture me.

Hughes.

It wasn't a great photograph. He was half turning away from the camera and wearing some kind of ridiculous cowboy hat, but I would have known him anywhere. It was his face I looked for in every crowd, his description I typed into endless searches online, his voice overheard in bars, my hand clenching around a non-existent gun, yearning to put a bullet through his traitorous skull.

I leaned forward, my lips dry, my mind icily calm.

'This photograph was taken eight hours ago,' said Gambon.

'You know where he is.' I was surprised I could speak at all, let alone in a voice that didn't shake with fury.

'I found him, yes. It wasn't easy. Mr Hughes had put a great deal of effort into covering his tracks.'

I bet he had.

'It took me nearly the whole morning.'

I grunted.

I'd been looking for that bastard ever since leaving the army. The first thing our Afghan torturers had done was to cut out the trackers in our armpits and destroy them. According to the military, Hughes was missing, presumed dead, the same as the rest of my squad. They'd dismissed my theory as the understandable rantings of someone who'd suffered extreme trauma. So it was down to me to find him. All my spare time, all my money, and every favour I could call in, had been spent trying to trace Hughes. He had bought himself a new identity and melted into some backwater forever. The fact I knew I would almost certainly never find him didn't stop me looking. It gave me a reason to keep living when the rest of my squad was dead.

I had been searching for Hughes for eighteen months. And Nicky Gambon had found him before lunch.

'Where is he?'

In the screen, Nicky waggled his finger in an amused admonition. 'Nah, I don't think so. That's your *fee*. You have to earn it first, Jo.'

I didn't hesitate. 'Earn it how?'

'I want you to say yes to the dickhead in VR who thinks he's God's gift. Clockwork Sherlock. He wants you to work for him. Accept the job. Then tell me who he really is.'

I glared at the screen.

'How did you –'

'If I can find your man Hughes, do you think having your email account hacked is beyond my means? I'm insulted, Jo.'

He didn't look it. He looked smug. All but the most basic email accounts are supposed to be unhackable. My email provider boasted *military-grade encryption*. Right. I'd been shot clean through my left thigh on an incursion where my squad's position had been protected by *military-grade encryption*. Fair to say I wasn't a fangirl.

'I've already turned him down,' I said. 'Sorry.'

Nicky sat back and folded his arms. The silence stretched out until it was thoroughly uncomfortable. For me, at least. It was long enough for me to start wondering if he ever blinked. Finally, he leaned forward again.

'There was broken glass in your room. A hole in the window. A door blown out with plastic explosive. You had some high-level help. Who would help you, Jo Barnes? You resigned your commission, you haven't held down a job since then, you're well on your way to being an alcoholic, and you're three months behind on your rent. But someone found you in one of my gaffs and broke you out. I don't know anyone with the skills or the balls to do that. Also, interestingly, you were missing for most of yesterday. I'm thinking you decided to meet our virtual friend. Now, I won't ask you again.'

Nicky was starting to look a little tetchy. It was a small step, for him, from tetchy to homicidal.

I considered my position. There was no way I wanted to be on Nicky Gambon's payroll. I may not have been the perfect soldier, but that didn't mean I had thrown my moral code away along with my Glock gen eleven. Besides that, playing off one of the most dangerous criminal bosses in London against the rumoured skills of the VR detective would be dangerous, unethical and bloody stupid. But Nicky had bought my twenty – or thirty as it now was – grand of debt and he knew where Dad lived. There was only one answer that would give me a chance of surviving the next twenty-four hours.

I sighed. 'What exactly do you want me to do, Mr Gambon?'

He didn't smile or nod. He didn't react at all. He had never doubted that I would do anything other than agree.

'Give him a call, message him, whatever. Say you've changed your mind, that you want to try working with him after all.'

I thought of the VR goggles I'd destroyed, and the bruise Miss Poplar would be sporting after my visit.

'I don't think he'll believe me. We didn't exactly part on good terms.'

The car rolled to a stop. 'Not my problem,' said Nicky. 'Get it done. Don't try to contact me. I'll find you.'

I didn't like the sound of that.

'When you've convinced Clockwork Sherlock you want the job, call your dad and say you're working security for a restaurant.'

He was almost certainly tapping Dad's phone then.

'I'll give you until this time next week.'

I had to check my smotch to find out that it was Saturday.

'Don't disappoint me.'

The screen went dark and the car door swung open. I climbed out and it purred away. I was standing under an old railway bridge, water dripping down stone walls under pocked and rusting iron arches. My smotch told me I was a mile and a half from home.

I had been walking for ten minutes before remembering I'd been evicted. I kept going. Mehmet would let me stay a night, surely, rent or no rent. I wanted to box up my stuff. Tomorrow I'd move back in with Dad, which would mean he'd joke I was desperate.

Truth is, I *was* desperate. I was homeless, jobless, I owed a significant amount of money to a dangerous gangster, and I had three days to convince a brilliant detective that I'd had a sudden change of heart, after turning him down twice.

As it turned out, I didn't have to.

CHAPTER THIRTEEN

I LEAD *my squad through forests, always careful to stay within earshot of the river. We know the Afghan landscape well, and we are a tight, disciplined unit. We make no noise, communicating with hand signals.*

I wave Hussein over. The ope lab is three miles east of our location, but that isn't where we are heading. We need to get south of it. Two and a half miles before the pot-holed supply road reaches the heavily guarded perimeter of the lab, a natural rock outcropping provides excellent cover for an ambush.

We've been planning this for months, but, in a shocking piece of bad timing, Pakistan and Afghanistan have called a temporary truce – the first in three years. The British government is one of the sponsors of the peace talks so it can hardly be seen to send a squad to assassinate an Afghan general. Not officially, anyway. But the opportunity is too good to miss, so our orders come with one proviso – the op is off the books. We're dark. No comms. No tech at all, so no way of tracing us. No way of identifying us, either. Our fatigues came courtesy of dead terrorists; our weapons from an intercepted convoy. As far as the British Army is concerned, we don't exist. Not for this op. If we are caught, we are on our own.

Hussein is the best scout I've ever worked with. We move away from the river, following his route. I don't see much of Hughes — he's covering our rear.

It's late afternoon when we spot the outcropping. It's familiar to all of us. Just before dawn, at the final briefing, I'd used satellite imagery to show my squad yesterday's photographs of our destination. It was the first time they'd been told where we were going.

General Harif's convoy will approach from the south-west. Boone, our sniper, will take out the drivers and the tyres. Reynolds and Gasparini will mop up what's left with rocket launchers. Then we can go back the way we came before the smoke alerts the ope lab lookouts.

The plan is simple. Simple is best. Easy to remember. Not much to go wrong. Unless one of you is a traitor.

As we near the top of the slope, I look south. We can see for twenty miles and an approaching cloud of dust will give us plenty of time to prepare for Harif. I scan the road, but nothing is coming. I check my watch — the dumb kind. Smotches are trackable. It's nearly 5 p.m. If our information is good, we have about thirty minutes.

General Harif isn't just an Afghan general. Despite public denials, we know him to be one of the leaders of True Islamic State, the most significant jihadist group to emerge after the implosion of ISIS. He has been cementing his power base lately, and ope production funds his ambition. He's spent much of the past year searching for the Factory, the biggest ope lab in Afghanistan, run by a secular criminal organisation. If he controlled the Factory, he'd run ope production in Afghanistan. He'd stop being a local annoyance and move up to being a major threat to international security.

It's up to us to stop Harif. Permanently.

We reach the top of the outcropping. I signal to the others to move into position and they respond quickly, quietly, efficiently.

Then everything turns to shit.

Someone whistles behind me. Before I can turn, thirty armed men stand up from concealed positions around the ridge. Boone half-raises her rifle and the nearest man, wearing fatigues identical to her own, shoots her in the knee. She goes down screaming as the echoes of the shot come back to us from distant hills.

Then they are on us. They say nothing, just club us to the ground. I have time to wonder who whistled, before a boot catches me in the back of my head and my face smacks into the dust, my thoughts dissipating like the birds that scattered at the sound of the shot.

The doorbell woke me. I was asleep on my couch because Mehmet had moved my bed into another apartment.

'But that was *my* bed.'

Mehmet had shrugged, a gesture that involved some hand-waving. 'I will knock it off the rent you owe me.'

The sofa wasn't comfortable but I'd slept a solid eleven hours when the buzz at the door dragged me back to the world.

I threw a blanket around myself, but by the time I'd opened the door, there was no one to see. Just a package wrapped in brown paper with my name handwritten in black ink. Genuinely handwritten, not a printed font designed to look that way.

I made coffee before opening it. I only put a single finger of vodka in the cup. Not an alcoholic, see?

I hadn't slept that long for months. My dreams clouded my thoughts as I tried to get a grip on the mess I was in. The usual mélange of torture, death and Hughes's face.

The threat to my dad was uppermost in my mind. He might be persuaded to take a holiday, but I'd never get him away from the shop permanently, which made him easy to find. Nicky had been very clear about the consequences of letting him down. My life might be a mess, but I wasn't going to let Dad get hurt. He was one of the few reasons I kept opening my eyes every morning, a constant reminder that people could be kind, funny, bright, interesting. Dad kept me alive, along with Hughes. And when I found Hughes, when I killed Hughes, there would only be Dad. I had to protect him somehow.

Then there was Clockwork Sherlock; a mystery, an irritation and, if I was honest, an intriguing opportunity. I knew perfectly well the real reason I'd turned him down. Because it was a second chance. And I didn't deserve a second chance.

I couldn't stop thinking about Hughes, about the photograph Gambon had showed me. He was alive, and from the look of his photo, in good health. Tanned. Living the good life.

Hughes may have been the one who betrayed us in Afghanistan, but I was in charge, which made it my responsibility. Eight of us went across the line that night. Two of us survived. Once I'd put a bullet in him, maybe I could move on. Until then, I couldn't think about the rest of my life. There was no 'rest of my life' until that bastard paid for what he'd done.

Which brought me back to Gambon. He'd promised me Hughes. In return, I just had to hand him Clockwork Sherlock, to whom I owed nothing, not really.

I noticed my hand was shaking, so added another finger of vodka to the coffee. Then I opened the package.

It was a first edition of Arthur Conan Doyle's *The Sign of Four* – the second Sherlock Holmes adventure. It was in superb nick, red calf leather, gilt letters on the spine. Dad had once had a copy, but not in this kind of condition. I remembered how to check it was authentic, finding the word *wishes* misspelled as *w shed*. It was there. I whistled, the same noise Dad always made when he found something *really* special. Before sliding it back into the box, I checked the first page, and wasn't surprised in the least to find it was signed.

The book was accompanied by a letter, my name handwritten on the envelope. I unfolded it.

I misjudged you, and for that I am sorry. However, I no longer have the luxury of time to put right my error with the diplomacy you deserve. I am working on a case of peculiar importance, with some quite striking features. I would very much like your help – if my clumsy approach has not already made that an impossibility. As a token of my regret, I enclose a gift. I've also taken the liberty of paying your rent for the next year. No strings attached, Captain Barnes, but should you wish to take up my offer, you can message me at the following number this morning.

I held the letter in front of my smotch and added the number to my contacts.

Then I had one more vodka and pinged over a message.

What case?

CHAPTER FOURTEEN

We were due to meet the client at a swanky Knightsbridge hotel. Even showered, a little made-up, and in my best suit, I still felt like an imposter.

It was a nice neighbourhood. Georgian townhouses and private cars, robot street cleaners and a security guard on almost every door. Private security out here meant good money. It was the kind of job I'd been considering to make a dent in my debts.

Shit.

Nicky Gambon's face floated out of my medium-term memory, and he didn't look happy.

'Call Dad,' I murmured into my smotch, waiting the usual minute and a half while he ambled over from whichever armchair he had chosen for the night's reading. If he was in the bath, he wouldn't answer at all.

I was about to give up when the familiar rumbly greeting came out of my smotch. 'If you're anyone but my daughter, you can bugger off.'

One of the security guys outside a house with a front garden full of exotic greenery and palm trees took a step forward, looking my way. I gave him a cheery wave and brought the smotch up to my ear to cut the volume.

'It's me, Dad. You okay? Was there much damage?'

'I'm fine, Jo. Like I said, I was lucky.'

I thought of the short guy's nasty little smile. 'Your locks good? Alarm working?'

'Don't be paranoid. Everything's fine. Storm in a teacup.'

'Fire in a bookshop, actually. A bit more dangerous. And you didn't answer my question about the alarm.'

He coughed and ermed and aahed a bit.

'Dad?'

'Well, it seems, that, well, probably, um, it could be that, well . . .'

'What did you do?'

'It wasn't connected. I must have turned it off somehow. I don't quite understand how. Anyway, that nice Mark chap found the problem and it's all working again now.'

Yeah. I bet he did.

I wondered if it would be him listening in to this call and passing on the details to Nicky.

'Dad, if that nice Mark chap pops in again any time, you will let me know, won't you?'

'Oh, I see. Taken your fancy, has he?' He chuckled. 'I thought you only liked tall men.'

I rolled my eyes.

'And don't roll your eyes,' he said. Infuriating when he does that. 'Fine, I'll let you know. Now, it's lovely to talk, but *Ulysses* won't read itself, you know.'

'You're reading it again?'

'Well, I still can't decide if it's the best novel ever written or a complete load of old bollocks.' He knew my opinion.

'I just wanted to let you know I've got a new job, Dad.'

My cheeks were hot despite the winter evening. This was the first lie I'd told Dad in years. The words were like stones in my mouth. I spat them out quickly. 'In a restaurant. Security. So, if you needed to get hold of me, I might be working, okay? I think I'll be pretty busy.'

'That's great news, Jo. I'm proud of you. I knew you'd pull yourself out of that hole –'

'Sorry, Dad, I have to go. Talk to you later. Love you, bye.'

I swiped the call away. Now Nicky Gambon knew I was working for Clockwork Sherlock. Nothing good could come of this. It was a dangerous mess, and I'd have to work out how to drag myself – and Dad – out of it.

Not now, though. Now, I had an appointment.

As instructed, I walked past the hotel's front door and into the alley leading to the trade entrance. A black van blocked most of the narrow street. The back door opened as I approached, and a huge arm emerged to help me up. I ignored it and jumped in.

'Tobes.' I nodded at the man who had sedated me twice in one day. His huge frame looked even bigger in the confines of the van and he was bent over to prevent his head smacking against the roof. He looked uncomfortable. Good.

Behind him, sitting in front of three monitors like she was auditioning for the part of a geek in a spy movie, was my blue-haired friend.

'Popper,' I said. They spoke over each other in reply.

'Toby.'

'Poplar.'

The two of them exchanged a look and shared a smile. I was jealous of their easy intimacy. It had been a long time since I had felt anything similar.

'Call me Tobes if it makes you happy.' The big man shifted his bulk and the whole van rocked. 'Look, I'm sorry about the whole drugs thing. It's not something I would normally agree to do.'

I let the awkward silence hang there before answering.

'If you're hoping I'll throw you a bone, you're going to be disappointed.'

He grinned at that, not only recognising the reference, but acknowledging he knew I had done the same. In the Conan Doyle books, Toby was a talented dog with an exceptional olfactory organ.

'He said you'd read the stories.'

I scowled at that. It was one thing recognising a reference, but quite another reminding me that the Clockwork berk thought he knew everything about me.

Ms Poplar's black eye was impressive. She hadn't tried to hide it with sunglasses or make-up. I liked that.

'You can call me what you like,' she said, then deadpanned, 'Just try to avoid beating me up.'

She had balls.

I didn't offer an apology and she didn't wait for one. She held out her hand. A small box and two familiar-looking flesh-coloured items were on her palm.

'A fresh set of contact lenses and in-ear monitors,' she said. 'A few extras this time. Mr Holmes needs to see what you're seeing, hear what you're hearing. You'll . . . um . . .' She looked around the interior of the van as if seeing it for the first time. 'You'll have to get changed.' Reaching under her chair, she offered me a cream shirt and a black jacket.

I didn't move. 'Something wrong with what I'm wearing?'

'No. No. It's very fetching.' *Fetching.* By this time, I was almost warming to her. 'But it doesn't have eight cameras, three mics and an array of sensors stitched into it. Or does it?'

In reply, I stripped to my stab-proof vest. The shirt she gave me was too tight over it.

'You'll have to lose the body armour,' said Toby. When I eyed him, he shrugged. 'I'm sure we can have some bigger ones made, but this is all we have today, and you have to wear it.'

I looked him in the eye, undoing the straps and letting it fall to the floor. I wasn't wearing anything underneath. He went the colour of a postbox and turned away.

'Didn't even have to slip something in my drink,' I said.

I checked the shirt for electronic equipment but found nothing. Poplar watched me look.

'Nothing there you could find easily unless you knew where we'd put them,' she said. 'Camera in the top button, a mic at each tip of your collar.'

I still couldn't spot the camera. The mics were invisible too, but I could feel a tiny lump, and when my fingers brushed over them one of the screens in the back of the van reacted, a blue line spiking.

'One, two,' I said, watching the blue line rise and fall with my voice. Then I put the shirt and jacket on.

Toby was having trouble meeting my eye. 'Just need to check the jacket cams and mics,' he said. 'Can you, you know, turn around?'

'If you want me to give you a twirl, you only need to ask.' I gave him a knowing smile.

Poplar's screens showed the interior of the van, a handful of windows opening to show different views. Although I couldn't see them, the cameras were on the shoulders and the edges of the pockets, judging by the angles on the screens.

One of the cameras must have been on my back. On-screen, I watched Toby's eyes drop.

'Are you checking out my arse, Toby?' I only said it to make him blush again, but he was made of sterner stuff.

'Nope.' Looked like that was the end of flirting for today.

'Watson?' Poplar said the word without a hint of ridicule. I had a momentary epiphany. How many times had they been through this? How many Watsons had failed to meet the grade? Surely I wasn't the first.

'These code names,' I said. 'I get it, even though I'm not in love with mine. But if the boss is Holmes, I'm Watson, and our muscly friend is Toby the dog, shouldn't you be Irene Adler? If we're sticking to the Conan Doyle characters.'

Toby answered. 'She hasn't read the books. Hasn't even watched the movies, or the TV shows.'

'What? You crazy? They're classics.'

Poplar grinned. 'You three are the weird ones. Why would I waste my time on a book? What century do you live in? I bet you've never even played a *MOSMA*.'

I was tempted to defend my geek cred, but she had me there. The idea of linking my smotch to every other gamer in a Massive Online Smotch Adventure had never tempted me. I'd seen exhausted gamers trawling abandoned tube stations in the early hours, half-starved and all stupid.

'So, where did the name come from?'

That grin again. It was defiant. 'I didn't really fit in at school.'

I recognised an understatement when I heard one.

'My nickname was Miss Popular. I wasn't mad about it back then. Now I own it.'

She showed me a small black bag. 'There's a hyjector in here. I need to give you a shot. It would be brilliant if you managed not to headbutt me this time.' She opened the bag. 'You'll like this. They're ennanomeds.'

My eyebrows raised of their own accord, despite my efforts to appear unimpressed. Investment bankers with annual bonuses who could buy an extra house or three could afford enhanced nanomeds. Not proles like me.

'Consider it your healthcare plan. There are certain hazards in this job, so we like to make sure you're in tip-top condition. We want you to have every advantage. *Every* advantage.'

'You mean they're . . . ?'

Poplar nodded. 'Top of the line.'

'Ah.' I sat down and let her inject me. I had read about the next generation of ennanomeds, but even the most optimistic pundits thought they were ten years away from reaching the market. Standard nanomeds kept you snot-free and monitored your body for early signs of disease, ennanomeds promised better muscle tone, faster reflexes and increased stamina. Behind what I hoped was an implacable exterior, my inner geek was turning cartwheels.

If I expected to feel any different, I was disappointed. Maybe it was a placebo. Actually, she could have injected me with anything.

Poplar handed me a briefcase 'Everything you need for this evening is in here.' She held out her hand. 'Smotch, please.'

When I hesitated, she rolled her eyes. 'I only need it for a minute.' I handed over my smotch and she put it on a square black pad. Instantly, a new window opened on the screen and she dragged and dropped a file onto an icon.

'Scrambles the location signal, sends a mirror file back when it's pinged.' She registered my blank look. 'It means no one can track you.'

I thought of Nicky Gambon and wondered if that were true.

Poplar pointed at the briefcase I was holding. 'You might as well get kitted up. This will take a minute.'

I moved to the back of the van. I had a ton of questions, but Poplar had turned back to the screens. Toby wedged his bulky frame into a folding chair next to her and put on a pair of headphones.

Inside the briefcase was a mobile phone that was vintage

when Dad was my age, a Bluetooth speaker and a small complast case identical to the one that had been lowered into my cell at Nicky Gambon's. I guessed that must have been Poplar or Toby. Clockwork Sherlock ran a very small crew, it seemed.

As if responding to my train of thought, Poplar spoke over her shoulder while her hand swooped and tilted an air mouse, manipulating software faster than I could follow. 'We'll be staying close tonight, making sure everything works, but this isn't standard procedure. Mr Holmes likes to work alone. Assuming the tech still functions as it should, this will be the only time we will be hanging around.'

I opened the small case, put in the contact lenses and slid the in-ear monitors into place. Holmes didn't appear, but I heard his voice as if he were standing at my shoulder.

'Good evening, Watson. I'm glad you had a change of heart. Shall we?'

Before I could respond, Holmes's voice moved to the computers at the front. 'Thank you for your time this evening, both of you.'

'Of course,' said Poplar.

'Any time, Mr Holmes,' was Toby's response. As far as they were concerned, the sun shone out of their boss's Victorian trouser-clad arse. I wondered what he had over them.

The next time Holmes spoke, it was directly in my ear. 'Mustn't keep our public waiting, Watson.'

'My name isn't –'

'I know. And my name isn't Sherlock Holmes. But pseudonyms have their advantages.'

With a nod towards the others, I opened the back door and headed for the hotel.

Why is it that only country and western singers and people who open doors for a living are comfortable wearing tassels? I almost asked the question of the brocaded doorman who waved me through to the palatial, marbled lobby.

'Interesting,' said a voice in my ear. I tried not to flinch.

'What is?' I said, to the surprise of the concierge, who said, 'Madame?' as I passed. I gave him a weak smile and kept walking.

'The plain-clothes policeman sitting at the bar.'

I looked across the lobby. He wasn't hard to spot. A burly, bearded man sitting alone in the corner, a cup of coffee in front of him. He stared directly across at me, making a voice note on his smotch.

The invisible detective continued to speak directly into my ear. 'Our friend upstairs may not be a suspect yet, but I imagine she's been asked not to leave town for a few days. Take the lift to the forty-fifth floor.'

When the lift doors opened, Holmes was waiting inside. It was going to take time to get used to the way he could appear out of nowhere. I pressed the button, the doors shut and the lift began a rapid climb in absolute silence.

Holmes was dressed in a beautifully tailored black suit. It was the same suit he had worn in the apartment, down to the white shirt and the red cravat. In a virtual environment, he could, of course, appear exactly as he wished to, but he had chosen to present himself in the identical outfit. I made a deduction of my own. Clockwork Sherlock, just as his chosen namesake in the stories, was only concerned with the problems presented by unsolved crimes. Anything else was a distraction.

'Watson. Since first making my existence known to certain representatives of the apparatus of state, I have solved seventeen cases. The oldest was a burglary committed over three decades ago. The most recent was a murder committed four years ago by a means so subtle and imaginative that Scotland Yard was unaware a crime had even been committed until I brought it to their attention.'

I wondered why he was telling me this. Then he made it clear.

'The murder in question allowed a rather unsavoury character to rise to a position of power within the government of one of Britain's closest allies. My exposure of this individual went a long way towards establishing my credentials and proving I could be trusted with the most delicate of problems. The case I've been given cannot be solved from the comfort of the virtual world. We need to talk to suspects, visit scenes, smell the air, get our hands dirty. I cannot do that.'

Maybe he was an AI after all.

'Which is where you come in. Think of this case as a trial period of employment. When it's over, if it's appropriate, we'll discuss our possible future working relationship. Then there's the matter of your remuneration.'

He named a monthly figure a plastic surgeon would be happy with. It's difficult to haggle when your mouth's hanging open, so I didn't try.

When the lift got to the forty-fifth floor, it stopped, but the doors stayed shut. I jabbed at the button. Holmes shook his head.

'I'm holding it for a moment. I want to prepare you a little before we meet the witness.'

'And you didn't think of doing that back in the van?'

He vanished. I flinched. Then his voice was back in my ear.

'I want your honest impressions, Watson. Foreknowledge can too easily feed our biases unless we rigorously police our mental processes.' *A test, then*. 'I'll be watching and listening. Our witness has gone to considerable pains to conceal the fact that we are meeting her. Getting her to enter VR, or even AR, is impossible.'

'Why?'

He ignored the interruption. 'Although she believes a crime has been committed, no evidence has yet emerged to confirm her suspicions. My initial review of the facts, however, leads me to suspect her fears are well-founded. Foul play is likely. Almost certain, in fact. But this case is politically sensitive.'

'How sensitive? And why would someone want to hide the fact that you're involved?'

Then he told me the name of the witness and I understood.

CHAPTER FIFTEEN

GRETA BLACKSTONE WAS nothing like I expected because she was *everything* she was rumoured to be. I'd heard it said about charismatic people – even those whose beliefs directly oppose your own – that they made you feel as if you were the only person in the world when they were talking to you. Of course, once the light of their attention moved to someone else, the effect was dissipated, but the glow might last long enough to half-convince you to go along with their dubious convictions, or – in extreme cases – vote for them. Greta Blackstone had built a support base numbering in the hundreds of thousands by touring the country, meeting local New Ludd groups and speaking at rallies. Within a few minutes of meeting her, I could see why she was so popular with the good folk of her London borough, despite a platform based on dragging us all back to the previous century.

'You must be Miss Watson,' she said, coming to meet me as I entered the suite. There wasn't so much as a security guard posted on the door. She really was keeping this meeting quiet. 'Or is it Ms? I know how irritating it can be if people address you incorrectly. Don't let me make that mistake.'

Her smile was convincing enough, and I responded, despite my misgivings about her. I shook her hand.

'Just Watson is fine.'

'Watson. Perfect. I've brewed a pot of Darjeeling. Unless you'd like something stronger?'

Tempting. 'Tea would be lovely. Black, no sugar. Please.'

She picked up a tray containing teapot, china cups and a pot of sugar lumps, and set it down on a long, low table in the middle of the room, waving me towards a curved wooden sculpture that I belatedly identified as a chair. Fortunately, it was more comfortable than it looked.

The suite was a minimalist masterpiece. Other than a rug bigger than the entire square footage of my flat, the floor was polished dark wood. A spiral staircase led to an upper area, and an archway to my left revealed a second room with a dining table that seated twenty. Other than the low table and four sculpture-chairs, this reception room contained a huge wall screen and a grand piano, which, judging from the absence of fingerprints on its polished surface, was never played.

The lift I'd arrived in only serviced the suites which occupied the top few floors, all facing the river. The corner windows were floor-to-ceiling and the view was breathtaking, but I barely took my eyes off my host.

Blackstone poured the tea, perched on the edge of a second sculpture-chair. Her charisma was nothing to do with her looks: she was short, stumpy even. Her long hair was streaked with grey and tied back into a ponytail. She wore navy trousers and a plain, white shirt.

'I'm staying here for a week or two. Robert and I used to split our time between his place and mine. I can't bear to be in either at the moment.'

I nodded understandingly, without knowing what she was talking about. Holmes wanted me, as he put it, untainted by any foreknowledge of the case. If Blackstone were to ask me a direct question, I'd look like an ill-informed idiot. Brilliant.

'I was informed that we would be using some form of . . . advanced technology to communicate with Mr Holmes. I made it clear where I draw the line.'

If I had been distracted by her charisma, these words, coldly delivered, reminded me who I was dealing with. If this woman and her organisation had their way, the most technologically impressive piece of equipment in this suite would be the coffee maker. I glanced up at the wall screen. In a place like this, I'd expect to see cutting-edge tech: a screen that didn't just provide entertainment, but linked to the hotel mainframe, connecting the guest to any of its services, as well as accessing the net, providing video communication, gaming, and the usual exotic array of participatory porn. Not here, though. The screen was not only turned off, it was covered with a blanket.

Blackstone saw where I was looking. 'Oh, I'm no technophobe. People often make that mistake. But the clothes I'm wearing, the room I'm standing in, the kettle that boiled the water for our tea; they are all the product of human ingenuity. Technology, properly used, is a force for good. No, I have no problem with human technology. It's when we cross the line and start letting *things* do our thinking for us that we go astray.'

Her eyes dropped to my smotch in mute disapproval. Which I didn't really get. Sure, every smotch has a basic AI, but when I say basic, I've met more intelligent dogs. It can add a date to my calendar or recommend a movie based on previous likes and dislikes, but it's not as if we sit up at night arguing about free will.

When she topped up my tea, her hand shook. I looked more closely at her and saw the tension in the jaw, the way her eyes moved rapidly for a few seconds as if searching for something, before settling into a dull gaze that saw nothing at all.

Grief. I knew what that looked like. As I watched Blackstone master her emotions, the polite, neutral mask dropping back into place, I wondered if what I had just witnessed was genuine, or a performance. Despite what Holmes had said about preconceptions, I didn't like this woman.

'So how does this work?' she said, her voice flat. 'I made it clear I won't go into Virtual Reality to meet him. Or it. God, that it's come to this. But I understand that your boss is the best there is. If he can find out what happened, then I have to know. I have to.'

I opened the briefcase and took out the Bluetooth speaker, which hummed into life at my touch, and set it on the table. The phone wasn't as simple. I looked at it, rubbed my thumb over the screen, even breathed on it, but nothing worked.

'There's a button on top,' said Holmes in my left ear. 'Press and hold.'

A button. How novel. I did as he asked and, after five seconds, the phone buzzed and the screen glowed, the word *Welcome* blinking. At least, I think that was the word on the screen. The resolution was so bad, it might have been *Wilson* or *Wellington*.

'Open Bluetooth. Connect.' Nothing happened. I brought the antique closer to my mouth. 'Pair Bluetooth.' Hopeless.

'It's pre-voice control,' said Holmes in my ear. 'Press *home, settings, connectivity, search for devices*. Then select *GX Speaker*, press *yes* to confirm.'

'I'm getting cramp in my thumb,' I muttered.

Blackstone blinked and looked at me. I shook my head. 'Nothing. Doesn't matter. I'm just waiting for –'

'Ms Blackstone.' Even through a small speaker, Holmes projected authority. I'd heard enough attempts at a commanding tone in the military to know that most people failed at it. Not Holmes. His calm tone, leavened with a constant note of repressed energy, conveyed focus, conviction, intelligence and competence. There was even a touch of empathy, as if he knew you well enough to understand, and have sympathy for, the decisions you'd taken, the mistakes you'd made.

Greta Blackstone swivelled towards the speaker as if it contained the detective. A look of contempt flashed across her features so quickly that I wondered if I'd imagined it. Her voice was steady and her words precise.

'Mr Holmes. Robert, my fiancé, died last night. I believe he was murdered.'

CHAPTER SIXTEEN

I OFFERED the usual empty platitude. 'I'm sorry.'

Greta Blackstone spoke over me, her tone flat. 'Robert's daughter came to see him that day. They met for lunch. They hadn't spoken in person for a year. Hours later he was dead. He didn't give her what she wanted so she –'

Holmes interrupted. 'Please, Ms Blackstone. It's important you focus on the facts. I've read your statement, but I want to check some details. Before we begin, I'd like to know a little about your relationship. How did you meet Robert Fairfield?'

Ah. The leader of the New Ludds, an organisation opposing technological progress, buttering the biscuit with the owner of the best-known technology company in the world. Yep, I could see how that might be tricky.

Greta Blackstone stood up. Any fragility she'd displayed was gone. Whatever her personal feelings were, she had evidently prepared for this meeting and spoke fluently, without hesitation. I knew she was a good speaker, but I'd expect someone in shock, numb, devastated by the death of their partner, to be less lucid. She laid out the facts. Or laid them out as she wanted us to perceive them, perhaps. I was determined to keep an open mind and was far from convinced that someone confined to virtual reality, watching through cameras and listening through microphones, could ever hope to match the skills of someone physically interacting with another human being.

I listened. No need to make notes as everything would be recorded.

'I met Robert at a party just over a year ago.'

As Blackstone spoke, I looked for the emotional response you'd expect from someone remembering the first time they met their murdered lover. I didn't find it.

'It was a political event in honour of some anonymous career politician going up to the House of Lords. I say yes to those invitations, as much as they bore me. I need political allies, and the real business of government is often done over a few glasses of Burgundy at a party. He introduced himself as Robert, I responded with my first name. Of course, I knew who he was, and I saw the same knowledge reflected in his eyes when we shook hands. We used to laugh about it later. He was in the garden. There was a summer house at the end of the lawn that concealed a swinging chair, the kind you picture on the porches of American houses. I asked if I could join him, and we sat there quietly for ten minutes. It was extraordinary, looking back. All anyone did at those parties was talk, work the angles, make connections, expand their network. And I'm one of the best. Or one of the worst, depending on your point of view. As public sensibility has shifted in our favour, I find I'm invited to more and more parties. Our politicians are as pragmatic as they are ambitious.'

It sounded like she was reciting a speech. Maybe she was distancing herself from any direct connection to the raw memories. Or maybe she actually *was* reciting a speech.

'Robert and I knew we were going to end up together by the time we said goodnight. We sat behind that summer house until the sun went down. As we parted, Robert said, "What do we do now?" I said we'd find a way to make it work. "Yes," he said, "I really believe we will." And somehow we did.'

We were interrupted by a sound most people – unless they grew up with a father like mine – never hear outside of an old movie. It took me back to Wednesday afternoons with Dad, half-day closing in the holidays, when he would make me hot chocolate and we would watch a classic film, or – if I got to choose – an episode of *Columbo*. It was a telephone ringing.

'Excuse me,' said Blackstone. 'I have to take this. I left instructions I was only to be disturbed if it was an emergency.'

She walked over to a small wooden table that must have been expressly designed for the purpose of holding the antique device perched on top of it. She lifted the top part of the telephone and held it to her ear. 'Hello?'

Blackstone turned her back and lowered her voice. She moved around the corner, stepping through the doorway into the neighbouring room.

'What do you make of Ms Blackstone?' I flinched at the sudden voice in my ear. It would take some getting used to.

'I'm not convinced,' I said. 'Something off about her. Then again, I'm hardly a fan of the New Ludds and every time I see her face on a smotchcast, I want to slap it, so maybe I'm biased.'

'Maybe. What about her appearance, clothes, this apartment? Any thoughts?'

I took a quick circuit of the room, but there was nothing to see. As Dr Watson had ended up looking like a dunce every time he'd tried his hand at deduction in the stories, I had no great desire to emulate him. I kept my thoughts to myself.

'Not yet,' I said. Holmes grunted.

Fearing Blackstone would catch me snooping, I returned to my chair moments before she came back into the room. I stood up when I saw the tension in her face.

'That was the police. The results of the autopsy. Robert died of a massive overdose of liquid amphetamine.'

'How was it administered?' Holmes asked. From his lack of reaction, I guessed the autopsy result wasn't news to him.

I watched Blackstone carefully. She hugged herself as if the room had turned cold. Her expression remained neutral, but I could see the tension in her neck and shoulders. I'd visited the partner of every member of my murdered squad, seen every reaction from disbelief to rage. I'd never seen anyone with the level of self-control exhibited by Greta Blackstone.

'His insulin injection. Someone replaced it with the amphetamine.'

'Insulin injection? Who the hell injects themselves with insulin?'

'It's partly my fault.' Her voice was thick, eyes downcast. 'He knew my opinion of nanomeds, so he had them flushed and went back to insulin injections. His doctor advised against it of course, but by then, Robert had changed his mind about so many things.'

I couldn't let that go. '*Partly* your fault? The nanomeds meant he never had to worry about his diabetes, and you had him go back to injecting himself every day. What's your problem with bloody nanomeds?'

She flinched, but her answer carried the conviction of all zealots. Idiot.

'An army of tiny robots inside our bodies capable of

making any biological changes they're told to make? Those creatures could kill us in our sleep if they chose.'

'But they don't. They're programmed to look after us. Average life expectancy has risen fourteen years in the past twenty since nanomeds were made available on the NHS. Fourteen years. That's what you're robbing your followers of. What the hell's wrong with you people?'

Finally, I'd riled the woman. She snapped back at me.

'Is that *you* defending the nanomeds or is it them? How would you know the difference? Your body is riddled with them, I assume?'

She took my silence as assent.

'So, tell me how you can be sure you're even speaking for yourself, when millions of tiny artificially intelligent creatures could be manipulating your brain chemistry?'

'Because that's bollocks. I know my own mind.'

'Do you? How can you be so sure?'

I thought of the nightmares, of the constant background noise that wouldn't fall silent until I had watched Hughes take his final breath. Nope. Definitely me.

'I'm sure. My nanomeds stop me getting ill or dying. And if Robert Fairfield had still had his, he might be alive now.'

'No! He was murdered. If this hadn't worked, she would have found another way.'

She stopped talking and sat down, pulling her shoulders back and taking some deep breaths. Her eyes fell back to the floor.

Holmes's voice cut in. 'You said she, Ms Blackstone. Who?'

She knew she couldn't backtrack. 'The only one who knew what he was planning to do – break up his company and publicly support the New Ludds. Beth. His daughter. He was ready to alter his will, ensuring the company would not survive him, and leaving much of his estate to my organisation. He was a changed man, Mr Holmes.'

'Who else knew about this?'

'Other than me? Only Beth and her husband Jack.'

'And you suspect they had a hand in this.'

Greta Blackstone looked up and the familiar steel was back in her expression. 'Who else?'

There was another possibility. I butted in with it. 'Fairfield Tech is one of the biggest companies in the world. This might have been a corporate hit.'

Blackstone shook her head. 'Why? What possible good would killing Robert do for Fairfield Tech's competition? He has never been any more than a silent partner. He had no interest in the business. The only person who would benefit from his death is his daughter. Beth hardly ever came to see him, especially since we told her about our relationship. Robert spoke to her on the phone in the summer. She pleaded with him not to break up Fairfield Tech. He agreed to think about it. Robert loves his daughter.'

She paused, looked away and swallowed. I watched the tendons in her neck tensing under her skin.

'Beth came up from Cornwall yesterday. He told her he was going ahead, that Fairfield Tech was finished. She murdered Robert.'

She put her head in her hands.

Clockwork Sherlock looked unimpressed – impatient, even – at this sudden display of emotion. If he wasn't an AI, he did a damn good job of impersonating one.

'Ms Blackstone, tell me about last night. Anything you can remember might prove crucial, however trivial it might seem to you.'

Blackstone took a few long, shuddering breaths and looked up. 'I made a full statement to the police.'

'I've read it. Let me check a few details. You spoke at a

rally in Greenwich yesterday morning, then spent the rest of the day at home catching up on correspondence. Alone?'

Greta Blackstone's voice had returned to the practised, fluid cadence of the professional politician.

'The gift of solitude is something you tech-slaves will never understand until you experience it.'

If this was her attempt at winding me up, it failed. When I didn't respond, she continued.

'No messages, no constant torrent of social media, no virtual meetings with people who won't make the effort to come and see you. It's blissful.'

'It also leaves you with no alibi.' Holmes at his most caustic. I liked it. Blackstone didn't.

'What are you suggesting?'

'Suggesting? Nothing. Stating a fact. You have no vid feed to support your account, no calls made to or from a trackable smotch. You successfully campaigned to have security cameras removed from your Knightsbridge street, so there's no way of proving where you were.'

'They're surveillance cameras, not security cameras.'

'Please, Ms Blackstone. You're not on the campaign trail now. It's not as if you're going to win any converts in the present company.'

Blackstone went very still for a moment, then decided it wasn't an argument worth having.

'By the time I was getting close to catching up with my correspondence, it was dark. I hadn't seen Robert all week, so I called him and he suggested I come over when I was done. I knew he'd met Beth for lunch. He said he'd tell me about it when he saw me.'

She blinked slowly. 'That was the last time I ever spoke to him.'

'How did you get to Mr Fairfield's house.'

'I took an Egg.' A curl of distaste at the corner of her mouth.

'You claim to have arrived at eleven thirty?'

'*Claimed?* Mr Holmes, if you're inferring –'

'My use of the word *claim* is not an inference, Ms Blackstone. Your rejection of technology means we have no recording of the call to Mr Fairfield. Eggs entered and left your street at intervals during the evening but privacy laws mean it could take some time to confirm your account. Your time of arrival is, at present, based solely on your statement and what you've said to me. That is a claim, not a fact. To treat it as a fact would be a disservice to finding the truth. And you want me to find the truth, do you not?'

There was a long silence. 'Of course I do,' said Blackstone.

'Then continue.'

'I was at Robert's door in about fifteen minutes. Went upstairs, straight to his bedroom. That's where I found him.'

'Did you go anywhere else in the house – before or after finding the body?'

'No. I called the ambulance and the police from the bedroom. I sat at the bottom of the stairs to wait for them.'

'Did you check his pulse? Why not wait with him?'

'Yes, I checked his pulse. But it was obvious he had gone. The colour of his skin, the way he had fallen. The expression on his face.'

I watched Blackstone carefully. She looked like a woman fighting to keep control. Her voice had tightened, and she was breathing more quickly. Holmes changed his line of enquiry.

'Your relationship was a secret. Were you planning on keeping it that way?'

'No. Not for much longer. We told our families last year. Robert invited Beth and her husband over to meet me. It didn't go well.'

'How so?'

'Beth runs Fairfield Tech. Robert was never much more than a silent partner after he inherited the company from his brother. But, ultimately, he controlled it. Beth and Jack could see our relationship was serious. They were terrified of the implications for their precious company if Robert listened to me. Which, of course, he did. I never thought she'd go so far to stop him.'

'Patricide is a rare crime, Ms Blackstone, and there's no record of any animosity between father and daughter. Beth Fairfield may indeed harbour animosity towards you, if her father was really about to get behind your cause –'

'If? I assure you, Mr Holmes, Robert was absolutely committed to –'

'Inference again, Ms Blackstone, inference. Please. Let me continue.'

Blackstone rubbed her eyes and looked at the Bluetooth speaker. Behind it, unseen by her and only an image on a contact lens for me, stood the Victorian detective, watching her gravely as if he were really there, rather than observing her through the cameras sewn into my clothing.

She huffed out an exasperated sigh, but let him speak.

'If Robert Fairfield was preparing to break up Fairfield Tech, it would be a major setback for his daughter, granted, but she is the CEO of one of the most successful companies in the world. She would not be short of job offers.'

'You don't know Beth Fairfield. Her father was standing between her and the love of her life.'

'Jack Bolton – her husband? How so?'

Blackstone snorted. 'Jack is a good boy who does as he's told. He is far from being the love of her life.'

'Then who claims that honour?'

'Not who. What. All Beth Fairfield cares about is her precious company and the money that comes with it. She knew she'd have to wait to inherit Fairfield Tech, but when her father fell in love with me, she saw all her plans put in jeopardy.'

'And what do the police think of your theory?' Holmes already knew what lines the police were pursuing. This question must have been purely to observe Greta Blackstone, measure her responses, add the data to the rest.

'They are going to interview her. When they find her. She wasn't with Jack when they called this afternoon with the news of Robert's death.'

'Interesting.' Again, I realised Holmes must already have known this. One aspect of what Blackstone said didn't ring true to me. Beth Fairfield was patently not stupid. If Greta's theory was correct, then Beth would hardly have murdered her father in a way that made her the most obvious suspect.

Holmes, if he shared my suspicions, didn't voice them. 'If your accusation is correct, the evidence will prove it.'

When I had packed the equipment away, Blackstone stopped me at the door.

'Who is he really? Now I've met him, I cannot believe he is a piece of software, however advanced.'

Personally, the jury was still out on that. I shrugged.

'And the cold cases he is supposed to have solved. Is he really that good?'

I was about to answer truthfully that I didn't know, when Holmes spoke into my ear. 'Tell her what I'm about to say, please, Watson.'

'He has something he wants me to tell you,' I said, slightly resenting being used as a mouthpiece.

She nodded, her expression puzzled.

'I'm just going to repeat exactly what he's saying, okay?' I said, then did just that. 'A couple of general observations: you were very close to your mother, and you've recently taken up a new form of exercise. Yoga or tai chi, most likely.'

Blackstone's jaw dropped open.

'One more thing . . .' When Holmes said this, and I repeated it, I got goosebumps. He'd just quoted a line from *Columbo*, my favourite television show as a child. 'I hope you've arranged for someone to look after the kitten.'

'Well, yes, my neighbour will pop in to feed . . . how on earth?'

'Feisty little thing, but very affectionate. A tabby, yes?'

'Yes, but how did you know? How *could* you know?'

Holmes knew how to make an exit. We left without another word.

CHAPTER SEVENTEEN

I MANAGED to hold it in until we were in the back of an Egg. Through the back window I saw the black van containing Poplar and Toby pull into the traffic behind us.

Holmes had materialised beside me. His smile was one of anticipation. There was a puzzle to be solved.

'Fine,' I said. 'I give up. How did you do that?'

'Do what?'

'The cat, the yoga . . . that.'

He closed his eyes. 'Deductive reasoning, to those who fail to practise it, often looks like magic. However, I should warn you that – very much like conjuring, in fact – once the method is known, the trick appears insultingly obvious and unsatisfying.'

'Spare me the lecture, Sherly.'

He flinched and fixed me with those keen grey eyes. 'Holmes, if you please.'

I sighed. 'All right. Please. Holmes. How did you do that?'

His head went back and his eyes closed again. I reminded myself that he saw nothing other than what he could see through the various cameras on my clothing and, perhaps, the security camera in the Egg.'

'Very well. What were your impressions of the room? And of our client?'

I thought about it for a moment. 'Both were tidy, well presented. No mess in the apartment. Spotless, the whole place. Blackstone dresses well; smart, fashionable. Her make-up was subtle. Apart from her jacket on the back of the chair, the suite looked like no one was staying there.'

'Quite so. My deduction was based on tiny, but obvious details.'

'Like what? How did you know about the yoga and the cat? And what about her mother?'

'The watch she was wearing.'

I thought back. There had been a watch on her wrist where the rest of us wore smotches. Small, silver, antique probably.

'The earliest photographs of her wearing it date back to soon after her mother's death.'

'Hardly conclusive,' I pointed out.

'It's broken,' said Holmes. 'The hands are stuck at four fifty. I noticed it was wrong when she shook hands with you, and I checked again before we left. Why wear a broken watch? Because it has great sentimental value.'

'Makes sense,' I said. 'Simple, really.'

'Simple if you bother to train your mind to pay attention. And so to the cat. What did you notice?'

I tried not to look stupid. 'Well, I was paying more attention to her manner, to the way she behaved.'

'Watson, there is often much to be learned from the way someone conducts themselves, and from the words they choose to use, but you must remember that people can, and do, project a fictional version of themselves, a facade they wish others to accept as their true self. You must learn to look beyond it. The yoga was a guess, but an educated one. She kept adjusting her posture, subtly sitting up straighter, bringing her chin back. Someone has told her to do this, but the instructions are recent as she has to consciously remind herself to follow them. Yoga can be practised in small spaces and without taking much time. She's a busy woman.'

'And the cat? I don't remember seeing any cat hair.'

'You weren't looking in the right place. Her trousers showed signs of being recently brushed, but only from the shins down. The obvious place to rid yourself of cat hairs would be in front of the windows where the light is best, and two tabby cat hairs were clearly visible there.'

Not to me they weren't.

'Cat hairs in one of the most exclusive hotels in the city would be unthinkable. They came from our client. The rest was easy. An otherwise immaculate suit was marred only by the tiny puckers around the lap produced by a contented feline extending its claws. Two tiny scratches on her wrist, one older than the other, suggests the animal is still playful.'

I was equally impressed and annoyed. Nobody likes a show-off.

'Watson, I liked the way you deliberately riled her back there. About the nanomeds, I mean. Making her angry, breaking through her self-control to see if she might reveal something useful. Impressive. Thank you.'

'Oh, that.' Probably best not to let him know that I was just monumentally pissed off that a seemingly intelligent woman's half-baked ideals got her boyfriend killed.

'Yeah, it's a military technique,' I said out loud. A thought struck me. 'Who's the client?'

Holmes looked amused. 'What do you mean?'

'The client. In this case. Greta Blackstone certainly wouldn't hire a detective who's probably an AI.'

Holmes didn't rise to the bait.

'Did the police ask for your help?'

'No. I have a complicated relationship with Scotland Yard. We put up with each other. Senior officers may complain about me, but they can't argue with results.'

'Then who involved you? And why?'

He paused to light his pipe. A pipe that wasn't real, filled with invisible tobacco. It gave him more time than the rest of us to gather his thoughts. The slower pace of conversations with Holmes took some getting used to. Perhaps that worked in his favour when interviewing suspects.

'Watson, old man, if anyone can be said to be the client in this case, it's me.'

'You? Why?'

'Because it presents a challenge, and a good one at that. There's a puzzle here. Ms Blackstone is cooperating fully, but it could all be a bluff. How much do you know about Beth Fairfield?'

'Not much. She's supposed to be a business genius and she gives lots of money to charity. I've seen a few interviews. She actually seems pretty nice.'

'Hmm. How many people do you think knew Robert Fairfield was injecting insulin?'

'Other than Greta? His doctor. And close family, I suppose.'

'Beth, then. She's an only child. And you just described her as a genius.'

'In business.'

'Quite so. But this murder was premeditated. Even if she is of only average intelligence, if Beth Fairfield planned to kill her father, do you think she'd do it herself using a method only she, Greta, and his doctor knew would work?'

I could see his point. 'Surely the same applies to Greta, then. Unless one of them is trying to pin it on the other.'

'Quite. Or unless someone else found out about the

diabetes and his lack of nanomeds. This is a dark, dense forest, Watson, and we must cut through it. Let's start with motive. We only have Greta Blackstone's word that Robert was planning on changing his will and that he was coming around to the New Ludd point of view.'

'And the flushed nanomeds.'

'True. But what if Ms Blackstone found out that he wasn't planning on breaking up the company after all? Motive enough?'

I didn't like Greta Blackstone, but I wasn't sure she was a killer. Then again, I had been convinced that Hughes was a good soldier and a good friend, and look where that had got me. At the thought of Hughes, my skin prickled and I dug my nails into my palms.

Holmes had said something, but I'd tuned out his voice in the earpieces as if it was a smotchcast I'd lost interest in.

'I'm sorry,' I said. 'Say that again?'

He pressed his lips together and frowned, looking peeved. His avatar had quite the range of expressions.

'I asked you about Beth Fairfield's motive.'

'She's scared of losing her company. She always thought she would inherit it, now she thinks her dad lost his mind after he met Greta because all his blood supply was diverted to his danglies. If Blackstone's telling the truth, that is.'

'What a marvellous command of the English language, Watson. Let me show you something.'

The Egg's screen brightened, revealing a freeze-frame of a room. It was the interior of a restaurant. Chandeliers, silver platters, waiting staff so discreet they were hardly there. The sort of place where the prices would be printed in Great British Pounds. They'd only accept unidollars, of course, but it gave the clients a nostalgic glow to pretend the old currency was still good. Probably served meat, too. Not the sort of place I usually frequent – I eat at joints with complast tablecloths where no one minds if you top up your juice with vodka so long as you don't bother the other customers.

Judging from the light streaming in at the large window, it was lunchtime. Only half the tables were occupied. Holmes pointed to one hallway along the side wall. A man was sitting alone there with his back to the camera.

'Robert Fairfield yesterday afternoon,' said my companion. I squinted. His shoulders and the back of his head were the only parts of his body visible. My deductive skills concluded that Fairfield wore a dark suit, his hair was thinning, and – judging from his jacket – he hadn't suffered from dandruff.

'Is there another angle?' I said, curious to see the face of the man whose murder we were investigating.

'No. This is Saveur, an establishment with a reputation for discretion. Officially, there are no registered cameras on the premises. Miss Poplar outdid herself to obtain this footage.'

I'd heard of Saveur. Describing it as discreet was a bit of an understatement. Dad said the poet Von Turing was rumoured to have squatted on a table one drunken evening and taken a shit during an argument about Yeats. The staff had removed the evidence, replaced the cloth and brought him a bowl of water, some soap and a new bottle of Armagnac for his guests.

'Beth Fairfield arrived at one thirty-six.' The screen unfroze. Robert Fairfield stood up as his daughter approached, stepping out from behind the table.

Beth was in her early forties, but could pass for ten years younger. She was physically fit – you could see it in the way she walked. She was known as much for her love of dangerous sports as she was for her business savvy and charity work. As a schoolgirl, she'd got her kicks by hacking the school database for her friends, trading doctored school reports for cash. Famously, she'd been expelled from her first high school when she went too far, doctoring HMRC records, leading to the headteacher's arrest for tax evasion. These days, she fed her adrenaline addiction with hang-gliding, caving, base-jumping, free diving, wing-suit flying and aerobatics. The media loved her, particularly because she often used her extreme sports adventures to raise money for charity.

I leaned closer to the screen. 'Straight from the hairdresser, I see.' Her long blonde hair had disappeared since the last press photo I'd seen of her. The pixie cut she'd gone for suited her.

The kiss and hug between father and daughter on-screen was a little tentative, perhaps, but hardly indicative of a serious feud. The image froze, then settled into the twitch and flicker of fast-forward, the time code turning minutes into seconds.

'I wanted you to see this.' Holmes returned the video to normal speed as Robert Fairfield left the table and headed towards the bathroom.

Beth checked her smotch while sipping her drink. After nearly a minute of wondering what I was looking for, I gave up.

'What am I missing? She's not doing anything.'

'Precisely, Watson.'

I thought about it for a second. Robert Fairfield's half-full glass of wine was right in front of her.

'Ah. I'm guessing there are poisons that would have done the job as effectively as the amphetamine.'

'Quite so. Particularly straightforward when the intended victim has no nanomeds. Ironically, hacked nanomeds would have been the perfect method of delivery. A simple matter for Beth to tip them into his drink. Especially in a restaurant rumoured to have no cameras.'

If this video was ever made public, Saveur's reputation would be in trouble.

'Why is there a camera?'

The screen flickered into fast-forward again.

'Saveur's proprietor never claimed an absence of security cameras, she just never denied the rumour that they had been banned from her establishment. And since no media story has ever originated from Saveur, its clientele has assumed the rumour is true. Here we are. Unfortunately, Robert Fairfield blocked our view of Beth for the entire lunch, so there was nothing for the lip-reading software to go on until . . .'

Beth Fairfield was leaving. Robert stood up as they said their goodbyes. The camera had a good view of her face. As she spoke, subtitles appeared on the screen.

I'm glad we sorted this out, Dad. Family comes first, you know that.

She listened to her father's reply, nodding and smiling.

No. Look, I won't lie to you. It's hard for me to accept her, because of her views, but it's not my business. If you love her and she makes you happy, then I'm happy too. Of course, of course . . .

Robert was talking again.

Yes. Absolutely. We will. I'll bring Jack. Next month sometime. It'll be lovely.

Whatever her father said next caused her to shake her head and take his hands in hers.

No, no, Dad. I've changed. Grown up a bit. Realised some things don't matter quite as much as I thought. I'll find new challenges; you know I will.

They hugged, then Beth Fairfield left, turning at the door to blow a kiss towards her father.

The screen went dark. 'Interesting,' I said. 'Kind of blows a hole in Greta Blackstone's theory.'

'Possibly.'

'Possibly?' There was no answer.

We drove on in silence. When I looked at Holmes, he had

closed his eyes. There was something unnerving about his stillness. When he spoke again, I jumped.

'I've been doing a little checking.' His eyes were open and alert.

'Checking what?'

'It seems Greta Blackstone was right about Robert Fairfield's daughter in one respect. She's spent the past year secretly negotiating a deal with Newton AI.'

If Fairfield Tech was the best-known technology company in the world, Newton AI wasn't far behind. The new kid on the block, its super-rich American founder had aggressively expanded the business, buying start-ups and establishing companies alike, determined to lead the market in Artificial Intelligence. Espen Nuerro had never hidden his ambition to own his British rival, but Beth Fairfield had been equally vociferous about her complete lack of interest in selling. According to Holmes, her public position had been no more than a bartering strategy.

'She's selling?'

'Not the company. The patent on a new application of the driverless algorithm, plus a prototype vehicle designed to deliver it. If the encrypted files of a battalion of corporate lawyers on both sides are anything to go by, she's four months away from three hundred billion dollars.'

I spent a few seconds trying to wrap my head around a number so large it barely made sense, then gave up.

'That's a lot of money.'

'It is. It's also a motive.'

CHAPTER EIGHTEEN

The Fairfield residence couldn't be seen from the road. A formidable pair of iron gates blocked our progress as we turned into a side street approaching the Thames. The window slid down as we approached, and I found myself looking at a frowning police officer.

'You'll have to turn around, I'm afraid. This property is currently part of a police investigation.' At rest, her face exuded bored hostility.

Holmes's voice came from the car speakers. 'We are expected. Call your boss. The name is Holmes.'

I coughed.

'And Watson,' he added.

The police officer stepped away from the Egg, half-turning while she spoke into her lapel. The Egg purred forward another two feet, stopping alongside a keypad.

'One one two, one eight seven,' said Holmes. I punched in the numbers and the gates opened noiselessly, closing smoothly behind as we drove down towards the river. There were cameras at the gate, but none at the door of the imposing Edwardian house that came into view as we swung left along a short, tree-lined driveway.

The rear-cam showed the police officer coming after us, registering something in her earpiece, then stopping while the gates closed behind us. The look of hostility was still there, but at least we'd relieved the boredom for a few minutes. I doubted she was grateful, though.

'Robert Fairfield replaced his security system with an older version, Watson. I would guess his fiancée was less than keen on the latest smart systems.' He nodded at the briefcase I still carried. 'Front pocket, set of keys. I must say, despite its inferiority to more modern methods, a key and lock is a wonderfully pleasing mechanism. Combine it, as Fairfield did, with a series of codes and it's hard to crack. Any intruder would not only have to have a physical set of keys copied, but would also need to discover the correct codes. Get it wrong three times and the house locks down while the police are alerted.'

The keys were on a leather fob: brass, heavy and cold to the touch. When we got out and stood by the door, I was surprised to see the Egg remain where it was, its motor powering down. Having an Egg wait for you was supposed to be impossible. A waste of resources and energy, a blow to the fabled efficiency of London's transport system. I thought of blue-haired Miss Poplar and wondered if her hacking skills extended this far, or if the detective had friends in high places.

Holmes stopped me at the doorway. 'No one has been allowed into the property since he was found, which makes life easier.'

He was walking around the perimeter, indicating that I should follow his non-existent footsteps, so as not to disturb any potential evidence. His expression was one of absolute concentration.

'Bring some light over here, will you?'

I patted my pockets for a torch, but as I reached Holmes, my right jacket cuff glowed, throwing a bright beam of light onto the house. Clever. Holmes didn't thank me.

'The killer was almost certainly known to the victim as they had the necessary keys and codes, but assumptions are dangerous creatures, Watson. It wouldn't do to pursue the one theory that makes sense without first making some standard checks that will eliminate other hypotheses.'

'Why couldn't it be a stranger? Keys can be copied. A drone could have filmed Fairfield inputting the security code.'

'Good thinking, Watson, if it weren't for one detail our victim kept secret from his fiancée.'

He walked away without elaborating, gesturing at me to follow. It was almost possible to believe we weren't in Central London once we were in the garden. The house itself stood between us and the Thames, and mature trees and hedges obscured the road we'd left at the end of the driveway.

Holmes had me pause at one of the flowerbeds that lined the neat lawn.

'Could you get closer, please?'

I knelt by a cluster of tiny white flowers. I'm not much of a gardener. They smelled cloyingly sweet up close. Ten feet behind me, four iron chairs were set around a table under a folded parasol. The flowerbed looked unremarkable to me, but I wasn't sure what Holmes was looking for. No footprints or marks where a ladder might have stood.

'Fine. If you'd stand up, please.' When I did so, there was a tiny whine from my left shoulder. I wouldn't have heard anything if the night hadn't been so still. I looked for an insect but saw nothing. Then I remembered the array of cameras dotted about my person.

'No fingerprints or marks on the outside of the bedroom window, no holes in the brickwork. No one got in that way.'

I peered up but could see nothing. A Virginia creeper covered much of this side of the house. I squinted. Another whine from my shoulder.

'Let's continue,' said Holmes, his avatar striding ahead.

'Wait, these cameras, can they zoom in?'

In answer, he merely waved me on impatiently. 'Come, come, Watson, we're hardly New Ludds, are we? Only the best technology for 221b.'

A camera hidden in a button capable of zooming in with enough resolution that Holmes could make out fingerprints on the window above me. And it must have a steadying mechanism able to compensate for my movements. Again, I wondered who was funding this operation and how Clockwork Sherlock could get his hands on technology a few years ahead of the rest of us.

I hurried to keep up with his long strides. His inspection of the rest of the exterior was cursory until he got to the river. The house was accessible from the water, an integral boathouse jutting out at the rear. It was inaccessible on foot from outside. Any approaching boat had to negotiate a floating harbour and an intercom to announce its arrival. A brick archway led from the water into the boathouse itself.

'There's a two-berth restored wherry inside,' said Holmes. 'Over a hundred years old, retro-fitted with an electric outboard. Licensed for a hundred hours of manual piloting per year.'

I whistled. The water was the last place in the UK outside a racetrack where humans could, if they had the funds, take full control of a vehicle. A hundred hours of freedom would cost a small fortune.

'River authority records show it hasn't been taken out for months,' said Holmes. 'The only other entrance to the house is in that boathouse. And any intruder would require the same code and key combination as the main door.'

He pointed across the river. 'Plenty of security cameras pointing this way. Miss Poplar and Toby have reviewed the footage and found nothing. Time to look inside.'

Back at the front door, a six-digit number on the keypad caused a panel to lower, exposing the keyhole. The lock opened with a satisfying clunk and we stepped into a cool, darkened hallway, heavy curtains blocking the light from the sinking sun.

'Lights.' The room remained in shadow. 'Lights.' When nothing happened, I waved my arms around to trigger the sensor. Eventually, I figured it out for myself.

'Oh, don't tell me,' I said. 'A physical switch?' It was on the wall next to the door. With a flick of a tiny metal nipple, the room went from dark to light. The New Ludds – as far as I knew – had no objections to modern lighting, so this must have been Robert Fairfield's personal preference.

The restored boat and the antique lighting were the first clues that the owner of Fairfield Tech didn't necessarily share his own company's love of the cutting-edge and the futuristic. Robert Fairfield's house looked like somewhere the original Sherlock Holmes would be happy to live. Everything was dark wood, tiled floors and Persian rugs. Huge gilt-framed oil paintings lined the vast wallpapered hallway, leading the eye up a staircase that wouldn't have looked out of place in a theatre. The portraits were uniform in size, hanging equidistantly in a perfect line. A burgundy leather chair stood in front of a large mirror at the foot of the stairs. Everything was immaculate. It looked like a photo shoot for the kind of poncey magazine I never downloaded.

I stepped forward, scanning the black-and-white tiled diamonds underfoot for prints. This detecting business couldn't be so hard. Just a matter of observation.

I followed the detective around the ground floor. He never hesitated, checking every room thoroughly, quickly and efficiently. He had the advantage of being able to follow a virtual floorplan. He also didn't need to open any doors, something I was quickly becoming accustomed to as he stepped through solid wood, waiting for me on the other side.

'Excellent,' he said after a brief tour of the downstairs rooms. 'Upstairs, I think.'

As we climbed the huge staircase, I asked the question that had been on my lips for half an hour.

'What was it Robert Fairfield didn't tell Blackstone?'

Holmes was absorbed in his own thought process, and all-but oblivious to my presence. He answered automatically without turning.

'He was one of the wealthiest men in the country. While I don't doubt his love and affection for Ms Blackstone, he wasn't a complete fool when it came to his security system.'

'What do you mean?'

Holmes curled his lips into a narrow smile. 'He kept a DNA-based lock, but he didn't tell Ms Blackstone about it. He must have added her genetic profile without her knowledge. I imagine she wouldn't have been best pleased, had she known. It was coded to the doorknob.'

'Sneaky.'

'Indeed. There is every indication that Mr Fairfield was killed by someone he knew intimately. He was a very private man, with only a few friends outside his family. Unless he let the killer into the house, they had the codes, keys and genetic profile necessary to get in uninvited. Yet neither the camera at the door, nor on the gate shows any record of a visitor. Curious.'

'Are you sure no one could get in by boat?'

'Any vessel that breaches the well-signed private jetty

ropes thirty yards out triggers the alarm. There are cameras covering all of this riverside frontage. Nothing came near.'

The bedroom was in darkness and it took me a few seconds to remember the antiquated lighting system, running my fingers along the wall until I found the switch. As light flooded the room, I blinked and tensed, adrenaline flooding my system and my feet automatically moving to a fighting stance.

Robert Fairfield's corpse was on the floor three feet from where I was standing. He lay where he'd fallen: near the fireplace, his torso contorted, upper body naked, the flesh grey and glistening with sweat. His hands were curled like claws in front of his chest; eyes wide open and staring in terror. I've seen plenty of dead bodies, but the sight of one can still make me recoil. When a soldier reaches the point at which death means nothing to her, that's the time to get out.

Holmes walked calmly through the corpse as if it wasn't there. 'If you could just move a little closer to the bed, Watson.'

I said nothing, but pointed at the rigid corpse, which had somehow found its way from the autopsy table back to the scene of its final breath.

'Oh,' said Holmes, 'don't mind that. A digital mock-up using the forensic team's photographs. I thought it might help. Please follow me and mirror my movements.'

Without waiting for an answer, he knelt next to the virtual corpse, putting his face close to the horribly staring eyes.

Determined to hide my discomfort, and deliberately slowing my breathing to bring my pulse back to normal, I stepped forward.

Everyone in military service receives basic medical training, but I had long since reduced my triage skills to three categories: wounded, dead and deadish. The first one got help, the third one got referred to someone who knew what they were doing, and the middle category didn't require immediate attention, which was where Robert Fairfield belonged. His eyes were staring, his nostrils were flared, and his lips were drawn back from a set of white, even teeth.

I followed Holmes around the room, kneeling by the bedside, then checking the windowsill and rug for marks.

The bed was unmade, the sheets twisted, crumpled and pulled half off the mattress beneath. The bedside table had been knocked over, water from a discarded glass leaving behind a faint stain on the cream rug. A hyjector, an air-pressure injector, lay next to the glass.

I couldn't help imagining Fairfield's final moments. Diabetics are at higher risk of heart attacks than the general population, and missing his insulin combined with inadvertently spiking his bloodstream with liquid amphetamine must have been a terrifying way to go.

Scanning the police report Holmes had forwarded, I projected the relevant section onto my palm. A phone had been found clutched in Fairfield's right hand. The pathologist had to break three of the corpse's fingers to release it. Fairfield had wanted to call for help, but the uncontrollable spasming of his body had prevented him doing it.

Holmes had not only fallen silent, but was standing still, looking down at the corpse. For a moment, I thought I saw compassion on the avatar's face.

'A violent and cruel death,' he said. 'The bathroom next, I think.' He blinked and Robert Fairfield's corpse vanished, leaving an imprint on my retina like the chalk outlines police used to draw around murder victims.

Fairfield's shower could comfortably have accommodated six people, had he so desired. The Victorian bath, with its clawed feet and high sides, was less ostentatious but still large enough for two, assuming they were good friends.

The bathroom was as tidy and ordered as the rest of the house.

The medicine cabinet was above the sink. I opened it to find the usual shaving paraphernalia laid out in size order, plus a shelf full of small glass vials. There were two vials per day, marked a.m. and p.m., enough to last a week.

The empty vials went into a box at my feet, to be returned to the doctor and reused. The p.m. vial on top was likely the candidate for the lethal dose.

'The insulin was emptied down this sink,' said Holmes. 'Traces of amphetamine were found. The murderer didn't bother washing it away. Which means it was switched yesterday, rather than at any stage before. Fairfield's private doctor delivered the insulin personally. He's been looking after the family for decades and was horrified when Robert elected to have his nanomeds turned off. By taking personal responsibility for the insulin, bringing it to the house himself, he hoped to persuade his patient to go back to the technology that kept him alive. It's all in the doctor's statement.'

'Why hasn't all this been taken to the lab?' I said.

'It has.'

I kicked the basket of empty vials. My foot went right through it, connecting solidly with the wall behind. 'What the f—'

'Full disclosure, Watson. The crime scene has been precisely reconstructed in Augmented Reality to make my job possible.'

He caught my look and corrected himself. 'Our job, that is. I have yet to convince everyone at Scotland Yard of my usefulness. It's human nature to resent someone who excels in a field in which you are hoping to make a name for yourself. Although ordered to give me total access, some senior officers find ways to show their lack of support.'

For a surreal moment, I was sure he was about to talk about Inspector Lestrade.

Holmes sighed. 'DCI Barnett is the senior officer assigned to this case. He's solid enough, but lacks the suppleness of mind necessary in more sophisticated investigations.' Damned by faint praise indeed. 'Barnett isn't a New Ludd, but, despite my results, he still distrusts my methods and my anonymity. He made his feelings plain to his superiors on this occasion, only to be told to step aside. His ego will be stinging a little today. I imagine you'll have an opportunity to meet him sooner or later, Watson.'

That sounded like something to look forward to.

'Forensics confirmed the insulin vial for yesterday evening had been replaced with amphetamine. The traces in the sink give us a timeframe, eliminating the possibility that the fatal switch might have been made in advance. Follow me.'

He disappeared through the far wall. I elected to use the door.

Fairfield's office was our penultimate destination that evening. Like the rest of the decor in his house, it looked like a room from a bygone era. The desk wouldn't have looked out of place in a National Trust property. It wasn't the size of it – in fact, it was no bigger than my dad's ancient flat-screen television – but its condition. The polished wood glowed warmly in the light of the standard lamp in the corner. The green leather top was worn and scuffed in places. Where I'd expected to see a computer, there was a line of old hardback books. As the daughter of a bookseller, I had to check them out, of course. Disappointingly, they weren't a collection of first-edition Dickens, but psychology texts.

If the study was notable for anything, it was its tidiness – just like every other room we'd seen. Spotless and symmetrical. An inappropriate thought struck me. I wondered if the horrified look on Robert Fairfield's face was down to the fact he'd knocked over the bedside table while his heart hammered out its last beats. The man abhorred a mess.

The books on the desk and shelves were dust-free, and alphabetised. The mantelpiece boasted two framed photographs. One was a candid shot of Greta Blackstone in happier times, her smile unaffected and natural. I nearly didn't recognise her. It felt like an intrusion even looking at it. The second showed a young woman in a business suit posing outside the headquarters of Fairfield Tech. Beth Fairfield, back when her hair was still long. I didn't need Sherlock Holmes to tell me that.

Our two main suspects lined up together. Very neat.

Holmes had me examine the desk, particularly where an empty glass stood. I pointed at it. 'Not really here?'

'Correct. Evidence.'

I poked my finger through the air where the glass should have been, then turned my attention to the desk. There were three circular indentations in a line from front to back where coasters must have rested over the years. Robert Fairfield's cognac glass sat within easy grabbing distance of his leather chair, the coaster sitting perfectly in the indentation nearest to him.

'Hmm,' said Holmes as I bent over the glass. His eyes had narrowed, and he was nodding. 'Well, that fits.' He straightened, and I took his place. If we already knew how the amphetamine was delivered, I wasn't sure what we would gain from examining the scene of his final nightcap.

'The glasses on the side, Watson?' He was standing by the cut-glass decanter where five identical glasses rested on a silver tray. I joined him, bringing my shirt cam close.

Holmes was smiling. 'A murderer who knew about Fairfield's diabetes and got in and out without being caught on camera is either an incredibly sophisticated assassin, or someone well-known to the victim, as Blackstone suggested.'

'Unless the killer *was* Blackstone.'

'Occam's razor, Watson? Very often the detective's best weapon. I suggest we reserve judgement until we have all the facts. Let's check the final piece of evidence.'

I followed him to the kitchen, then down a short passage leading to a heavy door with a keypad.

'Same code as the front door, Watson.'

'The boathouse? But the cameras across the river? You said nothing had –'

He'd gone.

'Oh. Fine.' I punched in the code and followed, muttering.

CHAPTER NINETEEN

It was pitch black inside the boathouse, but I was ready this time, finding the switch within seconds.

The security door had the same keypad on the inside. I looked at the door handle.

Holmes anticipated my question. 'DNA locked, the same as the front.'

The majority of the space, revealed in flashes as the lights flickered before warming up to full power, was taken up by *Bethany*, the wherry he'd mentioned outside. My nautical knowledge was limited to what I'd picked up from reading *Swallows and Amazons* as a child, and *Moby Dick* as an adult, neither of which were much help to me now. All I knew for sure was that it would have been expensive. Stupidly expensive.

It didn't take a VR detective to work out why its deck was covered in cobwebs; it had obviously been sitting idle for months. Robert Fairfield's nautical aspirations had fallen fallow after he'd found himself a girlfriend.

Holmes waved me over to where he stood on the far side of the *Bethany*.

'Walk from the door towards me,' he said. 'Slowly, if you please.' The note of command in his voice didn't annoy me as it came from a place of deep focus rather than a need to dominate.

The concrete floor was rough, dry and unmarked, but a mop thrown in one corner suggested that, if there had ever been any evidence of footprints to find, they would have been easy enough to remove.

The far side of the boat revealed a metal ladder of the kind found in swimming pools, the top two rungs out of the water, the rest beneath. No marks on it that I could make out.

'Fingerprints?' I suggested. Holmes didn't reply at first. I didn't know if he was deep in thought or playing online poker and checking his emails. 'Holmes?'

He blinked, then put his head on one side, frowning.

'No need to think like a police officer, Watson. That's what police officers are for.'

'Then how am I supposed to think?'

He didn't answer, walking briskly to the door, stepping straight through the solid wood and vanishing.

I caught up with him in the hall and repeated my question, annoyed now. What exactly was I here for? Producing a virtual pair of leather gloves from his virtual pocket, he pulled them on.

'Don't think, Watson, that's my advice.' It was the kind of remark guaranteed to wind me up. Then he flashed me a cold smile and fixed me with one of those disconcerting stares that someone who's not really there shouldn't be able to manage.

'Learn to pay attention first. Then you can move on to thinking.'

He disappeared through the door. I didn't follow.

'Facetious twat,' I murmured.

The detective's head reappeared through the wall a few seconds later, like a stuffed moose.

'A twat? Possibly, but I'm not being facetious, Watson. Successful deduction is dependent on how well you've paid attention. It's all here. Everything we need.'

Next moment, there was a high-pitched *ping*, and an orangutan wearing a police helmet materialised in the hall.

I stared and pointed. 'What the actual shit?'

'Mr Holmes?' said the orangutan.

'Good evening, detective chief inspector. To what do I owe the honour?'

The ape pursed its lips, looking so like a photograph of my great aunt Melissa, who — apparently — disapproved of everything, that I nearly laughed out loud.

'As a professional courtesy, I thought it only fair to let you know . . .' said the creature, one long limb delving between its squat legs and lazily scratching its genitals. I looked on in horror.

'Let me know what, Barnett?'

'That we've brought Greta Blackstone in for more questioning regarding the murder of Robert Fairfield. Between you and me, it's not looking good for her. Wouldn't want you wasting your precious time on something as uninteresting as a lover's tiff turned bad, eh?'

The orangutan stopped scratching, sniffed its finger, then resumed, more vigorously this time. I stared first at the ape, then at the head of the famous detective poking through the door, as if it had been stuffed and mounted by a Victorian explorer.

'Well, if that's the angle you're pursuing —' began Holmes, but the orange apparition interrupted.

'I suppose she's got you chasing the daughter, am I right?'

Holmes's silence was answer enough for the ape, who produced a truncheon from somewhere about its person and waved it in the air as he spoke. 'Well, don't let me stop you if, er . . . that's the angle you're pursuing.'

The orangutan, apparently, was blessed with a limited vocabulary.

'Thank you. I won't.'

'But you might be in for a hard time proving she did it.'

'Well. You have your methods, Barnett, and I have mine. You have been quite outspoken about the inherent flaws in the investigative powers of a VR detective. It's best if I allow my results to speak for themselves.'

The ape was smacking itself on the head with the truncheon now. 'Well, well, that's fine, Clockwork Sher— I'm sorry, *Mr* Holmes – but cold cases are quite different to the real thing, I'm afraid. Anyhow, must be off. Murder suspects won't interview themselves, you know.'

'Wait. You said it might be hard to prove Beth Fairfield killed Robert Fairfield. How so?'

The orangutan tucked its truncheon under one arm.

'Because Beth Fairfield is dead. And she died before her father.'

CHAPTER TWENTY

'You met Chief Inspector Barnett, then?'

Poplar smiled as she took the contact lenses I'd handed to her, dropping them into a beaker of cleaning solution. I had a fresh pair in a box, ready for next time. Apparently, the in-ear monitors could last for years and charged wirelessly, but the contact lenses were too delicate, and one pair could only be relied upon to stay charged for seven to eight hours.

The expression on my face was enough to save me having to answer the question.

'Oh, it's just a bit of fun. What's the point in living all your life in VR if you don't get to have some fun designing the avatars sometimes?'

Poplar swung around to face her screens, murmuring commands and touching the panel. The orangutan, complete with helmet and truncheon, appeared on the screen, hitting itself on the head just as it had when I met it in Robert Fairfield's hallway.

'Trust me, there's something very ape-like about the real DCI Barnett,' she said.

Toby handed me my stab vest. 'People have said the same about me.'

He held out his hand for my shirt, not blushing this time when I shrugged it off.

Poplar smirked. 'You're built like a gorilla, Toby, but that's not what I mean. It's the way he moves. Barnett, I mean. You've seen him.'

I put the vest on and buttoned my own shirt over it. 'So you designed an avatar for him. Do you do it for everyone?'

'No.' She waved a hand at the screen and the Barnett ape disappeared. 'If Mr Holmes speaks to someone regularly, they get their own avatar. It's template-based with basic facial expressions that correspond to tone, and mouths that mimic language in real time. Barnett can't see it, of course. That just makes it funnier.'

I made a noise.

'What?' said Toby.

I pulled my trousers on and thumbed the belt to tighten them. 'It's just, well, he's not exactly a laugh-a-minute, Holmes, is he?'

'His sense of humour is pretty dry,' said Poplar. 'But it's there, trust me.'

'And his famous detecting skills? The "once you eliminate the possible, whatever remains" crap?'

'We wouldn't be here if he couldn't do it,' said Toby.

Poplar nodded. 'I've never met anyone like him. It's scary, sometimes.'

For a second, I thought of Nicky Gambon and what he would do if I gave him Clockwork Sherlock's true identity. Nothing good. What was I getting myself into?

'You've heard about some of the cases he's solved,' said Toby. 'And he's been given access to many investigations at the highest level. If Mr Holmes can't solve it, no one can.'

The pair of them just looked at me. You can't buy the kind of loyalty those two had, however misguided it might be.

Poplar's body language was defensive, arms folded. 'He's not the one we need to worry about. You've got to get up to speed. You need to practise sub-vox.'

'Sub who?'

'Sub-vocalising. When you want to talk to Mr Holmes, you don't need to do it out loud. Shape the words as subtly as you can and use your throat as if you're speaking, but don't actually sound the words. Try it.'

'Arrgurr coda Doyle grieved a raries.'

'What?'

I repeated it. 'You know. Arrgurr coda Doyle. Ro Sherwah Ho.'

'I just told you not to say the words out loud. Just shape them.'

I tried again. It was a thoroughly strange sensation, completely unnatural. This time, no sound escaped my lips, which twitched as if I were having an allergic reaction to Botox.

'Arthur Conan Doyle believed in fairies,' said Poplar.

I found sub-voxing more amazing than becoming a middle-aged man with mutton chops and a moustache.

'Wow.'

'Don't get cocky. Your diction is all over the place. You sound like you're having a stroke. I'll put some mics in with your field kit. You need to work on it.'

'Right-ho. Will do. I'm off to bed. See you in the morning. I'll meet you at . . . that place where we all work. The one that I don't know where it is. That one. The one you don't trust me enough even to say what postcode it's in.'

Nothing. They just stared at me. I opened the back door of the van.

'We'll send an Egg for you at five,' said Toby. I checked my smotch. 12:52am. With luck, I'd get a solid three and a half hours sleep in. Smashing.

It might have been a few hours or a few days before I'm fully conscious again. Hard to say how long for certain, as the only window in the room has been crudely painted over.

I'm lying on a cement floor. A single bare bulb hanging from a wooden beam above me provides the only light, revealing a room about five metres by seven.

I lift my head from the floor and push myself into a sitting position. My head hurts. My neck hurts. My lips, when I open my mouth, peel apart audibly and I spit away flakes of dried blood.

I'm still wearing my fatigues, but they've taken my boots and socks. I bring my hands up to my ribs and press. The pain isn't sharp enough to take my breath away. Not broken. I try my face next. Puffy lips, swollen cheek, left eye half-closed. A lump on the back of my skull the size of a baby's fist. And I've pissed myself.

I'm desperate for water but I force myself to listen, to pay attention, to learn something of where I've been taken. I hear distant voices, too far away to make out any words. A faint, sweet, sickly smell, with vinegary undertones. Unprocessed ope. I'm in the lab.

It takes a few minutes to stand but I manage it without passing out. I take a step forward. I try to take another, but something stops me. I look down. My right ankle is tied with rope. The other end is tied to an iron ring screwed into the wall. I strain at it, my ankle protesting at the pressure, but it holds.

Someone is coming. I slump to the floor again.

The door opens.

'Water?' English. Educated. A slight accent. He repeats the question, then, 'I will return in four hours. If you wish to forgo a drink until then . . . well, it's your choice, Captain Barnes.'

I sit up, hold out my hand. He steps forward and hands me a chipped mug. I drink greedily, never taking my eyes off his face. I know it well. It was in all our briefings.

General Harif.

'You're going to tell me the location of the Factory. Or you will be tortured and killed.'

I stare at him. He nods.

'See you in four hours, Captain Barnes.'

My smotch woke me with *London's Calling*. I had it send the track to the bathroom while I showered. Old analogue bands like The Clash always have a restorative effect, along with early Stranglers or, at a pinch, Adam and the Ants. Straightforward, unpretentious.

I dropped the pair of monitors into my ears before leaving, saving the shorter-lasting contact lenses until I really needed them.

The Egg was in dark mode again and unresponsive to my attempts to find out where I was heading. At five in the morning, I guessed the lack of traffic meant we'd reach our destination – wherever it was – quickly. I might only have ten minutes quality snoozing time. I closed my eyes.

My body woke me after twenty minutes. We should have arrived. Instead, the Egg was accelerating, suggesting we had left the city streets.

'Light mode, show view,' I said automatically, not expecting anything to happen. To my surprise, the glass cleared. It was still an hour and a half before sunrise. The only light came from the solar signs and the gentle yellow glow of other Eggs. I leaned forward in my seat and looked for landmarks.

A sign flashed by. The Egg was heading west, leaving London on the A4.

The screen flickered and Holmes appeared, looking as

immaculate as ever. That was one advantage he would always have over me. Even if he'd hardly slept and felt like shit, it would never show.

'Good morning, Watson. Beth Fairfield was murdered in St Austell. Barnett is coordinating with the police there, but concentrating his efforts on Greta Blackstone. There have been a couple of developments.'

'What developments?'

'The timestamp on the footage from the cameras at Fairfield's house show Greta arriving at nine thirty that evening, not eleven thirty as she claimed.'

'Motive and opportunity. Can't be that hard to get hold of liquid amphetamine.'

'Not hard at all.'

The Egg slotted into the slip road for the M25.

'You said developments, plural. And where the hell are we going?'

'Change of plan, old man. Beth Fairfield was murdered. In St Austell. The luggage is in the Egg's locker. We're off to Cornwall.'

CHAPTER TWENTY-ONE

CORNWALL HAD BECOME QUITE a favourite for high-tech start-ups a generation ago when the improved network had been completed. Most business was conducted online, but if someone had a London meeting, even if they set off from the southernmost tip of the county, they could be within sight of the Shard in two hours.

There were no complaints from me about the last-minute trip as I'd seen the ticket pop up on my smotch. First class.

I knew first-class travel was a thing – and had even scowled with envy at the odd travel cast that showed the interiors of the carriages, never thinking I'd see one for myself.

Supposedly, the coffee was not only freshly ground, but actually roasted onboard. So I was trying not to smile as I dressed in the clothes that gave Clockwork Sherlock as many eyes as a fly and more ears than anyone could possibly need, and put in the contact lenses. He didn't need to know I was as excited as a kid on Christmas morning. There was another change of clothes in the small suitcase he'd provided. All of them new and unworn. How long was this jaunt going to last?

The Egg got up to full speed on the slip road to the

motorway and the waiting Feeder in the middle lane coordinated its approach to match our velocity as we joined the traffic. At a hundred miles an hour, the Egg whined loudly enough to be just audible in the virtually soundproof cabin.

The flat side of the Egg docked with the Feeder, a solid clunk and a hiss announcing a successful manoeuvre. The doors slid open.

Stepping into the Feeder, the doors sealed behind me. None of the eight seats were occupied, so I sat in the nearest one, pulling the restraint bar over my head. It clicked into place, then the air belt inflated, pushing me gently back into the padded seat. When the Feeder was satisfied I was safely in place, it sent the standard warning to my smotch. I thumbed my consent, agreeing that if I sabotaged the safety equipment in any way and managed to injure or kill myself or any fellow travellers, Fairfield Tech would suffer no legal consequences. That done, I placed my hands on the seat arms and braced myself.

The Feeder to Roadtrain section of any trip was the only time anyone got any real clue about the physics involved in whisking millions of people around the country at speeds approaching commercial airplanes. Although every care was taken to make the process as undramatic as possible, accelerating from one hundred to three hundred miles an hour in a metal box the size of a doctor's waiting room was still guaranteed to give most people the willies.

For me, it was the one time I had some sympathy with the New Ludds and their assertion that any use of artificial intelligence was another step along a road that led to the end of humanity as Earth's dominant species. It was hard not to ascribe personality to AIs that coordinated the transport network. The G-forces pushing me back into my seat felt like a giant hand effortlessly holding me down. With an effort, I could move my head forward half an inch. I was a doll in the hand of a giant, super-strong child. Out of the corner of my eye, as we approached the Roadtrain thundering along the fast lane, I saw graffiti on its side – a pair of handcuffs, the New Ludds reminding us we were becoming prisoners to the technology that was supposed to free us. In their view, of course.

The M25 Roadtrains were the longest in the country at fifty to eighty carriages, depending on demand. Three of them circled the 117-mile concrete necklace around the throat of the capital night and day, all year round. Two engines drove the beast – one at the front, the other halfway along its length. This meant half the train could go for maintenance or refurbishment and be immediately replaced with no interruption in service.

The bump as the Feeder docked with the Roadtrain was much louder than when the Egg had made the same manoeuvre. At three hundred miles an hour, the dirty air thrown off by the aerodynamic train made approaching it a turbulent business. Despite that, the Feeder smacked cleanly into its dock, my restraint lifted and a useful blue arrow directed me towards the carriage – in case I was tempted to try to exit through the window and roll down the motorway for the next mile or so instead.

The doors snicked closed behind me and a beautiful auburn-haired woman in the bottle-green Fairfield Transport uniform smiled and took my bag from me.

'Welcome to the M25 Roadtrain first class section, Captain Barnes,' she said. 'Please follow me to your private compartment.'

I followed meekly behind, half-expecting a tap on my shoulder and a demand that I return to the correct part of the train immediately.

The private compartment contained a chair the size of a single bed. A sign on the wall showed why – it was designed to lie flat should the passenger require a power nap. The wall screen scrolled stock market gains and losses while the British countryside streaked by like an abstract painting. The windows were kept half dimmed by default, as early passengers on the super-speed service invariably threw up seconds after an attempt to admire the view. As this was a compartment designed for single occupancy, I had the option of going fully dark should I wish.

'Can I get you anything to drink? We have twelve minutes before transfer to the Exeter Express. Plenty of time for a cup of tea. Or a spicy Bloody Mary, if you'd prefer?'

She winked. Flawless complexion, green eyes, and more than a hint of naughtiness. It had been a long time since I'd been intimate with anyone – of either gender, or none – too long. My last lover had been Hughes. That had to change. But I'd backed out of any opportunities so far. I looked the steward up and down appraisingly. The idea of the compartment going dark took on new possibilities.

A familiar male voice broke in on my nascent imaginings.

'Are you flirting, Watson? Not that I disapprove, although there's anecdotal evidence that such activities blunt the effectiveness of the rational mind.'

'I don't need anything,' I said to the Fairfield steward with a sigh.

'Shame,' she said, and left.

If this was first-class travel, it was going to be hard to go back to anything else.

'Holmes,' I said to the empty cabin. 'Care to fill me in on the new development in the case?'

'The death of Beth Fairfield?'

'Assuming nothing more significant has happened since last night, yes.'

Holmes ignored the sarcasm. 'She was strangled.'

I regretted my flippancy. 'When did it happen?'

The stock market ticker on the wall screen vanished, replaced by the Baker Street apartment. The detective was leaning against the mantelpiece, stuffing tobacco into his pipe.

'We'll get the details from the pathologist. But it would appear that Barnett was correct. She was lying dead in St Austell Harbour before Robert Fairfield injected himself with amphetamine.'

'Looks like someone really had it in for the Fairfields. You can see why the police are talking to the leader of the New Ludds.'

'Yes, logic suggests Greta Blackstone should be our prime suspect.'

'But?'

He lit the pipe with a long match. 'There's no "but", Watson. We are in possession of some of the facts. Far too early to draw conclusions. Currently, the available facts favour one theory over all others, but, like all true scientists, we must be prepared to abandon our hypothesis in an instant if new evidence throws it into question.'

'Well, at least we know Blackstone didn't kill Beth Fairfield. Personally, that is.'

'How so?'

He was being deliberately obtuse, but I ignored it. 'I'm not denying she's done some remarkable things in her life, Holmes, but nobody can be in two places at once, can they?'

He drew on the pipe, his long fingers tapping meditatively on the mantelpiece. 'Just so, Watson. Just so.'

The screen went dark.

Another Feeder arrived before I'd had a chance to try out all the seat positions, flick through a dozen movie stations and sample the complementary warm nut selection in the wooden bowl on the table.

I boarded the Feeder and strapped myself in. This time,

as we detached from the Roadtrain, there were no G-forces to contend with as the vehicle reduced speed, dropping to two hundred miles an hour before taking the next junction, and coming alongside the Exeter Roadtrain.

The Exeter Express was tiny in comparison, made up of ten standard compartments and two sub-divided first-class sections at the rear.

It might have been a smaller Roadtrain, but my private compartment – which was kept for the exclusive use of the Fairfield Tech directors and guests – was bigger than its M25 equivalent, with a wine rack, a fully-stocked fridge, a table, two chairs and a bed. There were chocolates on the pillow and rose petals on the duvet. The bed would easily accommodate two, if they were friendly. I thought of the previous steward and sighed.

'Thinking about the case, Watson?' Holmes had appeared on the far side of the table, legs crossed, lighting his pipe.

'Something like that,' I said, and sat down. My smotch vibrated and I swiped away a message as the door chimed to indicate we had a visitor.

The Exeter Roadtrain chief steward was a short man in his early sixties who introduced himself as Bernard. I wasn't sure if it was his first name or surname. Perhaps it served for both. He looked like a Bernard. Polite, solicitous, professional, and so quiet it was easy to forget he was there. I wasn't sure if he always wore a black tie or if he was in mourning for the death of one of his best customers.

'Mr Bolton said you had some questions for me.'

'We do. Thank you for coming by.'

Bernard showed no surprise at the voice coming from the speakers, responding with a shallow, all-purpose bow. Holmes wasted no time on small talk.

'How long have you worked on the Roadtrain network?'

'Seventeen years.' Bernard listened to Holmes's voice, but looked at me. After a moment's hesitation, he added, 'Sir.'

'And when were you promoted to chief steward?'

'Twelve years ago, sir.'

Holmes drilled down on the details of Saturday afternoon, the day Beth Fairfield travelled back to Cornwall. The day she and her father died, hundreds of miles apart.

Bernard had very little to tell us. Beth Fairfield had boarded as usual, but hadn't required him during the journey. Other than welcoming her aboard, bringing her the pot of green tea she drank on every trip, and saying goodbye when she left, there had been very little interaction.

'Not even when you brought the tea?' I said.

'No. She just gave me a nod. I did notice she wasn't working.'

'Was that unusual?'

'Well, Mrs Fairfield always catches up on some work during the journey, but on Saturday she just stared out of the window. She was extremely quiet. When she spoke, she whispered, and she told me she was very tired. I wondered if she was ill.' His eyes flicked between my face and the wall screen. 'Was that what happened? Was she ill? Should I have called the doctor?'

There was a catch in his voice. I looked at the way Bernard was standing, his hands flat against his sides as if on a military parade, and realised he was trying to stop his hands from shaking. He was worried he might have been able to prevent her death.

Holmes responded matter-of-factly, but I interrupted him. 'Sit down, Bernard. Please.'

The manner of Beth Fairfield's death had not yet been released to the press, but this man needed to know there was nothing he could have done. There's no easy way to break the news of violent death, but this wasn't my first time. He paled, looked down at his feet.

Holmes stopped him on his way out. His manner was softer now. I took it as an indicator of his humanity, then speculated that it could equally be a demonstration of machine learning.

'Bernard. There was something different about Mrs Fairfield on Saturday. Something you noticed. What was it?'

Bernard looked lost. His fingers went to his uniform automatically, brushing away a speck of imaginary dirt.

Holmes pressed him. 'Something trivial, perhaps.'

At this, Bernard's expression changed, and he looked at the screen. 'I didn't think it was worth mentioning, sir.'

'What was it?'

'She tipped me, sir. It's just that it was unlike her, sir. Not that she wasn't generous. I wouldn't want you to think that. She pinged a generous bonus to my smotch at Christmas last month, same as every year. But this was cash. Just thought it was . . . unusual. It's not my place to . . . I mean, I'm sorry if I . . . but you said to mention anything, even if it was trivial.'

'And you have been as good as your word. Admirable, Bernard, admirable. Thank you.'

When the steward had left, Holmes reappeared on the screen. He was smiling.

'Interesting, no?'

'The fact that one of the richest women in the world left a tip? And that she was quiet? What does that tell us? Maybe she had argued with her husband. Maybe the nanomeds weren't coping with PMT as efficiently as usual.'

'Maybe. You might be right, Watson. Time will tell.'

Like the most annoying kind of magician, Holmes sometimes gave the impression that he knew more than his audience.

'How did you know?' I said.

'Know what?'

'That Bernard had noticed something about Mrs . . . Ah.' I remembered my training in interrogation techniques, and the way they had been applied when I was captured. 'You didn't know he had noticed anything, did you?'

'No. It's a simple way to extract every piece of useful information. And in this case it worked splendidly. Very good, Watson.'

If he was going to carry on being this patronising, he and I would have to have a little chat.

It would be an hour before we reached the Exeter loop. Holmes was still talking. I shook my head, pointing at the bed.

'An hour's sleep and I'll be more help to you.'

He hesitated, which I took as a sign of disapproval.

'You're paying for my time,' I said, 'so it's up to you. But if you want me alert and paying attention, let me sleep. Haven't you got any deducting you can be getting on with?'

'How droll, Watson. Very well.'

He nodded and closed his eyes. I took that as a dismissal, and lay down without even bothering to move the rose petals. The message on my smotch had been from someone I'd added to my address book using the name Nicholas. Nicky Gambon's message wasn't something I wanted to read while wearing online contact lenses, in-ear monitors and an outfit bristling with cameras and microphones.

To my surprise, I slept for fifty minutes.

Five minutes after I'd woken up and thrown a handful of water on my face, we boarded an Egg at the southernmost edge of the Exeter loop and headed for St Austell where a grieving husband and a second murder victim awaited us.

CHAPTER TWENTY-TWO

THE COACHES WAS the kind of hotel I had sometimes guarded while doing casual security work, cash in hand, no questions asked.

It stood above the town of St Austell, overlooking it with an indulgent air, like a rich grandfather watching his grandchildren clamber round a playground. It was a collection of turrets, towers, long, low wings and walled gardens that should have looked like a mess, but somehow pulled off being grand instead.

By the time my Egg pulled up outside, Holmes was gone. He had spent the Exeter to St Austell leg of the journey filling me in on the death of Beth Fairfield.

Local police had been called the previous evening. St Austell's harbour master had found Beth's body on Sunday evening, face down in the boat she kept at the marina. When the first officer on the scene turned the body over, any speculation that her death might have been an accident was abandoned. The dead woman had taken a beating, her shattered face was swollen and there was bruising around her neck. DNA tests, her wedding ring, and a positive ID from her husband, confirmed her identity in the early hours of Monday morning.

The pathologist was confident about time of death. The physical evidence tallied with the final back-up from Beth Fairfield's smotch, which had been ripped off her wrist and crushed. She had died between seven and nine Saturday evening. Which meant that, at the moment Robert Fairfield's killer had tipped that night's insulin down his sink, replacing it with amphetamine, Beth Fairfield had been lying dead in her boat, three hundred miles away.

On arrival, my Egg was met by the hotel manager, an energetic, fit man in his thirties wearing retro jeans and a white shirt. He carried himself with a friendly, relaxed ease, taking my bag, welcoming me to the hotel, asking if I needed anything, and informing me that, as requested, a private room had been made available for lunch at 12:45 p.m.

The suite I was staying in was ridiculous. High ceiling with frescoes, four-poster, walk-in closets, blah blah blah. Whatever the source of Clockwork Sherlock's funding, it was substantial. The tech at 221b and in the van was a step or two beyond cutting-edge. And he had at least two employees besides me. If he was paying Toby and Poplar half of what had dropped into my account ten minutes after I'd accepted the job offer, his payroll must be eye-watering.

It was strange to unpack a bag full of clothes that someone else had picked out for me. Every outfit was more of a wearable surveillance suite than a fashion statement, but they were smart, too. I wondered who had been put in charge of shopping for me. The blue-haired Miss Poplar was more of a dungarees and denim shirt kind of gal. My money was on Tobes. The underwear was the same comfort-over-flirtation style I always bought, but far better quality than my usual five-for-a-coin bargains. I started speculating how much they'd found out about me by mining my shopping data, then stopped before I got angry.

As well as a dozen pairs of lenses and a spare pair of in-ear monitors, there was something new. A small box containing half a dozen band-aids. When I opened the box, it triggered a message on my smotch containing a set of instructions. I projected it on the wall and ripped open the first band-aid packet in accordance with step one. Step two was positioning the adhesive strip at a specific point on my throat. The plasticky rectangle was pink. For a second or two I wondered if the 221b team had missed the bloody obvious. Then the colour began to change, darkening, new shades flowing across it in waves like an octopus I'd seen on a nature documentary. When it matched my black skin, it effectively vanished.

'Clever,' I murmured.

'It is rather, isn't it?'

Holmes was standing by the window, looking out towards the town. I covered my shock and annoyance at his sudden appearance – I'd have to remember that he could show up on a whim when I was wearing the VR kit – and gestured at the view.

'You can't see anything out there.' His eyes and ears were attached to the outfit I wore.

He smiled at that. 'There are six cameras on this side of the hotel's exterior, Watson. We live in a connected and slightly paranoid world. Which is greatly to my benefit.'

'What is this?' I indicated the invisible band-aid.

'Sub-vox microphone. It's all in the instructions. I'd suggest you get in some practise. We're meeting Jack Bolton in an hour and I want you to review Fairfield Tech's history before then. What are you doing?'

It was the first time I'd ever heard a hint of panic in his voice. I was getting undressed. If I only had thirty-five minutes, I was going to have to prioritise. And practising using the sub-vox microphone was nowhere near the top of my list. Also, if Holmes was going to keep appearing, uninvited, whenever he fancied it, I was going to pretend it didn't bother me in the slightest. From the uncharacteristic display of bluster that followed, I figured he would ping me a message before materialising next time.

'Ah. Right. Very well. Yes. Um, Watson, I . . . I . . . perhaps I should, that is . . .'

I wondered what cam he was looking through as I peeled off my underwear and kicked them away.

'See you at lunch.'

And he was gone. There had been questions about the original, fictional Sherlock Holmes's sexuality, or lack of it. Judging from this version's reaction to a naked female body, I was veering away from the theory that Clockwork Sherlock was an AI, unless that AI had the sexual characteristics of an adolescent boy.

I touched the band-aid on my throat as I scanned the rest of the instructions. I hoped they'd thought to make it waterproof.

The shower had ten different jets of water in constant motion and was so powerful it almost made up for the missed opportunity on the M25 Roadtrain. I looked down at the yellowing bruise on my stomach where the stab vest had saved me from stitches. It seemed like months ago, but it was half a week. I pictured the lowlife who'd wielded the knife, which made me think of Nicky Gambon, and Dad. It took a big effort to drag my mind away from a fruitless spiral of wondering what the hell I was going to do. I pushed the thoughts into a box and locked it. Lazy pop psychology articles claim the ability to lock a problem away and not have it affect present circumstances is a peculiarly male characteristic. The lazy pop psychologists are wrong.

It's something survivors do, and it has nothing to do with gender.

A good shower is one of the few things guaranteed to make me happy, and this one was so exceptional that I actually broke into song, badly, with a medley of Eighties hits. Unfortunately, I only discovered the shower responded to voice control when I reached the chorus of 'Gold' by Spandau Ballet, at which point the water turned freezing.

There was a new document on my smotch, titled 'Fairfield Tech background – please read'. The doc contained text and video, so I pinged it on to the bedroom screen and scanned it as I got dressed.

I was hardly a follower of business news, but even I remembered the story of Fairfield Tech. It was hard to imagine a more ironic and tragic event than the one that indirectly led to Britain becoming the first country to move entirely to a self-driven networked transport system.

Fairfield Tech had led the way in self-driving technology, thanks to its groundbreaking adaptive algorithm. It had been dreamed up by Stephen Fairfield after he'd studied the intricate choreography of starlings while on holiday. As their fractal dance had skipped and dodged, twisted and soared, he had dictated notes into his smotch. Eighteen months later, the first networked self-driving prototypes had been publicly unveiled to a crowd of cynical journalists, none of whom expected to end the morning with a spontaneous standing ovation.

I watched the first video. I'd seen the footage years before in a documentary. A dozen Fairfield Tech employees, plus Stephen, his wife Fay, and their two children, John and Art, each climbed into an individual vehicle in the Fairfield car park to demonstrate the power of his algorithm. There were no steering wheels in these tiny vehicles, no accelerators, no brakes. No manual override of any kind. And they were fast.

This wasn't a cautious demonstration to illustrate the potential of Stephen's breakthrough. This was sixteen vehicles at speeds of up to forty miles an hour in a space smaller than a football pitch, hurtling towards each other with no regard for traffic rules or convention. Sometimes two or three cars were reversing while six or seven of their brethren convened on them from different directions. There were sharp intakes of breath, grunts of surprise and even a scream or two from the occupants of the complast chairs laid out at the edge of the car park.

When the reporters realised every car was reacting instantly to every other, that each was linked; an intelligent swarm that could think – and react – as one, they knew they were witnessing history.

The video stopped. I sat down on the bed and set the screen to auto scroll, slowing it occasionally to try to make sure I got the gist of Fairfield Tech's story.

Once the car-park footage was made public, people started calling them Eggs. Stephen Fairfield had named his invention Neurons, a desperate-to-be-cool name that everyone flatly ignored. The vehicles in question featured a tapered nose for aerodynamic efficiency and a rounded rear end to offer a spacious travelling experience for passengers. And they were white. They looked like eggs. From there it was predictable that the bus-sized versions would be known as Cartons. When it came to naming the autonomous high-speed motorway vehicles, Fairfield dropped any attempt at coolness and plumped for the merely descriptive. The slip-streaming three-hundred-mile-an-hour rockets in the fast lane were Roadtrains. Actual trains were quickly given over entirely to goods transportation, passengers preferring the speed, luxury and excitement of the Roadtrains. The Feeders were the most prosaically named of all: a similar size to a carton, but built for speed, designed purely to dock with

Roadtrains. Feeders spent much of their time on the hard shoulder, fast-charging before their next customers appeared.

Soon after the prototypes were unveiled, the British government entered into talks with Fairfield Tech. Less than a decade after that first demonstration, the final car driven by a human on a London street rolled to a stop outside Battersea Recycling Plant.

Stephen Fairfield didn't live to see his dream become reality. Shortly after the first demonstration of his revolutionary algorithm, he was returning from a wedding in Wales when an exhausted lorry driver on the M4 failed to notice the mile-long tailback forming in front of him. The coroner's report concluded the driver found the brakes less than a second before he ploughed into the Fairfield family's car. The forty-foot truck was travelling at seventy-four miles an hour at the moment of impact.

The lorry driver survived with a cracked rib. Stephen Fairfield, Fay Fairfield, and ten-year-old John Fairfield were all pronounced dead at the scene. Art Fairfield, sixteen years old, precociously intelligent and expected to follow his father into the business, was airlifted to the National Hospital For Neurology and Neurosurgery in central London with what the press referred to as 'life-changing injuries'. When his organs started shutting down, a last-ditch attempt to save him was made by transferring him to a specialist private facility, but it was too late. The entire Fairfield family was lost.

Robert Fairfield, Stephen's older brother and only relative, inherited the company. The car crash and the wave of public sympathy that followed led to negotiations with the government for a new vision of transport in Britain. Robert Fairfield, an academic lecturing in psychology before his unexpected inheritance, turned out to be a canny negotiator. And daughter Beth, who had demonstrated a flair for business and had been working for a tech start-up for two years at the time of the tragedy, became the youngest CEO in the FTSE 100.

I scanned through the reports on Beth Fairfield and Jack Bolton, then turned off the screen. Robert and Beth Fairfield's deaths wiped out what was left of a particularly unfortunate family. Time to meet the man who'd married into it.

CHAPTER TWENTY-THREE

JACK BOLTON WAS ALREADY SITTING at the table when I entered the private room. He had turned away from the plates of Greek olives and freshly baked bread, and was staring out of the window at the back lawn, which sloped away towards the cliffs and the sea beyond. We were probably less than a mile away from where his wife's beaten body had been found.

According to the pathologist's report, the cause of death was strangulation. Beth had been preparing for a night dive – scuba diving was one of her many hobbies – when she was attacked.

Jack Bolton had a look of shock on his pinched features. Understandable in a very recently bereaved husband, but it was the same expression he wore in almost every photograph I'd ever seen of him. Even when he was going for a confident smile, he looked like a man who'd just won the lottery and posed for photos, only to be told that his fly was open and his worldly goods were showing.

If the rest of the world had been surprised by the announcement that Beth Fairfield was marrying Jack Bolton, no one was more surprised than the man himself, it seemed. Beth had been nominated for Businessperson of the year six times, and had only lost twice. She was heiress to one of the biggest fortunes on the planet, and CEO of a company that had more power than many small countries. On the other hand, Jack Bolton was a shy, introverted Texan who'd grown up helping his dad rebuild classic muscle cars in the back of his scrap yard, before acing maths and science at school and getting a scholarship to MIT. After graduation, he'd moved to Europe, working in the team that integrated hardware with the brilliant software coming out of Fairfield Tech's AI unit.

Then the CEO noticed him. Within six months he was head of engineering and dating a woman of the kind he'd only previously met at office parties, where they usually assumed he was with the caterers. In interviews, when Beth had been asked about her love life, she'd admitted she had always been attracted to geeks. When she married Jack Bolton, everyone realised it was the truth.

He wore glasses. This was an affectation in most people, but not with Jack. He was short-sighted, but when he was working with engines or schematics, he liked the rest of the world to drift out of focus. Laser surgery, or adaptive bi-focal contact lenses could remedy his affliction, but he didn't want it remedied. His loss of depth of field, in his opinion, meant he could become absorbed in his work without distractions. All this was according to the interviews Holmes had forwarded. I'd read them after checking Nicky Gambon's message, which had been empty of content. That made it worse somehow. He was just reminding me he was there, waiting.

Jack Bolton looked up at my approach, dropped his napkin as he stood, bent down to retrieve it, then caught his glasses as they slid off his nose, placing them on the table. He was the archetypal puny, clever kid from old adverts for muscle-building courses. He was the *before* picture, but for Jack, there was no *after*. His mind had got him the job of his dreams, then it had got him the girl of his dreams. Why change?

He was slightly built, his dark hair refusing to submit to a side parting, instead sticking up in tufts. The reason for this was evident as he limply shook my hand – his left hand going nervously to his head and rubbing it.

'Dr Watson, or Miss Watson – is that right? When the police told me who was coming down, I couldn't believe it. Clockwork Sherlock. Even I've heard of him, and I'm not real good at keeping up with the news.'

'I'm not a doctor.' A voice in my ear prompted me. 'Why don't you just call me Watson.'

Jack grinned at that. 'Oh. Oh, I get it. Of course, ma'am. Watson it is.'

Holmes had asked me to bring down a small complast box. I put it on the table. Bolton opened it and rubbed his hands together. He inserted the in-ear monitors without hesitating and, after examining them up against the window for a minute, tipped his head back to drop in the contact lenses.

'We had a team working on something like this when I first arrived,' he said. 'Beth said they got a prototype off the ground, but the idea wasn't scalable. Too expensive. She closed it down. Shame.'

I had my first stab at sub-voxing. 'Is it my eegadganation, or has he agotten his wife's just deen durdered?'

'If I understand you correctly, then that shower did you the world of good, Watson. Yes. He's a bundle of contradictions, is Mr Bolton.' The voice was in my right ear only, as if Holmes were leaning over my shoulder and speaking directly into it.

'Ny nonitors aren't wooking cockerly.'

'They're working perfectly, Watson. Our friend Jack is

now part of the conversation. Should you want to say something to me privately, as you just did, sub-vox it. If I wish to speak to you exclusively, my voice will be in your right ear only. Got it?'

'Got it.'

'Got what?' Jack looked confused.

I was saved from answering by Sherlock Holmes making his entrance. He walked through the wall opposite the window, his stride purposeful, his face a study in serious intent. Bolton reacted with a delighted smile, which he quickly replaced with the look of shocked concern with which he had first greeted me. The grin flashed back momentarily when Holmes removed the greatcoat he was wearing and tossed it aside along with a sturdy walking stick, both of which vanished as they left his hands.

'Mr Holmes, I'll be honest, I never thought you were real. No offence. I figured you were a piece of software with a learning algorithm linked to the police database. I thought it was an interesting idea. Don't get me wrong – a piece of intelligent software is as interesting to me as a human being. No, I'm lying, usually it's more interesting. I figure you could still be software, right? Why not? You keeping the truth quiet? Sure, I get it. George in Engineering is never gonna believe there's actually a real Clockwork . . .' His voice tailed off when he met Holmes's stony gaze. 'Ah, you don't like that nickname, am I right? Sorry. Please, please, take a weight off.'

Holmes stood across the table from him, not moving.

'Um, I mean, sit down. If you want to. Guess it makes no difference. Your choice. Okay.'

Holmes sat and Jack did the same, still shaking his head in disbelief, then turning suddenly serious, as if remembering why this meeting was taking place. He rubbed his hair again. He was nervous. I wasn't sure I was buying the whole nerdy schtick. He was talking a lot. I've seen people do that when they're hiding something.

A waiter came to take our order. I was starving, but I didn't want to interrupt the interview. I was about to wave the waiter away when Holmes's voice spoke directly into my right ear. As his lips weren't moving at the time, it was disconcerting.

'You must be hungry, Watson. Go ahead, order some food. I insist.'

I wasn't about to argue. I ordered curried monkfish and a side of hand-cut chips. I raised an eyebrow at my dining companions, then remembered one was a grieving husband and the other wasn't really there.

'Better bring me a beer,' I told the waiter.

Bolton faced Holmes.

'Anything you can do to find out what happened, Mr Holmes, anything I can tell you that might lead us to . . . whoever would do such a terrible thing, just ask.'

'In your police statement, you said both you and your wife received regular death threats.'

'Yeah, sure, every company developing AI gets them. Anonymous emails.'

'You keep them?'

'They go straight to trash, but nothing is gone forever. You want to wade through them?'

'Not personally, but we have software that can look for patterns.'

'It's mostly New Ludd assholes, but I thought they were all mouth.'

'Maybe they were. Best to check, though.'

Bolton put his hands over his eyes, rubbing them.

'I still can't believe it's true. If I seem a little odd, it's just that I don't know how to behave, really. I still can't believe she's really gone. If I hadn't seen for myself . . . oh, Beth.'

He covered his face with his hands. Holmes leaned forward. If either Jack or myself expected a word of sympathy, we were to be disappointed.

'Once we've seen the pathologist, we may need to talk to you again. And Watson will need access to the VR suite at Fairfield Tech.'

'Um.' Jack Bolton looked up, flummoxed. 'Well, yes, of course. Anything I can do to help. Anything.'

'Good. Did your wife often go on night dives alone? I believe solo diving is somewhat frowned upon.'

Jack sat back, visibly relaxing. 'If you knew Beth, you wouldn't have to ask that question.'

'No?'

'No. Mr Holmes, Beth is a thrill seeker, plain and simple. Was. Was a thrill seeker.'

He paused, his glance dropping to the floor. We waited.

'Roller coasters, base jumping, caving, high-stakes poker games. If she could get a buzz out of it, she wanted to do it. She'd been into scuba for a couple of years before she tried a night dive. She loved it. Especially off-season, in the cold months when no one else was in the water. After a while, even that wasn't enough of a kick for her. The buddy system annoyed her. She wanted to be alone. She tried explaining it to me, and I kinda understood it was something she needed, but I'm more of a beer and a barbecue kind of guy in my spare time. I throw up on roller coasters. Anyways, the dive club weren't happy when they found out she was going out on her own, but no one could tell Beth what to do. They explained how dangerous it was, that any equipment malfunction meant she could die. The buddy system was there to prevent accidents like that happening. They didn't understand. The risk was kinda the point.'

'Did she let you know she was going diving when she got back from London?'

'No, but I wasn't expecting to see her until later, anyhow. I was out.'

He stopped again and stared out of the window. After a few second's silence, he spoke without turning.

'Beth would have been okay about dying on one of her night dives. I mean, she didn't have a death wish, nothing like that. She accepted there was a chance she might not come back one night, that's all. But it shouldn't have happened this way. Not like this. Someone killed my wife and we need to catch whoever it was.'

'Indeed. Mr Bolton, I assume you have heard about the death of your wife's father.'

'The police called me on Sunday afternoon, asked me to get Beth to contact them. I smotched a message for her to call me. Then I found out what had happened to Robert after I'd identified Beth. I haven't really had time to process it. What the hell is going on?'

'As Beth's next of kin, you now stand to inherit Fairfield Technology, don't you?'

'I hadn't even – really? I mean, no. That's not how the business is set up. Even if it was, so what?'

'I can see you're upset, Mr Bolton. The police will want to know where you were the night before last.'

'Well, that's easy enough. I was at a business dinner and fundraising auction right here.' He indicated our opulent surroundings. 'I got pretty drunk, took an Egg home at . . . I guess nearly midnight.'

Nearly midnight. What a party animal.

' I slept on the couch. There were about sixty witnesses, if that'll make you happy. Hey, you should be talking to that crazy New Ludd woman. Someone is trying to derail the best tech company in the world. Sounds an awful lot like the kind of thing those anti-science pricks would do.'

The waiter chose that moment to bring my food. Bolton

asked for a bourbon, then turned back to the window. The curry smelt amazing. I was going to need my strength, right? It tasted as good as I hoped, especially washed down with a cold beer.

We tried a bit of awkward small talk, which floundered until I got Bolton talking about software and he explained an idea he'd had for solar submarines that would come to the surface to recharge in much the same way whales come up for breath.

Holmes waited until my plate was clean before speaking again.

'We have to leave, Mr Bolton. A few more questions.'

'Shoot.'

'In your police statement, you said the last time you spoke to Beth was when she called from the Roadtrain. She told you about her lunch with her father.'

'That's right. It had been tense between them for a while. She said they'd made up. She was real happy about it.'

'Why?' I said. 'Robert hadn't changed his mind, had he? He was still planning to marry Greta Blackstone. Still breaking up the company, right?'

Jack shrugged. 'Right. But we'd talked about it before she left for London. Family is more important in the end, isn't it? We could easily start another company.'

I wasn't to be so easily deterred. 'But you're in the middle of a huge deal with Espen Nuerro. You'd lose it if he got a sniff of what might happen to Fairfield Tech.'

'Hey, it's only money.'

'About three hundred billion, I heard.'

He shrugged again. Holmes took over.

'How did Mrs Fairfield sound on the phone?'

'Fine. She was fine. Pleased about making up with Robert. Full of plans, as always.'

Bolton glanced at his smotch. 'Look, I really gotta go.

Beth would've wanted me to carry on working. There's something I have to take care of. I'll get lunch.'

Holmes stood. 'That's very kind, Mr Bolton. Watson and I may need to speak to you again.'

'Sure. Come by the office.' He walked to the door, getting the attention of the waiter and tapping his smotch to pay.

'Good,' said Holmes when Bolton had gone. 'Now let's go and see Beth.'

CHAPTER TWENTY-FOUR

EVA MOWBRAY, the pathologist, stood three feet eight in her steel-toe-capped boots. When I first saw the boots, I thought they might be a deliberate statement, projecting her wish to not be messed with. Ten seconds into our visit to the morgue, however, they were revealed to have a more practical purpose.

Beth Fairfield's body was on the table. Mrs Mowbray waved a scalpel and made an odd 'phtt phtt' sound to indicate we should follow her. When she reached the table, the top of which was almost exactly level with her grey and purple bob, she gave a wooden crate a solid kick, which sent it sliding to the top of the table. She hopped onto it and turned to face me.

'So he's here, then, girlie? The clockwork gobshite?'

I tried hard not to laugh.

I doubted either of us had ever been referred to in those terms before. I wasn't about to make a big deal about it. Eva Mowbray struck me as someone who gave the term 'no nonsense' whole new vistas of meaning. And she was holding a scalpel.

I nodded. 'He's here. Mr Holmes can hear everything you

say, and can see everything I see. We're looking for as accurate a time of death as possible. The police report said Mrs Fairfield's smotch was smashed during the attack.'

The pathologist had turned her back on me as I started talking, bending over the body. I wondered if she was hard of hearing. I tried again, louder. 'I said we're looking for as accurate a time of death as p—'

'Now listen to me.' My dad would have had the perfect description of the expression on Mrs Mowbray's face: she looked like someone had pissed on her chips. I let her talk.

As she spoke, she occasionally jumped off the wooden box and kicked it into place at a different part of the autopsy table. She did this with such unerring accuracy that I thought the Scottish national football team might have had a better World Cup qualifying record had she been included in the squad.

'Bethany Alice Fairfield. Forty-three years old, identity confirmed by a visual inspection by next of kin at oh one hundred hours yesterday. DNA and dental records confirm. DCI Barnett called me personally to make sure I was thorough. I look forward to giving him some tips on how to do his police work next time I'm in London, the jumped-up, insufferable prick that he is. My report covers the initial findings. Full biopsy and bloods will be back later today. She was beaten and strangled.'

Mowbray lifted one grey hand from under the sheet. 'Her body was found at eighteen forty yesterday. Time of death almost certainly between twenty forty-eight and twenty-one hundred hours Saturday night. Blood analysis of what's left of her smotch confirm it was smashed to pieces with the same rock used to attack her. Come closer.'

I stood beside her and looked down at Beth Fairfield's face. I had seen photographs and videos, of course. She had been a beautiful woman in life. Not so in death. Death lends a kind of slack emptiness to even the fittest, most chiselled of features, but this was far worse. The woman I was looking at – her blonde hair leeched of its shine – had such puffy features it was hard to tell whether she was old or young. Her lips were split and swollen, and some front teeth were missing, visible because her broken jaw caused the mouth to sag open. Her face had lost the symmetry that had made her so photogenic. One cheekbone was crushed and bloody. Both eyes were closed and looked as if they had sunk into her face where the flesh around it had puffed up.

When I'd seen enough, I turned away. Holmes could look on with the cams provided, if he could stomach it.

'Measurements taken from the wounds, together with fragments found inside some of the deeper cuts, show her assailant attacked her with a rock. The first blow was from behind. It didn't land squarely, but it was hard enough to cause a concussion. Bruises on her knees suggest she fell at that point, but didn't lose consciousness. Blood from her head wound spattered the side and deck of the boat. She was on her back when he strangled her. When she turned to fight him off, he hit her multiple times, causing the broken cheekbone and jaw, plus the other injuries you saw. He was wearing gloves, but we have his DNA under her fingernails.'

'He?' I said. 'How can you be so sure?'

She gave me an unsympathetic smirk. 'Your wee boss not tell you everything, hen?'

'Barnett only shared the security camera footage with me ten minutes ago,' said Holmes privately. 'He's following orders to include me on his progress, but he's going to some lengths to be less than helpful. The footage from the marina shows a tall man in a hooded raincoat following Beth Fairfield at just after eight forty-five p.m. on Saturday night. The boat itself is out of sight of the cameras. The hooded man returned twelve minutes later. Beth Fairfield did not.'

I remembered to sub-vox. 'And en er oo tinking arout telling ne dis?'

Eva shook her head and hopped down from the box to stand in front of me. The fact that her glare originated from someone who came up to my waist did nothing to diminish its effectiveness. 'Are you just pissing about, or are you practising ventriloquism? Cos if you are, I'm here to tell you you're shite at it.'

I tried to regain some poise. 'If the smotch was smashed, how can you be so sure about the time of death?' Even the cheapest NHS nanomeds would trigger a smotch to send a beacon in a medical emergency.

Eva's sigh communicated her disdain as effectively as her glare. 'Your little bleepy bloopy boxes can't do everything just yet. We're made of meat, petal. The particular stages of rigor mortis, the rate at which blood dries — I have some books on post-mortem chemistry if you're interested.'

I let the sarcasm go by without comment.

She walked to the morgue door. 'As for the smotch, it was high-end, keeping a rolling back-up every minute. The last back-up was at twenty forty-eight. The nanomed update in that back-up shows Mrs Fairfield's heart rate up from sixty-seven to a hundred and thirty-six beats per minute. A sprint might show the same, or particularly vigorous sexual intercourse, but — given the other known factors — I'm putting my money on fighting off her killer, which suggests a fairly tight window for time of death, unless you have any pertinent insights that might persuade me to change my professional opinion, based on over three decades of experience, hen?'

I swear she didn't blink or take a breath during that sentence.

'Any other stupid questions before you go? Maybe something that gets right to the heart of the matter and reveals what a shoddy job I made of the autopsy? Wait — don't tell me

– Moriarty is behind this, isn't he?' She pulled an overdramatic face, accompanied for no good reason I could think of with jazz hands.

When Holmes responded, his tone was sombre. 'Mrs Mowbray, I can only commend you on your excellent work. I have a copy of your report and I cannot fault its thoroughness. Cornwall is lucky to have you.'

The expression on her face altered minutely, as if the bulldog had managed to spit the wasp out before it could sting.

'Just one more thing,' said Holmes through me.

'Out with it.'

'I gather the smotch was destroyed while she was still wearing it to prevent the emergency beacon.'

'It was.'

'May I see her hand, please?'

Mowbray returned to the table, kicked the box into place and lifted the sheet to reveal Beth Fairfield's right hand. The wrist was clearly broken, and scratches along the thumb showed where the smotch had been yanked off before the killer had finished the job of smashing it to pieces.

'Thank you,' said Holmes. 'And her left hand, if you please.'

The pathologist muttered, but kicked the box around the corpse and did as she was asked.

'Oh, shit,' I said involuntarily. It was worse than the right. The whole hand was a mass of bruising and blood. It looked like every finger had been broken. Even the wedding ring had been hit so hard, it had pierced the skin beneath.

'Interesting,' said Holmes blandly. 'We've seen enough. My thanks once more. Good day.'

As I left the building and turned left to head towards the seafront, glad of the tang of fresh, salty air in my nostrils, I turned to see Eva Mowbray watching me go from the window.

She must have booted her box over there. I raised a hand and she gave a curt nod in return.

Holmes was silent for the ten minutes it took to reach the front, spot the marina and head towards it. When he finally spoke, it was with a cold fury I hadn't expected.

'The pieces begin to fall into place. We will bring the guilty to justice, Watson. The perpetrator of this crime will soon learn there are consequences to such callous disregard of a human life's value.'

I stayed silent until we reached the marina. Then I asked the obvious question.

'I understand why the murderer destroyed the smotch. But why smash her other hand as well.'

The avatar only I could see nodded gravely. 'Precisely, Watson, precisely. Why?'

CHAPTER TWENTY-FIVE

It was one of those winter days when the weather seemed designed to depress everyone who ventured out. The rain came down half-heartedly, but the wind occasionally managed a big enough gust to throw a stinging cupful of cold water in my face. My clothes repelled the liquid, of course, but human hair and skin finds ways of retaining water, and I felt cold and miserable as I trudged towards the waiting boats.

The harbour was quiet, only a few tourists taking the air, heads down as they danced around the puddles.

I walked straight to the harbour master's office, following Holmes, who walked in his own bubble of dry, fine weather.

Cal, the harbour master, was living proof that clichés gain traction for a reason. He was white-haired, bearded, had skin like a wrung-out chamois, and was wearing an Aran jumper under a navy coat. He offered me sweet tea in a pewter mug. I hate sweet tea, but what else can you drink with a man straight from the cover of *The Famous Five Go Smuggling*?

The office was a mess, the desk covered in paper, rope and a lobster pot. It smelled like the sea. Not in a romantic, refreshing, invigorating sense. It stank of salty dampness and old fish.

Cal kept a toothpick in his mouth. I'd never seen anyone do that in real life. He didn't remove it to speak, or even when he slurped his tea, when it hung from his bottom lip like a line of drool. I tried not to stare.

'Mrs Fairfield often went out at night.'

Cal pointed through the window at the boats on the north side of the harbour. They all looked alike, but it wasn't hard to spot Beth Fairfield's, as it was marked off by police tape. A single police officer guarded it.

'I warned her, of course, but she wasn't one to take advice. She was a very determined woman was Mrs Fairfield. She stood her ground; told me she knew the risks. It was her business, wasn't it?'

'Are you here every day?'

'Me or Johnny. We knock off at four during the winter months. If we're needed, all the owners have our smotch tags. We've got the camera for security. Not that we use it, really. There's a newer marina three miles out of town where the billionaires keep their toys. We're mostly fishing boats, and the pleasure cruisers in the summer season. And a few dive boats, of course. Not much crime around here. Not until . . . this, anyway.'

'You handed over the footage from Saturday evening to the police?'

'That I did.' Cal looked up from his tea and his expression hardened. 'We got some good shots of the bastard, even though he was wrapped up in a big coat. The police were on that boat straight away, dusting for DNA and that. Found my fingerprints – and a few of Johnny's – but the psycho was wearing gloves. She was a nice woman, was Mrs Fairfield. When I think that the murdering scumbag must have walked right past this office, it makes my blood boil. What did you say you were? A consultant?'

'That's right. We're helping the police with the investigation. I understand it was you who found Mrs Fairfield's body.'

'That it was.' The toothpick stopped bobbing between the harbour master's lips, and he looked down at his desk, staring through it, his expression distant.

'Do you always check on the boats?'

He shook his head as if to clear it, then looked at me again. 'Twice a day in season. Not so much in the winter. Every other day, maybe. I'd been outside and seen the dive boat was there, so I assumed she'd come back as normal. That's what I told the police. Never crossed my mind to think she'd never gone at all.'

'When did you find the body?'

'Not till the evening. I was in The Ship.'

The harbour master noticed my confused expression. 'The Ship – it's my local. I'd had a pint, about to order a second, when I thought maybe I should check Mrs Fairfield's boat.'

'Just out of curiosity?'

Cal's already florid complexion reddened further, and he chewed the toothpick more vigorously for a few moments. 'To be honest, I thought I should have checked the security footage. Mrs Fairfield always lets me know when she's taking the boat out for a dive. Just drops me a message. If I'm nearby, I go and help out, make sure the boat's running okay. Not that night, though. She went out without a word. Anyway, I was in The Ship, like I said, and Molly – she works for the Fairfields –was saying Mrs Fairfield was s'posed to be coming home the day before, but she hadn't turned up. I thought maybe I'd better check the security cam. Came down here and had a look. Camera covers the front of the harbour but not the jetty itself. I skipped through the evening footage until I found her. Then I saw the fellow who followed her.'

Cal bit through the toothpick, spat it into the bin, replacing it with another from a tin on his desk. He nodded out towards the poor sod guarding the murder scene. 'One of the police guys told Johnny that the psycho smacked her around something awful. Broke bones in her face. What kind of sick bastard . . . ?'

Holmes prompted me. 'When you'd watched the footage, you checked the boat?'

'I did. For some reason, when I found her, I wasn't surprised. It was like I knew she would be there. Once I'd seen the video of that bastard following her out.'

'Describe what you saw on the boat.'

'She was on her front. One arm flung out, like she was waiting for someone to help her up. Fingers all busted up. I boarded the boat, took her pulse, but I knew. She was so cold. So cold. I called the police. You know the rest.'

I put a hand on his shoulder. Holmes was still asking questions. I sub-voxed my objections.

'Giggim a loody second, will you?'

When the harbour master had taken a few longer breaths, I went back to the questions. 'Did Mr Bolton ever go diving with his wife?'

Cal snorted. 'Hardly. Not the type. Chalk and cheese, those two. Not that it seemed to matter. They used to rub along well enough. At first, anyway.'

'At first? What about more recently?'

The harbour master looked a bit sheepish, tugging on the end of the toothpick. 'Not really my place. I don't want to speak out of turn. I'm no gossip.'

Which, in my experience, meant Cal was a seasoned gossip and couldn't wait to share his opinion on the state of the Fairfield–Bolton marriage. I gave him an encouraging smile.

'Anything you can tell us might be useful, Cal. You're the one with the local knowledge. There's a murderer at large. Any information that might help us find him, even if you don't think it's relevant, isn't gossip, it's background information.'

The toothpick wandered from one side of Cal's lips to the other.

'Background information,' he repeated, sitting up straighter. I'd just given him permission to gossip. 'Right. I get you. Well, if you really think it'll help . . . ?'

'I do.'

'All right. It's not as if it's a big secret or anything. Word is that Mr Bolton and Mrs Fairfield have been a bit out of sorts with each other for a while. Not spending so much time together. Separate beds, according to Molly Ward. She cleans for them. She says they're barely in the house together anymore.'

Holmes wanted details. I repeated his question. 'When you say "for a while", how long do you mean? Be as precise as you can.'

'Well, let me see. I was chatting to Molly at the fete, and that was start of August. She said the atmosphere had been sour for a couple of months up at the house. No rows or nothing, don't get me wrong. Just not happy, that's what Molly said. She's four husbands in, so she should know a thing or two about marriage.'

He chuckled, then stopped abruptly as if remembering why we were there. 'Molly gave them a year. She was right. This isn't what she meant, though. Terrible business. Terrible. You don't think Mr Bolton had anything to do with it, do you?'

'No. We're just gathering information, that's all.'

'All right, then. I mean, he's not my cup of tea, but I reckon he's a good 'un at heart. He certainly wasn't after her money. The papers said he insisted on signing one of those, what do you call them?' He pulled at the toothpick again, before saying, 'Peanut. One of them peanut agreements.'

Holmes spoke into my right ear. 'What on earth is he talking about?'

'Prenup,' I said aloud. 'He signed a prenup agreement.'

'That's the one,' said Cal, at the same time as Holmes groaned, 'Give me strength.'

Holmes walked alongside me as we made the ascent to the hotel. The rain had eased off, but the wind was bitter.

'There are some pieces still to locate and put together. I've asked Miss Poplar to check Beth and Jack Fairfield's movements last year. They certainly attended fewer functions as a couple according to the data available online, but that might mean nothing. Separate beds would explain why Jack Bolton didn't notice his wife was missing.'

Holmes rubbed his hands together and lengthened his stride. I kept up with him. Holmes could walk at any speed he liked. He could probably fly if he wanted to. By the time we reached the top of the hill, I had worked up a light sweat. Considering the reduced physical exercise and increased physical abuse I had pursued since leaving the military, I was in better shape than I deserved to be. I hadn't had a proper drink for two nights, and a mental image of an ice-cold vodka tonic kept me going.

'Watson, I'm going to arrange for a little tour of Fairfield Tech in the morning. I hope it'll prove useful. They have a VR suite almost as advanced as the one at 221b. I think –'

He stopped talking, stopping in mid-stride. Literally mid-stride. His body defied gravity, hanging in mid-air, his rear foot pushing forward off its toes, the front foot six inches above the pavement, frozen in place.

I took another couple of steps before noticing, then stopped and looked at him. He looked ridiculous, his mouth open, mid-sentence. Then he vanished, simultaneously reappearing at my elbow. I jumped, despite myself.

'Can you try not to do that, please? It's bloody annoying.'

Holmes indicated an old woman with a miserable-looking dog, looking at me from across the street. 'You really should be sub-voxing, old man.'

'Oh, huck ock.'

The detective whirled round until we were eye to eye. He was smiling.

'The police have just shared a DNA match for our killer, Watson. Francis Turren. Forty-six years old. An ex-marine. No permanent address. He wasn't in the police database. His DNA was on record after being treated for a head injury sustained nearly thirteen years ago during the Iver Heath riots. He's lived off-grid completely since then.'

A tog. He couldn't be tracked easily, then. Total off-gridders were hardcore anti-tech, anti-surveillance, anti-pretty much everything. They tended to live a nomadic existence, squatting or sleeping rough. A few of my former army pals had slipped off-grid after failing to reintegrate when dropped back into their former lives. I wasn't entirely unsympathetic.

'Any leads on his whereabouts?'

'None yet,' said Holmes. 'The police are raiding squats, searching homeless shelters. It might take months. In the meantime, the case against Greta Blackstone has just grown stronger.'

'Why?'

'Francis Turren wasn't just caught up in the riots thirteen years ago. He was one of the instigators. His wife and daughter were coming back from a trip when the Roadtrain they were travelling on was wiped out at Iver Heath. There were no survivors. His daughter was ten years old.'

'Oh, shit.'

'Quite. He was a popular and active member of the New Ludds for a few years. They suspended his membership when they chose to broaden their appeal to the mainstream. Turren's calls for direct action and his increasing use of violent and inflammatory language, talking of battles and war, became an embarrassment to the New Ludd leadership. When they discovered he was making bombs and hoarding weapons, they expelled him. That was eight years ago. Since then, very little has been heard from him. Until now.'

'Okay, so an ex-New Ludd extremist kills the boss of the best-known tech business in the world. How does that strengthen the case against Blackstone? She was in charge when they kicked him out, right?'

'Yes. But for about a year, shortly after he joined the New Ludds, he and Greta Blackstone were a couple.'

'Oh, shit.'

'You should consider broadening your vocabulary, Watson. It hardly does you credit at times. The point being, if any recent contact between Turren and Blackstone can be shown, things will look very bleak indeed for Greta.'

'And what do you think?'

That half smile twitched at the corners of his lips. 'I think this case is fascinating, Watson. If we could find Mr Turren, I'd be very interested to talk to him. But I'm in the hands of the police. Total off-gridders are rather outside of my remit.'

'But not mine. Isn't that why you offered me a job?'

He looked at me appraisingly. 'You're right, but I can't afford to spare you, old man.'

'I wasn't thinking of me.'

'No?'

I waggled my smotch at him. 'We maladjusted ex-military types have a bit of an informal support network, you know.

I'll put the word out. Where did he live when his family was alive?'

'Bermondsey. But he could be anywhere by now.'

'Leave it with me.'

He nodded. 'Very well. Interesting. A network of anti-social ex-soldiers. It could be very useful to have them working for 221b. I might even call them the Baker Street Irregulars.'

'You might. But not to their face, unless you want to get headbutted. I'll make some calls now.'

'Excellent. Then get some rest. I'll join you for breakfast before we visit Fairfield Tech. Eight o'clock. I'm going to have a busy night, I think. Until then.'

And he was off. I waited, in case he was going to reappear and pull an extra 'jump scare', but he had gone for good this time.

I made my calls, sent some messages. Some of the men, women and enbies I'd fought alongside lived on the fringes of society, keeping to the shadows. If anyone could find a man like Francis Turren, they could.

When I was done, I turned my face towards the hotel, the bar within, and the very large vodka tonic that awaited me.

CHAPTER TWENTY-SIX

I was trained to resist torture. What this means in practice is attending seminars on torture, because it's against international law to torture anyone, so if the British army started torturing soldiers to teach them about torture, it might be bad for morale.

The first time I find out if I'm equipped to withstand torture is when General Harif comes back, accompanied by two men, one of whom carries a car battery.

I've heard the others screaming. I know my turn is coming. And I know they're leaving me until last because I'm the leader. If I give them what they want, I can spare my squad more pain. I can grant them a quick death.

I know the others will tell Harif they don't know where the Factory is. And there's no way he could know that we're lying.

My squad found the Factory seven months ago. But no one knows we know other than the CO of the platoon. And my squad members, of course.

For the first time, I consider the possibility that we have a traitor in the squad.

I watch the two men place the car battery on the floor. When they approach me, I fight, but I'm already weak and I can't stop them. They slip rope nooses over my wrists, tossing the ends over the beam above. They hoist me to my feet with all the emotion of a butcher hanging meat to mature. When my toes are just scraping the floor, they attach the rope to iron rings in the wall. Then they go back for the electrodes.

I think of my own training with a taser. I know my personal pain threshold is higher than most.

They rip my clothes open and attach electrodes to my chest, my armpits, the soles of my feet. In a stupid, pointless show of bravado, I clench my teeth when the fire lances through my body, stripping my nerves then filling them with acid. When I don't scream, they shrug and do it again. I whimper but I don't break.

The third time I scream, because there's nothing else I can do. I scream and scream but I don't tell them anything.

Later, I realise that Harif didn't ask a single question.

I was on the floor of my room at the Coaches, rolling to a crouch. Ready.

I lashed out, punched a hole in the wall. Shocking build quality. My suite was designed to look like it had been that way for hundreds of years, but the wall of the en suite was a recent addition. There was no way Jacobean builders – or whatever they were – would have used MDF.

The ice in the bucket I had borrowed to bring the rest of the vodka bottle back to my bedroom had long since melted, but the water was still cold enough to bring some instant relief to my bloodied knuckles.

My body was not a good place to be. I was dehydrated and my head was pounding. That was down to the vodka. My pulse was racing, my nervous system was flooded with adrenaline, and I wanted to kill someone. That was down to Hughes. The dreams always left a lingering sense of Hughes, but I always woke up before I could imagine finding and killing him.

I didn't expect the shower to work the same magic as the previous day, but hoped it would make a start on making me feel half human again. I took a pint of cold water in with me and gulped at it while the warm jets pummelled my body. Some soldiers swear by ice-cold showers to reboot the system. They can keep them.

About two minutes into the shower, something so odd happened that I turned it off, went to the mirror and checked my face. It looked exactly like I felt: great. The headache had gone, my eyes were bright and clear, my skin was practically glowing with health and I was as alert as an airport sniffer dog who'd accidentally ingested a snoutful of cocaine. I looked at my bloodied knuckles. They had been washed clean. No cuts, no bruises, perhaps a tiny bit of swelling if I squinted.

'What the –?' Then I remembered. The ennanomeds. They worked. Not only did they work, they were bloody fantastic. I was reborn. Even the dream, the malodorous after-effects of which usually clung to me for hours like a needy sloth with abandonment issues, had faded to a manageable level.

I celebrated by leaping back into the shower and launching into a rousing rendition of *Wild Boys*.

At breakfast, I dutifully dropped a fresh pair of contacts in and awaited the appearance of the great detective. After five minutes had gone by with no sign of him, I killed time by consuming six sausages, a three-egg omelette, a bowl of porridge, a pint of freshly squeezed orange juice, and more coffee than was good for me. When Holmes still wasn't there after twenty minutes, I ordered three *pains au chocolat*. From the speculation I'd read, top-end ennanomeds were rumoured to be able to strip nutrients out of any food, discarding unwanted fat and letting it pass through the body without leaving any deposits around the hips or waist. If they hadn't cost as much as a three-bedroom house, they would have ended the dieting industry. If the rumours were true, of course. I was putting them to the test.

My smotch buzzed. Time to go to geek central: Fairfield Technology. I called an Egg for pickup in five minutes.

I stood up. My stomach made some alarming noises. The ennanomeds weren't wasting any time processing the nutritionally useless elements of breakfast. I pinged an update to the Egg. *Better make it fifteen minutes.*

Fairfield Technology wasn't much to look at from the outside, but I'd been expecting that. The headquarters had been built on what was left of an abandoned industrial estate three miles outside St Austell. It had been constructed in the most low-impact, energy-efficient way possible. The only visible building was a long, single-storey reception: a subtle, bleached wood and glass structure at the end of a long drive. There were no overt security measures, but an invisible automated surveillance ring, five miles in diameter, surrounded the complex, meaning anything that moved was filmed, scanned and catalogued immediately. They already knew exactly who I was. If I hadn't had an appointment, the Egg would have been automatically powered down and locked until the security team came to ask some pertinent questions.

As we pulled up in front of the reception, I was acutely aware of my wearable tech. As I had been allowed to proceed unhindered, they must have been pre-warned that I was practically a mobile TV crew.

Twelve hundred people worked at Fairfield Tech. Hard to

believe looking at the reception area. The frontage was just for visitors – everyone else arrived at a no-doubt less pretty entrance on the far side of the complex.

Behind the reception was a slope, rising about fifty feet before levelling off. That was where the helipad was, plus the hangar for the famous new drones. The rest of the building was underground, using the natural properties of the hill to provide heat and ventilation for five floors of employees. Two of those floors were truly underground; the upper three could be spotted by the wide, narrow windows cut into the side of the hill.

There was no front door, just an opening big enough to drive a Carton through. I had read about this, too. The explanation had gone over my head, but it involved an artificial weather system inside the reception building, which responded in real time to external conditions, keeping the ambient temperature constant. However it worked, it was doing its job. The rain was back, but as I crossed the threshold, the drops around my feet sank into a floor magically free of puddles. I knelt down to check, running my fingers along the hard surface as the rain splashed around me. The floor was dry.

'Impressive, isn't it?'

The boss himself was there to greet me. Jack Bolton looked as if he had enjoyed a good night's sleep, which was odd given the circumstances. I wondered if his failing marriage was as amicable as he claimed, or if there was a darker reason for his equanimity. If the harbour master was to be believed, the Fairfield–Bolton household was far from the fairy tale the blogs suggested. Most relationships broke down when there was a third party involved. Was this the case here? If so, it gave Jack a motive for having his wife killed. The prenup took money out of the equation, but plain old jealousy had turned plenty of wronged spouses into murderers.

Perhaps the deaths of Robert Fairfield and his daughter weren't linked after all. DCI Barnett evidently thought so as he was still questioning Greta Blackstone. On the face of it, the leader of the New Ludds surely stood more to gain from the deaths of two giants in the field of cutting-edge technology than most people.

'I'll let you into a little secret, Dr Watson.'

Bolton was enjoying the whole Sherlock Holmes scenario a bit too much.

'Just Watson, please. What secret?'

'This.' He waved at the doorway. 'The weather thing. I don't know how it works. Not my field. That's what makes this place great, though. A bunch of specialists in incredibly narrow areas of technology who know nothing about what their colleagues do. This way, please.'

The reception area was only remarkable in that it lacked a single receptionist. No human receptionist, anyway. Three circular desks in the middle of the room glowed with a muted violet light. The nearest one brightened as we passed it. Jack slowed and spoke to it.

'This is Captain Barnes. Please tag her as Watson. Top-level visitor pass for today only.'

'Certainly, sir.' The voice that came from the desk was gender-neutral, but the accent was American. 'Welcome to Fairfield Technology, Watson. I hope you enjoy your visit.'

'Thank you,' I replied automatically.

'You're welcome.'

I stopped walking. The voice had been the same, but the accent had changed. British, specifically London. I gawped at the violet glow, then back at Bolton.

'Did that . . . thing just . . . ?'

'Yes. Sam is a fast learner, and people are more at ease

around people who talk like them. AI is much less intimidating, when it sounds like your friend. Or should I say "mate"?'

The AI receptionist was far better at accents than its boss, who sounded more New South Wales than Southwark. He stopped walking.

'Look, I want to apologise if I was less than helpful yesterday. This is all . . . pretty raw, and there's a lot for me to process. The only person I've ever lost I was real close to was my dad, and that wasn't a shock. He'd been sick for months. But this, this is different. I don't know how I'm supposed to feel. My emotions are outta control. First I'm numb, then I'm in denial. Next thing I'm mad as hell and looking for someone to lash out at. And now I'm supposed to run the company. So. I'm sorry if I was out of line.'

He looked genuinely lost. 'No need to apologise,' I said.

'Yeah, well. Let me make it up to you by showing you our secret underground lair. Oh.'

'What?'

'I'm afraid I can't let you in with the amount of wearable tech you're packing. Industrial espionage is a big deal for us. No cameras, no recording equipment. No fancy contact lenses either. If you'll just step into the cloakroom, you'll find a set of engineering overalls in your size. There's a tray for the contacts. Sorry. Can't make any exceptions.'

I felt strangely naked walking back out in a dark-green set of overalls. He hadn't said anything about the in-ear monitors, and no one knew about the sub-vox plaster on my throat, so I didn't mention them. Jack nodded his approval.

A more traditional automatic door swung open as we approached. We entered a large lift. 'I'm glad I can help with the investigation. When Mr Holmes got in touch, I moved a couple of meetings around so I could help.'

That was big of him.

'Our VR facilities are the most advanced in the country.'

I let that one go without comment. I doubted he knew about the VR facilities at 221b.

The lift doors opened, and Jack led me out into a geek's paradise.

'Mr Holmes is waiting for you. Right this way.'

CHAPTER TWENTY-SEVEN

I'd been half hoping there would be a short tour, but my guide had other ideas. He threw out the odd word of explanation as I followed him along a wide, glass-sided gantry that afforded me a tantalisingly brief view of the open-plan floors beneath.

The Fairfield Technology recruitment process must have screened out anyone with vertigo. Drifting to the edge to get a better look, I saw something that looked like a steel spiderweb beneath me, with multiple strands on different levels stretching out to various enclosed sections. A few people were walking on the floors below.

'This way.'

I jogged to catch up. 'This is *some* building,' I said.

He shrugged non-committally. 'I guess you get used to it pretty quickly. I hardly notice anymore.' He stopped suddenly. 'What have you found out about who killed my wife?'

I reminded myself of Holmes's instruction to pay attention, tried to see what I could glean from Bolton's abrupt change of subject and the tension of his posture. The police evidently hadn't shared Francis Turren's identity with Bolton, so I didn't mention it.

'We saw the pathologist,' I said. He flinched. I remembered that he'd had to look at Beth's ruined face when he identified the body. 'And we visited the harbour master. Holmes is pursuing some leads. I'm sure we'll have some news for you soon.'

'Good.' Back to being perfunctory. Jack Bolton was an odd man. He walked on for another ten yards before taking a fork in the path that led off to the south-west corner of the facility. I wanted to keep him talking, see what I could find out. There was one cast-iron guaranteed way to make an engineer more communicative: ask them what they're working on.

'Where are the Honeydrones?' I said. I'd been looking, but had seen no sign of Fairfield Tech's latest baby.

Jack was as voluble as I'd hoped, and for the next ten minutes we talked about the project he'd been working on for the past five years. Well, I asked the questions and Jack talked. The Honeydrones were supposed to do for airspace what the Eggs, Cartons, Feeders and Roadtrains had done for the roads. Named in honour of the bees who could always find their way to the most promising flowers and back to the hive, the Honeydrones used an upgraded version of the original Fairfield algorithm to allow tens of thousands of unmanned aircraft to communicate with each other while they shared the same airspace. In theory, a swarm of electric Honeydrones was safer, more convenient and far more economical than any other form of airborne transport. In practice, the Honeydrones had some heavyweight opponents from the aviation industry, politicians, and – predictably – the New Ludds.

Fairfield Tech's most pressing problem was a practical one. Just like the electric road vehicles, the Honeydrones could only work if they were the sole type of aircraft allowed within a specified corridor of altitude in domestic airspace, each drone constantly aware of the position and velocity of its fellows. It was all or nothing. For now, despite some convincing demonstrations with swarms of small prototypes, they were still grounded.

A door opened as we talked, and Bolton led me into a familiar-looking room. The first thing I noticed was a dentist-style chair – the twin of the one at 221b. Then I saw an additional two identical chairs. The computer monitors were built into the walls rather than the desk-based workstation Poplar used. The whole room was like a clichéd sci-fi movie scene. It was white, spotless, futuristic. Even the floor was white and completely free of dirt or dust. Whoever did their cleaning deserved a pay rise. Although, judging from what I'd seen so far, it was probably a robot. They deserved an oil change, then.

'I'll leave you to it. Even at a time like this there are meetings I can't avoid, decisions to make. It's what Beth would have wanted.'

I hadn't asked him to justify himself to me. As the door hissed shut behind him, I said, 'Who's going to show me how to operate all this?' But he had already gone.

'I'll show you the ropes, Watson.' That androgynous London accent again, coming from a violet disc the size of a side plate on the far wall. 'If you just step up to the chair. Mr Holmes and your colleagues are waiting for you in an encrypted dataspace. I'll ping them a message, let them know you're on your way.'

The disc glowed brighter as I approached the chair. 'Just sit normally, Watson, and place the visor firmly over your eyes.'

The visor was on a small table. Same deal as the one at 221b. So light as to be almost unnoticeable when you were wearing it. I leaned back on the chair and pressed the sides of the visor down around my eyes. It stuck in place.

'Do I need to press any . . . ah.'

The room around me darkened smoothly and slowly. The chair gripped my arms and legs – not enough to make me feel imprisoned, but enough to manoeuvre me into a standing position. For a moment in the darkness it was a little eerie. I could hear nothing, see nothing. Then the picture slowly brightened, colours, shapes and textures coming into focus around me. Within seconds the illusion was complete. So complete that my mind, despite knowing none of it was genuine, treated the new environment as if it was as real as the Cornish hill I was actually sitting inside. Although I knew I wasn't really where my senses were telling me I was, it made no difference.

I was standing in a corridor at the top of a flight of stairs. In front of me was a door. Dark wood, possibly mahogany. Muffled grunts and heavy breathing came from the room behind it. I brought up my hand to knock. A hairy hand emerged from a starched white shirt with cufflinks inside a tweed jacket. I brought my fingers up to my face. The sideburns and moustache were so realistic I could feel individual hairs. Holmes had referred to this as *suggestive VR* at our first meeting. It had sounded like an online porn term at the time. This time I understood what was happening: my brain was cooperating with the hyper-realistic environment by filling in any missing sensory details.

A familiar voice called out from within.

'No need to stand on ceremony, Watson. Come on in.'

Offering up a silent prayer that the noises were due to him indulging in some sort of VR exercise regime, rather than anything dodgier, I pushed on the door. When nothing happened, I twisted the handle and tried again. Door handles. So nineteenth century.

CHAPTER TWENTY-EIGHT

THERE WAS a fire spitting and crackling in the grate. Oil lamps had been lit and the curtains half-closed against a blizzard outside. It had been raining in Cornwall. Holmes could have whatever weather he wished for here. I wondered if he found hypnotic heavy snowfall an aid to the deductive process.

I didn't speculate for long as my attention was caught by the two strangers in the room, and by what Holmes was doing with one of them.

Leaning against the mantelpiece was a slim, Asian woman in an elegant peacock-blue suit, watching the proceedings impassively.

In front of the fire, Sherlock Holmes, stripped to the waist and glistening with sweat, was face-down on the rug underneath a hulk of a man a head taller and at least fifty pounds heavier than him. Bald, ugly, also half-dressed, this gorilla-like creature had Holmes in a headlock and was grinning with triumph.

'Be with you in a moment.' Holmes sounded fairly cool given the circumstances, but he had to gasp the sentence out due to the constriction on his windpipe. In a virtual environment where he could turn into smoke and have his opponent's limbs rearranged by a team of ninja mice, I wondered why he chose – mostly – to stick to the rules of the physical universe.

'Now then, at this stage you're confident you have me at a slight disadvantage, correct?'

He was talking to the hulk.

'Slight?' said his opponent. 'I could tear your head off.'

'Mm. You sense victory and that's the perfect time to show you that your confidence' – he jabbed up into the sweaty armpit above him with two straightened fingers – 'is premature.'

The bald man's eyes widened in surprise at the same moment his arm relaxed. Holmes rolled to the side as the big man fell forward, every limb floppy and useless, hitting the rug nose first with a spray of blood and a jolt that made the floor tremble underfoot.

'Ow.'

The Asian lady applauded without removing her soft leather gloves. It sounded like someone patting a dog. 'Nice moves,' she said.

'Seriously,' said the giant on the rug as Holmes reached for his shirt from the back of a chair. 'Ow. That really hurts. Can you stop it?'

'It'll wear off in a few minutes, as you know.' Holmes picked up his shirt. The Asian woman threw him his jacket. When he checked his reflection in the mirror, the sweat evaporated and his unruly hair returned to its customary slicked perfection.

The hulk groaned.

'Oh, very well,' said Holmes, and a moment later, the defeated man pushed himself to his knees. His nose – surely broken – looked fine and the blood that had accompanied the crunch of his fall had disappeared. The New Ludds would have hated this.

I looked again at the two strangers and made the obvious connection.

'Poplar,' I said, waving at the Asian woman. 'Tobes.' With a nod to the giant now getting to his feet.

'Close,' said the hulk, now looking down at me. If he'd gone for a Mohawk rather than skin, it would have been flattened by the ceiling. 'We can choose whatever avatars we want in here. I'm Poplar.'

I leaned out to peer around the cartoon barbarian. The diminutive, glamorous Asian woman raised an eyebrow. 'Don't judge,' she said.

I pointed at my abundant facial hair. 'I wasn't about to. Not that I was given the same choice.'

'You look marvellous, Watson,' said Holmes.

He smiled up at Poplar. I was having a hard time equating the blue-haired girl with the hulking bald-headed man. It didn't help that she now spoke with a bass profundo growl that rattled the furnishings.

'What did you do to my armpit?'

'Oh, it's a long-forgotten technique from the Polynesians. Eight hundred years old, at least. I'll show you next time. You're improving.'

'What's the point?' I asked. 'None of this is real.'

'Oh, but it is, Watson. As real as anything back there in RR as far as the brain knows.'

He noticed my quizzical expression.

'RR – Real Reality,' he clarified. 'When I'm there, I'm a ghost, unbeholden to the physical laws that govern the rest of you, but equally unable to manipulate solid matter the way you can. Augmented Reality has its limits. In here, even though you know it's not real – and we can argue that point long into the night – your brain treats it as if it is. If I were to break your finger, you would emerge unscathed once you exit VR, but the pain will be every bit as convincing as if your bone had genuinely snapped.'

I put my hands behind my back. 'But last time I was here —'

'You were coming round from a sedative. Your first impressions were dreamlike. Your brain was not fully immersed. Now it's different. Rub your eyes.'

'Sorry, what?'

'Your eyes, old man. Give them a rub. Quickly, please, we have work to do.'

Fine. I rubbed my eyes, then shrugged. 'So?'

'Think about it.'

I shrugged again. 'What is there to . . . oh.' I wasn't here, I was sitting in a VR chair in Fairfield Technology, near St Austell, Cornwall. And there was a visor on my face that covered my eyes. Only, I'd just rubbed my eyes and there'd been no visor.

'Oh indeed, Watson. If you remind yourself strongly that you're not actually here — if you picture your surroundings in RR vividly enough — you can exit at any point. And the visor will be there when you feel for it. Not now, though.'

I'd been lifting my hand towards my face. I let it drop again.

'Wait,' I said as a thought occurred to me. 'If I'm in St Austell, can I be overheard? Recorded? I don't know who's in that room with me.'

'No danger of that. We can speak freely.'

I wondered at his confidence. I was in a VR suite in the middle of the most high-tech company in the world, yet my employer wasn't in the slightest bit worried that his privacy could be breached. I filed the information away for future consideration.

Holmes had removed his jacket again. 'Since we're all here, how about some training, Watson?'

'Training?' I looked at Poplar and Toby. They were grinning. 'Ah,' I said. 'Well, that depends.'

'On what, old man?'

'On whether you agree to obey the laws of physics.'

Holmes had removed his shirt again. He had chosen a wiry, lightly muscled torso. His chest was hairy, which was not only historically likely, but also brought him in line with the current fashion for body hair.

'Very well. For the first bout, we will obey the laws of the natural world. But Watson?' Holmes adopted a fighting stance in front of the fire and beckoned me over. 'I should warn you. I have studied unarmed combat methods from all eras and locations. You may find yourself at somewhat of a disadvantage.'

Our audience's smiles broadened as I took off my jacket and shirt, revealing a white vest over a similarly hirsute chest.

Holmes bobbed on his toes, his eyes flicking from my face to my arms, ready to exploit any weaknesses he could find. He looked every inch the experienced fighter. I had faced his type before. And I had done so in the real world.

'Begin,' he said.

I brought up my arms as if I were about to mirror his stance, but instead – immediately after he had spoken – I punched him sharply in the chin. It was more of a jab than an uppercut, not a tremendously powerful punch, but placed perfectly. The detective stumbled backwards, fell over an armchair and hit the floor, hard.

'Bloody hell,' breathed Toby. He and Poplar stared at me, then at Sherlock Holmes's supine figure.

Holmes lay still for a few moments. When he did move, it was to raise his hands in the air and applaud. He laughed, but

I knew I wasn't imagining the irritated note of shock in his voice.

'Ha! Excellent, Watson, excellent.' He stood up and took up his guard, making sure he was just out of range. 'Shall we say best of three?'

I intended to say, 'Fine with me,' but only got as far as, 'F—' when Holmes dropped, pivoted on one outstretched arm and swept both legs under mine. I was surprised, but I had an answer ready as I fell. Instinct tells you to break your fall, but a trained fighter learns when to ignore it. I reached out to grab his legs and regain the advantage. To my amazement, Holmes anticipated the move, keeping his legs moving, turning the initial sweep of his legs into a full 360-degree manoeuvre. I hit the floor hard with my left shoulder a fraction of a second before his shoe connected with the back of my head.

My grunt of pain turned into a drawn-out groan. 'Nice move,' I said in a tone fairly dripping with threat.

'Thank you, Watson. Had enough?'

I rolled onto my knees, then got back to my feet. 'You said best of three.'

'So I did. So I did.' That satisfied smile was twitching at the corner of his mouth. The original Sherlock Holmes was an excellent boxer, and this version obviously prided himself on matching, or even improving on, the Conan Doyle model.

We circled each other more warily this time, looking for an opening. Most one-on-one fights I had been involved with had lasted as long as it took a meathead to say, 'Do you want to take this outs—'. Fights against multiple opponents involved more than just speed and accuracy – they called for a modicum of strategy. Very, very occasionally, the same level of strategic thought had to be brought to bear in an encounter with a single opponent. This was one of those occasions and I found myself in the unenviable position of having to think like Sherlock Holmes.

Clockwork Sherlock wasn't driven by anger. He was as dispassionate an opponent as I'd ever faced, which made him formidable. If there had been an element of showboating in his last attack, it was gone now, and his calm grey eyes watched me steadily and shrewdly. He wasn't talking anymore, and Poplar and Toby might as well have been on the other side of the world as Holmes and I prepared to engage.

Classic fights have been likened to games of chess, but I think it's a weak analogy. Poker is a far better comparison. In chess, a thousand variables are held in mental stasis simultaneously, and games between masters are demonstrations of deep, multi-layered, supple thinking. Heads-up poker is simpler, particularly when each player has some knowledge of the other. Rather than thinking many moves ahead, as the chess players do, the poker player tries to get into the mind of their opponent, using informed speculation based on imperfect information to choose the most effective play. In a well-matched fight, as in a poker game, the combatants are always trying to think like their opponent. Average players play the cards they've been dealt. Better players play their opponent – the cards are secondary. The best poker players tell a story to their opponents, knowing that their opponents are doing exactly the same thing.

My left hook has ended many fights, arriving just after a right jab. With a good opponent I would signal the hook, but never unleash it, instead using the slight pull-back of my left shoulder as cover for shifting my weight to my left foot, freeing my right to deliver a crotch-squishing kick. I'm not much of a one for the Queensbury rules.

I had misjudged Holmes. The way he'd put me on the floor had been inspired. Creative. Annoyingly effective. He had anticipated my actions. What would he do with the jab and hook? He knew I was an excellent fighter. He'd expect the hook to be a feint and defend against the kick, wouldn't he? So I should make the hook real. Or would he expect a double-bluff and be ready for it?

In the end, I decided that in a fight with an opponent who could out-think as well as outreach me it was time to let instinct back into the equation. And my instinct knew exactly what to do.

I jabbed with my right. Holmes read it beautifully, his head moving backwards as his eyes flicked across to my left hand and the approaching hook.

I don't know what defence and counter he had planned. Something imaginative and painful, I imagine. But when I suddenly dropped my guard completely, I was close enough to see the moment of doubt in his expression. I fell forward, deliberately off-balance, before pushing with both legs as he reacted and tried to step back.

Too late. I was inside his reach, my arms were wrapping round his waist, and as he prepared to counter-attack, he suddenly went very still indeed.

I would have loved to use the moment to say something witty, but as my teeth were closed hard enough on his windpipe to prevent him drawing air, neither one of us was in a position to deliver a bon mot.

Two seconds passed before he delivered the double tap on my shoulder acknowledging defeat. I released him and stepped away. Toby and Poplar regarded us with jaws hanging open.

'Shitting hell,' said the Asian woman, for a moment actually looking more like Toby.

Holmes rubbed his throat ruefully. There was no mark, of course. He shook his head as he buttoned his shirt.

'I knew you were good, Captain Barnes, but it's quite something to witness your skills first-hand. And it's a good exercise for me to limit myself to the same physical laws that govern the rest of you.'

'The rest of us? Why don't they apply to you, then?'

Holmes didn't rise to the bait.

'The more time you spend in VR, the more you'll learn to transcend the limitations you bring in with you. This is all data after all. We're participants in a programmed environment. The limits are in the code. But those limits can be stretched, particularly if you wrote the code.'

The door of the apartment opened and a second Sherlock Holmes walked in. He nodded at the first, then walked up the wall and onto the ceiling, tilting his head to look down at us. Or up at us.

'For your brain to buy in to the simulation,' said upside-down Holmes, 'your physical body has to match your virtual body to a certain extent. Back in the VR suite, you are standing up, supported by the chair. If I were to challenge the illusion . . .'

I floated away from the floor, my whole body rotating as I did so. I came to rest on the ceiling, eye to eye with the second Holmes. I looked down at the first one, and at Poplar and Toby. I felt dizzy and stumbled forward. If I fell, I didn't know if I'd end up on the floor or the ceiling.

I put out a hand to regain my balance, but my limbs seemed to belong to someone else. I experienced a sudden, violent antipathy towards the body I was inhabiting, like a transplant patient rejecting every single organ at once.

'Steady, old man.' The second Holmes took my arm. 'Shut your eyes. Please.'

The room was beginning to spin, so I did as he asked. When he released me, I opened them to find my leather-shod feet back on the carpet where they belonged.

The two Holmeses regarded me with the same concerned expression. 'Better, Watson?' said one. I nodded.

'It takes time to ignore some of the basic building blocks of your consciousness. You can't survive in the physical world without making certain basic assumptions at a level so deep you don't even know you're making them.'

'But they don't exist here,' added the second Holmes. I rubbed the bridge of my nose, wondering if I had a headache coming on.

'Sorry,' said one of the detectives. 'It's disconcerting at first.' He dissolved into a cloud of dark smoke, before darting into the fire and up the chimney.

'There will be plenty of time for you to learn the lack of limits in here,' said the remaining Holmes. 'I hope. The fact that you have accepted your avatar so quickly shows you have potential. Remember –'

He vanished. At the same moment, I felt a cold blade press on the skin of my throat. I froze.

'It's VR, Watson. The rules don't have to apply.' Holmes stepped away from me, folding a cutthroat razor away as he did so. 'You fight extraordinarily well, Watson. But I let you win.'

So that was what all this was about. A bit petty. Still, I wondered if he had given away more than he intended with this demonstration. The theory that Clockwork Sherlock was an Artificial Intelligence was now number one on my list. I wondered what Nicky Gambon would make of that.

Holmes turned to the woman by the fire. 'To business, Toby. What did you find?'

'Follow me.' Toby led the way out of the room. I followed, Poplar squeezing her bulk through the door behind me. I hurried to catch up with Toby. She/he smiled as she led me down the stairs. I was struggling with pronouns. I decided to do what I'd do in Real Reality: refer to them as they presented themselves and ask if I wasn't sure. So, for now,

Toby was *she* and Poplar was *he*. Simple enough. As for Holmes, that was anybody's guess.

The staircase ended in a narrow hallway with dark-red wallpaper and burgundy and cream diamond floor tiles.

'Saturday evening,' said Toby, and opened the front door. When I saw what was out there, I gasped.

It wasn't snowing. It wasn't the end of the nineteenth century. And it wasn't London.

CHAPTER TWENTY-NINE

Even though I knew where we were, it took a few seconds for it to fully register.

We were standing outside the harbour master's office in St Austell. When I'd looked out at the snow from the rooms at Baker Street, it had been daytime, but now it was a moonless night. The only light came from the street lamps above us, the nearest of which housed the security camera.

I was uncomfortable but didn't know why. It was like having an itch that desperately needed attending to, but not knowing what part of my body to scratch.

Holmes was closing the door behind him.

'It can take a little getting used to,' said Toby. Her voice matched her appearance and I couldn't picture a fit, ex-military male when she spoke, so I stopped trying. 'It's easier to bounce out of a mock-up. Takes more concentration to make it work.'

'Mock-up?'

Poplar answered this time while Holmes glanced up at the camera and positioned himself on the path below it.

'The Baker Street rooms environment was constructed from the ground up, every detail thought about and programmed. Feature-rich, if you like. But this' – he flicked his eyes left to right – 'is a mock-up. We have this camera here, plus other street cams that give us different views of the area and we can access all the latest stills and videos online. All of which means the algorithm can build a convincing environment, but the tiny details are absent. We might not know it, but our brains miss the little things. Oh, and there's the lack of people or sound or variations in temperature. We don't bother with stuff we don't need.'

That explained my discomfort. I relaxed a little. The part of the illusion I found the strangest was the acoustics. We were standing in the open, near the sea, but there was no crashing of waves, and Poplar's voice had sounded like we were still standing in Sherlock Holmes's rooms.

'Let's start with Beth Fairfield,' said the detective.

Suddenly I was in a zombie movie. Jerking, stuttering figures appeared. A man walking a dog, a woman with a pushchair, head down against the rain I couldn't see. They flickered like old home movies, blurring and sharpening, sometimes vanishing completely before reappearing a few feet further on.

'Sorry about the quality,' rumbled Poplar. 'Here we are. Eight forty-three that night.'

A private car pulled up under the street lamp and a woman got out with a heavy canvas bag. She put it on the floor and watched the car leave. Her hair was wet but she didn't use an umbrella. Beth Fairfield. She froze as if someone had pressed a pause button – which was, I supposed, exactly what had happened.

'Nice clear image under that light,' said Toby.

Holmes walked closer to the woman in question. It was hard to equate those well-known features with the unrecognisable corpse I'd seen in the morgue. 'Yes. A very clear image indeed, considering. Carry on.'

Beth Fairfield turned and walked towards the jetty, heading for the dive boat. Ten yards before reaching her goal, she vanished.

Poplar turned to Holmes. 'And that's the limit of the security cam footage, sir. There are no more cams along that part of the jetty.'

'How long before Francis Turren follows?'

'As soon as she's out of sight. He must have been watching from one of the alleyways opposite.'

'Show me.'

I turned to look at the houses over the road and yelped in shock. A hooded figure stood three feet away from me. Before I could move, it walked into me. Instinctively, I brought my arm up to defend myself, but there was no impact. I blinked and he had gone. When I swung around to the others, I saw his retreating back. He had walked right through me. I shuddered and reminded myself this was just a virtual crime reconstruction, and he was just a recording. It didn't really help.

As the figure passed under the street lamp, the image froze. Holmes, Poplar and Toby gathered around it. I called over to them.

'Thanks for the warning. Not that I mind murderers walking right through me or anything, but . . .'

They ignored me. I rolled my eyes and joined them.

'No view of his face at all,' said Holmes. 'The clothes tell us nothing: generic, probably purchased online. Same with the boots. They're not anything a fisherman would wear. Is this all the detail we can get?'

Poplar answered. 'The security system is a generation older than anything I've ever worked with. The definition is appalling. I've enhanced it as much as I can. We only got that good shot of Fairfield because she stood still for so long.'

'Yes, she did, didn't she? Continue.'

We all watched the hooded man take the same route as Beth Fairfield, staying close to one side, out of the light as much as possible. He vanished at the same point she had.

'What about the other footage I asked for? What did you find?'

Toby leaned in towards me. 'It's about to get weirder. Don't freak out.'

I was readying a pithy response when the world changed. The sky lightened and the rain stopped. The boats, the harbour master's office, the entire harbour itself, vanished and were replaced with another street. The only constants were the four of us.

I took a pace to one side to steady myself. Toby looked up at me in concern.

'I'm fine,' I said. 'Fine.'

'Good. I threw up the first time that happened. Don't throw up in VR, Watson. It's bad.'

We were standing at the top of one of the sloping streets leading down to the harbour, over a mile away from where we'd been standing seconds before. A few people populated the scene, but they were frozen. Another mock-up, this one with even less definition than the first. I fancied I could make out individual pixels on the sweating face of the woman jogging across the road.

'How hard was he to find?'

Poplar's bald beef-cake avatar responded. 'The software picked up thirty-seven possibilities, which I reduced to twelve by filtering out those who showed up on subsequent security cams and were identified as locals. When I narrowed the search to the approach with the fewest cameras, I found a match within the window you specified.'

'Excellent. Is this the camera?'

He pointed up at a fixed camera mounted above a coffee shop. It looked as if it would capture anyone approaching the cafe, covering the pavement and road in front, and opposite, a short alleyway between two houses.

Poplar nodded at her boss. 'That's it. There's a series of alleyways at the back of the houses. If you follow that route down to the sea, there's only this camera and the one at the harbour to worry about.'

'No household security cams?' I said.

'Plenty,' said Poplar. 'Funnily enough, there was a brief Wi-Fi outage on Saturday evening. Might have been triggered by a mobile blocker. It was back on within ten minutes, but that's plenty of time for Turren to run down to the front. Then all he had to do was wait.'

'Show me,' said Holmes.

He turned towards the alley as Poplar pressed an invisible pause button and the scene came to life. We all watched a hooded figure cross the space between the two buildings, head down, walking fast. Holmes headed down the alley and we followed.

'St Austell GBR station is the other side of these trees.'

We emerged into a surreal hinterland. The buildings around us were no longer photo-realistic, but representational. They looked like architects' drawings. A dense patch of trees appeared real until I noticed it was actually the same tree reproduced many times. The ground underfoot was unnaturally flat, and the grass had the uniformity of AstroTurf.

Toby walked beside me. 'No cameras here, and no need to mock-up anything convincing.'

Holmes stopped ahead at the artificial treeline. A crude path was visible at one end, leading to a fence with missing panels.

'Turren travelled by railway. Smart move if you wish to remain unseen.'

Within cities, autonomous driverless vehicles were the only choice, but longer trips presented a second option. The railways. Passengers could be unofficially added to a freight train for very little cost. It was an uncomfortable way to travel – no lighting, no heat – but it was dirt cheap. Officially, railway travel no longer existed, but it was an open secret that a small cash bribe at the major stations would secure a space on one of the empty carriages. A bigger bribe would get you your own private space in a freight truck, maybe even a cushion.

Evidently this was how Francis Turren had arrived in St Austell. GBR didn't run security cameras, and the cooperative that ran Britain's rail network was a notoriously keen litigious defender of the right to privacy. Turren could easily have made his way out of London anonymously. Even the talented Miss Poplar had only managed to find one camera shot of him between the station and the harbour.

'So we know how he got here. And he got out the same way?'

Poplar nodded. 'Retraced his route, right down to the Wi-Fi outages. I have the same cam shot of him heading back, but the angle's even worse than on the way in. He must have caught the night freight to London.'

'Damn it. He could be anywhere.'

No GBR trains boasted of their speed, but the night trains were notoriously slow, running at twenty to forty miles an hour, which made economic sense and meant they could offer their cheapest rates overnight. If Turren had travelled on the overnighter, he could have alighted at Exeter, where the freight was transferred to the London line, or jumped off at any point between Cornwall and Paddington.

'Theoretically,' I said.

'What do you mean?' Holmes walked away from the fence and back towards me.

'I mean I'd put money on him being back in London.'

'Explain.'

'When people lose someone close, once the initial shock has passed and they have to carry on with their lives, they react one of two ways. They either make a clean break – move away, go somewhere where they won't be reminded of what they've lost every time they open their front door. Or they stay put because they don't want to forget. Turren didn't leave after he lost his family. He's gone back to Bermondsey.'

'Hmm. Maybe.' Holmes may not have been convinced by a conclusion not based on deductive reasoning, but I knew how people behaved under stress. I was sure I was right.

Toby's avatar appeared at my shoulder. She looked me up and down, from my prematurely balding scalp to the leather boots strapped over my breeches. Oh yes, I cut quite the dashing figure. 'Look, when everything settles down, do you fancy going for a drink somewh—'

She was interrupted by a repetitive high-pitched chime.

'Who is it?' said Holmes.

The bald, muscle-bound Poplar pulled a sour face. 'DCI Barnett.'

'Very well. Please answer.'

The orangutan appeared in a doorway. He had a half-eaten banana in his hand and bits of it were dotted around his hairy features.

'Hope I'm not interrupting anything important, Mr Holmes.' The sycophantic grin looked incongruous on his banana-splattered face. I reminded myself that, as an audio caller, not only could he not see any of us, he was unaware of Poplar's choice of avatars.

'I always have time for you, Barnett, you know that. We

may approach matters differently, but we are pursuing the same end, are we not?'

'Absolutely, Mr Holmes, absolutely. That's why I wanted to tell you personally. Save you carrying on with this wild goose chase. We've got our murderer. '

CHAPTER THIRTY

THE DETECTIVE CHIEF inspector struck a dramatic pose, arms folded across his chest. He smirked knowingly at Holmes, Poplar, Toby and me. If he'd known he was an orangutan, he would have realised why his showboating was ineffective.

'I don't think this case is worthy of your superior methods, Mr Holmes.'

Barnett put some emphasis on the word *superior*, as if afraid we might otherwise have missed the sarcasm.

'Well, I appreciate you taking the time out of your busy schedule. As we are investigating two murders, might I ask to which you refer?'

'To both, Mr Holmes. It might not have been the same hand that did both deeds, but it was the same scheming mind behind them. I must say, although I am a great admirer of your work – a great admirer – sometimes simple police work gets the job done sooner. Real life isn't, as it turns out, stranger than fiction after all. All too often it's the obvious solution that turns out to be correct.'

'You'll have to spell it out, I'm afraid, detective chief

inspector. My deductive skills have fallen behind your own, it would seem.'

'We've just charged Greta Blackstone with the murder of Robert Fairfield, and with plotting the murder of Beth Fairfield.'

'And your evidence?'

'With Mr Fairfield, it's just as I said from the beginning. Motive, opportunity, means. Blackstone has the full set. She's the head of the New Ludds, Mr Holmes. Her professions of love for the deceased were a lie. She was manipulating him, persuading him to join her organisation, turn against technology. She wanted Fairfield Tech finished.'

Holmes shook his head. 'Come come, inspector, you can do better than that. I doubt a jury would bring in a guilty conviction on such flimsy evidence.'

The orangutan grunted. 'True. But we checked Blackstone's story and it doesn't hold up.'

'How so?'

'She claimed she didn't get to Robert Fairfield's house until eleven thirty. Used a credit coin to pay for her Egg, so there's no record. No cams in her street either, remember?'

'Yes, I remember,' said Holmes. 'You're hardly building your case here.'

'Ah! But Robert Fairfield didn't take out every camera like she wanted, did he? He left one on his gate. So we have film of her turning up at his place. Guess what time it was?'

'Well, judging from your air of excitement, and the fact that you are making no attempt to hide your delight, might I hazard a guess that Ms Blackstone didn't arrive at the time she claimed in her statement?'

'Ten out of ten, Clockwork!' The ape stamped his feet for emphasis. 'Go to the top of the bloody class. She got there at nine thirty. Plenty of time to kill the poor sod, wait a while, then pretend she had just found his corpse. Didn't think to check that, eh, with that big brain of yours?'

'You may be right,' responded Holmes. 'It's certainly possible I missed something.'

I stepped in. 'It's a bit odd, if you think Greta Blackstone didn't know about the camera at the gate, that she would commit murder, then wait around at the scene before calling it in, don't you think? She could have just gone home, left the body to be discovered by someone else.'

Barnett wasn't going to allow his triumph to be diluted. 'Not at all, not at all. Planning a murder is one thing, but actually carrying it out, seeing a fellow human being die in front of you, that's quite another. Blackstone might be a murderer, but she isn't a seasoned killer. She probably went into shock, started behaving irrationally. What does it matter, anyway? The facts all point to her.'

'I bow to your superior knowledge of human psychology,' said Holmes without a trace of sarcasm. 'Any news on Beth Fairfield's murderer?'

'We'll have him soon enough. The togs might be harder to track down, but even they can't avoid justice. There's a manhunt in progress across the country. If we don't find him the old-fashioned way, with boots on the streets, the facial recog software will get him. He can't avoid every camera forever, and we only need a glimpse for that program to nail him. It's an amazing bit of kit. We'll have Turren soon. And we'll be asking him when he last spoke to his old girlfriend, Greta. Don't you worry, Mr Holmes. I'm sure another case will come along that's a bit more suited to your special talents, eh?'

Holmes smiled at that. 'I expect you're right, inspector.'

The orangutan grinned broadly and vanished.

'Bollocks,' said Poplar at the same time as Toby muttered, 'Dickhead.'

Only Holmes seemed unfazed. 'The police will be keen to show that Blackstone and Turren were still in touch with each other. I also have a question I'd like to ask Mr Turren.'

He fell silent, closing his eyes, and didn't expand further. I hadn't yet decided whether keeping his reasoning and speculations to himself, occasionally tossing out frustrating hints about his internal processes, was a quirk of his own or if he'd based it on the original Sherlock. Either way, it was bloody irritating.

Holmes opened his eyes. 'Today's headlines, Miss Poplar?'

The hulk shut his eyes. When he opened them again, newsfeed headlines drifted across the sky like time-lapsed clouds.

DO YOU RE-GRETA KILLING HIM, BLACKSTONE?

FAIRFIELD FAMILY CURSE STRIKES AGAIN.

NEW LUDD KILLS TECH GIANT'S BOSS

'That's enough. thank you.'

The headlines disappeared. Holmes stood quietly, looking at the ground, his cane tapping rhythmically on the pavement. I didn't remember him bringing a cane. VR had its uses.

'Scotland Yard has its murderer, as does the media.' It was evident that Holmes didn't agree.

'Er, boss? Just a thought, but . . .' Toby's voice died as the detective's head swung sharply in his direction. She coughed and tried again. 'It's just, well, the New Ludds would have you shut down if they could. I know Blackstone said she wasn't against all technology, just AI, but she doesn't speak for all of them, does she? You've read the graffiti, seen the protests. Some of them won't be happy until we're rubbing sticks together to make fire and sending smoke signals to communicate.'

'So?'

'So . . . all I'm saying is, even if you reckon she didn't do it . . . er, do you reckon she didn't do it?'

'I am not yet in full possession of the facts, Toby. Let's just say I have doubts.'

'Doubts. Right. But, well, what's the rush? I mean, this whole thing is going to damage the New Ludds. I don't know if you've noticed, but they're big news since Greta Blackstone turned them into a political party. They might even get a seat in parliament. This case could stop them getting too powerful.'

Holmes remained silent. Toby shuffled nervously.

'I mean, I'm not saying leave her to rot. Just, well, let her sweat a bit first.'

Holmes, looking down again, shook his head slowly. Then he looked at me. 'You've read the Conan Doyle stories, Watson.'

It wasn't a question. 'More than once,' I admitted.

'Toby isn't our friend here's real name. When he joined 221b, a clean break with the past was necessary. Toby let me choose a new name. Do you remember who Toby was in the stories?'

Of course I did. I looked at Toby, who even in his Asian female form retained the ability to blush adorably. I smiled at him as I answered.

'He was a dog.'

'He was. And I borrowed the name for two reasons. One was the original Toby's gift for sniffing out criminals with extraordinary tenacity. The second was more of a general characteristic associated with the canine species. Loyalty. My Toby would put his namesake to shame in that department.'

Toby shuffled her feet.

'But,' said Holmes, coming closer and looking Toby in the eye, 'certain principles must take precedence over loyalty. Without exception. One of these is justice. Justice is not enslaved to any idea, any agenda. It even supersedes any legal system that tries to enshrine its values. When artists personify justice, they portray her as blind. Blind to status, wealth, power or transitory political concerns. I thank you for your loyalty.' I half expected him to pat Toby on the head at this point. 'But if I took your advice and ignored the way justice is currently being abused, I would be unworthy of that loyalty. No. We will find the truth. Any personal cost must be disregarded. Back to 221b with you. I'll be there shortly to brief you.'

With a nod to Holmes and a brief glance in my direction, Toby disappeared.

'Poplar.' The big bald head swung in his direction. 'Double-check the St Austell footage, then get me access to the Newton AI facial recognition program. Watson, you're with me.'

He walked up to the nearest door, which happened to be that of a small newsagent with fishing rods and beach balls hanging outside its window. When we walked inside, we were back in Baker Street, the snow falling and the flames bright in the hearth just as we'd left it. Holmes paced in front of the fire and when he spoke it was with a peculiar intensity.

'The next few days are crucial. The pieces are falling into

place, but we must be careful. Right now, the murderer has no reason to suspect we are drawing close.'

The murderer was in good company, then.

'One diabolically clever escape has already been pulled off. If alerted to our lines of inquiry, another may be attempted. We must be circumspect, but we must act quickly.'

He looked at me as if only then remembering I was there.

'Nothing more to be gained here. Come back to London, Watson.'

Baker Street darkened at the same rate as the VR suite in Fairfield Tech swam into focus around me. A flutter of panic knotted at my guts, but I was better prepared this time. Also, there was no one available to headbutt, my only companion still the glowing violet disc and the disembodied voice that accompanied it.

'Welcome back, Watson. I hope your meeting went well.'

I peeled the visor from my face and dropped it on to the seat as the chair gently tipped forward and deposited me on my feet. I had a paranoid thought.

'I'd like to review the recording, please.'

'Oh. I'm sorry, Watson. Your meeting wasn't recorded. Our VR suites offer the very latest in privacy settings. Your environment was encrypted by Mr Holmes. Everything that happened inside during the past forty-six minutes and thirty-three seconds was scrambled. Wonderfully effective encryption, too, I must say. Very sophisticated. Made me quite jealous.'

She was positively enthusing about being blocked from listening in. Again, I wondered who Clockwork Sherlock was, and where the money came from to finance an operation that could impress a Fairfield Tech AI.

'Oh. Your smotch has just pinged an alert to our system. You have an urgent message.'

My throat tightened. Was it Dad? Had Gambon lost patience?

'Can I take it here?'

'Certainly. I'll patch a secure remote feed to the terminal by the door.'

I ran over and punched my code into the keyboard, confirming with a ret-scan. It wasn't Gambon. The message was from Crabby463. Sean Crabbe had been my first sergeant in the army. He'd been in civvies for a decade now.

Found your man, but he's jumpy. Police are looking for him too. I think he's spooked. He's heading back to his squat. I'll keep him under surveillance, let you know if he bolts.

There was an address attached. Shit. If Turren went on the run before I got back to London, we might never find him. But even if I left now, it would take me close to three hours to get to Bermondsey. And Holmes needed me to talk to Jack Bolton.

'Aha!'

I was so pleased with myself, I actually said it out loud. Some ideas are so crazy, you know you have to try them. I sub-voxed. 'Poplar? You there?'

A three-second wait.

'Yup. 'sup?'

I told her what I wanted to do. When she'd stopped laughing, she agreed to help.

I was about to get in a lot of trouble. It felt good.

CHAPTER THIRTY-ONE

I spoke to the Fairfield AI as I left the VR suite.

'Sam? I'd like to see Mr Bolton before I go. Is he available?'

'Certainly. He asked me to show you to his office when you were done.'

It was only when I was back on the walkway, leaving the glowing disc behind that I wondered how exactly it intended to show me the way. Then a subtle violet line appeared at my feet, heading to the right. Clever. The line faded and disappeared behind me as I walked.

The light led to a second lift, which took me down five floors. The doors opened straight into the reception area for the CEO's office. I didn't move at first.

It wasn't what I was expecting. No chrome, no concrete, no 'distressed' wood. It was beautiful. On my right, water splashed over a rock wall, landing in a pool where koi carp swam lazily beneath lily pads. In front of me and continuing to the left were trees: tropical, verdant, lush. I squinted disbelievingly. No, not trees, just the most hi-def wall screen I'd ever seen. A parrot, long tail feathers streaming behind it, launched itself from a nearby branch and disappeared from view, squawking. The sound was too quiet to be real. This curated piece of the Amazon looked like the real deal, but the volume was kept low so as not to distract the boss.

I stepped out onto grass. At least, it looked like grass, and it felt like grass to walk on. I crouched and twisted a few blades between my fingers. It smelled like grass, too.

'It's grass, Watson,' said my host. A piece of wall the size of a cinema screen had risen silently in the trees ahead, revealing a room beyond with a desk, a comfortable seating area, a table that could seat twelve, and, incongruously, an Egg.

'People like to get out into nature. Creative people in particular. Can't always be done when you're working hundred-hour weeks tweaking software or finding complex mathematical solutions to problems no one else has even anticipated. So we bring nature to them. At least, that was the plan. The treatment needed to make flooring suitable for this genetically modified grass is still crazy expensive. We're working on making it cheaper. Meantime, I get to enjoy it even if no one else can. Come on through.'

I turned back to find the lift had vanished. I could just make out the regular line of the doors behind green vines.

Bolton offered freshly ground coffee. While he poured it, I looked around his office, which until a few days ago had belonged to his wife.

An ergonomic smart chair for the boss, complast-moulded vegan-leather-covered seating for guests. Every wall bar one was a smart screen, and a privacy visor and headset were hooked on a stand. The only odd touch was the framed photograph on the wall behind the desk. Later, it occurred to me that it was hanging on the only wall where the CEO of Fairfield Technology couldn't see it.

The photograph showed the Fairfield family. Not Beth

and Jack, who were childless, but Stephen, the founder, with Fay and their two boys, Art and John. It must have been taken a few years before the car crash that killed them, as Art, sixteen when he died, looked twelve, maybe thirteen.

Jack saw me looking. 'Robert insisted we keep that thing up.' He quickly added an addendum. 'Not that we didn't want to, of course. It just doesn't fit with the whole rainforest vibe Beth went for, that's all I mean. No disrespect. This whole place is here because of that man's mind. And who knows what might have come next if Art had survived. Everyone said the kid was a genius.'

He handed me the coffee. 'Update me,' he said in the confident tone of someone who always got what he asked for.

'I can't.'

Once he'd processed this unexpected statement, he frowned. I cut him off before he could protest.

'Mr Holmes doesn't operate like anyone else. He doesn't answer to anyone, and he doesn't share his reasoning as he works.'

'Just like the character in the movies.'

'The books, yes.'

We looked at each other. He glanced into his palm, read something on his smotch. 'I doubt you know much about his reasoning one way or the other, since you haven't even worked for him for a week yet.'

He waited. I said nothing. He broke first.

'I had a call from Scotland Yard thirty minutes ago. They've made an arrest.'

'I know. Greta. You met her, right?'

'Sure. Once. We didn't see eye to eye. I'm all about human potential, she's a big fan of the Dark Ages.' It was a bit too slick, that line. Like he'd rehearsed it.

'You think she killed Robert?'

He put his coffee down. 'Blackstone says the New Ludds

don't support violent protest, but I don't see her condemning those who do. I think that woman is a liar, and I think she'll do anything to advance her agenda. Yes, she could have killed Robert. Beth, too. Or ordered someone to do it. It's the same thing. And if she did, I hope they find a prison cell just the way she'd like it. No heating, no modern comforts. A stinking dark pit where she can rot for the rest of her days.'

His demeanour had changed. I knew he wasn't faking how he felt about Greta Blackstone. Didn't surprise me. If the New Ludds had their way, he'd be back rebuilding vintage muscle car engines in Texas.

Holmes had warned me to remain neutral. 'I'm sure justice will be done,' I said.

'I hope so. If she did this, the New Ludds are finished. Greta Blackstone made a big mistake. Guess she overestimated how clever she'd been. I mean, claiming Beth killed her father. That woman deserves everything she's gonna get.'

'It's odd, though.'

'What is?'

'Why would she have Beth killed before Robert, since that makes it impossible to pin Robert's death on his daughter?'

He shrugged. 'If criminals didn't make mistakes, they'd never get caught, right? Or maybe the nut job she hired to kill my wife did it earlier than she had wanted. I don't know. I'm sure Mr Holmes will work it out.'

'Yes,' I agreed. 'I'm sure he will.'

He stood up. 'Well, I guess there's nothing more for you to do here. I hope the VR suite was useful.'

A voice whispered into my left ear. Poplar. 'I'm in.'

Time to put the crazy plan into action. I transitioned into geeky fangirl. 'It was *amazing*. This whole place is amazing.'

'You got that right. Best company in the world.'

'But wasn't Beth trying to sell part of it?'

'Only to take it to the next level. Look, I'm a mechanic. A good one, maybe a great one, but Beth was a visionary. Always looking ahead. Three years, five years, ten, twenty. She knew it was time to expand, and the deal she negotiated means Fairfield Tech's future is assured. You think what we've come up with so far is impressive? You won't believe what the next fifty years will bring.'

He was on his soapbox now, but I wondered if he really believed it. After all, the deal, if it went through, would probably make him one of the richest individuals in the world, but Beth was gone and he wouldn't have a hand in running things anymore. Would that be so easy to give up?

'But the Honeydrones sound amazing. Why sell them? Was going to Newton AI your idea?'

'No. That was Beth. It took me a while to come around to it, but she was right. The UK may be ahead of America on driverless ground transport, but the regulations on air travel are gonna take years to sort out. In the US, Nuerro has a whole state to play with, ready to sign up for a fleet of Honeydrones. The British government screwed this one up. Politics, Sugar. That's your problem right there. If you didn't have an election every five years, your politicians wouldn't have to appease Blackstone and her New Ludd assholes.'

I let the *Sugar* comment go. And I didn't rise to the bait about politics. America's ten-year presidential terms were hardly a triumph for democracy.

For the next five minutes, we talked about Honeys. Well, I asked the right questions and Jack talked, warming to his theme. 'American states have different laws. It'll only take one of them to start using Honeydrones and the rest will follow. Britain will lose its lead as an innovator. It's a shame and it's mostly *her* fault.'

I didn't need to ask who he was referring to.

'The piece I read in *New Scientist* said they'd seen a full-size prototype,' I said. 'But I think they were making a lot of stuff up. They said it looked incredible. And they said they watched a test run, the Honeydrone was nearly silent at low speeds.'

'It is! You can barely hear her until she hits eighty miles per hour.' Suddenly I could see the little boy proudly helping his dad in the workshop, showing him something he'd made. 'You wanna see it before you go?'

'I'd *love* to.'

'Great. Come and see my favourite toy.'

Gotcha. Now for the dangerous part of the plan.

CHAPTER THIRTY-TWO

The drone team worked on the top floor – naturally – underneath a section of roof parallel to the helipad, which slid open like something in a Bond film. I knew this because Jack Bolton ordered them to show me, standing by proudly as sections of the ceiling pivoted away from each other like a giant, slo-mo camera shutter.

The acting CEO of Fairfield Tech looked as relaxed as I'd seen him yet. Glancing round at my surroundings, I could understand why. The Honeydrone team worked in a room that was an engineer's wet dream. Schematics were projected on every wall, a dozen huge desks held parts of sophisticated electric engines, the individual functions of which I couldn't begin to guess. Robot arms danced above a dark carbon fibre shell in one corner, performing adjustments at such a speed that its movements were a blur.

We passed a few employees on our way to the centre of the room where our goal lay shrouded under grey silk. Jack offered a word or two of encouragement to everyone we passed. Dark eyes and rumpled clothing suggested they were putting in long hours, but the confidence and optimism was palpable. They were ready to take the Honeydrones to the next logical stage: getting a swarm of them into the air with human passengers. Britain might not be ready, but the possible deal with Newton AI meant the engineers in this room knew their baby might soon be taking to the skies by the thousands. Jack's claim that selling the patent to Nuerro gave his fleet of intelligent drones the best chance of ushering in a new era of aviation rang true to me. At least, it rang true from his point of view. Part of the deal was that he would remain in charge of the project for the first three years. But while Jack might come across as a little naive, Beth Fairfield was as sharp as they come. She would have known when negotiating with Newton AI that the likelihood of Espen Nuerro – America's King Geek – allowing her husband to continue calling the shots for long was negligible.

When Jack pulled the sheet away, I forgot all about the corporate machinations and selfish motivations. I even forgot about the murders. When it comes to technology, I've always been an early adopter, and the piece of engineering in front of me set every nerve-end tingling with anticipation.

My first thought was that the design team had learned the lessons of Fairfield's road-going efforts. No one would be nicknaming this beauty a Chicken, writing articles comparing it to the Eggs, and asking which came first. Nope. If Fairfield Tech wanted this to be known as a Honeydrone, then Honeydrone it would be. If another nickname ever did catch on, it would be something cool. Unbearably cool. Because this was the coolest machine I'd ever seen.

It was matt black. The surface wasn't just non-reflective, it seemed to *absorb* light. I couldn't stop looking at it. The insect inspiration had only been allowed to inform the name. This was no bee. The cabin was long, narrow and aerodynamic. It reminded me of the vehicles in the twentieth century, and even early in this one, that were built to break land speed records on vast salt flats. This had the same kind of latent energy about it. It looked like it wanted to go somewhere right now, fast as hell.

But what brought the unforced smile to my lips was what they'd chosen to do it with the wings. There were four of them. They formed an X. I thought of the movie trips of my formative years, of the blockbusters whose origins stretched back to my grandparents, and I giggled.

'I know,' said Jack proudly. 'We're all like that the first time.'

No photographs had been allowed out yet. Not of the full-sized prototype.

'It's . . . beautiful.' It was all I could manage.

'Step towards it.'

I looked at him. 'Go on,' he said.

I didn't need to be asked twice. When I was six feet away from the Honeydrone, my grin broadening with every step, there was a gentle hum and a gull-wing door unfolded itself from the cockpit, revealing a single seat.

I stopped.

'I can't let you take her up,' said Jack. 'We're allowed manned flights on our private land, but only with qualified pilots.'

I found my voice. 'Could I . . . ?' I pointed. I didn't have to pretend. He recognised a fellow enthusiast when he saw one. I was glad he hadn't let the conversation get too technical as I barely knew one end of a screwdriver from another. I just bloody loved technology.

'Hey, you're here now. Why not? Something to tell your grandchildren about.'

Before he could change his mind, I walked closer to the Honeydrone. With an elegance that surprised me, the X folded together, bringing the sill of the cockpit closer. The seat itself pivoted, staying parallel to the floor.

I got in, and the wings reversed the process so smoothly I was barely aware of any motion. The fan-like electric engines that would keep it aloft were neatly hidden within the wings. I put the seatbelt on and gave Bolton a cheesy double thumbs-up. He shook his head, laughing.

There were no controls, just one very comfortable seat. That would become between two and twenty seats once the Honeydrones were in production. Two-seaters for the insanely rich, twenty-seaters for the well-off who were in a hurry.

'The cabin is gyroscopically mounted,' said Jack, walking around the Honeydrone. 'Once in flight, any banking manoeuvres can be smoothed out. You'll know when you're climbing or descending, but most of the bumps and jolts of other aircraft don't happen in a Honeydrone. You can keep the windows transparent, even turn off the gyroscope if you want to know that you're really flying. Or you can shut off the outside world and get where you want to go without even knowing you were a few thousand feet up.'

There were instruments in the prototype, of course, but they were just there to take measurements. In flight, a swarm of Honeydrones would be controlled in much the same way the Eggs, Cartons and Roadtrains were: a hive AI mind to which every vehicle contributed, and a static backup on land.

'Don't get used to it, Watson.' There was a smile in his voice. 'Come on, time to go.'

I gave him a little wave of acquiescence while sub-voxing, 'Poplar? Please tell me you're ready.'

In answer, the Honeydrone's engines hummed into life, and – almost instantly – I found myself six feet up.

Bolton was the first to react, shouting, 'Close roof!' When nothing responded to his voice command, he sprinted to a control panel and pulled an honest-to-goodness red lever. I would have laughed, but my throat dried up when the roof started to close.

'Shit!' I screamed. 'Poplar?'

'It's mechanical,' she hissed in my ear. 'Can't override it. Smart guy.'

I looked up. The irises were whirring and the view of the sky was already frighteningly small. I wasn't going anywhere. I hoped Jack Bolton would think it was some kind of malfunction. I was already preparing my speech when the Honeydrone's wing rotors tilted, the nose swung up, and I found myself staring straight at the shrinking patch of cloudy Cornish sky.

'Poplar? N—' The rest of the word was lost as my ability to speak, breathe or move disappeared along with Bolton, the engineers and the room they were standing in. As the drone shot through the narrow aperture like a ferret with a firework up its arse, I didn't even have time to wonder if I was going to die. I swear sparks came off the tips of the wings when the drone left the building.

Once clear, the Honeydrone banked as its kinetic energy dissipated, then – at the moment that it hung motionless in the sky like the most expensive kite in history – the rotors whirred again. I was pushed back against the padded seat as we bumped through the thermals, climbed to just under cloud level, and rocketed towards London.

'Yeeeeeee–haaaaaaa!' I yelled as I looked out at the wings, then down at the hedges, fields, roads and houses flashing by beneath. 'Let's go blow up the Death Star.'

'Do what?' Poplar sounded amused and pleased with herself. With good reason.

'Nice one, Popples, you're a bloody genius. How long to Bermondsey?'

'Forty-nine minutes. The Honeydrones aren't linked to the web yet, so there's no way to access your messages. I'm streaming security cams in Bermondsey but I don't know where to look. We won't know if Turren is still there until you arrive. There'll be an Egg waiting with a new smotch for you.'

She'd thought of everything. 'Poplar, did I mention you're –'

'–a star? Yes, you did. Don't forget it, Watson. Now enjoy the ride.'

My adrenaline was spiking so badly, I swear I could actually feel the ennanomeds in my system trying to tamp it down.

I grinned. No net, no Holmes, no Nicky Gambon, no bodycams or contact lenses, just the whistling of the wind outside the cockpit of the most advanced flying machine I'd ever seen. And, at the end of the trip, a chance for me to do something more proactive than take orders from a fictional detective.

Yes, I was going to enjoy the ride.

CHAPTER THIRTY-THREE

THE HONEYDRONE ATTRACTED a fair bit of attention on its journey from Cornwall to London, but by the time anyone had heard the distant hum, looked up, seen us streaking through the sky and pointed, we were out of sight. It was only when we were landing that anyone could get close.

The drone showed no signs of slowing as we skimmed across the M25 and over south-west London, by which time we had begun a steady, but fairly steep, descent. I'd never before realised how many parks there were in that part of the city. The only one I was sure I'd correctly identified was Richmond Park, simply because it was so huge, running into Wimbledon Common to the east.

When I spotted the sparkling Thames snaking through the skyscrapers ahead, I knew we were about to land. Finally, the fan-like rotors on the wings dropped in pitch, tilting as we slowed. The vehicle I was sitting in was designed to be a comfortable, safe form of public transport, so I expected our landing to be gentle and undramatic.

I was mistaken.

'You're coming down in a school playing field,' said Poplar.

'Your arrival will probably attract attention. The Egg will be waiting. Get to it before you're swamped with curious kids. Brace yourself.'

I looked down and spotted the school in question, its football pitch about the size of a playing card. Then the rotor slowed again before stopping completely. It was a moment exactly like the *Roadrunner* cartoons Dad and I used to watch, when Wile E. Coyote runs off a cliff, hangs there for an impossible second or two, then succumbs to gravity and plunges out of the sky. I'd like to claim I'd thought of that simile as I was sitting a thousand feet up in a prototype vehicle that had just lost all power, but it wouldn't be true. It wasn't until later that the image popped into my head. At the time, I didn't even have long enough to contemplate my mortality as my stomach decided to stay exactly where it was while the rest of my body plummeted to the ground below.

What made an already unpalatable situation worse was the fact that the Honeydrone elected to make its descent nose-down. I've read fiction where the ground *rushed towards me*, but I have to disagree. I knew very well that the cold, hard ground was doing what it did best: it was sitting there, waiting. All the rushing was being done by the Honeydrone as it dropped like a broken toy.

I can't judge the moment that it happened, as my eyes were closed, but I heard the scream of the rotors and felt the drone virtually stop before righting itself. All the skin on my face tried to move to the rear of my skull. Two seconds later, we thumped onto the grass.

I only opened my eyes when Poplar said, 'Go!'

The cockpit glass swung up and the wings folded as the Honeydrone sank to one side. I released the seatbelt and half jumped, half fell onto the playing field. On my knees, I looked up and saw the promised Egg waiting on the far side of a fence. I walked towards it, then stopped.

There was a strange high-pitched roaring noise behind me. For a moment, I wondered if the Honeydrone had developed a fault. I looked over my shoulder to check and saw hundreds of kids pouring out of the school behind, heading for their futuristic visitor.

I broke into a run, but they weren't interested in me. They all wanted a piece of the Honeydrone. From the frenzied sound of their screaming, some of them literally wanted a piece of it.

As I reached the fence, climbed over it and landed on the pavement beyond, the excited screams turned to yells of disappointment. I scrambled into the Egg. When it pulled away, I looked back to see the Honeydrone streaking back the way it had come, building speed by the second, a crowd of waving children watching it until it was a speck in the distance.

'Good as new,' said Poplar in my ear. 'I'm sure Bolton will understand once he's calmed down. We are trying to catch his wife's killer, after all.'

I opened the complast box on the seat. A new smotch, a pair of contact lenses, and two tiny cameras and a mic mounted on disks with adhesive backing. My hi-tech multimedia outfit was back in Cornwall. There were no instructions, so I stuck one cam and the mic on my chest, and the other cam behind my neck. I thumbed and ret-scanned the smotch and, while it downloaded my profile and data, put in the contact lenses.

When the smotch buzzed into life, there were two new messages from Crabby463.

He's in the squat. Packing.

Then, four minutes ago, *He's nearly done. Where are you? What do you want me to do?*

I brought the smotch to my mouth to reply. *Go knock on*

the door. Come up with some excuse to delay him. I'm – I checked the map on the screen *– two minutes out.*

His reply was nearly instant. *Roger that. Will do what I can.*

Holmes materialised on the seat next to me. 'Excellent work, Watson.' He rubbed his hands together. 'The game is afoot, eh?'

The squat was in an abandoned warehouse that had been divided into units on a tatty, unloved industrial estate. I spotted Crabby immediately. Ginger hair, no neck, angry looking. The door of the warehouse was open. I got my first glimpse of Francis Turren in the shadows within. Unshaven, dark hair buzzed short. He was shaking his head. As I got out of the Egg on the opposite side of the street, Crabby glanced over his shoulder, but didn't acknowledge me. Turren looked from me to Crabby, then swung the door shut and disappeared. Crabby stopped the door closing with his shoulder.

I broke into a run, and Crabby stood aside, kicking the door fully open.

'Need any help?' he called as I sprinted into a narrow passage, both sides of it lined with complast bags and cardboard boxes.

'Cover the front for me,' I shouted back to him. I couldn't see Turren, but I could hear him thumping up the stairs, so I followed, taking them two at a time.

I caught a movement and turned my head to see Holmes behind me. He wasn't bothering with realism, floating rapidly up the staircase like a helium balloon.

'Judging by the layout of this building, I'd imagine he's heading for the roof. This warehouse has a fire escape to the north. Turren is probably intending to use it. What are you doing, Watson?'

I had stopped. Turren's footsteps continued to climb the stairs above us. I looked at the detective.

'Please, Holmes, piss off and let me do this.'

He looked affronted. 'Watson, do I have to remind you that you work for me? I appreciate your experience in, er, confrontations of this nature, but –'

The footsteps were getting fainter. I folded my arms. 'He's getting away.'

Holmes gave me one last, pained look and disappeared.

I sprinted after Turren, unable to stop a tight smile appearing on my face. This was my element and it felt good to be back. I was breathing hard by the time I'd climbed four floors and reached the door to the roof, but I wasn't panting.

My quarry was an ex-marine with extremist views. He'd never been arrested, but he'd been questioned several times after New Ludd attacks on property. His name was highlighted in one of the police files Holmes had downloaded as a possible leader of a New Ludd splinter group. Specifically, the True Ludds, who had claimed responsibility for a spate of tech company bombings. He might be armed. And if he was, he certainly knew how to use a weapon.

I rolled through the roof door, staying low, and took cover behind a rusting air-conditioning unit before taking a quick look around, pulling my head back fast. It was clear. I heard him before I saw him – the roof was metal, and every footfall echoed and vibrated. I looked a second time, then broke cover when I saw Turren thirty yards away. He had no visible weapon but was carrying a rucksack.

I stood up. There was no cover other than another two identical air-conditioning units and another doorway leading back into the warehouse. To the north I saw the metal rungs of a fire escape, but that wasn't Turren's destination. There was no fire escape on the east edge of the building, but that's where he was heading.

Rain started to fall, hitting the metal with a white-noise hiss. I started jogging after Turren, jinking left to keep the next air-con unit between us. I upped my pace to close the gap. My body came alive, the muscles in my legs handling a near-sprint without complaint. The ennanomeds again. They were quite something.

There was a two-foot-high protective lip around the edge of the building. It prevented me seeing what Turren was running towards until it was too late. I should have known he had anticipated problems and set up an escape route.

Between the warehouse and its neighbour – a similarly anonymous building – was a twenty-foot gap. An aluminium extending ladder provided a makeshift bridge between the two. Turren barely slowed when he reached it, despite the rain and what I judged to be a fifty-foot fall if he slipped. Either he had the sure-footed confidence of a mountain goat, or he didn't care if he fell to his death.

As soon as he'd reached the far end, he pulled the ladder away and let it fall clattering to the ground below. Turren locked eyes with me for a moment, before turning and jogging away.

What I did next seemed logical at the time. I didn't consider any other options, such as messaging Crabby to follow his progress from the ground while I came down the fire escape. I like to think I made the decision instinctively, knowing my own capabilities, but sometimes I wonder if the microscopic machines in my bloodstream released a confidence-boosting rush of endorphins and adrenaline to nudge my decision their way.

Whatever the reason, I didn't slow down, I accelerated. The metal roof under my boots sounded like a drum solo in a death metal tribute band. My arms pumped as I pelted headlong towards the edge. Ten paces from the drop, then five, and I was visualising my right leg flexing and extending to send me soaring into the void a fraction of a second before it happened.

I was aware of the alleyway below me as I threw myself

into the air, but it, the sky, the building behind me and everything other than the foot-square piece of roof I had fixed for my landing-point was washed-out, faded, inconsequential. I held my breath, chest thrust forward as if it could defy gravity and drag my body into flight.

I landed paratrooper-style, falling to one side, legs absorbing the shock, turning the impact into a roll across the roof. Two rolls, three. On the fourth, I let what remained of my kinetic energy propel me into a crouch, before I stood up, ready to run again.

Turren had stopped running when I hit the roof behind him. I'd been right about him being armed, but there was no time to congratulate myself when I was staring at the Glock seventy-two pointing towards me.

I was too far away to stand a chance of disarming him, and too close to avoid being hit if he took a shot. The barrel was steady and was pointing at my upper torso – the biggest target. He couldn't miss.

'Who are you?' Turren looked older than forty-six. His dark eyes were surrounded by lines sunk into a grim visage. He looked like he hadn't slept well in a decade. Then I remembered what had happened to his wife and daughter. There was tension in his voice, but it was controlled. He hadn't forgotten his training.

'Mr Turren, please put that away. I'm not with the police.'

He ignored my request. 'Didn't ask who you weren't. Asked who you were. Talk.'

He didn't click the safety catch off for emphasis. Gang kids do that, people in movies do that. In real life, if you're going to point a gun at someone dangerous, you'd better have the safety off already and be ready to fire.

I didn't think it was just curiosity that stopped him shooting. A gunshot in London would bring a swift response from the police, so he'd only do it if he knew he could put me down and still be able to complete his escape. I thought of Beth Fairfield's ruined face. This man was a murderer. If he could beat and strangle an unarmed woman, the thought of shooting me would be unlikely to bring on an ethical dilemma.

'My name is Jo Barnes. I'm ex-army.'

If there's no honour among thieves, there is, usually, a little understanding between ex-military people. Turren's features remained fixed. I might as well have told him I was a part-time librarian. I kept talking.

'I'm working with . . .' Ah. I was talking to a hard-line New Ludd. He was probably already speculating about body augmentation after he'd watched me leap between buildings. If I followed that up by telling him I was working for a VR detective who was widely believed to be an artificial intelligence, I had no doubt he'd put two in my chest then one in my head to make sure.

I tried again. 'I'm working with a private detective. We're not connected to the police.'

'You know the police are looking for me, right? They released my name. My face is everywhere.'

'Yes, I know.'

Holmes faded into existence on Turren's left side. I didn't react, but gave a slow nod to show I saw him. His voice was for my ears only.

'Watson, your rooftop chase was seen from a neighbouring building. It won't be long before you have company.'

'Any suggestions?' I sub-voxed.

Turren was losing patience. 'I asked you a question.' The gun barrel remained steady, but his voice was tight and hoarse. His pupils were tiny. I sub-voxed again.

'He's high.'

When I heard the shot but remained standing, simple physics told me I was uninjured, but it didn't stop me flinching and taking a pace backwards. Turren had deliberately fired wide. Now he took two paces forward.

'The next one's in your chest. How did the police get my name?'

'DNA,' I said. If I tried lying I'd probably hesitate. I had a bad feeling about what would happen if I hesitated.

'Impossible,' he said. 'You're lying.'

'It's the truth. I know you're off-grid, but the DNA on file was from the Iver Heath riots. You were treated for a head injury. Police kept all DNA gathered in the riots.'

'Liar!'

For a second I was certain he was going to fire. His eyes dropped from my face. I decided I would drop to the left and twist, anticipating the shot, in the hope that it would hit me in the shoulder rather than the heart. It was the best I could hope for.

Just then, the first police drone rose from the north side of the roof. I'd heard that the latest generation carried tasers. I wondered if Turren knew this. His response suggested he did. He brought his left hand up to join his right on the pistol, swung both arms towards the drone and squeezed off two quick shots. Both of them hit their target and shattered carbon fibre and complast exploded, hissing, into the rain. By the time the main body of the drone had hit the ground four storeys below, the gun was back in its previous position.

'Nice shooting,' I said. Sometimes my mouth says things my brain should have stepped in to prevent.

'You know about Teera and Sash.'

'His wife and daughter,' said Holmes.

'Yes,' I said. 'I'm sorry.'

He didn't acknowledge the socially acceptable platitude. 'They died five days before the riots,' he said. 'I know exactly where I was and what I was doing during those riots. Want me to tell you?'

Even staring at the wrong end of a loaded gun, I knew a rhetorical question when I heard one. I waited. He kept talking.

'The riots started the same day I identified them. They'd brought all the bodies from the crash into a warehouse in Uxbridge. I took a train out there. It was a food distribution warehouse. It had been cleared out, but it still smelled of onions. R thirty-four.'

He went quiet, but his jaw was working, chewing on the memory. He swallowed. The rain was getting harder. When he spoke again, I strained to hear him over the percussion of the water hitting the roof.

'R thirty-four. That's where they were. Column R, row thirty-four. Under a sheet. Together. Surrounded by dead strangers. I couldn't take them, they wouldn't let me. I just had to tell them they were right, that was my wife and daughter, killed by the technology they promised would make life better. I walked away. Kept walking. By the time I got home it was dark. I saw fires burning on the other side of the river, heard the shouting, the chanting. But I didn't feel the same anger as them. Not then. That came later. When I got stronger. That night, I was weak. I got drunk. Weak.'

I knew how that worked. If he'd looked at me, he might have seen it in my face. But his gaze had dropped to my feet.

'When I woke up, it was light. I could see my Teera's jacket on the back of a chair, Sash's schoolbag by the door. I went out, bought more booze, came back and kept drinking. By the time Teera's brother came and found me and got me cleaned up, the riots were over.'

He looked at me again. He had spoken in a monotone and there were no tears. He looked empty.

'So, explain again how they got my DNA.'

'I don't know. That's what they told us.'

I believed he was telling the truth. Especially because he

hadn't denied murdering Beth Fairfield. Turren wasn't protesting his innocence and he wasn't showing any remorse. He just didn't think he'd get caught.

We both heard the whine of a second drone. Not the police this time. It was white with the News UK logo spinning round its frisbee-like body. Turren swung the gun towards it, then —when he saw what it was – walked over, keeping the gun trained on me.

'Stay,' he said. I stayed.

The drone danced away as he approached, keeping its distance. 'I'm not going to shoot. I want to talk.'

The drone moved closer as Turren reached the edge of the roof. He looked into the camera.

'People like Beth Fairfield and her company are handing the future of our species to artificial intelligence. Who really runs this country? The government, or the algorithms they use to tell us what to do? Wake up, all of you. Every day, you let artificial intelligence take a little bit more freedom from us. What do you think will happen in the end? We're heading for extinction. No, we're asking for extinction, and we're helping it happen. Open your eyes, see what's really happening. Think for yourselves! No soul, no solution.'

As soon as he trotted out the tired old New Ludd slogan from a decade ago, I knew what he was going to do. I was moving before I had a chance to think about it, but I was still five yards away when Turren stuck the Glock's barrel under his chin and pulled the trigger.

The small red cloud of blood, bone and brain hung in the space he had just occupied, while his body tipped back over the lip of the roof and fell. The drone followed it, still filming.

Movement to my right. I turned in time to see Holmes morph into the bald giant I had met in VR. Poplar ran to join me.

'I pixellated your face – you won't be identified. But three news drones and five police drones are inbound, and the ground crews won't be far behind. Use the internal stairs. The Egg is waiting at the north exit. Follow me.'

As I followed the avatar's broad back down the stairs of the second warehouse and out to the Egg, I kept thinking about what Turren had told me. He hadn't denied killing Beth Fairfield, but there was no reason for him to lie about where he was during the Iver Heath riots. So how had the DNA of a total off-gridder ended up in the National Health database?

CHAPTER THIRTY-FOUR

CRABBY HAD RUN at the sound of the first siren; he was no fan of the authorities. I fired off a quick thank you as the Egg cruised sedately against the flow of screaming emergency vehicles, then called Dad. He could tell something was off but Dad had always been sensitive to my mood. He asked a couple of questions and didn't push me to expand on my monosyllabic responses. I just wanted to hear his voice and I think he knew it.

Holmes had the sense to leave me alone for a while. Instead of appearing beside me, he sent a message to my new smotch. *The news drone suffered an unfortunate malfunction, so Toby had time to search the body before the police arrived. We have the burner phone Turren used. All messages deleted, of course, but Miss Poplar has been able to trace the thread. The messages were all sent via a similar burner. Unlikely it will ever be found, but the messages suggest that Turren knew their sender well. Not enough in itself to convict Greta Blackstone, but it adds fuel to the fire.*

When I arrived at my flat, it felt like I'd been away for a month, rather than one night. Nothing had changed. Although I hadn't expected anything different, there was always a part of me that found it hard to accept the world could be so oblivious. I had just watched a man kill himself, but – other than a few pieces on the rolling newscasts – everything carried on as if it had never happened.

When the police announced the suicide victim's connection to the Fairfield case, some notoriety would be attached to the name Francis Turren. But for most people, his death – and that of his victim – was a mild source of titillation, a background noise. I sought refuge in the shower. I'd once been interviewed by an army psychologist who described the desire to shower after witnessing violence as a symbolic act, an attempt to cleanse the body, mind and conscience. I disagreed. For me, it's a reminder that I'm alive, that I don't have bullet holes in my chest, that my throat hasn't been cut or my limbs blown off. It's the ritual of a survivor.

Thought of survival led me back to Hughes, but I firmly and deliberately stopped myself pursuing it. My mood was brittle. I craved a drink.

I tried to distract myself by speculating about Clockwork Sherlock's sexuality. Some tongue-in-cheek critics had suggested that the original Holmes and Watson were a couple. I'd never bought that theory myself. Not just because Watson was married and went into some detail about the circumstances around his falling in love with his wife. No. There was a famous section in the earliest stories where Holmes describes the human mind as an attic, which the owner furnishes with facts of his or her choosing. Holmes is of the opinion that there are hard limits to the amount of information a brain can contain, so those facts must be carefully chosen.

Sherlock Holmes doesn't know that the Earth travels around the sun, but he can identify 140 varieties of pipe, cigar and cigarette ash. As a consulting detective, the latter information is of use to him. The former merely unnecessarily clutters up head space. Surely he'd made the same decision regarding sex and love – human predilections that are notorious for playing havoc with rational thought?

I didn't know about my own companion's preferences, but the original Sherlock Holmes had chosen celibacy to enable him to better perform his duties as a detective. That might have changed after he retired, of course. For all I knew, *bee keeping on the Sussex Downs* might actually have been code for humping everything that moved in an effort to make up for lost time.

Thinking about Holmes made me realise I was seriously considering accepting the Watson job on a more permanent basis. Of course, that meant I needed to devote some thought to Nicky Gambon.

Gambon, instead of choosing between the carrot and the stick to get my help, had approached me with both. If I gave him Clockwork Sherlock's identity, Dad would be safe. And I would get Hughes.

The thing was, Dad would never be safe again. I wasn't so naive to believe Gambon would leave me alone once he'd got what he wanted. So what would come next? This was how people got dragged into crime. If I was going to stop it happening to me, I would have to get Gambon out of my life, keep Dad safe, and – somehow – find out where Hughes was, so I could put a bullet in his treacherous skull.

Then the images started coming, and I slid down to the base of the shower, wrapping my arms around my knees.

They torture me three times in all. On each occasion, I'm left weaker.

There is, I guess, at least a day between sessions. In between times, every five to six hours, a guard brings a tray with fruit, bread and water. He appears minutes after the torturers leave, while I'm unconscious. Or rather, while he thinks I'm unconscious.

After both of the first two torture sessions, through half-closed eyes, I watch the solitary guard come in with the tray. He has a knife in his belt. He doesn't linger. Even if I were to attack him, he knows the limit of the rope on my ankle and he stays out of range.

The first time he comes, I eat the food, sleep for an hour, then spend the rest of the time twisting and pulling at the iron ring in the wall. There's just enough give in it to give me hope.

When the guard comes back for the tray, I sit in front of the iron ring, hiding the brick dust and flakes of paint. He indicates that I should slide the tray towards him. When I've done it, he retreats quickly, locking the door behind him. I sweep the floor with my hands, scattering the evidence of my labour.

About eight hours after the third torture session, the iron ring comes loose so suddenly it takes me by surprise and I fall backwards as it slides out of the wall.

Then I wait for the next tray of food. And while I do so, the killing starts.

The shower head was still dripping onto my back when I opened my eyes. It had been months since my dreams had spilled into my waking life. My previous responses to these intrusions had been predictable, depressing and ineffective. They had involved alcohol, drugs, and violence, in any combination. Not this time. Whether it was the ennanomeds, or the fact that I wanted to see this through and find out what conclusion Holmes would arrive at, I wasn't sure.

I stood up and walked back into the bedroom, stopping suddenly when I saw the figure sitting in the chair by the window.

'Hello, Jo. I was in this neck of the woods, so I thought it was about time we had a little catch-up.'

Nicky Gambon grinned at me, his fingers drumming

lightly on the top of a net-blocker. He obviously didn't have the same issue with nudity as Holmes.

Nicky Gambon was true to form. He had a reputation as a ruthless killer who knew how to keep his hands clean so he could stay out of prison. His personal acts of brutality had always taken place behind closed doors. Anything more public was delegated, be it extortion, drug dealing, money laundering, fencing, beatings or murder. And if anyone in the organisation was caught, no one ever ratted on Gambon. Anyone who did time for him knew their family would be looked after while they were inside. The implication being that their family might suffer a different fate should Gambon's name ever get mentioned.

Nicky Gambon was virtually untouchable. And he was clever. Even sitting in my flat, he was never overtly threatening. He asked after my father, enquired how work was going, then reminded me that he had the current address of an old friend of mine. A friend, he reminded me, who had a habit of moving around since his time in Afghanistan. A friend who might decide to live somewhere else at a moment's notice.

His parting shot was more direct. 'I'm not a patient man, Jo, and I'm not going to waste time chasing your friend around the world if he decides to up sticks. Bring me something by the end of the week or our next chat will be less polite. And you'll lose your chance at Hughes.'

He was concentrating his efforts on the carrot rather than the stick, then. Smart guy. I was sick of waking up in the night with Hughes's face in front of me. Sick of him hijacking my life. Sick of the fact that he was still alive when everyone he'd betrayed in Afghanistan was dead. Everyone except me.

Gambon sat there while I dressed. I tried to stop my

hands shaking. It wasn't fear, it was anger, but I didn't want him to see how he was affecting me.

My smotch buzzed. Gambon pointed at it.

'Better pick that up. Might be our mutual friend.'

It was.

The political situation is escalating fast. We need to act on the evidence Barnett has chosen to ignore. Prove what really happened on the night Robert and Beth Fairfield died.

Gambon watched me as I spoke my innocuous response.

What do you need me to do?

I've sent an Egg. It's waiting outside with a change of clothes and all the tech you'll need.

I looked at the door, then back at Nicky Gambon.

'Your master calls?' he said. 'Good. Time is running out, Jo. Off you pop. I'll see myself out.'

I didn't look back as the door closed behind me. Another message pinged in as I reached the waiting Egg.

You're off to Colorado, Watson. You're going to catch a murderer.

CHAPTER THIRTY-FIVE

THE EGG HEADED west across town, taking a series of side streets. It wasn't rush hour, so our circuitous route could only mean the vehicle was avoiding a problem en route.

It wasn't raining anymore, but the clouds had a yellow heaviness that threatened snow. I set the windows to dark mode and looked inside the rucksack in the footwell. Complast cases with spare contacts and in-ear monitors. Underwear, toiletries, and shirts, trousers and a jacket equipped with cams and mics.

Holmes didn't make an appearance for the first five minutes, for which I was grateful. It gave me time to think. Not that I was making much headway in that department. Gambon wanted Clockwork Sherlock's real identity. Assuming I could get what he wanted, how much damage would it do, really?

I sighed at my own question. For Nicky Gambon to take a personal interest, Holmes must be a genuine threat to his organisation. If no one knew who Holmes was, then no one could get to him. Simple. You couldn't threaten, bribe or blackmail a ghost.

I didn't want to put Holmes in danger. But, even more than that, I didn't want to put Dad in danger. And, more than anything, I wanted to stop seeing Hughes every night in my nightmares and every day out of the corner of my eye.

Holmes appeared beside me.

'Sorry to keep you. We should reach Heathrow in seventeen minutes.'

'What? Er . . . yes. Fine.'

'Are you unwell, Watson?'

'No, no. I'm still not used to the way you appear out of nowhere like that.'

'My apologies.' He didn't sound like he meant it. He was immaculately turned out as always, although the cravat tucked into his detached white shirt collar was a burnt umber this time. *A man? A woman? Non-binary?* I realised I'd rejected two possibilities already. One was that more than one person was behind the mask of Clockwork Sherlock. His personality was too particular, too consistent. And I didn't believe an AI could fool me for so long. It was the tiny things, the idiosyncrasies. When I stripped off in front of him, if he'd been able to blush, he would have. No. I was in the presence of a human being. I was sure of it.

Holmes was eyeing me curiously. 'You seem distracted. Have you seen the headlines?'

I connected my smotch with the screen in the Egg and selected the news pages. I didn't have to hunt for the right story.

FRESH EVIDENCE LINKS GRETA BLACKSTONE TO MURDER OF BETH FAIRFIELD.

NEW LUDDS LEADER CLAIMS INNOCENCE

. . .

NEW LUDDS PROTESTS CONTINUE FOR SECOND DAY IN CENTRAL LONDON, EXTRA POLICE DRAFTED IN

I watched newscasts from Trafalgar Square where a crowd had gathered around a makeshift stage. According to the reports, their numbers had swelled from a few hundred to over a thousand during the last twenty-four hours. It looked to be bigger than that in the live footage. Different speakers took turns to denounce the police, the government and – naturally – the powerful corporations they believed pulled the strings of power. A few pieces of public smotch footage were played, showing scuffles between the more enthusiastic protesters and police in riot gear. I wondered at what point the protestors would cross the line between *restless crowd* and *angry mob*. I wouldn't want to be there when it happened.

'The link between her and Turren gives Scotland Yard more time to keep her in custody. Barnett is confident in the chain of evidence. She'll be formally charged in the next forty-eight hours. At which point, things could turn distinctly nasty.'

I watched a big man, the NL handcuff logo on the back of his coat, push the riot shield of a police officer, sending him sprawling backwards. The officer tripped on a kerb and sat down hard, automatically grabbing his taser. A colleague helped him up, shaking his head. The big man stared them down, then moved away as the line of police reformed.

'A riot would mean violence, injuries, damage to property, looting. The government would be under pressure to delegitimise the New Luddite movement. The consequences of this case could be far reaching.'

I said nothing. If the New Luddites had their way, I would be sitting in the back of a car driven by a human being.

On their very best day, a human driver would be alert, careful, respectful of other road users and conscious of a thousand random factors that might impact our journey. At their best. At their worst they might be hungover, angry, depressed, sleepy, coked-up or fighting a bad cold. They might be inattentive, careless or sloppy. And however good they were, they wouldn't know anything about the other vehicles sharing the route they were taking. The Egg, on the other hand, didn't sleep, eat, drink or take drugs. It didn't take shortcuts for the benefit of its single passenger, instead following a route that took into consideration every other vehicle that might affect its journey. If a Carton broke down three miles ahead, blocking a street for ten minutes, all vehicles amended their routes automatically. I'd seen a film shot from a helicopter once showing London by night. Self-driven vehicles didn't need headlights, of course, but each of them glowed in the dark to alert pedestrians to their presence. From above, when the film was run at ten times normal speed, the tens of thousands of pinpricks of light looked exactly as Stephen Fairfield had pictured them: a murmuration of sci-fi starlings.

The New Luddites wouldn't stop at transport, of course. The data network also drew their ire as it used elements of AI. The smotch would probably go. Perhaps they would issue us all with our own animal skins, and heavy wooden clubs would replace dating apps. Ah, the good old days.

'Watson. Is there something on your mind?'

'No. Not really. What makes you say that?'

'You're on your way to America, and you've yet to ask me why.'

'Why am I on my way to America, Holmes?'

'That's a very good question, Watson. It's because of Amy Stone.'

'Who?'

'Amy Stone. American. Thirty-five years old. Unmarried, single, no children.'

'And she's in Colorado?'

'Yes. Poplar followed her trail to its end three hours ago.'

'You said I was going to Colorado to catch a murderer. Amy Stone?'

'Yes.' Holmes straightened his cravat. 'And no.'

Our speed had slowed to a crawl. Unusual. The traffic ahead was stationary.

'Stop talking in riddles,' I snapped.

'And spoil all my fun?'

There were times when Holmes sounded less like a middle-aged man and more like an annoying adolescent.

'Watson, we have sighted our quarry, and they have no idea we are coming for them.'

In an instant his mood switched from excitement to sombre reflection. 'A cold-blooded, heartless crime. If it hadn't been for Beth Fairield's left hand and the tip on the Roadtrain, it might have deceived even me.'

'Who is this bloody Amy Stone?'

Holmes tilted his head to one side and brought his hands together under his chin. He looked at me as he spoke, but I might as well have not been there.

'Amy Stone left her home in Los Angeles last Friday night, flying to London for – according to her sister – a job interview she wouldn't say anything about. Only that it would mean a move to Britain and more money than she'd ever dreamed of making. But she cut her trip short. Very short, in fact. Six hours after arriving in London, she boarded a flight to Colorado via Berlin. She was healthy when she touched down in Britain. When she returned to America, she was dying of cancer, and was taken by private ambulance to an exclusive facility.'

'What?'

The Egg interrupted us, its soothing voice a product of thousands of hours of customer trials. 'Please remain calm. We are three-point-six miles away from our destination. We are currently unable to continue our journey. The police are aware of the situation and their advice is to remain in the vehicle until help arrives.'

I'd been so focussed on Holmes's surreal monologue that I hadn't paid attention to what was going on outside.

'Light mode.' The windows cleared and I saw the problem. There were stationary Eggs and Cartons on all sides. I could hear chanting and angry shouting somewhere ahead. The white cloud drifting past us wasn't snow. It was smoke.

I recognised where we were. Through the rear window I could see the Thames. We had come to a stop trying to turn left towards the airport, which meant the large park in front of us was Hampton Court Park and the series of buildings I could glimpse between the vehicles, and the trees beyond them, was Hampton Court Palace of the Future.

Ah. That would explain the angry mob, then. And the fact that one of the buildings was on fire.

When Hampton Court Palace had burned to the ground seventeen years ago, a national poll had led to the establishment of the Palace of the Future, a public/private enterprise that became Britain's newest national museum when it opened its doors six years later. Celebrating the UK's growing reputation as the home of bleeding-edge tech, the Palace was financially supported by a number of leading companies. The biggest single donor, with one of the halls bearing its name, was Fairfield Technology.

Not surprising, then, that the Palace had also become a focus for New Ludd protests. Now their leader was accused of murder, and since most Ludds ate up every conspiracy theory the net could throw at them, it stood to reason that they'd seize on Greta Blackstone's arrest as an attempt by computer-loving, weak-minded technosheep to shut them down.

'Disengage locks.'

I stepped out of the Egg. Most of the action was confined to the park. I could see placards being waved. None of this tight-beamed local smotchcasts for the New Ludds. It was a wonder they could organise themselves at all with all the tools they left on the table.

It looked like most of the action was centred around Fairfield Hall. It wasn't on fire, as I'd first suspected. The flames came from a bonfire in front of it. The mob's displeasure was made plain by the figure burning on top of the makeshift pyre – a human-sized Artie Robot, from Fairfield Tech's corporate logo.

Police drones were buzzing above, keeping their distance to avoid being taken down by makeshift missiles. The distant thrum of 'copters was just audible above the yells of the crowd. As they got closer, I could feel the rhythm in my gut, a deep bass that rattled windows. That meant the big bastards – fossil 'copters. It was the army, not the police. The government was taking no chances. In five minutes it would be tear gas, warning shots, and a ring of unsmiling, armed soldiers with full face masks and riot shields. They were going to swat the protesters hard and fast, sending a message that rioting would put you in prison, hospital, or worse.

Definitely time to go, then. If I had been in any doubt, the sight of an Egg being pushed onto its roof four cars ahead was enough to get me moving.

I was aware that Holmes was standing beside me. 'Canary Wharf and the Square Mile are at a standstill. The rest of London is fairly clear.'

'I'm going to get there on foot,' I said. 'We'll talk later.'

Holmes vanished.

I swung the rucksack on to my back and smotched a map onto the exterior of the Egg. I'd barely used the brand-new smotch and this was the moment I discovered it could project 3D holograms. A representation of my quickest route, with real-time adjustments for traffic and weather conditions, appeared between me and the Egg. I twisted my hand, and the image rotated. Moving my hand away increased the size; bringing it close did the opposite. I was grinning at it when a voice shouting, 'Oi!' made me look up.

Two cars away, two men, the bottom half of their faces concealed by bandanas, were laying into a Carton with cricket bats. I had a moment to wonder where the bats had come from before I spotted a third man pointing at me.

I turned off the smotch. Perhaps this hadn't been the best time to derive a nerdy thrill from a new AI-augmented holographic route planner.

Ignoring the shouty man, I jogged west. Running would look panicky, so I kept my pace relaxed. Terminal Five was under ten miles. I was wearing running shoes – I'd never understood why anyone would wear anything else by choice. If I took it easy, even allowing for a detour or two, I could easily be there in ninety minutes. With the ennanomeds' help, maybe even quicker.

'Oi!' Louder this time. I shot a look over my shoulder. Shouty man was pointing my way, but he was looking back, waving someone else on. Two someones. Both on bicycles and carrying a snooker cue apiece. Perhaps the riot had started as a celebration of British sport.

'Oh, bollocks.' I increased my speed. The cyclists had to negotiate the stationary Eggs. I hoped to get enough of a head start that I could duck into an alleyway or through a shop doorway and lose them.

When I rounded the first corner, I groaned. A wide street, terraced houses. No shops, no alleyways.

Whooping behind me. In their voices, I heard the untrammelled aggression born of adrenaline, endorphins, mob mentality and peer pressure. They'd spotted me, knew they were catching me, and could see I wouldn't get away.

What they didn't know was that I didn't intend to try. A lamp post ten yards away would do for what I had in mind.

I stopped. One of them was faster than the other and was already three bike lengths ahead of his colleague. I sprinted directly towards the street light. As I'd hoped, my pursuers read it as an act of panic and increased their speed.

As soon as I passed the lamp post, I dodged sideways, putting it between me and the lead guy. Then I faced him.

He probably wasn't a mindless thug, but the human brain can't make complex decisions when all the synapses concerned with fight or flight are behaving like a boxful of firecrackers in a metal bin. There was just enough time for a hint of confusion to mar his game face before he had to decide whether to go left or right to avoid the lamp post.

He went left – my right – disturbing his balance so he couldn't take a swing at me. When his brain freed up enough computational power for him to question why I had stopped, and to re-evaluate my victim status, he hesitated. Perfect.

The kick I stopped him with was straight out of my first ever karate class. Weight on my left leg, ninety-degree angle as my right leg shot out, the tread of my trainer leaving a clear imprint on his jacket. His breath left his lungs, his body left his bike, then his breakfast left his stomach. The bike careered up the street.

I stepped forward and plucked the snooker cue out of the hands of the prone figure.

The second, slower, rider had made his decision. Yes, his friend had paid a price for his hesitation, but he wouldn't make the same mistake. He accelerated, went right rather than left, swinging the cue towards me. I jogged backwards, watching him closely, making sure I was just out of reach.

Without the ennanomeds, which by now I was convinced were sharpening my senses and reactions, I might not have risked what I did next. As it was, I didn't think twice.

I hefted the pilfered snooker cue like a javelin and sent it towards my jousting opponent. Not directed at him, though. My target was the front wheel and my aim was true. Two or three spokes broke before the wheel stopped dead, launching the cyclist unceremoniously into the air. His brief flight ended face-first, after which he groaned a lot and spat blood and teeth onto the street. A New Ludd had just flown without the use of technology. You'd think he'd be pleased.

The second bike's front wheel was badly bent, but the first bike had come gently to rest in a hedge. I stole it and was at Terminal Five in a creditable twenty-seven minutes.

It was only when I was safely onboard that I checked my smotch. Holmes had sent a photograph of Amy Stone. At first I thought he'd accidentally sent the wrong file. The short blonde hair was identical. Then I noticed the subtle differences. She looked a little older and the eyes were darker. The smile was smaller, less confident than the one I'd seen so many times in the press. Other than that, I was convinced I was looking at Beth Fairfield.

CHAPTER THIRTY-SIX

WHILE THE PLANE taxied to the runway, I stared at the woman who could be Beth Fairfield's twin until my head hurt. Pieces of information drifted in and out of focus – Turren's disputed DNA, Beth's mangled left hand, Greta Blackstone's claim that Robert Fairfield had been about to break up the company – but no neat solution emerged. I turned off my smotch. If Clockwork Sherlock wanted a grand denouement to rival those of his fictional counterpart, let him have it.

I embarrassed myself on the plane.

First-class hypersonic air travel was all I'd hoped it would be, and I availed myself of the hot towels, the warm nuts and the ice-cold spring water. After ordering a light supper of sea bass, asparagus and new potatoes, I watched the clouds fade through orange and pink to blue-grey, into darkness. I was about to turn down the vodka martini aperitif when I remembered the ennanomeds. I called back the steward and ordered two, followed by a New Zealand Sauvignon Blanc to accompany the fish, with a twenty-one-year-old single malt to follow.

Unfortunately, the ennanomeds decided over-indulging in alcohol at an altitude of ninety thousand feet was unwise, and I remained tediously sober. Still, I supposed, it might be better not to arrive in America with a hangover and a mouth like a hamster's arse.

My fellow passengers looked like they belonged in the first-class cabin of a hypersonic jet. They were part of a club with unwritten rules and secret entry requirements. It was a strange club in many ways. Its members avoided eye contact and conversation. Noise-cancelling headphones were the norm, even though hypersonics, once at cruising altitude, are pretty quiet. The headphones, I concluded, were like a badge, or a membership card. They were there to announce the wearer's right to be where they were, and to discourage anyone from talking to them.

There was a parallel in the Sherlock Holmes stories – the Diogenes Club, of which Mycroft, Sherlock's older brother, was a member. Members of the Diogenes Club, once inside the walls of the building, were guaranteed minimal contact with their fellow members, and no conversation whatsoever. Some things hadn't changed much in a couple of centuries, it seemed.

Within five minutes of the seatbelt sign being switched off, everyone knew I wasn't a member of their club. Moreover, they wouldn't be handing me a membership form and a pair of headphones any time soon. My fellow passengers scrupulously ignored me as I tried out every position of the automatic seat, watched the first few seconds of a dozen movies, and used the bathroom five times, choosing a different scent and hand cream each time. I smelled like a bagful of tester strips in a perfumer's bin, but I was having a good time.

The noise-cancelling club watched me sidelong, their heads swivelling smoothly away if I glanced in their direction.

After ninety minutes, the cabin lights dimmed. A two-hour nap was encouraged before landing in Denver. It was quite nice being treated like a toddler in day care. I wondered if there would be milk and carrot sticks later.

I pressed the button to lie the seat virtually flat, then had a thought and called the steward. He was very polite, soft-spoken and unobtrusively attentive.

'Look, er, Edward,' I said, looking at his name badge. 'I'm going to have a kip now. I should warn you, I don't sleep so well. I usually deal with it by self-medicating with vodka. Tonight, I'm unexpectedly sober and may treat you to a little bit of twitching, kicking and an occasional shout. It's nothing to worry about. One word of warning, though . . .'

The poor boy had already paled.

'If you need to wake me up, do it very, very gently. That's particularly important.'

He nodded dumbly and withdrew.

I know my nightmares have a tendency to spill out of my subconscious into reality. After a few complaints from neighbours in Mehmet's building, I had pointed my smotch's camera towards the bed one night and whizzed through the footage over breakfast. Three times in seven hours I had punched invisible assailants. Once I shouted something incomprehensible and thrashed about like a landed fish. The problem was made bearable for the neighbours by moving my bed a few feet away from our shared wall. I didn't have that option now.

But I thought I might need the clarity a couple of hours sleep would bring, since Holmes had warned that some of the more physical elements of my skill set might be required in Colorado.

I gave the businessman opposite, with the carefully

trimmed stubble, what I hoped was a reassuring smile. He didn't act quickly enough to pretend he was looking elsewhere and was forced to make eye contact. The look he gave me suggested I'd just used sign language to offer him a colonoscopy.

I pulled the eye mask on, lay back and wondered if there was any chance my subconscious might do me a favour and put together the solution to the murders Holmes had already apparently grasped. I wasn't optimistic.

The last time I'd slept on a plane, I'd been in the back of a transport, strapped upright, weapon in hand, bumping and roaring towards a drop zone at four a.m. This was a touch comfier. I closed my eyes.

The screams from the room down the hall stop after a while, as they always do. I'm trying to identify each member of my squad from the sounds they make when the electrodes are applied, or the soles of their feet beaten, or worse. The only screams I'm sure I've never heard are those of Hughes. My right-hand man and – for the last few weeks of this tour – my lover. I suppose I already know why I never hear him being hung from the beam in his room, why I never hear him beg or cry. I just can't bring myself to believe it. Because if I do, I might give up.

I wait for the screams to start again. It's Hockney. I know it, because I heard her suggest a novel use for one of the torturer's guns. She's as tough as they come, but everyone cracks in the end.

They always come for me about an hour after Hockney. Always the same order. They want us to know our turn is coming.

Only this time, the screams don't start again.

Male voices from the room where they're torturing Hockney. Calm. Like they're discussing the weather. A burst of static from their coms. A short conversation. Then a single gunshot.

I stand up, face the locked door. And while I stare at the two inches of wood between me and the other human beings who have shared my life out here, another shot punctures the silence. Footsteps moving away. A third gunshot. A minute passes before the fourth. Then a fifth and a sixth.

Two of us left. And they want me to hear it all.

The key rattles in my door and my jailer comes in. Seeing me standing, he gestures angrily at the floor. I squat, muscles bunched in readiness.

As soon as he bends to place the tray on the floor, I am on him, the iron ring flying out of the wall as I pounce. I'm weak, injured and sleep deprived. I take advantage of his shock and grab his knife, my reflexes so slow it's as if I'm drunk. I try to slit his throat, but he's already moving, scooting backwards on his arse towards the door. I throw myself after him and the knife goes through his neck. He slumps and I run.

At first I run towards the rooms where I heard the shots, but as I round the corner, I see three guards, machine guns slung on their shoulders. They have their backs to me.

I pull back and flatten myself against the wall, look the other way. There's a breeze in this corridor – an open window at the far end. I know if I don't go now, I will die here.

I run down the corridor, half jump, half fall through the window, and limp away.

When I woke up, I was straddling Edward. Everyone in the Diogenes Club was looking at me, their craving for privacy trumped by the sight of a sweating woman in T-shirt and knickers – I must have kicked my trousers off under the blanket – pinning a first-class steward to the carpet, a complimentary bag of toiletries held threateningly against his throat.

'Oh, shit. Sorry.' I rolled off and Edward scooted away on his backside before getting to his feet, giving his waistcoat a sharp pull downwards and offering me a hand up. An impressive recovery. Another tick in the first-class travel box. The stewards' training must be wonderfully comprehensive.

'That's quite all right. You did warn me. I just put a hand on your shoulder to let you know we're landing in fifty minutes, and to ask how you'd like your eggs prepared. Next thing I knew, we were on the carpet.'

'A few of my relationships have begun exactly the same way.'

The sweet boy blushed.

'I am sorry. Poached, then.'

'Pardon me?'

'The eggs.'

'Ah. Of course.'

The rest of the flight was uneventful. The descent was made with a hypersonic's famous swiftness, dropping briskly to a few thousand feet above sea level before straightening and gliding the final ten miles. The flaps came up, the landing gear went down and the jets whined at a new pitch ninety seconds before we squealed onto the tarmac at Denver.

America has a confusing attitude to self-driving cars. Some states do, some states don't, which means all vehicles that need to operate across state lines have to be able to handle both. It still came as a shock to me when the door of the cab the police department had sent opened to reveal a human being sitting behind a steering wheel.

My driver was big, bearded and amused at my shock.

'From England, right?'

I nodded my assent.

'Welcome to civilisation. I'm Dwayne. You guys always look at me like that. We're not quite ready to let a bunch of robots take our rights away. Not in Colorado.'

For the three minutes it took us to get out of the airport complex and on to the freeway, I held onto the seat, my feet bracing for impact. It wasn't that he drove badly, it was just that I knew he was only capable of looking in one direction at any given time and he couldn't have any idea what any other driver around him was going to do next. What if another driver had a heart attack and lost control? Even a momentary lapse of concentration could cause a crash.

I only relaxed fully during the ten minutes we were on the I-70, when Dwayne thumbed a button on the dash and took his hands off the wheel. When he returned to manual in time to take the downtown exit and join the thousands of cars crossing the city every which way, I wanted to scream.

Despite the air con, I didn't stop sweating until we reached police headquarters, and was glad to step out into a cold breeze.

'Thank you,' I said without conviction as Dwayne opened the door for me to get out.

'My pleasure, ma'am. Enjoy your stay in Denver.'

He smiled but didn't move.

'Oh, shit,' I said, remembering another strange custom America had hung on to. I patted my pockets as if some cash might magically materialise. I hadn't touched a physical banknote in years.

Dwayne met my apologetic look with an irritated one of his own, then got back into the car to rejoin the lottery of human-driven vehicles.

I stood on the kerbside for a couple of minutes. Something to do with the case had just slotted into place in my brain, but wasn't quite ready to reveal itself fully.

I jogged up the ramp to the police headquarters.

Whatever influence Holmes had in London was powerful enough to extend to our American cousins. Once I'd made myself known at the main desk, I waited for less than a minute before a tall, lean woman in her forties approached, hand extended.

'Captain Barnes, I'm Detective Mills. Lois.'

'Hi, Lois.'

Her handshake was firm. Probably because of the American detective series I'd grown up watching, I'd always pictured dishevelled, tired, scruffy types, but Lois Mills wore a navy suit, black boots, and no heels or make-up. I followed her through a security check into a long corridor.

'Your boss has some fans this side of the pond, captain. We thought no one would ever get anything to stick to the Witch.'

'Yeah, I remember that. Before my time, though.' Esme Stradelli – the Witch of Wall Street – was currently serving seven life sentences – a peculiar feature of America's justice system – for perpetrating a series of frauds that nearly bankrupted a number of prominent financiers and a small South American country. She had been a careful criminal, confident that nothing illegal would ever be traced back to her. And it never was, until a twenty-year-old cold case caught the interest of Clockwork Sherlock.

Lois ushered me into a small office. This was more like it. Three half-drunk coffees in paper cups, an overflowing wastepaper basket and files dumped anywhere there was space, which didn't leave much room for anything else.

'Christ, O'Hanley. I said to leave it tidy.' Lois swept some of the debris off the desk. The computer monitor brightened. It was open at the sports results. I could already picture Lieutenant Columbo leaning back in the weathered and ripped swivel chair, chewing a cigar.

'This is perfect, Lois. Thank you.'

She was picking up the coffee cups. 'He's a good cop, but he's a slob. Sorry, captain. You hungry? Thirsty?'

'Some water would be great.'

'Coming right up. Any idea how long this is going to take? I have two officers standing by for when you need us.'

'Thanks.' I looked at my smotch. Three forty in the afternoon in Denver. Nine forty at night in London. Holmes had messaged saying he was starting his presentation at ten. And that was as much as I knew.

'I'm not sure. How do I reach you when I'm done?'

'I'm in the office next door. It's fifteen, twenty minutes out to Thoughts and Prayers.'

'Where?'

'Sorry. The Holistic Wellness Centre of Positivity and Prayer. It's a last-chance saloon for people with terminal illnesses, no hope, but plenty of money. We call it Thoughts and Prayers. What can I tell you? This job makes cynics of us all in the end. Holler if you need me.'

'Thank you. I will.'

Ten minutes later, I had changed into the cam and mic-equipped outfit in the rucksack and put in the contacts and monitors. As I was sticking the sub-vox band-aid in place, a familiar bald giant appeared. Still made me jump.

He winked at me. 'You all right?'

'Hello, Poplar. How are things?'

'Busy. And about to get a little bit crazy, I hope. You ready?'

'I suppose that depends on how you define "ready". If you mean am I prepared to join a virtual version of Sherlock Holmes as he explains something I've barely grasped to a police inspector who thinks he's already solved the case, then go somewhere I've never been to find someone who can't be there, then yes, I'm ready.'

'Good.' She was either too harassed to pick up sarcasm or she didn't care. 'The contacts are an upgrade. Three settings. I need to talk you through them.'

'Go ahead.' I sat back.

'You're in Augmented Reality now, which is mode one. Please sub-vox "mode two".'

When I did so, a black rectangle appeared on the wall. If I moved my head, it moved with me.

Poplar explained. 'Mode two works alongside mode one. You're still in AR, but you can link with us in VR through the screen. Put the screen wherever you want it; pinch to zoom, three-finger swipe to close. Try it.'

Holding a finger over the screen meant I could slide it to the floor, pinching reduced it to the size of a playing card. I expanded it until it took up half the office, then reduced it to its original size.

'Clever,' I admitted. 'What's it for?'

The screen came alive. I was looking at the Baker Street rooms. Toby, in his Asian female form, was standing by the mantelpiece. Barnett, or rather his orangutan avatar, was sitting in an armchair looking at Holmes, who was consulting a pocket watch. He looked directly at the screen.

'Watson?'

'I'm here.'

'Excellent.' I wondered what they could see of me. Later, Poplar explained that a static version of the Watson avatar stood in the corner of the room for most of what followed. Not creepy at all, then.

Poplar spoke directly into my right ear. 'Sub-vox "mode three".'

I did so and was instantly in Baker Street, standing up, facing Holmes. I stumbled in shock, and he sprung forward to grab my arm and keep me upright. I felt nothing physically when he touched me, and I was simultaneously aware that I was falling in one place, while still sitting in an office in Denver. It was thoroughly disorientating.

'All right, old man?'

'Fine. Thank you. I've got it now.' There was no way for

me to move around, of course. I wondered how Poplar was going to compensate for that. She – or rather he, in his bald muscle-bound form – was standing by the window, having appeared at the same time as I did.

Holmes addressed his audience.

'DCI Barnett, thank you for joining us. The purpose of this meeting is to prevent you making a catastrophic error.'

The orangutan looked decidedly put out. 'Now listen, Mr Holmes, you know I've been an admirer of yours since the beginning. For someone to be able to come in, with the benefit of new technology and without any other demands on their time, and help us out with some of the old, less important cases, well, it's been a big help. I'm not too proud to say so. And I know you'd be the first to admit you've had a fair bit of luck on your side.'

'Luck, Detective Chief Inspector?'

'Luck, yes. The fact that Andrews was still playing online chess with the Russian after twenty-seven years. And what about the Fegenvelle Embezzler? You couldn't have possibly known she'd go to that particular charcutier – of the thousands in Paris, I mean.'

Holmes looked amused. 'Quite an astonishing run of luck, really. But please don't misunderstand me regarding this evening's revelations. I am not only preventing an error that could stop your career in its tracks, I am handing you a case that could see you rise to superintendent, possibly even chief superintendent. I have no wish to take any credit for any of what I am about to impart.'

Barnett blustered a little about having the evidence he needed and not requiring help, but the fact was, the orangutan wouldn't have turned up if he didn't suspect Holmes might have an ace up his sleeve.

Holmes waited for the insincere protests to subside. 'I

will send my notes and any relevant recordings over to you when we are finished here.'

He took two steps forward into the centre of the room. The black suit was immaculate, the white shirt topped with the same red cravat he wore the day we met. He placed both hands on top of the cane, closed his eyes and dropped his chin, as if in prayer. When he lifted his head again and spoke, his voice carried that quiet authority I was growing accustomed to.

'At first, although the solution to this case was obvious enough, it seemed impossible. I had no doubt Beth Fairfield killed her father, Robert.'

Barnett stood up.

'Sit down, Barnett. I do not want to be interrupted.'

The ape briefly considered expressing his outrage, but – and I imagine this had much to do with the recent prospect of promotion – retook his seat without a word.

'Good. Now, how can someone murder someone else if they themselves are already dead?'

He clicked his fingers and Baker Street disappeared.

CHAPTER THIRTY-SEVEN

WE WERE in Robert Fairfield's study, exactly as it had been when we were last there. The single cognac glass was on its coaster on the green leather-topped desk.

Barnett was still in his armchair, peeling a banana. Poplar had had far too much fun with his avatar. I could see her smiling at her handiwork. Toby stood behind, hands behind her back. Holmes addressed his audience.

'No forced entry, no footprints in the flowerbeds or grass outside. There was no frost, so they would have been clearly visible. No scuffs or marks on windows. The only people with the necessary code were Greta Blackstone and Beth Fairfield. Greta Blackstone had no firm alibi and the timestamped video showed her arriving at nine thirty, rather than eleven thirty. Blackstone claimed that when she arrived at Robert Fairfield's house, he was already dead. Circumstantially, the evidence is not in her favour.'

Barnett grunted. Holmes ignored him.

'However, timestamps can be faked.'

'Impossible!' Barnett wagged a hairy orange finger at the detective.

'Not quite, Barnett, not quite. Improbable, certainly, but not impossible for a talented hacker, particularly if you have unfettered access to the leading technology company in the world. And, once we've eliminated the impossible, whatever remains, et cetera, et cetera. We all know the rest.'

From the look on Barnett's face, it was clear he didn't.

'And there are the street lights, of course. I'm sure you would have noticed them eventually.'

'Street lights?'

'All London lamp posts switch automatically to low-light status between the hours of eleven at night and six in the morning. Correct?'

The orangutan looked nauseous. Holmes didn't wait for an answer, instead pointing at the wall where a screenshot of the timestamped footage appeared. The street lights behind the Egg were dimmed.

Holmes clicked his fingers and the screenshot vanished.

'So. The timestamp has been discredited.'

Old-school deduction. I loved it. At that moment, I was proud to be Watson.

'If Greta Blackstone killed Robert Fairfield,' continued Holmes, 'we are being asked to accept she poisoned a man she had recently agreed to marry, before calling the police to report his death from the murder scene.

'A ruse! She did it to throw us off the scent. She . . .' Barnett caught Holmes's eye and stopped talking.

'As you were gathering evidence to convict her, rather than examining the facts, I turned my attention to the other possible suspect: Beth Fairfield. The cognac glass was the first obvious clue.'

Barnett was taking the instruction not to interrupt more seriously now. I was under no such restraint.

'What about it?'

'Its position, Watson. We know Robert Fairfield was a

tidy man of scrupulous habits. The office we are standing in is an intimate space. Two chairs only, one on each side of the desk. Miss Poplar?'

The cognac glass on the desk disappeared.

'This image was captured after the glass was removed for forensic examination. Look at the indentations where the coasters stood.'

We looked. There were three circular indentations on the desk where coasters had been placed countless times. The nearest one to Robert Fairfield's chair, and the one closest to the guest chair, were shallower than the one in the centre of the desk, where the leather had actually worn through to the wood beneath in a couple of places.

'Robert Fairfield appreciated symmetry,' said Holmes. 'Everything in his house, and particularly here, in his inner sanctum, suggests a man who liked everything in its place. His books, his paintings, the rugs, the position of the chairs. Symmetry. Even down to the position of his nightcap. A cognac before bed. If he's alone, the glass is placed in the centre, here.'

Holmes pointed, then moved his finger along the leather surface to the indentation where Robert Fairfield's glass had actually stood that night.

'If he was entertaining a guest, a pleasing symmetry was achievable by placing his glass here and his guest's glass directly opposite. Hence the lighter indentations in those spots. Mr Fairfield had enjoyed his nightcap alone for many years. And yet his glass was found here. He wasn't drinking alone that night. Which means he had a visitor before Greta Blackstone arrived. A visitor he knew well enough to share a drink with. The second glass was obviously washed, wiped clean, and replaced on the side. But Robert Fairfield's glass remains, and its position tells us what happened.'

I thought back to our night in Fairfield's house. No one

had been caught on camera and Holmes had said a boat couldn't get close without setting off alarms. I could buy the thing with the drinks, but that wasn't the main problem with his theory.

'How did she get in?'

'The boathouse, Watson.'

'But you said –'

'– I said nothing about a boat. Miss Poplar?'

And we were standing in the boathouse.

Someone knocked tentatively on a nearby door that wasn't there.

'Mode two,' I sub-voxed, and was back in Denver, looking at the London boathouse on a screen floating in the corner of the office. Detective Mills put her head around the door.

'You okay in here? Can I get you a drink or anything?' She looked around the office, as if my famous boss might materialise.

'I'm fine. Thanks.' I tapped my ear. 'Conference call.'

'Are you all right, Watson?' Holmes said into my right ear.

'Yes. Sorry.'

Lois withdrew, shutting the door quietly behind her. I sub-voxed myself back to the boathouse. Holmes stood on the far side of the boat, which was gently bobbing in the water.

'We checked this room and found nothing,' I said.

'Exactly.' Holmes pointed at the cobwebs across the beams, in every corner of the room, on the boat, and even stretching between the boat and the sides of the jetty. 'It had been many months since Fairfield had taken out the boat. It was here for the winter. The boathouse, and the restored wherry it contained, were due to be cleaned and prepared for the season in late April. Look here.'

He was standing over the ladder down to the water. 'This

VR room has been constructed using images taken from Watson's cameras. What do you see?'

Wondering how I was supposed to walk, my point of view suddenly changed, and I was looking down at the ladder alongside Holmes and the others. I didn't want to be the one to answer this time. Holmes said it for me.

'Nothing. The top two rungs of this ladder, and the bar used to pull yourself out, are never in contact with the water, yet there's nothing here. No cobwebs, no dust. Actually, that's not quite true.'

He pointed at the ladder and a magnified picture took shape immediately. We could all see cobwebs on either side of the ladder, strands hanging down where they'd been broken by someone climbing up.

'Beth Fairfield was an accomplished solo diver,' said Holmes. 'She had been diving alone at night for months before the murder. It's the only way to enter the house without being caught on camera or triggering alarms.

The police-ape laughed. 'So her corpse swam here from Cornwall a few hours after she was strangled?'

Holmes didn't repeat his injunction not to interrupt. He just treated Barnett to a humourless smile.

'Not quite.' He looked at me. 'Watson?'

I was blank for a few seconds, then the fog cleared. 'Not from Cornwall,' I said. 'She never left London.'

'What?' said Barnett.

'We'll come back to that,' said Holmes. 'St Austell first.'

I was better prepared this time. I blinked, night became day, and we were standing on a street in St Austell.

'Miss Poplar, please run the footage from when Beth Fairfield arrived at eight forty-three that evening.'

For the second time that day, I watched the CEO of Fairfield Technology walk out towards her dive boat, followed by the hooded figure we now knew to be Francis

Turren. The image froze and Holmes looked at the orangutan.

'DCI Barnett. You identified Francis Turren as the murderer.'

'There can be no doubt about it, Mr Holmes. No good trying to convince me otherwise. We have DNA from Beth Fairfield's fingernails when she tried to fight him off, and his suicide when tracked down was tantamount to a confession.'

'The DNA of a man who lived totally off-grid? Rather fortuitous, wouldn't you agree?'

'Hardly. He was injured during the Iver Heath riots.'

'He claimed otherwise.'

'Well,' chuckled Barnett, trying to regain some of his lost credibility, 'he would say that, wouldn't he? But DNA records prove him a liar.'

'And who provided the software that runs the National Health database? Our leading technology company.'

The ape waggled his finger again, but there was less conviction behind it this time.

'Rewind, please, Miss Poplar.'

Turren walked backwards away from the harbour. When Beth Fairfield followed him, Holmes held up his hand. 'There!'

The frozen image had caught Beth Fairfield looking around, her face clearly visible.

'Beth Fairfield, Mr Holmes. We know who she is.'

'Inspector, do you not find it odd that Mrs Fairfield would stop and have a good look at her surroundings? She's lived in St Austell for over a decade and had only been away for a day.'

'Not particularly. Why?'

'Because it's more like something a tourist would do, wouldn't you say?'

'Possibly.'

'There's no possibly about it, Barnett. In isolation, this

means very little, but it is another link in the chain of reasoning that has led me inexorably to one conclusion.'

'Which is?'

'Beth Fairfield didn't die that night. Amy Stone did.'

'Who?' said Barnett.

Holmes didn't answer him. 'Time for you to leave, Watson. Let's put an end to this.'

CHAPTER THIRTY-EIGHT

I WATCHED Holmes on my virtual screen with Detective Mills beside me as we drove to Thoughts and Prayers, which was located in the foothills just outside Denver limits. The two officers in front, one of whom was driving – which I was doing my best not to think about – kept quiet as instructed, so that I could concentrate on what was being said in London.

It was a surreal juxtaposition I'll never forget; the winter sun already dipping behind the mountains as the houses gave way to scrubland, farms and white fences, while back in Baker Street, Sherlock Holmes talked through the deductions that had led me here.

He explained how Amy Stone had been found by Beth Fairfield using Espen Nuerro's pioneering facial recognition program at Newton AI's headquarters.

'I had Miss Poplar run the same program,' he said. 'It came up with six possible matches for Beth Fairfield. We checked them all. The only match we couldn't locate was Amy Stone, who had gone to London for a mysterious job interview. Beth swapped their DNA records. She was remarkably thorough. There were only a few discrepancies in the tale she told us, but, added together, they were too strong to ignore.'

Holmes started pacing while he spoke, his hands clasped behind his back. The orangutan watched with his mouth hanging open.

'Beth's haircut. In itself, unremarkable, until you know that the style she chose that morning matched Amy Stone's.

'Then there's the Roadtrain trip to Cornwall. The chief steward noticed Mrs Fairfield was unusually quiet, claiming she had a headache. Specifically, whispering. A whisper covers an accent quite nicely.'

'But why would she pretend to be Beth Fairfield, if what you say is true?' The orangutan shook his great, shaggy head. 'You said she was in the UK for a job interview.'

'That was what Amy Stone told her sister. It doesn't mean it was true. I dislike speculating, but my guess would be that Beth told Amy they resembled each other, claiming there were times when a double might take her place for public appearances enabling her to spend more time at the helm of the business. Amy would have been expecting someone to meet her at the boat – possibly Jack, to see how convincing Amy was – how close he'd have to get before he realised she wasn't his wife. Hence the secrecy. Amy played along. A large deposit in her bank account gave her ample motive to do so. The clothes she wore, the smotch, even the wedding ring, were Beth Fairfield's – no doubt left in the Egg that met Miss Stone at the airport. Amy thought she was auditioning for a lucrative new role. Instead, she had been lured to her death.

'While onboard the Roadtrain, a single encrypted inward call was registered to her smotch. This was almost certainly Beth Fairfield asking Amy to meet her at St Austell, to come to the harbour.

'It was on the Roadtrain that Amy made a mistake. She

left a cash tip for Bernard, the chief steward. It was Miss Stone's first trip to Britain. She didn't know how rare tipping is, or that Beth Fairfield would certainly never tip in cash. I immediately thought we should be looking for an American.'

Barnett stood up. 'Now come on, Mr Holmes. You've got the cheek to tell me my case is based on circumstantial evidence, but what do you call this? Sounds like fantasy to me.'

Holmes responded with a smile quite unlike the tight, closed-mouth affair he usually favoured with us. This was a genuine grin, a visible sign of his inner delight. Seeing it, I knew he was absolutely confident he was right. And I'd seen enough of the way he worked to believe him.

'If something sounds fantastical, the common mind will reject it. Perfectly normal, inspector.'

DCI Barnett huffed at the implication that his mind was common, but sat down again and scratched his genitals.

'However,' continued Holmes, 'if we treat the fantastical explanation with the same dispassionate logic as the mundane, our minds remain open, and systematic deduction will inevitably lay bare the true facts of the matter at hand. Which brings us to the post-mortem.'

Holmes paused to light his pipe. The man was showboating, no doubt about it.

'We can discount any technological evidence as tainted. A sobering thought, perhaps, but Beth Fairfield can twist the facts any way she pleases when it comes to any evidence not directly in front of us. Security cameras, smotches, emails, transportation, even DNA. It was tampered with to tell the story Beth Fairfield wanted us to believe. So, let's ignore it for now and examine the physical evidence. The left hand of the corpse was smashed, stamped on by the murderer. If we ever recover the emails that persuaded Francis Turren to commit this crime, we will find instructions exhorting him to break the fingers of the victim's left hand. Particularly the wedding ring finger. The sender of those emails – whom Turren believed to be his former lover, Greta Blackstone – probably claimed the ring contained similar technology to the smotch and could summon the emergency services. Turren did as he was told.

'The real reason was to prevent the obvious conclusion, when the wedding ring was removed, that it had only recently been placed upon that finger. A ring worn daily for years leaves an unmistakable, indelible mark. Amy Stone had never married, never worn a ring on that finger. When I examined her hand, the ring had been stamped into her flesh, snapping the finger beneath.'

The switch of the DNA records of Beth Fairfield and Amy Stone would take forensic data analysts weeks to confirm, if it was possible at all, since it had been done by the company who supplied the hardware and software that contained the database concerned. But, Holmes assured Barnett, that didn't matter. The next half an hour would settle everything.

'We'll be there in two minutes, Captain Barnes,' said Detective Mills.

My stomach knotted and I nodded. Holmes had better be right about this. 'Can you pull over?'

The car stopped at the side of the road. It was getting dark fast.

'Detective Mills? I'm going to go back to the conference call. Sorry you're only getting one side of the – Holmes?'

'Watson?'

'Any way we can share this with our American cousins?'

'I don't see why not. Poplar?'

Half of the squad car's windscreen went dark, then, alongside the Colorado mountain backdrop, a dark path leading down to water appeared, thousands of reflected lights twinkling on its surface. It looked bizarrely incongruous against the arid, dusty foothills outside the car.

'Jeepers creepers.' They were the only words the driver said all evening.

'Where is that?' said Lois Mills.

Holmes's voice came from the radio. 'It's the Thames. Central London.' We all jumped. 'Thank you for your help, Detective Mills. Officers.'

The two men in the front nodded. Lois managed a throaty, 'You're welcome.'

'Watson will be joining us in virtual reality. You can observe onscreen. We are about to recreate the events of January the twenty-ninth.'

'Watson?' whispered Mills, looking at me.

'It's a long story.'

I sat back firmly, placing the back of my head against the rest.

'Mode three,' I sub-voxed. I closed my eyes as my vision darkened, the mountains, the car and my companions disappearing.

When I opened them, I was floating about two feet above the Thames. Holmes, Poplar, Toby and Barnett were doing the same – their bodies hanging in space above the water.

The scene was silent, making it eerier.

'The following reconstruction should clear up any remaining questions, Barnett. Rather than interrupt, if there's anything you don't understand, please ask at the end.'

I looked at the hovering orangutan. Now that Holmes was warming to his theme, he wasn't bothering to conceal his opinion that Detective Chief Inspector Barnett was somewhat of a dullard. Barnett himself was doing as he was told for now. Thinking of that possible promotion, no doubt.

I looked to my right and, in the distance on the far bank, spotted the hologram memorialising the London Eye attack.

We were facing south, then. In front of us was an old wooden building. Canoes were chained to the side of it. A faded sign on a padlocked door was almost impossible to read, but I could make out the word *club*.

Hidden from the street behind by the wooden building, a woman was climbing into a drysuit, pulling a cowl over her short, blonde hair. Beth Fairfield. She checked the contents of a small bag before tying it to her wrist with a length of cord. Then she pulled a mask over her eyes, put the regulator in her mouth, and waded into the water, quickly disappearing under the surface. As she dived, we watched the small, black waterproof bag, almost invisible on the water, follow her progress across the river.

Our strange party – Sherlock Holmes, Dr Watson, a big bald man, a small Asian woman, and a bemused orangutan – floated across the Thames to the opposite bank, entering Robert Fairfield's boathouse. We watched Beth Fairfield climb the ladder, shed the drysuit, and open the bag to reveal a change of clothes and a glass vial, which, once dressed, she pocketed.

'We know what came next,' said Holmes. 'The same day, at lunch, she and her father had reconnected. I'm sure he was delighted that Beth had dropped in to say goodbye before going home. Only Beth, Greta and Robert himself could unlock the house. She probably called up from the bottom of the stairs and he assumed she'd come through the front door. Then they drank together in his study. She wiped her glass clean and removed it after killing him, but didn't move her father's glass, which gave us the clue that he had had a visitor that evening.'

'Let me get this straight,' said Barnett. 'You reckon Beth Fairfield killed her father, had some other poor sod murdered to frame Blackstone and the New Ludds, then waltzed off without anyone seeing her? Beth Fairfield? One of the most famous businesswomen in the world? Even my mum would recognise her, and she stopped watching smotchcasts after *Midsomer Murders* was cancelled.'

'Well done, DCI Barnett.' Holmes patted one hairy orange arm. 'I knew you'd get there. That's exactly right. Let's skip forward.'

With a flourish – he was definitely having too much fun – the boathouse dissolved around Holmes, and we were back across the water. Beth was stuffing the drysuit into the bag along with some diving weights. She waited for a boat to pass, then launched the bag as far as she could. She watched the splash, then turned to a waiting Egg. Even its night-time glow was turned off, which was supposed to be impossible. She got in. When the Egg reached the main road, it pulled into traffic and began to glow again.

'Yes, yes, whatever. This proves nothing. She can't just disappear. It's Beth Fairfield.'

'Right again, inspector.'

Our surroundings darkened suddenly, before brightening to resolve themselves into the familiar environs of Baker Street. Toby was by the mantlepiece, her immaculate jade dress designed to draw the eye. She winked at me.

The orangutan decided it was time to re-exert his authority.

'If I didn't know you better, Clockwork Sherlock, I'd think this was an elaborate joke on your part. Beth Fairfield is dead. Francis Turren killed her. I am not interested in magically disappearing doppelgängers. You're wasting my time. I have other matters to attend to.'

He stood up, his orange fingers going to his face to remove the visor and return to Real Reality.

'As you wish,' said Holmes imperturbably. 'If you want to save yourself the trouble of watching what happens during the next thirty minutes or so in Colorado, it's your decision. I can easily bring in DCI Powell.'

I had no idea who Powell was, but there was clearly enough professional rivalry between them and Barnett to make the latter resume his seat without much more than a grumbled, 'Colorado. What's bloody Colorado got to do with anything?'

Holmes folded his arms.

'The final piece, inspector. Over to you, Watson. Time to visit the sick.'

CHAPTER THIRTY-NINE

I SUB-VOXED MODE ONE. I didn't want a screen restricting any part of my vision.

When the windscreen of the car cleared, we pulled back on to the road. Two minutes later, a sign for The Holistic Wellness Centre of Positivity and Prayer directed us to a road that was better maintained than the public highway.

'I don't really foresee much trouble,' I said. 'Maybe you guys could wait out here?'

Lois gave them a nod and opened her door. 'I'm with you, Watson. I have a warrant. I brought the dogs, as instructed. They're in the trunk.'

The 'dogs' were the search bots most police forces and military used to investigate potentially hostile environments before humans were sent in. Based on a variation of the Fairfield Egg algorithm, they worked as a team, each fist-sized bot in constant communication with all of its siblings as they rolled through their surroundings, packing an array of sensors.

'Detective Mills, Denver Police Department,' said Lois, showing her ID to an unimpressed-looking young woman at the reception desk. 'This' – Mills projected a document from her smotch onto the white reception desk – 'is a warrant issued by Judge Moynes this afternoon. I suggest you get your boss down here, pronto.'

The bored-looking girl didn't look so bored now. She murmured something into her wrist, then glanced up at one of the cameras capturing the scene. I got it. The boss would review the last minute's footage to check the warrant was real before deigning to join us.

It didn't take long. Less than a minute and a half later, a woman in her fifties stepped into the reception.

'I'm Meri Lightfoot. I'm in charge here. What can I do for Denver's finest this evening?'

The fact she'd addressed me and hadn't so much as glanced at Mills, suggested this woman was making a point. Although Mills was the one wearing a uniform, Meri Lightfoot had decided I was in charge after reviewing a few seconds of video footage. *Don't underestimate me*, was her message.

'I have a warrant from Judge –' began Mills, but I held a hand up.

'Thanks, Lois. Maybe there's an easier way to do this than a noisy search, or sending in the dogs. A . . . quieter way.'

Meri Lightfoot held my gaze. 'What do you suggest?'

I swiped my smotch and projected a recent photo of Beth Fairfield onto my palm. 'Any new patients in the past week? Female, in her forties? Rich enough to demand absolute privacy? Possibly with an upcoming slot booked in your surgical facilities with her private physician.' For some subtle but effective plastic surgery, I thought. 'Ring any bells?'

She took a little time to calculate the response likely to do her business the least damage. I knew which way she'd jump.

'Your smotch, please,' she said, holding out her hand.

I gave it to her, and she placed it on a circular pad on the receptionist's desk. It chimed with an update. When she returned it, she pointed to a door on my left.

'Take that corridor. At the end there's a door leading to the private wing. We have one patient there.'

I moved. Mills joined me, but Lightfoot called her back. 'Not you, detective.'

Mills protested, but I put a hand on her arm, keeping my voice low. 'It's okay. You can watch from the car. If you think I need help, kick some doors down.'

When I got to the first door, I noticed there was no handle. It slid open as I got close. Security linked to smotches. Very nice.

Meri Lightfoot tapped me on the shoulder. 'Please be respectful. I've seen this patient's records. She's very, very sick.'

Lady, I thought, *you don't know the half of it*.

Then I stepped through the door and went to meet a murderer.

Poplar's voice was in my ear as soon as the door closed behind me.

'All cams and mics are working, and I'm piggy-backing the police car's signal to stay in touch, but it's a bit patchy out here. I'm boosting it with any device I can find in the building itself, but the pickings are a bit slim. We won't lose you, but there might be dropouts.'

'Thanks for the heads-up.'

The door to the private wing slid open, as did the next. Everything in Thoughts and Prayers reeked of money, but this section was at a new level. Zen gardens, indoor waterfalls cascading into pools where I spotted turtles skimming the surface. Paintings on the walls from artists even I had heard of. And they looked like originals. White carpets made from that material that sucks in dirt and passes it into an under-floor system before it's jettisoned into the atmosphere. Smart windows. This was the place rich geeks came to die.

The last door opened into an open-plan living area with a dining table, sofas and four of those beanbags that mould to your shape. A huge transparent TV screen hung on thin wires in the centre of the room. One wall was all window, showing the mountains beyond. Four doors led off the room. Bathroom, bedroom, kitchen for the private chef, er . . . treatment room, maybe?

Horrible New Age music, sounding like someone had dropped dead and fallen on a synthesiser causing the same chord to drone on and on, added precisely nothing to the ambience.

I tried the first door. Bathroom. My initial burst of self-congratulation was cut short by a fist that, despite some impressive ennanomed-boosted reactions on my part, still managed to hit the top of my head. I was shorter than the fist's owner had expected. Wouldn't be the first time that's played to my advantage.

'Hostiles!' Poplar's voice was breathless, and one and a half seconds too late to be useful.

I rolled with the momentum of the punch and sprang back to my feet five feet away. 'Yeah. I noticed.'

'Plural. G'right!'

Go right. I'd been in the military long enough not to have to stop and think about it. I dived to my right just as a shape hurtled through the space I'd recently occupied.

'Any other surprises?'

Poplar sounded far more excited than me, and she was thousands of miles away. Still, that never stops professional gamers losing their shit when they win a tiddlywinks tourney against someone on another continent.

'I don't think so,' she said. 'I've hacked the security

system. Should be able to use the motion sensors to . . . got it. Just you and the three of them.'

'Three?' I counted my opponents and kept getting two. One was the guy who'd punched me. Six feet tall, black, blue crewcut and matching goatee. He looked like something out of a century-old video game, right down to the all-black, skin-tight ninja outfit.

The woman who'd rushed me from behind was shorter than me, but looked as if she'd started life a couple of feet taller, then been compressed. Natural blonde this time, cut short. Female fighters with long hair only exist in fiction. Another tight ninja outfit. Maybe henchpeople get a discount at the same online store.

The two of them moved away from each other, circling me. Neither of them were going to see their twenties again. Experienced, careful fighters. And almost certainly enhanced. *My nanomeds are better than your nanomeds.* At least, I bloody hoped they were. Anyone who could afford to stay in the private wing of Thoughts and Prayers could pay for the best bodyguards on the market.

'There's someone behind the third door to your right,' Poplar said. 'But they're not moving. I've alerted the Denver cops. They're on their way in. Can you hold the hostiles off for a couple of minutes?'

Great moment for a rhetorical question. Poplar sounded stressed. 'I think our third friend has joined me in the building's datasphere. Someone's trying to block me and seal the internal doors. Ha! I'd like to see –'

Silence. I was on my own. In the second that followed, I heard the door I'd come in click locked. That didn't sound good. I hoped Poplar was as talented as Holmes thought she was.

I'm good, hand-to-hand. Great, even. No need for false modesty. But two good fighters against one great fighter will win every time if they work together. And these two were good.

They moved fast, but I was faster. I was looking at the woman when my peripheral vision picked up a tiny movement from her colleague. His right thumb touched his ring finger. I reminded myself to sit down with Poplar at some point soon and ask what the tiny beasties colonising my body could and couldn't do. I knew I was faster than normal from the way I'd avoided the worst of that initial punch. I also knew my eyes were relaying more information to my brain than was normal. I'd never have seen Blue signal to Blonde without the help of ennanomeds.

I dived forwards as they lunged to close their trap. It was the one direction where they were vulnerable. It gave me an advantage that could be measured in milliseconds, but I made the most of it. Rolling, I swept my left leg under Blonde and, while she was falling, punched Blue hard in the middle of his right calf. It's a sensitive spot. If you hit it hard enough, the entire muscle cramps, which is agonising. It also has an adverse effect on mobility. Which was lucky as apart from a brief *hiss* of pain, Blue didn't seem unduly bothered by the move. He pivoted and aimed a kick at my ribs. That meant putting all his weight on the newly-injured leg. An unenhanced opponent would have fallen over. Blue didn't, but his aim was off. As his left leg sailed over me, I treated it to the same punch with which I'd attacked the right.

Blue stepped backwards and leaned against the wall for support. I rolled, ready to get to my feet, just as a shoe made contact with the right side of my face.

I went limp and fell to my left. Thank you, Sergeant Brookes. She had trained me in mano-e-mano combat at Sandhurst, and the most useful lesson she'd ever taught was how to get hit.

Only suckers spend all their time on attack and defence. There's always going to be a time when your attacks have failed and your defences are down. In ninety-nine per cent of fights, that's the end. Be the one per cent.

Whatever footwear is issued to ninja bodyguards, there's not a lot of give in it. Even with my dive in the same direction as the kick, with every muscle in my body suddenly limp, the side of Blonde's shoe hit me with enough velocity to send my skull crashing into the vulnerable brain within.

It hurt.

I didn't black out, but everything went a bit slow and sticky. I heard a church bell ring in my cranium and someone smeared Vaseline on the lens of the world. Shapes lurched around me. Everything swirled around me. Everything except one black silhouette.

My body moved before I gave it permission, and before the silhouette could finish the job.

When my vision cleared, I was on my feet, running. I've been stunned before and it's always discombobulating to come around. Time loses much of its meaning, and it can take a few seconds to remember where you are. And when you are. And who you are.

It's even weirder when you have to do all that while sprinting around the perimeter of a luxury apartment, splashing through the habitat of some indignant turtles, and trying to stay ahead of someone who wants to kill you. It was lucky Blonde wasn't built for speed.

When my brain brought me fully up to date with current events, I realised staying on my current path would bring me directly into the arms of my friend Blue. His calves meant he wouldn't be joining in the pursuit, but he wouldn't have to at this rate.

I changed course, heading for the centre of the room, with the huge TV and beanbags.

'Can you? Can you? Let me know if you can hear –'

'I hear you, Poplar.'

'Doors are unlocked. Backup will be with you in twenty seconds.'

Blonde didn't want to wait. Something heavy hit my left leg. I spun and went down, hitting the carpet hard. I saw what had hit me. A sculpture, in stone, of a pair of buttocks. Probably worth millions. I'd been brought down by an arse.

I was face down. Before I could roll, something much heavier than a stone bum landed on my back and knocked the air out of me. Blonde. The pressure eased and I instinctively pushed up with my arms, to give my lungs a chance to get some air.

Bad idea. I gasped in one breath before Blonde wrapped her powerful arms around me and squeezed. She was strong. Not strong enough to break the ribs of an ennanomed-protected chest, but strong enough to cut off the air supply.

I pushed up with my legs, managing to stand, despite the monster on my back. I twisted and saw Blue, smiling now, limping towards me.

'Ten seconds.' I was positive Poplar was enjoying this. Was she never going to forgive me for that headbutt?

'Beanbag,' I gasped with the last of my breath, hoping Poplar wouldn't think it was a term of endearment.

'Got it.'

I jumped, pushing myself backwards. Blonde fell with me, her grip as strong as ever. She could keep that grip despite a fall to the floor. She didn't know that wasn't my plan at all.

When we hit the beanbag, she must have had a moment to think it was her lucky day. What better way to break a fall in comfort? If it did occur to her that it was a smart beanbag, linked to the building's datasphere, it didn't happen until it was too late. Her weight carried her deep into the expensive piece of furnishing. At the same time as her momentum ceased, the bean bag closed over her body like a clam. Instead of moulding into a shape for maximum comfort, it identified pressure points in her neck, which, when triggered, break the signal chain between brain and arms. She went limp and I rolled off, the beanbag tightening to hold its prisoner.

I looked up into the face of Blue. He was still smiling. He flicked his wrist and an extendable fighting stick appeared. It crackled with energy. Oh dear. His smile widened.

'Drop it, asshole!'

Now, as a native English speaker, and a voracious reader since childhood, I will defend the beauty, power and sheer expressiveness of my language to anyone daft enough to question it, but even I will admit that *asshole* is a far better expletive than *arsehole* in certain circumstances. This was one of them.

Blue dropped the truncheon.

'On your knees! Hands behind your head.' Lois Mills moved forward and cuffed Blue, as her two colleagues, guns drawn, entered behind her.

'You okay, Watson? Holmes told us the building was locked down. We came through as soon as we could.'

I stood up. I was sore and couldn't quite take a full breath yet, but I was alive. I nodded my thanks and walked to the third door.

Time to end this.

CHAPTER FORTY

IT WAS A BEDROOM. Dressing table, a desk, one door to an en suite and another, open, leading to a walk-in closet.

Lying in bed, a drip leading to one arm, was a very ill-looking woman.

I stopped at the foot of the bed, suddenly unsure. The patient was bald. No eyebrows, either. All of the medical developments of the past couple of hundred years, and we still treat certain cancers by poisoning them, along with the rest of the body.

Her skin glistened with sweat. She appeared to be asleep. Sweating with illness or because she had spent the past few minutes engaged in a hacking deathmatch with Poplar?

The wall next to the closet glowed into life. It showed footage from multiple cameras in an airport. Holmes's voice came from the speaker.

'Four flights left City Airport on the night of January twenty-ninth. The final flight is the one we are interested in.'

On the screen, the multiple camera shots collapsed to one, overhead at the check-in desk as a woman in a wheelchair approached. The quality wasn't great but she was a dead ringer for the woman in Thoughts and Prayers. I looked across at the bed. Her eyes were still closed.

'The passport used belonged to Amy Stone. The flight was to New York, via Berlin. In New York, our passenger caught a connection to Denver.'

'City Airport is on the Thames, seven miles east of the point Beth Fairfield emerged from the river and got into the Egg. Saturday night traffic is slow. Plenty of time for Beth to shave her head and get changed. The woman travelling as Amy Stone arrived at City Airport forty-eight minutes before the Berlin flight departed.'

The screen changed to show a sped-up piece of footage of the exterior of the airport, Eggs arriving every second, disgorging their passengers before moving off again.

'Where better to complete her transformation than in the back of an Egg, the vehicle invented by her uncle, using software supplied by her own company? Toby spent a pleasant afternoon counting the Eggs that arrived at City Airport that night. Three hundred and forty-seven of them, extending the possible timeframe to its absolute limits. According to TFL, only three hundred and forty-six Eggs crossed the airport's perimeter.'

The bald woman in the bed stirred, opened her eyes, looked at me in alarm and pushed herself weakly up onto her pillows.

'Who are you? What's going on?' Her accent was American. Having said that, even I can do a passable American accent.

The screen went blank, then a live image of the patient replaced the security cam footage. My bodycams were still working then.

The sick woman tilted her head towards the screen. Detective Mills stood in the doorway and looked too.

Eyebrows appeared on the face first, then some make-up

around the eye, a little lipstick. Lastly, beautifully maintained blonde hair, styled into a pixie cut.

Detective Mills walked past me to the bed where the woman had slumped.

'Bethany Fairfield, under the Anglo–US law enforcement treaty, I'm arresting you for the murder of Robert Fairfield and conspiracy to murder Amy Stone. There's a whole bunch of fraud and other charges too, but hey, it's late.'

She cuffed Beth Fairfield as the CEO of Fairfield Technology sat meekly on the edge of the bed. She stared ahead numbly. She'd never expected to be caught.

Sherlock Holmes appeared on the screen. Lois Mills practically squealed with delight. Fangirl.

'Watson, are you all right?'

'I've had worse.'

'Good. Thank you for your cooperation, Detective Mills.'

'Oh, sure, I mean, it's a pleasure, an honour, any time, and I mean that sincerely, Mr Holmes, any time at all.' She realised she was gushing when she saw how her colleagues in the next room were looking at her, and she ended with one last, quieter, 'Any time.'

'Watson, back to London with our prisoner. Excellent work.'

CHAPTER FORTY-ONE

THE DETAILS of Beth Fairfield's trial, and the exoneration of Greta Blackstone, are a matter of public record.

For a while it looked as if the Fairfield killings might give the New Ludds the last push they needed to tip public opinion in their favour. After all, the most successful tech company in the country had tried to frame Blackstone for murder. Details such as the switching of supposedly encrypted medical records sowed seeds of serious doubt about the level of the country's dependence on technology, and the matter was raised in Parliament.

Any potential political capital for the New Ludds was stymied by the posthumous conviction of Francis Turren for the murder of Amy Stone, believing he was killing Beth Fairfield. The movement's attempt to move into the mainstream of British politics took a serious knock.

It was Greta Blackstone herself who unexpectedly punctured the final political aspirations of the New Ludds by stepping down as leader after declining to stand as a member of parliament. The vacuum left by her departure was filled by a more extreme, less media-friendly candidate, and the movement lost coherence for a while, succumbing to in-fighting over where exactly the line should be drawn on resisting new technology.

Blackstone's line on her departure was the oldest chestnut in the chestnut tree: personal reasons. Her grief over Robert's death had hit her harder than she knew, and the fact that his own daughter was the murderer had caused lasting emotional damage et cetera, et cetera, and so on and so forth. Yeah, right. I couldn't help wondering if that wasn't all bollocks. I'm a cynic.

Robert Fairfield's last will and testament was somewhat of a surprise to everyone. Not the will itself, but the estate to which it referred. The handwritten document in his safe left everything to Greta Blackstone. Everything turned out to be the house on the Thames, the boat, a tidy amount of cash and nothing else. Robert didn't own Fairfield Technology. He never had. The real owner had prized his, her, or their anonymity so highly, they had been prepared to pay Robert Fairfield a significant salary to pretend otherwise. Why anyone would want to do that was a mystery, and financial journalists had been unable to unpick the maze of shell companies and blind alleys around the true owner.

Beth's plan, thinking her father had been about to ruin Fairfield Tech, had been to steal the essentials from her own company and start again with the man she had fallen for when negotiating a deal that past summer – Espen Nuerro. A search of her rooms at Thoughts and Prayers uncovered a quantum drive containing the entire Fairfield Tech database. Since no evidence emerged implicating Nuerro, the Honeydrone sale went ahead. It was rumoured that Nuerro would be constructing a swarm of Honeydrones and testing them above the Arizona desert.

Beth Fairfield traded the wilds of Cornwall for a

minimum thirty-year stay at her Majesty's pleasure in Holloway.

Barnett, as Holmes had promised, took the credit for the successful investigation. At one point I couldn't check the news without seeing his smug face popping up. Looked like that promotion was going to be a sure thing. Couldn't happen to a nicer orangutan.

I got to spend the night, and most of the next day, in a Denver hospital, being checked over. The ennanomeds had minimised the damage, but they're not miracle workers. I had concussion, severe bruising on my ribs, and various cuts and scratches.

I flew home alone. First class again. I started in on the free booze with a vengeance after Poplar told me I could turn off the ennanomeds' automatic functions with the correct sub-voxed passwords.

About halfway through the third vodka, I started thinking tentatively about the future. It was a curious sensation. I tried to put the Nicky Gambon problem aside for ten minutes and imagine what the next few months, or even year or two, might look like.

For the first time in years, I had a job that challenged me, I was working with people I liked, and . . . well. Not completely true. I liked Toby. I liked Poplar, now that I thought about it. Clockwork Sherlock I wasn't so sure about. I respected him. Who wouldn't? He may not have been the detective of the Conan Doyle novels, but the world was a very different place to late-nineteenth-century London. It was no good knowing the colour of every brand of tobacco ash when nobody smoked. It was a good disguise, granted. His reputation was drawing more attention all the time, yet no one was close to finding out whose face was behind the mask.

And that was a problem for me. I wanted to know who he was. And I wasn't the only one.

After the fifth vodka, when everything was getting soft around the edges, my thoughts went where they always go. I started thinking about Afghanistan again. My squad. My friends. Only this time I couldn't get any pin-sharp images in my mind. I could remember the way they screamed when tortured, I could remember the shots I heard when they were executed. But I couldn't remember their smiles. I couldn't hear Boone's laugh anymore. I could remember Pollock's obvious nickname, but not his face. Harris had got into my bed one night after an IED narrowly missed killing us all, but I couldn't tell you if her hair was long or short.

But Hughes . . . Hughes I remembered. I remembered how his voice sounded, I remembered the jokes he made to defuse the tension on patrol – the sicker the better. I remembered the ancient hip-hop he used to insist on playing in the mess. I remembered the way he kissed me, and the way he looked at me when he thought no one else could see. And I remembered the moment I found out who my lover really was, when I saw him laughing with the guards; free, unhurt and relaxed on the night I escaped. Yeah, Hughes I remembered.

The problem was, he was all I remembered.

I waved away the stewardess when she came back with the bottle. I mumbled to activate the ennanomed codes and stumbled to the bathroom to piss away the alcohol and let my system clear itself.

By the time the plane bumped onto the tarmac at Heathrow, I knew I couldn't go on like this. My life had changed.

But I hadn't.

. . .

I'd only been away half a week, but my flat felt unfamiliar. I found myself trying drawers in the kitchen to find a corkscrew that had been in the same place since I'd moved in. Everything looked wrong, somehow. The bed was too big. The fridge was too small. My clothes belonged to a stranger.

Dad kept leaving messages. Nicky Gambon only left one.

Jo. I hear congratulations are in order. Nice work. If I don't hear from you before the end of Saturday, I'll pop over.

It was Thursday.

That night I toured a few of the pubs I used to hang out in. Turned off the ennanomeds. Drank too much, took some uppers, followed by downers. Drank some more. Announced to a table of strangers in a nightclub that they were my best friends. Got kicked out of that nightclub. Took some pills I bought off a guy outside a falafel place in Whitechapel. Threw up. Bought a bottle of vodka and tried to get on a Carton. Walked home when the doors wouldn't open for me, the other passengers looking out at me with a mixture of fear and pity.

Lay on my bed and stared at the ceiling until it started exhibiting strange, unlikely behaviour not normally associated with ceilings, such as growing mouths and singing death metal medleys in the style of a barbershop quartet. I was determined not to let the ennanomeds step back in this time, so I let myself drift into unconsciousness without reactivating them, half-hoping I might not wake up again.

I'm standing in front of my CO and trying not to punch him.

He's not a bad sort, Curtland. Fair. Approachable, but keeps enough distance to be able to maintain discipline.

Our camp in Tajikistan is large enough to maintain a small hospital, and that is where he heard my report, forty-eight hours after I returned alone from the op where I'd lost my entire squad. They pumped some drugs in to help the basic military nanomeds do their job, dressed my feet, cleaning and sterilising the cuts under my missing toenails. Then they gave me something to help me sleep. When I woke up screaming two hours later, they supplemented it with something stronger. Much stronger. I slept through the next day and night.

Curtland shows no emotion when I tell him they're all dead, and that Hughes betrayed us. As I describe what happened in detail, he turns his chair to the window to watch the light fade behind the trees outside.

When he finally speaks, he does so without looking at me. He reminds me of the nature of our mission. As far as the British government and the army are concerned, it never happened. The outcome of the failed op is the worst possible. Not only has the squad been lost, but a highly-placed terrorist leader now controls ope production in Afghanistan.

Curtland tells me there is only one thing I need to remember about what happened: it's over. It can never be spoken of again. We all understood that the mission had to be deniable, hence the clothes, the lack of ID, and the complete lack of traceable technology. It never happened. The families of the dead will be told their loved ones died in a training accident.

I tell Curtland that I want out. I'm finished with the army. I'm finished with all of them.

He says nothing for a long time. He's never been one to rush. He reminds me that the army considers me a potential candidate for promotion. I think of the screams I heard, the gunshots. The silence. He asks if I might be better taking some leave, a few months perhaps, so that I might give time a chance to put recent events into perspective. I think of the smotch Hughes said was broken, and I see him laughing with the guards who tortured and killed my squad.

'No, sir,' I say. 'Thank you, sir. But I've made up my mind.'

He doesn't argue with me.

I go home by truck, by train and by boat. I don't speak to anyone if I can avoid it. I feel as if I died back there. When I look inside, I can only find one part of Jo Barnes still living. It's a dark, twisted thing, a stunted, coiled figure, born of rage and despair. I might be dead, but it is very much alive, and it gets me up every morning, forces me to my feet, won't let my heart stop beating, my skin go cold. It waits impatiently for me to come back to myself, to start to function as a human being again. Because then I can help it with the only thing it wants, the entire reason for its existence.

I can find Hughes. And kill him.

Turns out the ennanomeds have an automatic override in an emergency. I woke up fresh and healthy with my smotch listing a combination of legal and illegal drugs in my system that would, had it not actually killed a horse, at least have caused it to take early retirement in a nursing home offering twenty-four-hour care. I deleted the message.

'Preachy nanny med bastards.'

I drank coffee and had to open the windows to get rid of the reek of whatever it was the meds had caused me to sweat out of my body overnight. I was cold. Sober. Angry and scared. I was avoiding doing something about Gambon because I just couldn't see a way out without someone getting hurt. And, every time I closed my eyes, I still saw Hughes.

I grabbed the first edition Sherlock Holmes stories the clockwork version had given me and sat cross-legged on the floor in front of the window, shivering and turning the pages, flicking through at random, reading sentences here and there. I'd loved the stories when I was twelve, and they'd had the rare quality of delighting me all over again when I reread them in my twenties.

The book was a beautiful object. Dad says reading a classic first edition is a spiritual experience. We know it's a classic decades or centuries later, but – at the time of printing – no one knew how the book might be received. People were reading it for the very first time. Imagine being one of the first readers to travel with Betsey Trotwood to the cottage at Blundeston for the birth of David Copperfield. Or seeing the world through the eyes of someone living in Iain M. Banks's Culture universe? Or even following a war-weary doctor looking for lodgings in London and meeting the consulting detective Sherlock Holmes.

The breeze blew the pages as I sat there. Occasionally I looked down and read a little, or simply admired the original illustrations. I've never been a fan of pictures in books, for the same reason I will always read the novel before seeing the movie: I want my imagination to supply the images. That's its job. But these drawings captured something of the spirit of the times – London was a dark, brooding character that came through as strongly as Holmes, Watson, Lestrade or Mrs Hudson.

I looked at a picture of Holmes disguised as a clergyman, his distinctive features unrecognisable somehow with the addition of a pair of round spectacles and a silly hat.

Something nagged at the edge of my consciousness, an itch I couldn't scratch. It was as if I was craving a cold beer on a hot day, but I'd forgotten what a beer was, didn't know the word, couldn't even picture it. Or I had a really important appointment, but couldn't remember with whom, or where, or why.

I paced around for ten minutes, splashed water on my face, watched ten minutes of the latest Japanese extreme game show.

I took my coat from the back of the door and went out for a walk. Walking usually helped me think through a problem. Not today, though. Today it made me colder, no less confused, and miserable. Also. My feet hurt. I looked down to see bare toes. I'd forgotten to wear socks. Or shoes.

Back at the flat, I sat down in front of the window again,

picking up the Collected Stories. I couldn't focus, reading the same lines over and over. It would seem even reading was denied me as a distraction. With a sigh, I shut the book, stood up, and looked out of the window until it got dark and my own reflection stared back at me.

'*Shit.*'

I knew what to do.

CHAPTER FORTY-TWO

They both agreed to meet when I called them. I suppose it was the equivalent of an office party. They weren't to know it was a leaving party.

I met Poplar and Toby in a Spitalfields bar, not as rough as the places I normally frequented, but not so trendy it made me want to punch someone.

They were waiting for me in a booth around the corner from the main bar. The decor was light industrial, as if the place had recently been converted from a workshop whose stock-in-trade involved sheet metal, examples of which lined the walls and hung from the ceiling. It was a look that had been all the rage a decade ago. The beautiful people had moved away a few years back, leaving uglier, less successful, more interesting drinkers to keep the place in business.

'I got a pitcher of beer,' called Toby, waving me over. 'Unless you want a house cocktail with an umbrella in it? They're two for one tonight.'

'What's the house cocktail?'

Toby looked puzzled. 'It's green, if that helps. Tastes foul. I've had four.'

I demurred, so he poured me a beer.

For a couple of hours we shot the breeze. That's another tick in the American language box. The equivalent British English expression is, I suppose, *chewing the fat,* but it just doesn't have the same carefree sound to it. Who would want to chew some fat if the alternative was shooting some breeze?

The green cocktails made Toby chatty. A lot of it was down to the post-match high the three of us were sharing. There's nothing quite like it. No drug comes close. I only found myself in truly dangerous, life-threatening situations four times in my army career. On the three occasions that I came back unscathed with my squad, the buzz was so intense, we didn't know what to do with ourselves. Our commanding officers knew better – we were shown to the nearest bar and left to indulge in activities that had been the cultural norm in the northern hemisphere for thousands of years. Garish cocktails had featured in my litany of bad decisions on all of those occasions. Hasty, ill-considered choices of sexual partner had also been somewhat of a speciality.

We talked about the case, of course. It was still in the news, but once all the memes had been mined, the national gaze would turn to the next scandal, the next crisis, the next big sporting event. Very few people knew the whole story, and most of those people were currently sharing a pitcher of beer in Spitalfields.

A few drinks in, and we agreed, now that we'd had a chance to think about it, that it was obvious from the start who'd killed Robert Fairfield, and – once you knew that – everything else fell into place logically.

'Yeah,' I concluded. 'Anyone could have seen that Beth Fairfield must have found a woman who looked just like her so she could scuba dive into her dad's house to kill him, then fly to America to hide for a while, before getting her face changed and getting together with her new geek boyfriend.'

'Well, when you put it like that,' said Poplar.

'Yeah, well, it's easy to solve impossible cases when your whole life is spent in VR, playing the role of the greatest detective of all time. What does he do when he's not being Holmes, anyway?'

Toby ignored the question. Poplar shrugged and took another sip of beer. Who the hell sips beer? 'You were good in that fight,' she said. 'In Denver. I mean, Mr Holmes said you were perfect for Watson, but I'd checked your records and everything, and I wasn't sure ab—'

She stopped talking, her face reddening. I patted her arm.

'Hey, don't worry. I didn't exactly make the best first impression. To be honest, that's the usual story with me. But I'm glad I stuck around. And I'm glad you let me. You're amazing with all these . . . miniature cameras and mics and contact lenses and VR and AR and computers and shit.'

We smiled at each other. She was a nice kid. I'd miss her.

Toby was eyeing me over his pint glass. I gave serious consideration to encouraging him. After all, this would probably be our last chance. I thought about it all the way through the first couple of beers, then decided I liked him too much. I'm a huge fan of meaningless sex for the fun of it, but taking Toby to bed had the potential to turn into meaning*ful* sex, and that I could live without.

Apart from his unsubtle sexual signals, he gave very little away. He batted aside my question about where he grew up and shrugged when I asked whether he'd been an army grunt or something a little more rarefied. When I asked him directly how he'd met Clockwork Sherlock, he'd been just as direct in response.

'That's a story I'll never tell anyone. If Mr Holmes wants to talk about it, that's his decision.' And he stumbled off to the bar for more beer and bowls full of nachos.

Poplar was more forthcoming, but not by much.

'Five years ago, Mr Holmes caught me committing an undetectable, victimless crime. He didn't threaten to turn me in or anything. He told me that if he'd noticed me, so would others – eventually. And those others would want me to work for them. If I was lucky, they'd be sophisticated, professional criminals. If I wasn't, they'd be the government's computer crime department, and they'd either jail me or recruit me. He offered me a job instead. When I found out what he wanted, and when he showed me the kind of tech I'd be able to play with, it was an easy decision. Never looked back.'

Which was all very sweet, but it wasn't everything.

'And?' I said.

She gave me a very steady look, as if deciding if she was ready to trust me. I held her gaze, despite knowing she couldn't.

'I never knew my mum and dad. Mr Holmes looks after me. He looks out for me. And I do the same for him.'

I squeezed her hand. It took some serious daddy issues to accept a technological fiction as a substitute father.

Toby came back laden with goodies and we got loudly, happily drunk before weaving out into the freezing February fog and hugging. We got into separate Eggs. I let them take the two waiting in the rank and stood outside until the cold was physically painful, before smotching a ride for myself.

I never expected to see them again.

CHAPTER FORTY-THREE

SOME PLANS ARE fun to come up with and fun to execute. That morning's plan? Not so much. If everything went as expected, it would leave me back where I was before meeting Holmes. Well, not exactly. My rent had been paid for a year, my bank account was in credit, and I owned a handsome first edition that Dad could probably sell for a tidy sum if I needed the cash. Which I would, to fund a last-ditch attempt to find Hughes. Because after today, there was no way Nicky Gambon was going to hand over the information.

I was up early. I ran for an hour. It had been too long since I'd had a good run, but my body didn't protest as much as I expected. Another gift from the ennanomeds. That was a positive thought, considering the ocean of shit I was about to jump into.

I showered, ate four pieces of toasted sourdough with peanut butter, had a mug of coffee and opened my wardrobe. I put on a pair of combat trousers and a vest, then picked out one of the shirts supplied by Poplar. I stuffed the rest into a big bag.

I sat at my small table after clearing the books off the only other chair I owned. Even if he wasn't really here, Holmes would look weird if he sat on a pile of classic pulp sci-fi.

I dropped the monitors into my ears and blinked the contact lenses into place. Then I thumbed my smotch on and shot a message across to Holmes.

I need to speak to you, right now.

If I had wondered where exactly I factored into Holmes's universe, the fact that he responded to my message in less than a minute provided a fairly unequivocal answer.

There was a knock at my door. A virtual knock.

'Come in.'

Holmes walked through the door. The novelty of seeing him pass through solid matter had worn off.

'Good morning, Watson. I trust everything is all right? I interrupted an entertaining session studying African shipping routes to come and see you, so I hope this is important.'

I indicated the spare chair and he sat down, with that little hitch of his trousers. He looked genuinely put out. I studied him without speaking. He was immaculately turned out as always, since any imperfection, any virtual scuff on his virtual shoes, or any virtual stain on his virtual suit, could only be there by choice – which would be an odd choice.

I saw intelligence, energy and curiosity in those grey eyes, but none of it was real. The avatar sitting opposite had offered me the chance to be John Watson to his Sherlock Holmes. It was a better offer than the original Watson had accepted. I didn't have to share rooms with him, my life was my own.

I'd joined the army because, in my naive way, I had believed the world contained its fair share of bad guys and someone had to stop them screwing everything up for everyone else. It had taken nearly a decade and the deaths of six friends to disabuse me of that fallacy. I'd been looking for a world with clear lines. Good/bad. Right/wrong. Loyal/traitor. The world didn't always work like that, and I learned that lesson in the hardest way possible.

Now here was someone who appeared to have the clarity I'd lacked. Someone who could remain detached from the human mess that confuses the rest of us. Someone who wanted justice for those who had been wronged and had the skills to ensure it prevailed.

And he'd offered me the job of my dreams.

'Still want me to be Watson?'

'Of course.' He said nothing else. He knew I hadn't finished.

'I can only do it if you trust me. Completely.'

He was totally still, his attention entirely focussed on me.

'Trust has to be earned, Watson.'

I was ready to throw some outrage his way in reply, particularly as I'd taken some damage on his behalf while bringing in the murderer, but he got there first.

'And you've earned it. What do you need from me?'

And here it was.

'Your name. Your real name. I can't work with someone who hides their identity from me. I won't.'

He stood up then, paced my flat, ending with his back to me in front of my bookshelf.

'You're sure?' He sounded disappointed and I knew why. The anger came back then, which made it all much easier.

'Yes. I'm sure.'

'Very well.' And he disappeared.

Right.

I made more coffee and waited. What if I was wrong? I went over everything again, every meeting, every conversation. No. I wasn't wrong.

Before I'd finished my coffee, there was a knock on the door. I didn't think it was virtual this time. I was right.

Toby wasn't smiling this morning.

'Hello, Toby. How's your head?'

He didn't answer, just handed me an envelope, turned his back and left.

I looked down. There was no name on the envelope. It was unsealed. I squeezed it open between finger and thumb and looked inside. A single, folded piece of paper.

I brought my smotch up to my mouth.

'I have what you want, Mr Gambon. But I will only give it to you in person. I'll be in my flat for the next twenty minutes. The door is wide open.'

Nicky Gambon walked into my flat eight and a half minutes after I sent the message. Blue suit, matching tie over a dazzling white shirt. He looked like an advert for cologne. *Machete, because even murderous bastards should smell sexy.*

Considering what was inside the envelope on the table, you'd think he'd be pleased. He didn't look it. He looked like a man who'd confidently placed a very large bet only to find the odds had moved against him. He looked like a man who'd made a big mistake.

He didn't waste time on niceties.

'Well? Who is he?'

'I don't know.'

He took a long, slow breath, and fixed those soulful brown eyes on me, as if he was already feeling sorry about the way he was being forced to torture and kill me.

I didn't flinch, just nodded at the envelope. 'In there.'

'Open it,' he commanded, his voice flat and emotionless.

'No.'

He'd been looking at the envelope when I said it. It seemed to take an age for him to drag his eyes up to meet mine, but when he did, they were filled with the kind of cold rage that had proved to be an effective laxative on many occasions.

'I beg your pardon, Jo?'

'You heard me, you cloth-eared dolt.'

Gambon was like a human statue. For a fraction of a second I doubted myself. Too late now.

'I said "no". You want to know his real name, it's right there. Open the envelope and read it. I'm not stopping you.'

His eyes continued to deliver their promise of prolonged dismemberment for another five seconds, then he walked up to the table, put his fists on it, and looked at the envelope.

'That's it, Nicky. Clockwork Sherlock's real name inside that envelope. C'mon. If it was worth going to all the trouble of having me kidnapped, surely opening a teeny-weeny envelope isn't too much of a stretch. Is it?'

He didn't say a word. I picked up the envelope and waved it under his nose.

'What's the matter, dipshit? What, you can run Whitechapel, but you're scared of stationery? You want to know the truth? You *can't* open the envelope, can you? You can't even pick it up.'

Finally, Nicky Gambon lifted his head and looked at me.

His eyes weren't brown anymore. They were grey.

CHAPTER FORTY-FOUR

'How long have you known?'

As Nicky Gambon hitched up his trousers and sat opposite me, the blue suit changed style and colour, becoming black. The blue tie was a red cravat. For the first time since I'd met him, Holmes didn't look completely sure of himself.

'The penny dropped yesterday.' I pointed at the bookshelf. 'The illustrations reminded me.'

'Ah. The sailor, the elderly woman. The opium smoker, perhaps?'

'The priest.'

'Of course. Excellent work, Watson.'

'I should have worked it out earlier,' I said. 'The fact that both times I met Gambon in person, I was wearing my VR gear didn't occur to me until yesterday. And the pretend net-blocker. Nice piece of misdirection. What happened to the real Nicky Gambon?'

Holmes lit his pipe. He had recovered his poise remarkably quickly.

'Massive heart attack five months ago. A word with the coroner, and the Commissioner of the Met, and I was able to step into the role. It won't last forever, but I intend to keep it going as long as possible as it's an excellent way to pick up information. Gambon's most trusted lieutenants agreed to play along in return for lenient sentencing later. They were the pair you put in hospital after the kidnapping. I, er, hadn't anticipated how, er, *firm* you would be during your escape.'

'I thought they would kill me.'

'Quite. It was an error of judgement, for which I apologised to them, and now do the same to you.'

'You've got more than that to apologise for.'

'Watson, I'm –'

'And you can stop calling me Watson. First of all, your hired muscle tried to knife me.'

'I knew you wore a stab vest, and he was removed from the team for his actions.'

'Then you threatened my father.'

'I assure you, Wats— Jo, that he was never in any danger. The tiny fire was set to convince you the threat was real.'

'Worst of all, you promised me the traitor. You promised me Hughes. You were lying to me all this time.'

I picked up the envelope and walked into the kitchen.

Holmes followed. He had regained his customary poise and was rubbing his hands together.

'This is splendid. I spent months looking for the perfect candidate and even when I found you, I underestimated your capabilities. Normally the kind of trust and loyalty I'm looking for has to be built over years. This way, I put you under a great deal of pressure to betray me, but you resisted it. You are a woman of rare character. And the level of intelligence –'

I interrupted him. 'How many?'

I only knew my question had surprised him by the pause that followed it. His avatar appeared unperturbed.

'How many what?'

'No more games, Holmes. You know exactly what I mean.'

The great detective shook his head and leaned towards me. 'Very well. You're the fourth. Would it have made any difference if you'd known?'

'Maybe. Maybe not. It's hardly the point. You should have told me. What happened to the other Watsons?'

He walked out of the kitchen, stood with his back to me. 'The third Watson couldn't deal with AR and VR – just wasn't agile enough mentally. The second left because they, well, we . . . there was a personality clash. We didn't get on.'

I couldn't let him stop there. 'You mean not everybody is impressed by your winning smile and friendly banter?'

'He said, and I quote, that I was "a twat pretending to be an even bigger twat". He had a way with words, I'll give him that.'

I suspected I'd get on quite well with the second Watson. 'And the first one? What happened there? Told you to piss off too?'

'She died.'

Holmes turned to face me, his posture more rigid than ever. 'I was there when it happened.'

I was never more aware than at that moment that I was talking to an image projected on to my eyeballs, that I had no idea who, or what, was behind this puppet. He either felt no emotion, or he was deliberately concealing it.

'At first I wondered why you didn't just use Toby as Watson,' I said. 'You obviously trust him. He can fight, and he's ex-military like me. But I get it now. You didn't want to risk losing him. You need someone dispensable. Someone like me.'

He knew me well enough not to deny it.

'At first, maybe. Yes. Not any longer. Not for a while, Jo . . .'

. . .

He hesitated. Then he stepped forward, clasping his hands in front of him, every inch the confident detective. I had seen him unsure and doubtful, and now he tried to shake that impression off like a dog coming in from the rain.

'You surpassed my expectations, Captain Barnes. I never expected you to see through my disguise.'

'You underestimated me, all right.'

I turned on the stove and placed the envelope on it. Within a few seconds the edges began to curl up. A brown shadow in the centre, then a lick of flame at one corner. I watched it burn to ashes.

'I don't know who you are. And I don't want to know. It's over. Find yourself a fifth Watson.'

I took the in-ear monitors out first, placing them on the hob. They fizzed before cracking and blackening. Holmes was still watching, right up until the moment I popped out the second contact lens and tossed it alongside its twin to burn.

The spare contacts, monitors and sub-vox band-aids, I threw down the flat's communal rubbish chute, along with the bag of clothes. The shirt I was wearing went last. I wondered if anyone was still watching.

I didn't want to be alone in my flat after that. I pulled a winter coat out of the wardrobe and slung it over my vest. Then I walked out, giving the door a satisfying slam behind me.

I didn't tell Dad what had happened. We've never spoken much about my work. He knows he's a refuge, an escape, somewhere familiar and comfortable where I can talk about books, watch classic twentieth-century movies or TV shows with a mug of tea and a box of biscuits. He'll ask the odd general question, but he doesn't pry. I love him for that.

He waited until we'd ordered takeout and were halfway

through an unexpectedly spicy madras to ask something he probably considered safely innocuous.

'How's the new job. Security, wasn't it?'

I burst into tears.

In the end, I told Dad a few bits and pieces. Not enough to worry him. No, that's not true. He was already worried. I hadn't cried in front of him since Mum died. I told him enough for him to understand that I felt as though I'd been mistreated. I didn't need to tell him he was safe, as he'd never been aware he'd been in any danger. Come to think of it, he'd never actually *been* in any danger.

I poured the rest of my tea away and went to his wine rack. We shared a couple of bottles of Bordeaux and talked about fictional detectives. After some shouting, a lot of laughter, and a third bottle, we agreed the best fictional detective in literature or on-screen was, without a doubt, the Parisian, Inspector Jacques Clouseau.

We didn't finish the last bottle. I told the ennanomeds where to get off and fell asleep on the sofa watching *Columbo*. The last thing I remember was Dad tucking a blanket round my shoulders and kissing my forehead while, in the background, Columbo said, 'Oh – ma'am? Just one more thing . . .'

When I woke up, I had slept through at least three episodes on the Columbo channel. Something had woken me. I lay quietly and waited for it to happen again. Twenty seconds later it did.

The alert chime on my smotch, tucked into my shoe.

I had only set one alert. It was on the email account I used for information about Hughes. I sat up, groaned, and muttered the codes to clear the booze away. Almost immediately, I craved water and needed to pee.

I picked up the smotch, thumbed the alert and read the email without even thinking about it.

The email was signed *Holmes*. It contained an address. Nothing else.

I got dressed. Dad caught me as I was opening the front door.

'You okay, Jo?'

'I'm fine, Dad. I have to go.'

'At four in the morning? Where are you going?'

'Australia.'

CHAPTER FORTY-FIVE

FIVE DAYS later

I unscrewed the hip flask and took a long swallow of vodka. Other than the slight warming sensation, I barely noticed it going down. It was more of a tradition than a necessity. One last shot before the job.

It was an hour until sunup. I'd spent the previous forty-five minutes getting into position after yesterday's reconnaissance of the ranch. Hughes had spent his blood money carefully, not doing anything to draw too much attention. According to his closest neighbour, twelve miles up the road in the ranch country of North Western Australia, he was a quiet man who valued his privacy. They didn't call them ranches, but stations, which had confused me at first.

He wasn't called Hughes now, of course. Rod Burns, which I was convinced he'd only chosen because it sounded like a porn star, was the name on the mailbox at the end of the long drive. Hughes's sense of humour had always inclined towards the schoolboy, and dick jokes were his favourite. If I had needed a clincher, this would have been it.

The evidence Holmes had attached to the email was comprehensive. Hughes, the traitor whose sell-out had led to the death of my squad and days of torture for me, lived here, in Australia, on a four-hundred-acre station, in luxury. His immediate neighbour, with whom I'd sunk a few beers the previous night, didn't know much about the rich eccentric up the road. Hughes's ranch was the only one in a hundred miles with no livestock. That was considered odd, not sinister.

I took one more sip of vodka for luck and pushed the flask into my rucksack. There was a faint line of light on the eastern horizon. I looked through the telescopic scope. No lights on in the house. No sign of movement. But Hughes had been in the army for a decade when I'd met him. He would be awake early. My research last night had turned up one particularly useful nugget of information. Friday was market day, and Rod Burns was always there when it opened for his weekly supply run.

He wouldn't be making that run this morning. Or ever again.

I tucked the scope into my jacket pocket and put my gloves back on. The west Australian nights were cold, and it would be hours before the sun started baking the hard, flat landscape. My hands barely shook at all.

I was sitting cross-legged behind a line of scrubby bushes. The sun would rise behind me, meaning there was no danger of Hughes picking up a reflection in the scope of my rifle. Not that he would be looking for it. Or me. He must have known I would come for him. I bet he spent the first six months constantly looking over his shoulder. According to the traces I'd been able to find, he'd kept moving for nearly a year. By now, his paranoia would have faded. I had no doubt

Hughes was still careful, and always would be, but when over a year had passed with no hint of discovery, he must have adjusted his perception of the threat level.

I waited, hidden from the low, long building of the ranch a quarter of a mile away.

I guessed I had twenty minutes to wait. I spent the time remembering what Hughes had done. The screams I'd heard, day after day, from the other members of my squad. Trying, and failing, to stop my own screams, knowing my comrades were listening. And the silence that was worse than any scream.

I repeated each of their names to myself as I waited. Boone, Pollock, Gasparini, Harris, Hussein, Reynolds.

I whispered those names over and over, watching that door. The moment Hughes walked out, I could bring the whole sorry mess to an end.

When the door did finally open, I was lying facing down, the rifle braced against my shoulder. Insects bigger than the mice back home had crawled across my body and face, but I wasn't moving. Not for them, not for anyone.

He walked out onto the porch, an ugly old hat pulled down on his head. Instead of walking straight out to his pickup truck, he looked out towards me, pulling the brim down to shade his eyes. It was as if he were looking right at me. I knew he couldn't see me; he was watching the sun come up, squinting against the light. He looked older, skinnier.

I slowed my breathing as his face filled the scope, the cross hairs coming to bear on his forehead. I was a decent shot. Not the best in the squad – that had been Boone – but not bad. And any one of us could hit a target like this in our sleep.

Some snipers fire as they breath out. Others don't care when they fire once they've lined up the shot. Me, I like to be sure I'm not going to miss before holding my breath and squeezing the trigger.

I held my breath.

CHAPTER FORTY-SIX

The way I remember it, that winter in London stretched through February, March and into April. White flakes twitched past my window at night. By day, the sun produced enough warmth to make the trees crack and pop, branches occasionally shuddering as they shrugged off a layer of snow. I often stood at my window, looking down into the tiny patch of garden behind the flats, blinking against the solid slab of white, seeing a hard-edged dark square at the centre of my vision when I turned back to my dark room.

I didn't think about Australia. I was empty. I was done.

I took a job as a security guard in a gallery. Not for the money. Not for the company, since I worked alone. I took it because I could be around people without being noticed. They walked into the room and looked at the paintings hanging on the walls. Some did it as if it were a chore, something to be crossed off a to-do list. Some stopped at every painting and stared for the same amount of time before moving on, their faces blank. Some came in pairs, talking about what they were seeing, discussing influences, techniques. Others came alone to see one painting, ignoring the rest, sitting or standing in front of it as if nothing else existed. I liked them.

My favourite visitors were the ones who were surprised. Often part of a family group, they looked disengaged and dutiful as they shuffled around the room. It was usually something in their stance that gave them away. A moment when they looked at some daubs of colour on canvas put there hundreds of years before, and something touched them. Across the centuries, the different cultures, something cut through the noise; an invisible finger reached out, penetrated skin, muscle and bone, and came to rest on a stranger's heart. Like falling in love. *I know you.*

The surprised ones always came back, and they were always alone the second time. Like they were embarking on an affair.

They didn't see me. Nobody saw me. But I saw them and that was enough. It felt like a first step towards something, although I couldn't have said what it was.

The thaw came after Easter, and I started taking my sandwiches to nearby Holland Park. There was a bench facing a pond in the Japanese garden. The squirrels begged for crumbs and brave sparrows swooped if the squirrels were too slow.

People walked in front of me, crossed the little bridge across the water. I caught snippets of conversations. Sometimes I wove them into little stories while I sat there. Sometimes I didn't.

On a Tuesday lunchtime in May, a man detached himself from the ever-shifting human flow. The unusual break in the pattern registered itself in my brain. He came closer. I was looking at the water. I recognised the way he moved, but I didn't look at him.

He sat down next to me, placed a paper bag on the bench between us.

'Hello, Jo.'

Sometimes, I could go a whole day without speaking. My voice sounded strange to me, distant, unfamiliar.

'Hello, Toby.'

'You look well. You working near here? How are things?'

I blinked, sighed and looked at him. He was smiling. Sincere, loyal Toby. Named after a talented dog. I liked him. There was no point pretending otherwise. But there was also no point in him being there. I smiled back.

'What do you want, Toby?'

He reached into the paper bag, pulled out a pair of over-ear headphones, the kind with a mic attached. The kind helicopter pilots use. As far from in-ear monitors as it was possible to get.

'He wants you to meet him, Jo.'

Holmes had emailed dozens of times. I hadn't opened them. He'd messaged me directly. I'd blocked him on my smotch. So he had kept his distance. Up to now.

'No. Tell him no. And make sure he understands it's final.'

I stood up, took a few steps away from the bench. I heard Toby get up. Half a second before his hand touched my shoulder, I stopped, took a pace backwards while twisting, jabbing an elbow into his solar plexus at the same time as gripping his fingers and pushing them up and back. He dropped to his knees. It was either that or two broken fingers.

He didn't resist. He looked up at me. After a second he laughed.

'I've missed you.'

I let go. 'I'm not interested.'

I walked away, heard Toby run back to the bench for his bag, then hurry to catch up. I didn't stop. At the gate out of the park, he said my name. I stopped. Before I could say anything, he put his hand on my upper arm. I let him do it.

'Jo. You don't understand. He wants you to *meet* him.'

When I didn't move, he placed the headphones in my hand. 'Please.'

I watched him leave, walking back into the park until I lost him in the trees.

I looked at the headphones for a long time. There was no great internal debate going on. It was more like I was back in front of my flat window at night, watching the snow falling. Not thinking. Not doing. Asleep with my eyes open.

I don't even remember deciding to put the headphones on.

'No more secrets, Jo,' said Holmes. 'I'm waiting for you.'

CHAPTER FORTY-SEVEN

HOLMES'S VOICE directed me across the street. I walked through a narrow alley between billionaires' houses, crossed a tiny patch of grass in a square I'd never seen before to stand in front of a building that might have been a school or an embassy. Four storeys high and as wide as three terraced houses, its walls were constructed of large bricks, faded terracotta and pale pink, on which were projected the dancing shadows of two of London's ubiquitous plane trees.

It was the kind of building on which you'd expect to find an elegant brass plaque announcing its function, but there was nothing.

'I'm here,' I said into the mic and climbed the elegant stone steps to the large olive doors.

'Not the main steps, Jo. The basement.'

I looked over the balustrade and saw narrower steps beneath. The door they led to was smaller than the one above, but no less imposing up close. It was steel. There was no handle. It swung open as I approached and shut silently behind me as I stepped into darkness.

The lights were automatic, warming up quickly, going

from dying embers to a yellow brightness. I followed a featureless corridor with two doors on each side. At the far end was a dark-wood staircase leading up to the main building.

'It's the second door on the left.'

I tried the first as I passed it. Locked. I ignored the second door and went to the end of the corridor, going up the staircase far enough to see that it led to another steel door. This one had a retina scanner.

Back in the corridor, I tried the two remaining doors. One opened into a bedroom: neat, tidy, impersonal. A man's winter coat hung behind the door. The room next door was packed with computer hardware. Quantum computers were so small now, Fairfield boasted you could run the whole of Britain's transport system from hardware no bigger than a shoe box. In which case, this was the equivalent of a shoe shop's storeroom.

'Are you lost?'

'No. But I'm nosy. And suspicious.'

'No need. You're in my home now. Please. Come straight through.'

I crossed the corridor, put my hand to the door, oddly reluctant to go further now that I was here.

I pushed the door open.

The room beyond was a cross between a hacker's lair and a pharmacy. Two of the walls were screens, displaying information I didn't recognise or understand. The wall with the door to the corridor was lined with shelves containing vials, sterilising equipment, medical fridges – one of which contained hanging blood sacs – rows of boxes and tubes. Enough medicine for a small hospital.

The fourth wall, to my left, was bare, apart from a sink. There was a final door, which must lead to the room behind the locked door in the corridor. On a small table to the left of the door was a surgical mask.

'You can take off the headphones now. Just put them on the shelf.'

I did as he asked. His voice came from flat speakers on the walls.

'It's good to see you again. Please wash your hands with the soap provided, put on the mask and come through.'

I washed, twice, then put my hands into the slot above as instructed. It was a dehydry – the first I'd ever used. Too expensive for the mass market. It felt like someone was peeling a really thin pair of rubber gloves off my fingers. The process took less than a second, leaving my hands dry and missing a molecule-thick layer of skin.

I put the mask on. The final door clicked and swung open, shutting automatically as I went in. There was a muted hiss like an airlock closing.

The room I stepped into was so stark, strange, yet unexpectedly familiar that I didn't know what to say.

'It isn't much,' said Holmes's voice from the wall, 'but it's home.'

It was white. The room was white. Almost all of it. The tiled floor, the walls, the ceiling, the bed, the machines, the table next to the pillow. I held my hands in front of my face as if to remind myself that I hadn't been washed out by this blinding whiteness.

My surroundings were familiar because they were like the room near the end of *2001: A Space Odyssey*. The bit that people still argue over. When, after ten minutes where you think your drink must have been spiked with a hallucinogenic, everything goes bonkers. When the astronaut is in a white room, in bed, and he's suddenly ancient, dying. That bit.

Only in *2001*, the room had paintings, statues. And the

bed wasn't white. In here, everything was white apart from the bedcover, which was baby blue. And the guy lying in the bed, whose skin was the colour of bone. Off-white. His dark hair was long, a shock of contrast on the pillow. A bandage hid his eyes. Tubes came out of his arms, leading to the machines surrounding him.

I took a step closer. Was he breathing? I waited until I saw the sheet over his chest rise slowly, almost imperceptibly.

Another step. He made the dying astronaut in *2001* look positively healthy. His sallow skin did little more than suggest the skull beneath.

I looked closer, gasped involuntarily. What I had taken to be his hair was nothing of the sort. Thousands of wires penetrated his scalp and trailed over his pillow, hanging from the back of the bed before pooling below. I stepped to one side to trace their route. The wires collected in what looked like a circular drain in the rear corner.

And the bandage over his eyes?

I took another step. It wasn't a bandage. It was made of material I didn't recognise, a few millimetres thick, and it stuck to his skin like a high-tech leech.

Another step. I bent over him to see more clearly. He had the face of an ancient boy.

'It's a version of the visor you wore in 221b.' The voice came from all around me. 'My eyes are in excellent condition. Twenty-twenty. Unfortunately, the same cannot be said for the rest of me.'

His body was entirely concealed by the bedclothes. I wondered if I should hold his hand. I went to lift the corner of the sheet.

'NO!'

I dropped it and jumped back. The body on the bed hadn't moved, but something in his neck had twitched.

'I'm sorry. I just . . . I want you to know me as I am, Jo.

I'm not what you see here. I haven't been for twenty-five years. When I was able to make a choice, I chose to be someone new. I chose my identity. Please. I am Sherlock Holmes.'

I had edged back to the bed as he spoke. I looked at his throat, at the band-aid there.

'My sub-vox skills are superior to yours, Watson. Which is hardly worth boasting about.'

I smiled and I let the *Watson* go by without comment.

'Twenty-five years?' I said. There was something about that quarter-century that flagged up a memory. An anniversary. Around the time of the court case. Something . . .

'Why didn't you kill Hughes?'

I went very still. I had asked myself the same question for weeks. I'd probably keep asking it for the rest of my life.

I'd put my rifle down that morning, watched the traitor who'd got my squad killed drive off his property and head for the market. I'd caught a flight home, but not before paying a visit to the British Consulate in Perth.

Hughes was quietly extradited ten days later, and his flight was met by British Military Police. His trial was scheduled for the summer. It would be a closed trial because of the nature of our mission, but word was he would be in prison for the rest of his life.

Boone, Pollock, Gasparini, Harris, Hussein, Reynolds. I wondered what they would have made of what I'd done.

'I don't know,' I said to Holmes. 'But I couldn't kill him.'

Neither of us spoke for nearly a minute. I could hear the hum of the machines that kept him alive.

'Who are you?' I said finally.

'Open the drawer.'

The table next to his head had a single drawer. I slid it open. Inside was a photograph. I took it out and looked at it.

I'd seen it before. In Jack Bolton's office. A family group.

Stephen and Fay Fairfield, with their sons Art and John. The tragic Fairfield family, wiped out in a car wreck. Except . . .

'You're Art Fairfield.'

I looked at the boy in the photograph, his hand resting on his brother's shoulder, their father and mother standing behind them. My eyes flicked back to the face on the pillow. I could see the resemblance now, but what was left of Art Fairfield looked as if all the life had been sucked out of him long ago.

'Not anymore. Not for a very long time.'

'Why? Why let everyone believe you were dead?'

'Because by the time Toby connected me to VR, I knew that my body was finished. And I'd had time to get past despair and self-pity and realise there was still something I could do with my life. Something that I could do most effectively if no one knew who I was.'

I thought about the sixteen-year-old Art Fairfield losing everyone he loved and everything he knew.

'My deductive skills were formed in adolescence. It became somewhat of an obsession. Dad thought it was a phase. Toby knew better.'

'How did Toby, I mean, what did Toby . . .' I struggled to form a coherent question.

'He worked security for the family. The crash killed Petra, one of his colleagues. Even though he wasn't there, it nearly killed him all the same. He barely left my bedside for months.'

Holmes laughed. I couldn't think of him as Art, despite looking at the shrunken man–boy on the white pillow.

'What's funny?' I said.

'Toby. I signalled to him by blinking Morse code with my one functioning eye, but it took him nearly three days to realise what I was doing. I still tease him about it. He arranged the transfer to a private clinic – right here, in fact – where I'd offered the owner a generous salary and a job for life. He organised a death certificate and my tragic demise was announced.'

My brain engaged with some of the new facts and I tried to prioritise my questions.

'Robert Fairfield?'

'I needed him. To run my company.'

'My god. You still owned it.'

'Yes. As far as the trade press was concerned, my father's will left Fairfield Tech to a trust he'd set up. Robert never knew that I controlled the trust since he never had any real interest in the business. He was content to act as figurehead and titular owner, particularly after the trust suggested his daughter would make an excellent CEO.'

I couldn't resist. 'She turned out well, didn't she?'

'Very droll. Actually, Beth was a first-rate hacker, and a smart negotiator.'

'And homicidal.'

'So it turns out, yes. I let her run the company, occasionally carefully stepping in via Robert to direct research in the direction I wanted.'

'The VR suite?'

'Among other innovations, yes.'

My mind raced to make sense of this information. I couldn't take it in.

'I did what was necessary to be able to reinvent myself,' said Holmes. 'I became Clockwork Sherlock.'

'I thought you hated that nickname.'

'It could be worse.'

'Wait. This case might have helped the New Ludds. Greta Blackstone. You couldn't have known what would happen when you proved her innocence. She might have got into Parliament. If the Ludds got their way, VR might be banned.

Why did you do it? You still owned the company? Why risk it? What was in it for you?'

I should have anticipated his answer, of course.

'Justice.'

Toby was waiting when I got back to the corridor. I didn't know what to say to him.

Holmes's voice interrupted any awkwardness.

'Why don't you two pop out for a spot of dinner? My treat. There's an Egg waiting.'

I looked down at my security guard uniform. Toby offered me his arm, bowing. We walked down the corridor. The door swung open as we approached.

'There's been a spate of robberies in London's comic-book shops,' said Holmes, in one of his customary non-sequiturs. 'They always steal the same comic. *Quantum Callgirl* number thirty-nine. Nothing else. The case has some intriguing peculiarities. It would be very useful to visit the scene of the latest theft. And I think we might want to interview the comic's writer, Alan Frank. Could you come in to 221b Monday morning? I'll send an Egg.'

Toby and I hesitated at the door.

'Why not?' I said.

'Excellent. Then I'll see you Monday, Jo.'

I got the last word in as the steel door swung shut behind us.

'Call me Watson.'

AUTHOR'S NOTE

This novel started life as an audiobook, so thanks to everyone at Audible for seeing the potential of a futuristic Sherlock Holmes, and for letting me geek out about self-driving transport and virtual reality.

Thanks to Julie Crisp for her fantastic editing and invaluable suggestions.

And thanks to Manuel Clément for his help with AR, VR, and RR!

I'm currently writing more of my Bedlam Boy series (Jack Reacher meets Jekyll and Hyde). For a free story to whet your appetite (and the occasional email from me), click here: The Las Vegas Driving Lesson

If this is a paperback, don't click, you'll look daft (although we've all done it). You might be better off finding me at my website - ianwsainsbury.com, or emailing me at ianwsainsbury@gmail.com

Clockwork Sherlock will return...

ALSO BY IAN W. SAINSBURY

Thriller

Bedlam Boy 1

Bedlam Boy 2

Bedlam Boy 3

Psychological Thriller

The Picture On The Fridge (Winner of the 2019 Kindle Storyteller Award)

Science Fiction

The World Walker (The World Walker 1)

The Unmaking Engine (The World Walker 2)

The Seventeenth Year (The World Walker 3)

The Unnamed Way (The World Walker 4)

Children Of The Deterrent (Halfhero 1)

Halfheroes (Halfhero 2)

The Last Of The First (Halfhero 3)

Fantasy

The Blurred Lands

Printed in Great Britain
by Amazon